GEMS OF IXORA

OF BLOOD AND GARNET

2

JESSICA HOFFA

OF BLOOD AND GARNET

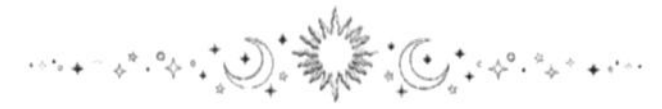

When love exists on a soul level,
it becomes something else entirely.
Unfathomable.
Unbreakable.
Undeniable.
Eternal.

-N.R. Hart

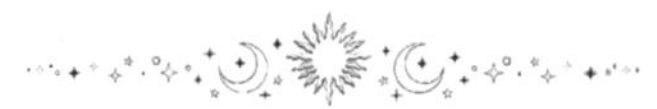

This is for the readers. The ones who took a chance on a new author, dove into the world of Ixora, and came out craving more. The ones who found a new book boyfriend in Daemon, and a best friend in Piper. The ones who are *very* mad at Auraelia (and probably me). I promise there is a happily ever after, it just might hurt a little first.

This world would not exist without you. So, without further ado, welcome back to Ixora.

Welcome *home*.

Content Warning

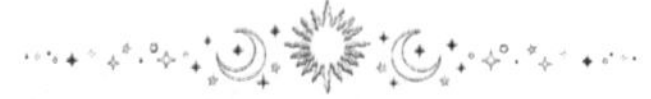

The following lists all of the trigger/content warnings that you will come across throughout Of Blood and Garnet. You will encounter themes of vulgar language, explicit sexual scenes, edging, bondage, breath play, anal play, blood, poisoning, violence, murder, anxiety, depression, grief, and death of a parent. Your mental health is extremely important, so please take care as you dive into the world of Ixora.

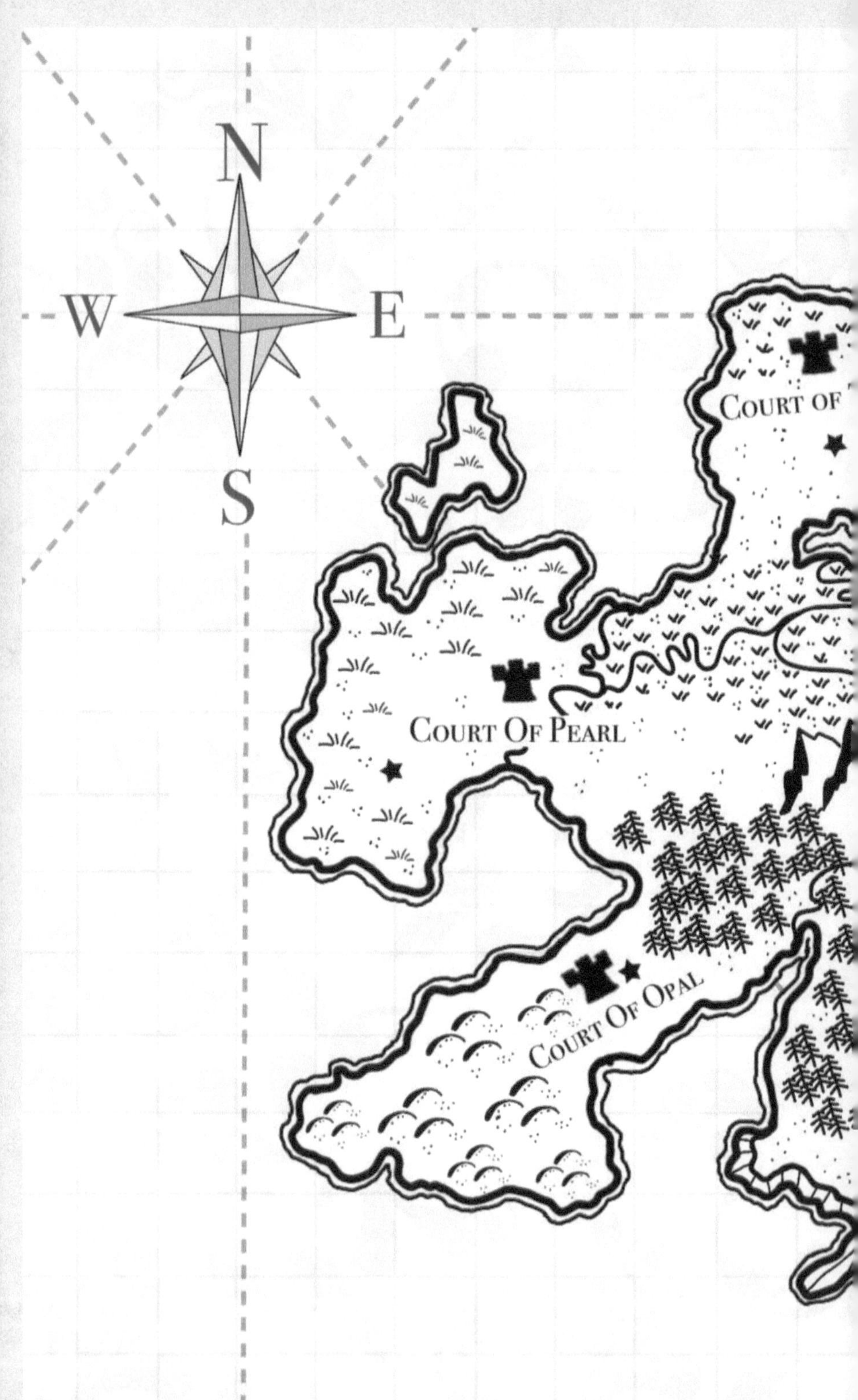
N
W
E
S
Court of
Court Of Pearl
Court Of Opal

Ixora
Court Of Garnet
Onyx Mountains
Lyndaria
Kalmeera
Cerulean Sea
The Court Of Sapphire Isles

Pronunciation Guide

The Court of Emerald

AURAELIA "Rae" ROSE MORWEN: Ah-rAe-lEE-ah "r-Ay" Mor-win

XANDER "Xan" MORWEN: ZAn-der "z-An" Mor-win

ADELINA: Ad-eh-lEEn-uh

PIPER: PI-per

SYLVIE "Vee": Sil-vEE "vEE"

SER AERON KOA: Sir Air-on KO-a

ARAMIS: Air-a-miss

HARLAND: Har-lAnd

OPHELIA: O-fEE-lia

RIONA: REE-O-na

DEMIR: De-mEEr

ASTRAEA: Uh-strAe-uh

ALARIC SOREN: Uh-Lar-ik Soar-en

ELIZA "Liza": EE-LI-z-ah "LI-z-ah"

ORION: O-rI-un

JASIRA: juh-sEE-r-ah

The Court of Sapphire Isles

DAEMON ALEXANDER: DAy-mon a-lex-an-der

AIDEN: Ay-den

YVAINE "Vaine" CORDELIA: E-vAi-n "v-Ai-n" cor-dEEl-ia

AVYANNA: Ah-vEE-ana

EVANDER: E-van-der

RANEESE "Neese" GARRETH: Ra-nEE-ce "nEE-sEE"

CASSIUS: Cas-EE-us

SYRUS: SI-rus

SIMON: SI-mon

SARIAH: Suh-rI-uh

JODIE: Jo-dEE

ERIX: Air-ix

KILLIAN: Kill-EE-n

DARYA: D-ar-EE-ah

The Court of Opal

AESIRA: Ah-sEEr-ah

ARLO: ar-low

IRIDESSA "Dessa": Ear-uh-dess-uh "dess-uh"

The Court of Pearl

KAEMON: KAy-mon

LAVENA: Luh-vEE-na

The Court of Topaz

ORNA: Or-nah

BLYANA: BL-I-ana

The Court of Garnet

DAVINA: duh-vEE-na

CAIUS: kI-us

KYRA: kI-rah

Goddesses of Arecelia

RAYNE (Goddess of Love and War): RAy-ne

NARISSA (Goddess of Sea and Sky): Nuh-riss-ah

MORANA (Goddess of the Dark Side of the Moon): Mor-ah-na

ESMERAY (Goddess of the Face of the Moon): eh-z-me-ray

DALIA (Goddess of Fate): Dah-l-EE-ah

KERES (Goddess of the Underrealm): K-Aer-ez

INARA (Goddess of Warriors): i-NAR-uh

Places

IXORA: ick-soar-aH

LYNDARIA: lyn-dar-EE-ah

KALMEERA: Cal-meer-ah

ARCELIA: ar-cEE-lEE-ah

MALAENA: Muh-lAy-nuh

LYNARIA: Loo-nar-EE-uh

LILURA: LI-loo-r-uh

Contents

Prologue

Daemon

One week following the death of Queen Adelina...

"Fuck you," Daemon seethed as he stormed into his father's office, the door ricocheting off the wall from the force. "I'm not marrying Davina. And I'll fucking abdicate right now if you try and push the issue."

"Son, I suggest you calm yourself and have a seat." His father's voice was eerily calm, and he kept shifting his gaze to the room's far corner.

When Daemon turned, Davina was leaning against the wall with her ankles crossed, her hands clasped innocently in front of her, and a menacing grin on her face.

"What the hell is *she* doing here?" Daemon asked through gritted teeth. His shadows thrashed beneath his skin and began to pool at his fingertips.

Davina pushed off the wall, her head tilted coyly to the side as the corners of her mouth pulled downward, a look of faux hurt slowly spreading across her face. "Ouch. That's not a very nice way to speak about your future wife and queen."

Daemon snarled and loosened the grip he had on his magic. "I'm not fucking marrying you, and over my dead body will you ever be queen of any part of this realm."

Her frown morphed into a sinister smile that sent a chill down his spine. It was the same smile she'd given Auraelia when she said, '*I am dying to play with you*' after she'd orchestrated the poisoning of Queen Adelina.

He straightened his spine and hardened his gaze as she slowly made her way across the floor.

"That can be arranged."

As soon as the last syllable crossed her lips, her wrist flicked to the side, and ice surged in his veins. His magic stilled under his skin, a feeling so cold it burned radiating through his limbs until finally, it squeezed around his heart, slowing the thunderous beat to nearly nothing.

The sensation had him clawing at his chest and gasping for breath as the frigid sensation took over his lungs. His knees buckled beneath him, and he collapsed to the floor as a vice-like grip squeezed against his skull.

Daemon groaned through gritted teeth against the onslaught.

Pain shattered his world; his entire being felt like it was being crushed.

Once Davina was in front of him, she squatted down to his level and lifted his chin so that he could see her face. Eyes that once resembled Auraelia's were now a deep blood red, and her lips were stretched into a feline smile.

"Let's get one thing straight, *my love*. I can squash you like a grape and walk away with a smile. You don't have to like me—hell, I don't care for you much either—but you *will* show me respect. Or the next time you cross me, I won't be taking it out on *you.*"

Even with the venom in her words, her tone was sickly sweet.

Davina stood and stalked toward the door, pausing briefly to look over her shoulder at where Daemon was still on the floor on his hands and knees. "See you soon, *my love.*"

The door clicked shut behind her, and whatever hold her magic had on him dissipated. He took great gulping breaths into his lungs as he crumpled to the floor and rolled onto his back.

Minutes passed before he was able to form a coherent thought. His mind raced over the effect her magic had on him.

"That's who you decided would make a good queen of our kingdom?" Daemon pushed up from the floor and onto his feet, then walked toward the door. With his hand on the knob, he turned and let his gaze rake over the man who sat behind the large mahogany desk.

This wasn't the man who had raised him. It wasn't the man who had taught him what it was to be a man and how to be a good king.

This man did nothing but bring a foul taste to his mouth.

Daemon scoffed and shook his head. "You better hope Auraelia can take her down, because if not? Not only did you just sign thousands of death certificates for our own citizens, but you've just damned the whole of Ixora."

Daemon opened the door and walked away, not even caring enough to pull it closed behind him.

Chapter One

Auraelia

Two months later...

"Fuck!"

Thunder rumbled through the sky outside the council chambers as Auraelia slammed her hands down on the table, frustration rolling off her in waves.

"Majesty," the sound of Ser Aeron's deep baritone cut through the field of red that was creeping into her vision. She could feel her magic swirling just beneath the surface of her skin. The static of her lightning made the hair on her arms stand on end.

As she lifted her head, she was met with the sharp intensity of Ser Aeron's amber gaze. His brow was furrowed, and his lips had set into a hard line. Though with all the severity of his expression, concern swirled in his eyes.

Auraelia blew a breath through pursed lips and bobbed her head to let him know she was okay.

The sound of thunder lessened, and the clouds began to part as she sat back down in her mother's—in *her*—chair.

It'd only been two months since her mother had been poisoned.

Two months since she'd regrettably walked away from the one person that could ground her with a single touch.

In those months, she and her council had come up with little to nothing when it came to Davina. And that day had been no different.

What they *did know* was that she was attempting to extend her reach into other courts.

Mister Aramis had been going from court to court, enlisting the help of his many contacts throughout Ixora to ensure that Auraelia could keep tabs on her cousin. But even with the extra sets of eyes, Davina was practically a ghost.

No one could pin her down in one spot for long enough to get intel, and Auraelia had a feeling it was because of the person who helped her escape all those nights ago.

She needed someone, *anyone*, to give her some kind of lead to help her through this mess.

She'd already lost her mother, and the ache in her chest was a constant reminder of the love lost when she pushed Daemon away. It didn't matter that she did it to try and save him and his people. To save *her* people. She *missed* him. But every time she let her thoughts travel back to him, the chasm in her heart opened wider and the hold on her magic slipped.

She needed to focus before she lost her kingdom, too.

"My apologies. Where were we?" Auraelia leaned against the carved back of her chair, the cool wood seeping through the thin linen of her tunic as she listened to the advice from the council.

As the meeting came to a close and people filtered out of the space, Auraelia closed her eyes and sighed. Between the death of her mother and everything that had happened since, she hadn't slept much and it was starting to catch up to her.

Her head throbbed as a migraine began to set in, and she pressed her fingers into her temples in an attempt to alleviate the building pressure.

She'd started getting them around the time her world came crumbling down around her, and they'd become more frequent as her powers continued to grow and expand.

When was the last time I ate or drank anything?

Ser Aeron had stayed behind, the concern in his eyes from earlier never ebbing, and she could feel that intense gaze on her face.

Keeping her eyes closed, Auraelia braced herself for the question that she knew she needed to ask. She'd been avoiding it for months and couldn't put it off any longer.

After her mother's death, everyone in the council had been questioned extensively about their knowledge when it came to the Court of Garnet. They'd known about the former queen's half-sister—Lady Verena—the entire time, but they had only found out about Davina after Auraelia had traveled to Kalmeera.

Every single person on the council had known that Davina had been conspiring to take the crown, and every one of them kept that information from her.

She knew she couldn't lay all of the blame at their feet, but it didn't make them any less guilty.

The one person who hadn't been questioned was Ser Aeron. In the days of her catatonic state, Xander had sent him to fortify the army and make sure that they were ready for anything.

But now? She'd put it off long enough, and she needed to know. So, with a deep breath, she took the leap and asked, "Did you know?"

There was a small *squeak* as the foot of the chair shifted against the floor, and she cracked her eyes to peer at the man who had been in her life longer than he had been out of it. His eyes held so much sorrow, but it was the hint of guilt that slowly brought her anger back to the surface.

Auraelia sat up and rested her elbows on the table, her fingers steepled in front of her face. The burn from her lightning warmed the tips, and it took immense focus to keep it from forming into ribbons and spiraling around the digits.

Concentrating on the far wall, Auraelia spoke through clenched teeth. "How long?"

She saw him wringing his hands from the corner of her eye, something she'd never seen him do, before he clasped them together and released a long breath. "Auraelia–"

His placating tone made her blood boil, and she jumped from her chair. The abrupt movement sent it skittering backward and worsened her head's throbbing. "Don't. I don't want excuses; I just want to know. You've *never* sugar-coated anything with me. Never treated me like one of my mother's fragile flowers. Don't you dare start now."

She turned away from the table, her hands flexing at her sides, and began to pace.

One, two, three—she counted to ten in her head, then back down again, until her mind began to still and her magic settled. It was the only thing that worked anymore.

She could no longer use the memory of Daemon's voice to steady herself. Whenever she'd tried, all she saw was his face etched in pain as she walked away from him. All she felt was the icy cold hands of her heart being ripped out of her chest. And that was a pain she refused to let herself feel again. *Four, five, six*—

Ser Aeron stood slowly and walked over to where she paced in front of the windows that looked out over her mother's garden. What was once full of pink and white peony blossoms was now a wasteland of dying shrubs and wilted blooms.

"I've always known about Verena. Your mother—" he paused and walked closer, peering out of the window at the lifeless flora before continuing. "Your mother only told me about Davina a few years ago. I'm not sure how long she'd been holding onto that secret, but I'm almost certain she'd always known."

Auraelia stopped pacing and walked to stand next to him. "Why didn't you tell me?"

"It wasn't my secret to tell."

For a while, they stood there in silence. Watching the sun sink into the horizon as it painted the sky in pinks and purples, the stars began to poke through the last remaining streams of daylight.

"I tried, Auraelia."

The deep rumble of his voice cut through the silence, and she turned to look at him. He was still gazing out the window, but she could see the glassiness of his eyes and hear his breath's shakiness. When he finally looked her way, her heart broke, and her anger ebbed away.

"I tried to get her to tell you and Xander. I tried so many times. But your mother was a stubborn woman. And there were times when it was her greatest asset, but in this case, it was also her greatest downfall. I am so sorry that I wasn't there to save her."

Grasping his large hand in hers, she gave him a reassuring squeeze as tears lined her eyes as well. "It happened so fast that I'm not sure even you could have saved her. But none of this is *your* fault. Nor is it mine, though we both carry the weight of her decisions."

Pain that mirrored her own shone back through his eyes, and as he nodded, a lone tear ran down his cheek.

A soft knock on the door broke the silence that had begun to settle between them, and Auraelia called for whoever was on the opposite side to enter.

Piper poked her head in, her brow furrowed in frustration. "Rae, you skipped lunch...*again*. I'm here to force you to eat dinner."

Ser Aeron's gaze turned from sadness to annoyance. "You haven't been eating?"

At the mention of food, her head began to throb once more, and she cringed.

"You have another migraine, don't you?" Piper asked as she entered the room.

Auraelia nodded slowly, trying not to make any jarring movements, while Piper huffed out an annoyed breath and crossed her arms as she leaned against the table.

Ser Aeron squeezed her hand, pulling her attention back in his direction, and narrowed his eyes. "Go eat. I mean it. You have a lot on your plate, and I saw the hold on your magic slipping throughout the meeting as your emotions got the better of you. You need to be in control, not letting it control you."

Auraelia nodded and tightened her hold on his hand before letting go and allowing him to excuse himself.

When the door closed firmly behind him, Piper dropped her arms and released a heavy sigh. "Okay, food is in your room. We have enough time to eat before we have to meet Xan at the stables."

Xan. She still wasn't used to the nickname that Piper had given her brother. But she was the only one who used it, and it made him smile every time.

The two women hastily walked down the short hallway that led to the door of the queen's apartments—one that only the reigning queen could open.

Once inside, they practically inhaled their meal of roast and potatoes before they donned thick wool cloaks and snuck out through the queen's garden.

They had somewhere to be and not a lot of time to get there.

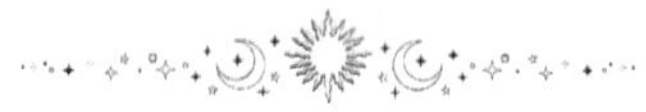

Walking into Vee's alone was one thing.

Walking in with an entourage was something else entirely.

Heads always turned when three people dressed in black cloaks with hoods drawn up entered a space.

Ignoring the curious gazes from those around her, Auraelia led Piper and Xander to the bar at the back where Vee stood, serving one of her patrons.

Waiting until the man left, Auraelia stepped up to the bar. "Is he here yet?" she asked in a hushed tone while Vee poured her a glass of honey whiskey.

"No, Your Maj–" she stopped, cleared her throat, and then shook her head, "No, I haven't seen him yet."

Auraelia nodded and grabbed her glass. Taking a swig before gesturing to her companions behind her. "Can you show us to the room?"

Vee dried her hands on the towel that hung from where it was tucked into the top of her apron at her waist, then called for one of her girls to watch the bar while she was gone.

She led them down a dark hall, then up a small flight of stairs to her private office on the main floor of the house. It was far enough away from the events happening below but close enough for an inconspicuous exit.

Inside was a small desk, a bookshelf, and an intimate seating area in front of a fireplace with a few armchairs and a couch. The sconces on the wall were dim but bright enough to see by, giving the space a gentle glow.

Vee closed the door behind her when she left, promising to bring a decanter of whiskey and wine back with her when the final member of their company arrived.

Auraelia took a seat in the chair closest to the fireplace while Xander and Piper took the settee—sitting on opposite ends of each other.

Idiots.

As time ticked on and there was still no word, Auraelia grew antsy. Twirling the queen's emerald around her finger as they waited.

"This is ridiculous. Of course, he's fucking late." Piper fumed from her seat.

She was slouched down on the cushions, her arms crossed over her chest as her foot tapped incessantly on the floor.

Reaching over, Auraelia grabbed her knee. "Would you please stop that? You're going to let everyone downstairs know we're up here, and I'm sure there's a good reason that he's late."

At least there better be.

As soon as the words left her lips, there were five quick knocks, and they all turned toward the sound as Aiden walked through the door.

"Sorry I'm late. Something came up."

There was a worried edge to his voice, and it put Auraelia on high alert. "What kind of something?" Her eyes narrowed, and the air in the room began to stir.

"Woah, easy. Everything is fine. It just took longer to get here than I had anticipated. That bitch has eyes everywhere."

The air around them settled as Aiden crossed the room and leaned against the mantle over the fireplace.

Odd.

This was the second clandestine meeting that they'd had with Aiden since everything fell apart. He was the one contact in the Sapphire Isles that Auraelia knew she could trust, and that was only because he wanted Daemon away from Davina as much as she did.

"Did you find out any more about what exactly her abilities are?" Auraelia asked. It was the one thing that none of their informants could catch wind of. Evidently, there weren't many people who had experienced Davina's magic and survived. And those who had either didn't want to—or were unable to—talk about it.

"Not exactly, but—"

"I may be able to shed some light on that." A voice as smooth as velvet and as dark as the magic that accompanied it swept through the room, slowing time to a crawl.

She'd know that voice anywhere, and her magic danced beneath her skin at the sound.

Auraelia looked to Aiden, who had an apologetic look on his face, before she slowly turned toward the door. Standing in the doorway's shadows was a man she would recognize until the day she died. Even with a hood covering his features, the broad set of his shoulders and the cocky lean against the doorframe gave him away.

No, it can't be. He can't be here.

The figure stood upright and pushed the hood back from his face, a Cheshire smile gracing his luscious lips.

"Hello, my star."

Chapter Two

Daemon

He watched as the color slowly drained from her face while she took him in. She looked at him like she was seeing a ghost, instead of the man who told her he loved her before she walked away.

He'd been angry for weeks after that.

Angry at her for turning her back on what they had.

Furious with his parents for putting him in the situation they were currently in.

And mad at himself for letting her go.

Squaring his shoulders, Daemon walked across the space and took the empty chair next to Auraelia.

"Wha–what are you doing here? You can't *be* here." Panic laced her voice as her wide eyes searched his face.

"You'll find that I can, *Princess.*" He smirked, and a faint blush crept across her cheeks. That simple wash of color made his heart race, and his shadows railed against the hold he had on them.

Noticing the way Xander kept clenching and releasing his fists, Daemon turned his attention to the couch. "Xander, Piper, good to see you both again. Now, if you'd excuse us. Her Majesty and I have some things to discuss."

"Excuse me?" Piper and Auraelia said in unison.

"Piper, you know I would never do anything to hurt her. You *both* do." The latter was directed toward Auraelia, but she turned away to keep from meeting his gaze.

As the minutes passed, he was confident that this wasn't going to go according to his plan.

When he found Aiden sneaking onto the Nevermore right at nightfall, he'd cornered him and demanded to know what was going on. Once he knew he would meet with Auraelia, Daemon decided to hijack their meeting. Aiden wasn't happy about it, but he'd get over it.

He needed to see her.

Needed to talk to her.

He was about to give up when Auraelia cleared her throat and straightened her shoulders. Slipping on the mask of the queen she was always destined to be, regardless of what her bat-shit crazy cousin seemed to think.

"It's alright. He wouldn't hurt me; if he tried, there wouldn't be much left to find." She let a few ribbons of lightning snake between her fingers as she spoke. It was meant as a reassurance to her family, and a warning to him.

All that Daemon saw was a challenge.

He sat as still as a statue, watching as the ribbons of light danced between her fingers. Xander and Piper slowly rose from their seats and followed Aiden out the door.

When the latch clicked into place, Auraelia pulled her magic back into herself and took a deep breath. "What do you want, Daemon?"

Her icy tone would have chilled him to the bone without the small break in her voice as she spoke. Like she was using every trick she had at her disposal to keep from falling apart.

She refused to look at him, instead focusing on her fingers as she picked at the skin around her nails. Her leg bounced with nervous energy as silence descended between them.

Daemon stood from his chair and took up the space that Aiden had just vacated at the mantel. "I just want to talk."

It was then that she finally looked up and met his gaze. The fire he loved and then watched get extinguished, once again burning brightly in her eyes. "Then talk. What do you know about Davina?"

He breathed heavily and then ran his fingers through his hair. "I, unfortunately, had firsthand experience with her power."

Her eyes widened in shock, and she shifted in her seat like she was going to stand and approach him but settled once more and averted her gaze.

He hated that she wouldn't look at him, at least not longer than a few cursory seconds. He needed to stoke that fire in her eyes. Needed to make her *feel* something, anything. Even if it was hatred. He needed to see the woman who held his heart and was the missing piece to his soul. But the woman who sat in front of him now was no more than a shell of the one he once knew.

Renewed anger at how she walked away those months ago resurfaced, and he continued when she didn't say anything. "After you sent me away—" venom dripped from his words, and the tiniest tick on her cheek let him know it hit his mark. "I went home and confronted my father. I barged into his office and told him I wouldn't marry Davina."

Auraelia shifted her gaze higher but still not to his face.

Progress, we're making progress.

"Little did I know, she was also in his office and, needless to say, she wasn't happy with my conclusion. So, when I told her that 'over my dead body would she ever be a queen in this realm,' she decided to show me that it was, in fact, a possibility."

That got her attention. Her eyes flew toward his, wide and full of worry and anger.

There she is.

"What do you *mean*?" she asked through clenched teeth.

"What I mean is that she made my blood run cold. It felt like ice was in my veins, and the frigid temperature *burned*. I couldn't access my shadows through the pain. Hell, I could barely breathe through it."

Auraelia's eyes grew wider with every detail, and the air in the room began to stir.

"Auraelia, breathe." He made sure to keep his voice low and steady. He'd seen how powerful she was when she reached into her well of magic, but he had no idea how deep that well ran.

She stood abruptly and began pacing in front of the desk. Mumbling something to herself, she rubbed at the darkened green tips of her fingers.

"One, two, three–"

Is she counting?

Daemon slowly crossed the room and gripped her shoulders when she made it back to her starting point.

The sudden contact jarred her out of her trance, and she jumped out of his grasp.

"Don't—" She closed her eyes briefly and took a quick breath. "Don't touch me."

The air around them was stirring the papers on the desk, and the hairs on the back of his neck were beginning to stand on end. "Auraelia, you need to breathe."

He could see the panic rising as her breathing became heavier, and the look in her eyes turned frantic.

Daemon began to stalk toward her, but she took one in the opposite direction for every step he took.

"Daemon—" There was a warning in her voice, but it was one that told him she wasn't in control. He didn't care if she fried him to pieces; he just wanted to try and calm her down.

When her back collided with the wall, he placed his hands next to her shoulders. Her eyes were squeezed shut, and she was still muttering numbers.

"Auraelia, my star, you need to breathe."

Her eyes popped open, and she focused on him.

The blue calcite of her irises was completely gone, replaced by a bright peridot green with streaks of champagne lightning coursing through them.

"Don't call me that." Anger burned in her tone, and every word was clipped. But anger was something that he would work with.

Anger was but a breath away from lust. And lust was but a step away from love.

He knew she loved him. She hadn't outright said it, and it may have taken two months apart for him to realize it, but he knew in his heart it was why she sent him away.

And if he could anger her, maybe he could get her to admit that she loved him.

Then *maybe* they could solve this problem together.

Daemon let a sly grin creep across his face and leaned in until their breaths mingled. "You think you scare me, Princess? Do you think that a little wind and some lightning are going to deter me? Well, I hate to be the bearer of bad news, but it won't."

He let go of the hold on his shadows. Let them weave their way around them, enclosing them in a cocoon of night.

"You sent me away. You let go of everything we had, and for what? What did it get you? I told you I *loved* you, and you still made me go. Why? Tell me *why*."

Ribbons of lightning wove around her fingers and arm, and Daemon sent some of his magic to play with hers. They twined together in a rope of light and dark. Opposites that shouldn't have worked, forming something new and beautiful. He leaned in further, his body close enough that when she breathed, her breasts brushed against his chest.

"I hate you," Auraelia seethed, the ferocity of her lighting ramping up as her emotions rose.

Daemon chuckled. "You know, I don't think that you do. But I can work with hate. Hate is just on the opposite side of the coin from love. And whether or not you're ready to admit it to me, even to yourself, we both know that you love me, Princess."

Her magic flared around them, ricocheting off his before they tangled together. He could feel the heat of her lightning as it danced with his shadows. Could feel the cool caresses of her wind as it battered against the shell of magic surrounding them. And it made all the blood in his body rush south.

Smiling, he closed the space between them until his body was pressing hers against the wall, and his leg was wedged between her thighs. Their gazes locked with a heat and intensity that could set the world ablaze.

Fuck this.

Daemon leaned down, but her hands flew to his chest when his mouth was but a breath away from hers.

"*Daemon.*"

His name was a breathy plea on her lips, and the heat from her hands on his chest was like a branding iron as burning streaks of light coiled around her fingers.

His eyes softened as he whispered, "I'm not afraid of you, Auraelia."

Then he crashed his lips to hers.

There was a fraction of a second where she tensed against him, and he'd begun to regret his choice to push her this far. But the moment passed faster than it came, and she melted into his touch.

Her fingers tangled into the loose fabric of his shirt before migrating upward to the nape of his neck where she held him to her.

Daemon added pressure between her legs with his thigh, and he felt the moan escape her lips and travel into his own.

But as soon as his hands landed on her hips, a gust of wind slammed into his chest and pushed him back until he hit the desk.

They stared at each other, breathing heavily as magic clung to the air.

"That shouldn't have happened." Auraelia finally spoke. Averting her eyes and breaking the connection between them.

"Aurae—"

"Don't. Just—don't."

"Fuck!" Daemon snapped as he ran both hands through his hair. Spinning around, he paced the length of the room a few times before coming back to stand a few feet from her. "Why? Tell me why, Auraelia. I fucking *love* you, and I know that you love me too, and you keep pushing me away. Why?"

Anger and pain filled every word, and he could see the walls crumbling down around her as his words hit home.

"Tell me!" he shouted.

"I can't!" she yelled in return. "*We* can't."

"Why?" He wasn't yelling anymore, but his voice was still raised and vibrated with all the pain he'd been holding onto for the last two months.

"Because of *her*! Goddess, Daemon. Do you not understand how hard this is? I *can't* be in love with you because *she* will use that against me. She will use it against you, and your family, and your people." Auraelia's head fell back as tears trailed down her face.

Daemon watched as the wall he'd just begun to tear down got built back up brick-by-brick until she squared her shoulders and pushed away from the wall.

"We can't do this. *You shouldn't* be here. This was a mistake."

"It wasn't, and I can see that nothing I say will change your mind. But *this*—" he gestured between them, "isn't a mistake. This is inevitable. We're two halves of the same soul, and I know you feel it. So, you can send me away again, but I'll be back. I'll always come back for you."

Daemon held her gaze for a moment more before turning and walking out the door.

The sound of it slamming behind him echoed down the hall as he returned to the stairs that led to the brothel below.

I need a fucking drink.

Chapter Three

Auraelia

The resounding *door boom* as it slammed into place reverberated through the air. Collapsing against the wall, Auraelia let go of everything she'd been holding onto for months.

Let go of the hold she'd kept on her magic.

Let the dam that had been holding back her pain and tears break and spill over.

Just...let go.

She'd kept everything bottled so tightly, tucked into the recesses of her mind, that she'd been able to fool herself into thinking she was fine. That she could get over whatever had been between her and Daemon. But the minute he stepped into that room, the minute his eyes locked onto hers, her resolve and the wall around her heart crumbled.

Tears streamed down her face as months of repressed magic bled out of her.

Wind spiraled around the room with enough force to slide furniture around and rip books from their homes on the shelves. Rain hammered against the windows, and thunder boomed in the sky while lightning twined up her arms until it encased her entire body in ribbons of crackling light.

Reaching for the one thing that could help, she closed her eyes and began counting.

One. Two. Three—

She needed to calm down. Needed to reign in her magic before she flooded the city or burned down the brothel with everyone inside. Every breath she took scorched her throat, and her lungs screamed for the air she was unable to find.

Four. Five—

She couldn't move.

Couldn't feel anything outside of the overwhelming grief that she'd been determined to ignore. Couldn't see anything past the anguish that, once again, twisted Daemon's handsome features.

Six—

Her eyes snapped open at the loud crash that echoed through the space as something rammed against the door to the office, and it wasn't long before Piper and Xander were barreling into the room.

Piper seemed to be screaming to her, but she couldn't make out the words over the wind's howling and the ringing in her ears.

Seven. Eight—

Her friend's face twisted into one of panic as she rushed across the space to kneel in front of her and froze. Piper's eyes quickly flicked over Auraelia's body before she said something to Xander, who was out the door the next instant.

Auraelia looked down at the coils of light that surrounded her body, and dread set in.

No. This can't be happening. I can't—I can't breathe.

Her breathing became more erratic as her panic rose, and for the first time since she discovered her lightning, it *burned.* The heat from the ribbons seared through the fabric of her tunic, and she couldn't stop it. It was as if her magic was actively fighting against her. Raging against the leash that she tried desperately to put around it.

Her vision blurred from the tears in her eyes, sizzling against her cheeks as they fell.

It wasn't until the world around her darkened and a pair of leather-clad knees knelt before her that she finally looked up.

Eyes the color of molten gold with the slightest hint of green around their edges stared back at her.

"Auraelia, let me help." Daemon reached a hand out toward her as he spoke.

She recoiled, but as she tried to back away, she collided with a wall of inky darkness. Shaking her head vigorously, she managed to inhale enough air to speak. "I don't want to hurt you."

Sadness filled his eyes, and his shoulders drooped as a sigh slipped through his lips. "You can't hurt me, Auraelia. Not any more than you already have. I just want to help you. *Please*, let me help."

Daemon slid closer, and as he reached out again, she felt her magic stretch toward him in return. Her lightning again twined with his shadows until they were wrapped in a sphere of burning light and velvety darkness.

The feeling of his hand on her cheek made her heart skip and grounded her long enough to suck air into her lungs.

Even after everything she'd said and done to push him away, he'd come back.

I'll always come back for you. His words from earlier echoed through her mind as tears streamed down her face once more.

"I'm so sorry, Daemon." Auraelia's words came out in hiccupped sobs as guilt crashed into her.

His hands were warm as he cupped her face and rested his brow on hers. "I know."

Those two words had the rest of her walls crumbling down.

She let him pull her into his lap. Let the beat of his heart and the rhythm of his breathing settle the storm in her soul. It was selfish to lean into his touch and seek solace in his embrace; she knew that but couldn't help it.

She craved being near him, held by him...even if it was for a short time.

Daemon stroked her hair as he spoke in hushed whispers, "We'll figure this out, my star. I promise."

She pulled away enough to glance up at him. "How?"

Reverently, he wiped away her tears and caressed her cheek as he gazed down at her like he was committing every fleck of color in her eyes to memory. "I don't know, but we will do it *together*."

When he pressed his lips to hers, it was like coming home.

As if everything they had been through and had yet to endure was nothing. Forgotten as their lips melded together and their souls healed.

It was a promise to be there with her through whatever and wherever this war with her cousin took them.

To be hers and for her to be his.

It took everything she had not to entirely fall apart in his arms.

With her emotions settling, Auraelia was able to wrangle in her magic. Calming the wind that still howled through the room. Easing the storm that raged outside. And finally, pulling her lightning from where it mixed with Daemon's shadows.

As their magic separated, the room around them came back into view. Piper's mouth dropped open as her eyes flicked between Auraelia and Daemon. "Rae, is everything okay?"

Sliding from his lap, Auraelia nodded to her friend, then dropped her gaze. Letting it land where her fingers were intertwined with Daemon's in her lap. "You should go."

"Auraelia—" Her name was a growl on his lips, and she winced.

"Daemon, please." She took a steadying breath before lifting her gaze to his. "Nothing has changed—"

"Everything has changed! Auraelia, *please*. Don't do this, not again." Anguish swirled in his eyes, and the chasm in her heart widened.

"Please try to understand. You *can't* stay here; it's not safe, not for you or for either of our people. If we have any chance at defeating Davina, we have to be smart about this. Which means you *need* to leave."

"She's right." Aiden's tenor cut through the room, causing Piper to jump.

"Goddess, dammit, Aiden. Could you *not* sneak up on people, please?" Piper growled out through clenched teeth.

Auraelia rolled her eyes before turning a pleading gaze back to Daemon.

He sighed, defeat settling in his eyes. "I know you're right. I do. But I feel like I just got you *back*."

Auraelia reached up and cupped his face in her hand. Relishing in the scratchy, soft texture of his beard beneath her palm. "Walking away from you was the hardest thing I've ever had to do—" She smiled and pulled his face to hers, placing a chaste kiss on his lips before resting her brow against his. "I won't do it again."

The words were acid on her tongue, and she knew that they were a lie as soon as they left her lips.

It may break her into a thousand pieces to do it, but she would walk away from him a thousand times if it meant keeping him safe.

Daemon stood and helped her to her feet as well.

Then, after another quick kiss, Auraelia watched as he walked out the door again.

Minutes passed before Xander broke the silence that had descended on their small group. "Lying through your teeth again, I see, sis."

Auraelia flinched at the bite in his tone before turning to face him head-on. "You would have done the same in my situation—" She quickly glanced at where Piper was picking up papers from the floor before staring back at her brother. "Would you not?"

Xander didn't respond, but the way his eyes lingered on Piper was an answer in and of itself.

Piper—oblivious to their conversation—straightened and turned toward them with a stack of parchment and books in her hands. "Would you both stop gawking at me and help? Vee is a tiny but terrifying woman. And I'd rather not get on her bad side."

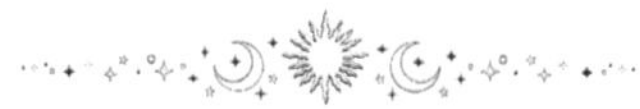

Back in her room at the castle, Auraelia stripped out of her riding clothes and took a long, hot shower before collapsing into bed. She was exhausted beyond belief, but her mind was a massive tangle of thoughts.

After tossing and turning for hours, she gave up.

Crossing the room to the writing desk that was nestled into a corner, she opened the bottom drawer and pulled out the wooden box that had been locked away since Daemon left. Inside sat the sapphire pendant he'd given her.

The one that had let them reach each other regardless of time or distance.

The physical reminder of everything she lost. Everything that she'd given up.

She'd tossed it into a box and locked it away the same way she'd locked away her feelings for him. Building a wall so high that she couldn't look back even if she'd tried.

Until tonight.

Bringing the box to her bed, she set it down on the coverlet and took a deep breath. As she slowly lifted the lid, and the contents inside came into view, her breath caught in her throat.

Surrounding the pendant were countless letters.

New letters.

She'd left the old ones on the side table of her former room, unable to bring herself to take them with her into her new chambers.

He never stopped writing.

Tears sprung into her eyes as she pulled them from the box one by one and placed them into a pile on the bed.

Cracking the seals on each one, she slowly worked her way through them all. Her heart broke with each one she opened. Anger, sadness, and cold indifference poured through his words, and the guilt of everything she put him through crashed into her once more.

Auraelia,

I don't understand why you sent me away. We could have done this together. Do I mean nothing to you? Does what we have mean nothing to you? I told you that I loved you, and you just walked away as if it meant nothing.

Fuck, maybe it did mean nothing to you.

I did as you asked. I left today.

I hope you're happy.

Daemon

Auraelia,

I confronted my father yesterday.

Let's just say that it didn't go to plan.

I wish you would just talk to me.

Daemon

Each letter got shorter as she read. No longer were there greetings or farewells.

Instead, he flipped between cursing her name and begging her to write back.

Fuck you and your reasoning behind this bullshit.

Fuck, Auraelia. Talk to me, please.

But the one that stung most was the final letter that she'd received.

My star,

I love you. I will always love you.

Even if the stars cease to shine and the world is cast into darkness, I will love you.

If you set the world ablaze, I will stand beside you, watch it burn, and love you while ashes fall from the sky.

You can tell me over and over again to stop, but I will only ever love you more.

I am yours, Auraelia. Whether you want me to be or not. I am yours.

I will wait for you, and I will always come back.

I can only pray that you will do the same.

Forever yours,

Daemon

Tears streamed down her face, landing on the parchment in her hand and smudging the ink scrawled across the page.

Picking up the pendant from where it lay on the bed, she let the chain slip through her fingers before palming the rich-colored stone. The sapphire warmed in her hand, the familiar feeling bringing her a sense of comfort.

She had no idea how to—or if she even could—repair the damage she'd done to her relationship with Daemon. No clue if there was a way for her to make it up to him. The one thing she did know was that it wasn't safe to try until she'd handled her cousin.

Piling the letters back into the box, Auraelia slipped back out of bed and padded over to her desk. After placing the box back in the drawer, she penned a response to Daemon.

She just hoped that one day, he would forgive her.

Chapter Four

Daemon

Despite the ache that settled into his soul the moment he walked away from Auraelia—*again*—warmth filled his chest as they pulled away from Lyndaria's harbor.

A smile tugged at the corners of his lips, and hope filled him. Hope that they were on their way past *this*. Hope that the connection they'd rekindled in that dark office of the brothel was enough to bring her back to him.

The warmth in his chest turned to a gentle, yet firm, tug. It was a feeling he hadn't had in months and something he hadn't fully realized was there until it was gone.

The pendant.

He'd felt it the moment she'd taken it off all those months ago. It was like a light had been dimmed, casting his world in a bleak shade of gray, and his shadows had shuttered at the feeling. Like they, too, knew that she'd cut herself off from him.

But now? Warmth filled his body, and shadows purred beneath his skin.

It wasn't long before the familiar feeling of magic twisted along his arm before dissipating into his pocket.

Daemon slipped his hand into the silk lining of his vest pocket and ran his fingers over the rough texture of the parchment and the warmth that still lingered on the wax seal.

Only, it wasn't the usual thinly folded letter.

This one was bulging on the sides, and it was like a stone weighing down his pocket.

A stone...

"Fuck," Daemon muttered beneath his breath.

Grasping the letter in his fist, he pushed away from the rail and headed toward his cabin below. Men scurried around the deck, shouting commands and acknowledging them, throwing lines and moving supplies, but all of that faded into the background as the letter in his pocket grew heavier and heavier.

Below deck, he slammed the door.

Running his hands through his already messy hair, Daemon sank down onto his bed and pulled the offending parchment from his pocket.

It lacked her usual finesse.

There was no sprig of lavender.

The seal was done haphazardly and warped around the odd shape of the bundle in his hand.

Taking a quavering breath, Daemon pried open the letter and gently pulled apart the folds. There, nestled in the middle, was the pendant he'd given her. His shadows, once swirls of living darkness in its center, sat stagnant and lifeless.

He lifted the stone and saw that beneath it, written in shaky script, were two words that would haunt him for the rest of his days.

I'm sorry.

Daemon balled up the paper and hurled it across the small space.

Pushing his fingers through his hair, he pulled at the roots. Needing physical pain to drown out the anguish in his chest.

How could she do this? How could she give up so easily?

He began to rock as pain bled into anger. His shadows began to seep out of him, filling the space around him until the entire ship was encompassed in the darkness that shrouded his soul.

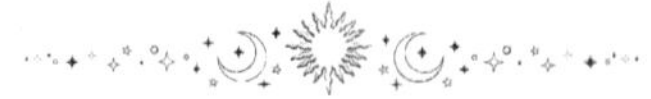

It took a full day and part of the following night to make it back to Kalmeera.

Daemon's fit of magic inhibited Raneese from seeing where she was going, and they had to stop until he was able to pull back his shadows.

Finally back at the castle, Daemon slammed the door to his suite as he crossed the room to the bar cart nestled between his floor-to-ceiling windows. It was late, and he was tired but needed a drink.

Pouring himself a glass of whiskey, he downed the contents, then rested his hands on the cold glass top.

"Rough night?" The cool, sultry voice that filled the quiet of the room made the hair on the back of his neck stand on end.

"What the *fuck* are you doing in my chambers?" Daemon ground out through clenched teeth. Standing up straight, he turned toward the offending sound.

His drapes still hung open, letting in the soft light of the moon, and there, stretched out on his couch with her long snow-white hair draped over the arm, was Davina, her lips tilting up into a sly smile that reminded him a little too much of Auraelia.

The family resemblance was eerie.

Their features were almost twin-like, the only outstanding differences coming from the color of their hair and the fact that Auraelia's skin was kissed by the sun, whereas Davina's was bathed by the moon.

They were the embodiment of night and day.

"I asked you a question, Davina. What are you doing in my chambers?" Daemon's hands balled into fists at his side, turning his knuckles white.

With a roll of her eyes, Davina sat up from her lounging position and propped her feet onto the low table. "Why, waiting for you, *my love.*"

Her tone was sickly sweet, and it made Daemon's skin crawl. "Oh, cut the crap. What do you want?"

"Where were you?" Her smile still sat firmly in place, but the slight tilt of her head suggested that she already knew.

"I don't need to explain myself to you," Daemon spat before turning back toward the bar and pouring himself another drink.

"Now, now—" she tsked, "there's no need to be rude. Maybe I should just go ask my cousin if *she* knows what you've been up to." Her statement was followed by a thud.

He only took half a turn to see what she'd tossed onto the table.

Months of correspondence with Auraelia sat at Davina's feet.

Months of personal information. Of hopes and dreams. Of *love.*

"Where did you get those?" he asked.

Davina pulled her feet from the table, her smile dropping a little as she looked at him. "I think I have a right to know where my *fiancé* is spending his time—and with whom."

"I'm not—"

"Don't even think about finishing that statement, Daemon. Or do I need to remind you of what happened the last time?"

Memories of the icy claws she'd dug into his heart and the frigid temperature that ran through his veins had his skin pebbling.

"Now, why don't you be decent. Pour me a drink, and we can *talk*."

Tonguing a canine, Daemon reluctantly grabbed two glasses and the decanter and brought it over to the sitting area of his study.

After downing his glass, he rested his arms on his thighs and glared through his lashes. "What do you want to *talk* about?"

Davina took an easy sip, then leaned back against the couch. "I want you to tell me about my cousin. I want to know her strengths and her weaknesses. You were once, quite possibly, one of her greatest weaknesses. The letters—" she gestured to the pile on the table, "prove that."

"Why do you think that's now past tense?" Daemon lifted a questioning brow before taking another sip.

"If you were where I suspect you were, your demeanor proves that she nipped whatever you had in the bud. So, I need all her dirty little secrets—well, not *dirty* secrets. I got my fill of those in your letters. Thank you very much."

Hearing Davina casually dismiss his relationship with Auraelia was a red-hot dagger to his heart. He knew that Auraelia had given up. He understood why...to an extent. And yet, hearing the finality come from someone who had no idea what was going on between them—hell, *he* wasn't even sure what was going on—hurt.

I need another fucking drink.

Daemon refilled his tumbler and downed the contents. Then he poured another and downed that one, too.

Davina watched with unveiled amusement, her feet crossed at the ankle as she sipped slowly from the crystal tumbler.

Hours passed, and Daemon continued to drink. He'd finished off the decanter of whiskey, all while Davina nursed her single glass and then moved on to a bottle of wine while they passed the time in relative silence.

Occasionally she would prod him for information about Auraelia, but it stopped when he'd begun peppering her with questions about Garnet.

After that, she'd sat comfortably on his couch while he nearly drank himself into a stupor.

Daemon's arms were heavy as he attempted to pour himself yet another glass of wine.

He wasn't sure when it had happened, but Davina was suddenly in front of him.

"I think you've had enough," she whispered as she moved the bottle and glass out of reach and gently pushed him back until he sat upright.

Daemon slumped down into the chair. He tried to keep his gaze on Davina, but his eyes were heavy as exhaustion mixed with the alcohol in his system.

"Poor, poor, Daemon," she cooed as she slowly ran her hands up his thighs.

Slate-blue eyes stared up through pale lashes, and through his inebriated state, he could almost pretend that they belonged to Auraelia...almost.

Daemon squeezed his eyes shut and shook his head, trying to shake the fog from his mind.

"I could make you feel good, you know. Make you forget." Davina's whispers ghosted across his ear as she slowly slid into his lap. His knuckles whitened as his grip tightened on the arms of the chair.

Get it together, Daemon.

Davina's legs settled in on either side of his own.

"Why are you doing this? Surely you know about the treaty," he whispered, surprised that he was able to make a coherent sentence.

The heat of her body pressed into him as she lowered her lips to his. But a moment before they touched, she replied, "The treaty was voided the moment your father sided with me."

Daemon stood abruptly, toppling Davina to the floor.

Laughter filled the otherwise quiet space as he shoved away from the chair on surprisingly steady feet.

"You hadn't figured that out yet, had you?" she asked through her laughter.

Daemon whipped around a little too quickly and staggered. "You're lying."

Davina stood and brushed off her pants. Her feline smile was firmly in place as she stared at him. "No, my sweet, I'm not. The moment your father sided with me; he was working against *her*. Which broke the treaty." Her smile twisted into a sneer at the mention of Auraelia.

Daemon stood wide-eyed as his thoughts spiraled.

We can be together.

The treaty doesn't matter anymore.

I need to tell Auraelia.

"Now, before you get a stupid idea of running off to tell my cousin. Let me remind you of one...little...thing."

His blood began to chill, and his heartbeat slowed as Davina took calculated steps toward him.

"I can and will demolish all that you love and care about if you cross me. Your people, family, friends. And even though Auraelia seems to have pushed you aside, the quickening of your heart when you found out about the treaty tells me that *you have* not. I will break her in front of you. Make you watch while I slow her heartbeat to a crawl and freeze her from the inside out." She accentuated her threat by doing the same to him. "Do I make myself clear?" she asked when she was standing before him.

The once slate-blue eyes that stared back at him were now the color of garnets. The same color of the very blood that she was able to manipulate.

Daemon managed a nod through the pain, and the next instant, it was gone.

"Good." Davina patted his chest as she sidestepped him and headed toward the door.

As she pulled it open, she looked over her shoulder at him, a Cheshire smile plastered on her face. "I think this is the start of a *beautiful* relationship."

The door latched behind her, and Daemon had the strong urge to purge the contents of his stomach.

Rushing to his desk, he pulled out a piece of parchment to pen Auraelia a letter.

He needed to let her know what he'd discovered.

But as he began to write, he remembered the sapphire in his pocket, its weight growing heavier with every passing moment.

Fuck.

Chapter Five

Daemon

Daemon winced as streams of sunlight danced across his face.

What the fuck?

His head throbbed, and his mouth felt full of sawdust. Pushing into a sitting position, he looked around the room.

He was still in his study, but he didn't remember falling asleep. Didn't remember much of the previous night if he was candid with himself.

What the hell happened last night?

He remembered Davina being there when he'd returned from Lyndaria. Remembered drinking—too much, if the pounding in his head was any indication. From there, it was a blur. Just flashes of memories. Of slate-blue eyes and sensuously curved lips that had almost managed to fool him into thinking it was whom he longed for. Of moon-white hair and snow-kissed skin as she'd climbed into his lap.

Fuck.

Daemon groaned and pressed two fingers into his throbbing temples. His head pounded with every beat of his heart. How had he let it get that far? Let her get that close to him?

He winced as he peeled his eyes open into thin slits and stood. He made sure to move slowly so that his head wouldn't spin. As he took a step, the sound of paper crinkling beneath his foot stopped him in his tracks. Looking down, he saw the letters from Auraelia scattered around the floor near his couch. The memory of Davina throwing his failed relationship in his face barreled back into his mind.

As well as her little tidbit of information about the treaty.

He still needed to tell Auraelia. Still needed to figure out *how* to tell her now that she'd given her pendant back.

Daemon rubbed at his sternum, at the ache in his chest that had nothing to do with the previous night's indulgence.

Stooping down, he compiled the letters and then headed into his bedroom. He needed to wash off the feeling of Davina's body pressing into his.

It didn't matter that nothing happened. It didn't matter that Auraelia seemed to no longer be interested in pursuing what was between them. He still felt like he'd betrayed her somehow.

Turning the water as hot as it would go, Daemon stepped into the streams.

The initial chill had a sobering effect, giving him a brief moment of clarity.

He couldn't stay in Kalmeera. Not while *she* was there.

Thankfully, it was his turn to check in on the Priestesses.

The wind whipped against his cheeks as the Nevermore sliced through the water. It would take two days to reach Lunaria, even with the wind on their side.

Daemon stood on the quarter-deck while his captain stood at the ship's helm.

"Any idea on how long we will be in Lunaria?" Raneese asked as she skillfully steered the ship through the waters.

Turning from where he was looking out over the crystal blue waters to lean against the rail, he crossed his ankles as he folded his arms across his chest. "Why do you ask?"

Raneese shrugged. "Just *seems* like it will be a longer trip than usual, I guess."

She gave him a side-long glance before turning her gaze forward once more.

Daemon rolled his eyes and pushed away from the rail, crossing to the opposite side. The sound of rope slipping through the riggings as his crew adjusted the sails echoed through the quiet that had fallen between him and his captain.

He'd never lied to her before; there was no reason to start now.

With a heavy sigh, he gripped the edge of his ship. Letting the feel of the smooth wood beneath his palms calm him. "I can't be there while *she's* there. Can't stand to see the way she turns my father into a cowering insect who bows to her will."

"Is that all?"

The tone in her voice said that she already knew it wasn't, but he blew a breath and answered anyway.

"I need to clear my head." Daemon paused for a moment and looked out over the Cerulean Sea. The water was calm, unlike the thoughts that spiraled through his mind. "I need to recenter myself. If I don't..." Shadows danced at his fingertips, swirling around his digits in inky ribbons.

A wary look crossed Raneese's face as she nodded.

He didn't need to explain. He didn't need to bring up what had happened when they left Lyndaria. He'd never had that happen before. Never lost such control over his magic, not even when it had first manifested.

His shadows had bled out of him in waves. It was as if his entire ship had been dunked in a bottle of ink so dark that not even the light of the full moon was able to penetrate it.

Daemon shivered at the memory and pulled his magic back into himself.

The trip across the Cerulean Sea was uneventful.

They'd stopped on Malaena—the middle island—the first night to grab the supplies that the Priestesses had sent word that they needed. And so that Daemon could reassure his people that he would do everything within his power to keep them safe from Davina.

By the time they reached Lunaria the following day, it was nightfall.

The moon was high in the sky, and the stars were out in full force.

With the lines that secured the Nevermore to the dock in place, Daemon dismissed his crew...all save for Raneese.

"I need you to do something for me," he said as they sat in the captain's quarters. The rest of the crew were already shoreside, most likely dining at one of the small taverns in the harbor.

"What?" The word was slightly drawn out as Raneese narrowed her eyes and took a large swig from her glass.

Daemon reached into his pocket and pulled out a piece of parchment, then slid it across the table to Raneese. "I need you to bring this to Lady Aesira of Opal."

Raneese sputtered, and the rum that was still in her mouth dribbled down her chin. "Excuse me?"

Daemon shifted slightly in his seat. "I need you to bring this—" he held up the parchment and waved it around in short movements, "to Lady Aesira in Opal."

"Don't talk to me like a petulant child. I *heard* you the first time, asshole. I meant, *why* do you need me to bring a letter to Aesira?"

An exasperated sigh left his lips as he ran his free hand through his hair. It had gotten longer, more unkempt, but he didn't care. "Because Auraelia returned this."

He reached into his pocket and let the sapphire dangle between his fingers from the slender, silver chain. The glow from the lamps in the cabin danced on the deep blue surface, but his shadows were still cold.

Still lifeless.

Balling up the pendant and chain in his fist, he dropped it back into his pocket. "I need to get this information to Auraelia, but since I no longer have a direct line of communication with her, I have to find another way to do it."

"What about Aiden?" she asked as she idly ran her finger around the lip of her glass.

Daemon shook his head. "Too obvious. And I don't know when, or *if*, he's going to have another meeting with her."

Raneese nodded, her finger still circling the rim.

"I need this to get to her as soon as possible, Neese. Opal is far enough away from Kalmeera that it wouldn't be the obvious choice. So while I'm here, I need you to be *there*. Please."

Raneese raised her eyes to meet his. Sadness and understanding mixed with the swirls of chocolatey browns that made up her irises. After swallowing the remaining contents of her glass, she snatched the letter from his hand.

"I'll do it. But only because you said please."

A smile tugged at his lips as he raised his glass of whiskey to his captain.

To his friend.

As a new day broke, and Raneese and the crew pulled away from the harbor, Daemon shadow-walked to the opposite side of the island where the Moonstone Temple of the Goddess Narissa and her priestesses stood atop the highest mountain.

A sense of calm washed over him as he reached the bottom of Mount Uttara.

He'd always felt at home here. Felt at peace.

Daemon pulled on his power and shadow-walked to the highest point that magic could carry him. When he reached the base of the sanctuary, he stared up the massive expanse of steps that led into the clouds and began to climb.

Long ago, wards had been set at the base of the stairs that led to the temple. Markings that temporarily stripped people of their abilities as they climbed the nine-thousand steps that led to the mountain's peak.

It was said that the Goddess herself placed the wards there to keep people from entering the sacred grounds unannounced. To test their mettle and their devotion.

And it was only once the final step was crossed that their magic was returned.

Daemon maintained a steady pace as he took step after step. Even though he did this every other month, sometimes multiple times during his stay, it never got any easier.

It's no wonder the priestesses never leave the damn sanctuary.

The air thinned around him the higher he climbed, making breathing more difficult, but still, he pressed on.

It was past midday by the time he reached the top.

Despite it being winter, the islands held the warmth of summer throughout the year, and he was dripping with sweat. Even the coolness that came with the high altitude couldn't soothe the heat of his skin.

After the first hour, he'd removed his coat. By hour two, his vest.

But by the time he reached the top, his chest was bare, and his skin glistened in the afternoon sun.

As he crossed the final step, it was as if a lead blanket had been lifted from his shoulders, and his magic flowed freely through his veins once more.

"Welcome back, Your Highness." High Priestess Darya's voice was as cool as a summer breeze. Her sky-blue linen robes draped down her body and pooled on the ground at her feet, the long billowing sleeves covering the delicately tattooed hands that were laced together at her waist. Encircling her hips was a simple silver chain adorned with crystals and shells that tinkled in the breeze.

Every priestess of the Sapphire Isles wore the same robes, but what set the High Priestess apart was the circlet around her brow. It was a simple band of silver with a modest tear-shaped sapphire in the center. But, simple as it may be, it marked her as the head of this temple.

Even as a prince, Daemon didn't mess with her authority.

"Good to be back, High Priestess. Is everything well?"

The priestess nodded, then turned on her heel.

He followed after her as she headed toward the largest of the buildings, taking in the scene around him. He would never get over the beauty of the sanctuary grounds.

Columns of opaque white stone, with large swirls of arctic blue and periwinkle, lined the path before the steps and shimmered in the sunlight. However, due to the high elevation, there wasn't much in the way of vegetation. But where there was a lack of greenery, there was an abundance of scenery.

Snow-capped mountains created jagged cuts through the horizon, and beyond them sat a glistening expanse of deep blue water that stretched as far as the eye could see.

Once inside, Daemon inhaled deeply. The smell of vegetable soup hung heavily in the air, which made his mouth water and his stomach grumble.

The space was warm and inviting. Long tables were nestled under beautiful multi-colored glass windows that depicted the visages of their Goddess. Intimate sitting areas surrounded the massive fireplace on the far wall, complete with blankets and floor cushions.

It was relaxing. A quiet and calm place, free from distractions, and just what he needed.

"Would you like something to eat, Your Highness?" The High Priestess asked as they made their way through the communal area, where a few priestesses and guests were finishing what was left of their meals.

"That would be wonderful, High Priestess, thank you."

She stopped and turned her head in his direction, a small smile playing on her lips. "As I've told you before, Your Highness. You may call me Darya."

Daemon chuckled. "And as I've told you, *Darya*, you may call me Daemon while I am here. Just as you used to."

He'd known Darya for years. Met her when he'd come to study at the temple after his magic had manifested three years ago. They'd spent meals together and trained together. She learned their Goddess's ways while he discovered his magic's ins and outs.

Since then, they'd only seen each other a few times a year when he came to the island every other month. And in that time, she'd risen from pupil to High Priestess.

She inclined her head in acceptance, then continued to lead him through the room.

Exiting the main building, they headed toward the sleeping quarters.

His room was no different from any of the others on the grounds. Simple, with no more than the necessities: a bed for one, a small writing desk, and an armoire that held simple ivory linen clothes that were required to be worn at the sanctuary.

There were no private bathing rooms on the grounds. Instead, there were a handful of communal areas for hygiene.

As Daemon entered his rooms, another priestess exited, having just brought him a washbowl and towel to clean up from his trek up the mountain.

Darya excused herself, leaving him to his own devices, but not before issuing promises of food and wine once he joined everyone else in the communal building.

By the time he'd curled into bed that night, the moon was high in the sky, and he'd fallen asleep with a smile on his face for the first time in a long time.

The cold stone floor of the temple bit into the soles of Daemon's bare feet as he paced frantically across the space.

He'd been at this for days.

Three days of going back through the basics of magic. Of trying to regain control of the shadows that coursed beneath his skin.

Three days of meditating beneath the stars, *trying*—and failing—to get a sign from the Goddess Narissa to show him where to go from here. And he had nothing to show for it.

This was his last night at the sanctuary, and as he came to a stop in the center of the floor, he tilted his head upward and shouted into the star-speckled sky, "Goddess, why won't you answer me!"

The temple was tucked away in the far corner of the grounds. Secluded from the rest of the compound to give privacy to those who wished to convene with their Goddess—even if they were yelling into the void of the night.

Made only of moonstone columns, with no solid walls or ceiling, it looked out over the sea below and to the sky above.

Daemon fell to his knees as he stared up at the inky black sky.

The swirls of colors and stars that filled the blank canvas above him no longer brought him the solace that it once did. Not since he'd laid his eyes upon *his* star.

His throat was sore from shouting, and his hands shook at his sides as anger coursed through his body.

Roughly, he ran his fingers through his hair and released an exasperated sigh as his head fell forward in defeat.

"There's no need to shout, my son."

A voice, soft as velvet, slid into his thoughts, causing him to snap his head up and glance around. But there was no one there as a silky laugh caressed the corners of his mind.

"Sit, Daemon. Close your eyes, and see *me. Close your eyes and look upon my face."*

He did as the voice commanded. Sitting on the floor of the Moonstone Temple, he lifted his face to the sky once more and closed his eyes.

His mind filled with the deepest blues before clearing away to reveal the bearer of the voice. Staring back at him was a woman clad in sky-blue and dove-gray robes, with pearls and tentacles woven through the auburn waves of her hair and a fisherman's net draped across her eyes. But when she pushed the veil aside, it wasn't the blank eyes of lore that shone back at him. Instead, eyes the color of the ocean's depths locked onto his.

His eyes widened as he stared back at the woman.

At the Goddess Narissa, herself.

"Hello, Prince Daemon."

"My Lady." Daemon bowed low to the floor, his heart pounding in his chest. As far as he knew, the only people alive who saw Narissa were her priestesses. Everyone else had been lured to their deaths—or so the legends say.

"Rise, my son. You have no reason to fear me."

Daemon rose and silently met her gaze.

"I've been watching you, Daemon. You and your *star.*"

"Why?" His voice was barely a whisper, and the Goddess smiled.

"That's not the question you wanted to ask me." Narissa began to take leisurely steps around the temple, weaving her way around the columns as she spoke. "Not the question that has plagued your mind and heart for months on end."

Daemon's heart clenched in his chest as he let the words tumble from his lips. "Why am I drawn to Auraelia? Why does it feel like my very soul fractures into pieces when I'm no longer near her? Why—"

Narissa appeared in front of him, mere inches from his face. "Because, dear boy, she is the other half of your soul. She is the one whose heart beats in time with your own. She is your soulmate, Daemon."

"Soulmate?" Shock radiated through his body at her words. Shock and...clarity.

The Goddess spun away and continued her lazy rounds through the temple. "Yes, your soulmate. Yours is a love that has been destined for over five hundred years. Yours is a love that was meant to bring all of Ixora together. But your ancestor, King Erix, spoiled that."

"The treaty," Daemon muttered under his breath.

"Yes, the treaty. For centuries, the souls of both yours and Auraelia's ancestors have been reborn. Given new life and a new chance at love. But they are kept apart in one way or another every cycle." She paused momentarily, then turned toward him, her eyes full of hope. "You and Auraelia have a chance at happiness, Daemon. Have a chance to bring the realm together. You just have to take it."

His shoulders dropped as he released a sorrowful sigh. "Auraelia doesn't want anything to do with me or us anymore."

"Do you honestly believe that to be true?" she asked, her tone skeptical.

He didn't respond. Didn't know *how* to respond.

Did he believe that? No. And despite her best efforts to push him away, he knew she loved him. But he also didn't know how to convince her of it either when she refused to let him in.

Narissa grabbed his shoulders, pulling his attention back to her. "The love between you is written in the stars, Daemon. Your souls are bound to each other, and only *together* can you do what needs to be done."

He didn't miss the stress she put on the word "together." Didn't miss the slight widening of her dark eyes as she said it.

Together? How the fuck is that going to work when she won't even talk to me?

But before he could ask her what she meant—she was gone.

The deep hues that clouded his mind while he conversed with the Goddess faded away, and Daemon blinked at the brightness of the moon that took their place.

His head throbbed like it had the morning after he'd found Davina in his chambers.

What the fuck was that about?

Chapter Six

Auraelia

In the two weeks since Daemon walked out of her life—again—Auraelia spent her free time doing anything, and everything, to drown the ache in her chest.

She threw herself into endless council meetings and trained harder than she ever had with Ser Aeron, but nothing was helping. Nothing masked the pain that came when she saw his eyes. Saw the anguish that stared back at her before he walked away again.

So, she'd decided to try something else.

As she sidled up to the bar inside Madame Sylvie's, Vee's eyes widened to the size of saucers.

"What are you doing here? Did you have a meeting tonight?" Vee whispered nervously, her eyes a constant swivel as Auraelia sat on one of the worn leather stools. Undoubtedly, she was looking for her usual companions.

"Calm down, Vee. I'm just here for a drink and a distraction."

"No one—"

"No, Vee. No one is with me. Now, would you please pour me a drink?"

Vee's shoulders relaxed a fraction, though her eyes still held a sliver of worry in their icy blue depths. "What kind of distraction are you after, girl?" she asked, her brows raising slightly as she poured Auraelia's favorite honey whiskey into a tumbler and slid it across the bar.

Auraelia took a long swig from the glass before setting it back down and shrugged. "Anything will work, really. I'm not picky..." Auraelia let her eyes wander to the women who roamed the floor and the sheer gowns that trailed behind them, reminding her of Daemon's shadows.

She wasn't lying.

She would be perfectly content sitting at the bar drowning her sorrows, but she'd be just as fine following the gentle sway of hips into a dark room.

She'd been with women before and usually preferred it, especially since most of the males she'd been with were more interested in chasing their pleasure than tending to hers.

But that was *before*.

Before moss green eyes with twin suns burned their way into her soul.

Before calloused hands and pillowy soft lips marked her body.

Before Daemon, and the way that their souls called to one another.

She hadn't been with anyone since him. Hadn't wanted to.

But tonight? Grief was a cruel bitch that chilled you to the bone, and being wrapped in the warmth of another was as tempting as letting herself drown in the never-ending torment that plagued her soul.

Vee watched Auraelia through an intent, narrow gaze, then rolled her eyes and pulled a step stool from where it had been tucked behind the counter. Climbing to the top step, she stood on her tiptoes as she reached behind the liquors on the highest shelf and pulled down a dusty, cobweb-coated, brown bottle.

Vee blew off the dirt, coughing as her feet returned to the floor. "Come on." She jerked her head to one of the girls walking around the floor, a silent indication to watch the bar while the Madame tended to other business.

Auraelia slid off her stool and followed the petite woman down the hall that led to her office. When they reached the door, she blanched as the memories of the last time she'd been there tumbled through her mind.

Vee's voice filtered out into the hall, "You coming or are you going to stand like a statue in the hallway all night?"

Steeling her spine, Auraelia stepped over the threshold.

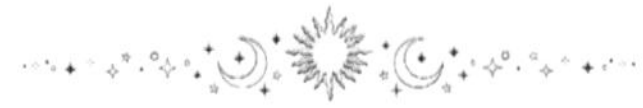

The following morning was torture.

Her head throbbed in her skull, and her body ached.

What the hell happened last night?

Auraelia gingerly sat up, rubbing her jaw as she cracked her eyes.

She was in her suite, still fully clothed in her tunic and trousers from the night before. But the faint scent of clove and cinnamon clung to the fabric.

Oh, fuck.

Falling back onto the mattress, she groaned.

"Yea, you look about as shitty as you undoubtedly feel." Piper's usually sing-song voice was as frosty as the morning air, making Auraelia wince.

"Good morning to you too, Piper," she said sarcastically, throwing her hand into the air in a mock wave.

Piper stalked across the room and tossed a towel onto her face. "Get up, you smell like tits and ass, and you have training with Ser Aeron in thirty minutes."

Removing the towel from her face, Auraelia pushed into a sitting position again. "What's got your panties in a twist today?"

Piper's glare was as frigid as her tone, and Auraelia had to suppress the shiver working through her.

"What's got my—" her friend inhaled deeply, her nostrils flaring with annoyance. "I'm pissed off because I got a letter from that tiny demon of a woman asking me to '*kindly remove Her Majesty from the premises*' at nearly three in the morning. What the fuck were you thinking, Rae? You're lucky that the guards don't open my correspondence—"

Auraelia's eyes widened slightly as she bobbed her head in understanding, but her mind wandered as her friend continued her tirade.

So that's *how I got home.*

Grabbing the towel, Auraelia crossed the suite to the bathing chamber.

The chill of winter had crept into the room, the cold tiles biting into her bare feet. At least she'd had the wherewithal to remove her boots the night before...or had Piper done that?

Piper was still raging in the bedchamber as Auraelia turned on the shower and stripped.

Just as she stepped into the warm streams of water, her friend barreled into the room. "Were you even listening to me?"

Auraelia tilted her face up into the warmth and sighed. "I'm sorry. I know that doesn't fix it or make up for it. But I am."

Her friend shook her head and crossed her arms. "Rae, I know you're in pain. I know there is a lot on your plate right now. But you're the *queen.* You can't be sneaking off to brothels by yourself. At least bring me with you."

Piper's usual humor bled into the end of her speech, and though she suspected that they were okay, she needed to ask anyway. Needed to hear it directly from Piper's lips to be sure.

"Yeah, Rae. We're fine. Besides—" a sly grin formed on her friend's face as she continued, "I don't need to stay mad at you. One look at you, and Ser Aeron is going to drill you until you puke."

Auraelia groaned as laughter flowed out of her friend.

As Piper turned to leave, Auraelia called after her. "Did Vee say if...if um—"

Piper's head tilted to the side, a look of understanding filling her eyes. "Nothing happened, Rae. Vee said that she saw a *look* in your eyes, and that's when she brought you to the office, plied you with goddess-only-knows-what kind of liquor, then sent for me. You didn't betray him."

"Not in that way," The words remained unspoken between them, but Auraelia read them in her friend's gaze. Felt them in the heaviness of her heart.

Auraelia's lips turned inward as she nodded to her friend, then returned to the shower.

She washed quickly, not wanting to freeze in her shower before freezing on the training pitch. After conjuring a warm breeze to dry her hair, she let her mind wander as her lady's maids readied her for the day.

Piper hadn't been too far off in her assessment from the morning.

Ser Aeron had run her through the paces until she was on her hands and knees, dry heaving over the cold hard ground.

The sun had long since moved from its high peak in the sky, now heading toward the looming horizon, and still, the sound of metal crashing together filled the air around the training pitch. Mud squelched beneath Auraelia's boots as she spun to parry yet another attack from Xander while keeping an eye on Ser Aeron at her back.

Channeling her magic, she pushed a gust of wind toward Xander in an attempt to move him away from her, but he'd thrown up a shield. Their clash of magics had the air funneling around the shimmering dome.

"What's wrong, brother?" Auraelia tried to keep the exhaustion out of her tone as she spoke. "Scared of a little *breeze*?"

Whirling around, she wove streaks of lightning tightly together in a makeshift shield. One that not even Ser Aeron wanted to go near.

Xander, just as winded as she was, smirked. "Wind? No. The sparkly ribbons of death that are currently twining around your forearms? Absolutely. I already had to cut my hair because of you."

His tone was lighthearted, and Auraelia had to stifle a laugh at the memory from the previous week of her lightning ricocheting off of Xander's blade and singeing his hair. He now sported a cut similar to Daemon's, though his was still long enough on top to pull back into a bun.

Her training had intensified over the last few months. Went from her usual rounds of sparring and light magic training with Piper to full-on, multi-partnered combat training.

Ser Aeron had seen the toll her newfound abilities had begun to take on her body and had insisted. Claiming it would be good practice for the impending battle with Davina and a good, *healthy* way for her to expend her magic.

He'd been correct—obviously. It gave her a healthy outlet to expel the magic that was built day by day and a way to work through the anger that followed her everywhere.

"Would you two—" Ser Aeron swung his broad sword at Auraelia's head, "kindly shut the fuck up."

She crouched just in time to miss the blade, and as her fist hit the ground, it trembled. Knocking the two males off balance enough that she could push them back with a strong gust of wind. As they fell to their asses outside of the muddy circle, Piper gave a triumphant *whoop* from the sidelines.

Xander's arms were propped on his raised knees, his eyes slightly wide. "Well, that was new."

"Indeed." Ser Aeron's deep baritone voice echoed across the pitch. "Where did that come from, Auraelia?"

She looked down at her hands, one covered in mud and the other still tightly gripped around her the hilt of her short sword.

Where had *that come from?*

"She's always been able to do that," Piper said from where she was perched on a bench, popping grapes into her mouth.

"What?" The two men asked in unison.

Rolling her eyes, Piper wiped her hands on her pants as she stood. "The day Queen—" she paused momentarily, then continued. "*That* day, when Rae's magic was bleeding out of her in the ballroom, the ground shook. You don't remember?"

The question was asked to the group, but Piper focused on her. And she saw it as she dug into the recesses of her mind, behind the wall where she'd tried to shove all those memories. She *felt* it.

Sheathing her sword in the scabbard strapped across her back, Auraelia trudged through the muck of the training pitch to the water table.

How many abilities are going to come out of the woodwork? Lightning, rain, wind, and now this?

She angrily took a sip from the water skin, then slammed it back onto the table.

Lost in her own thoughts, she hadn't heard Xander creeping up behind her, so she jumped as his warm hand clasped her shoulder.

"What's wrong?"

Auraelia leaned over to place her hands on the table. The wood scorched beneath her palms as her lightning settled at the surface. "It's just one more thing for me to learn. One more thing that I need to be in control of at all times. I just—" she sighed and shook her head. "I'm *tired*, Xander. So fucking tired."

Her brother gave her shoulder a reassuring squeeze. "I know. But, Rae? You're the strongest person that I know. And I also know that the Goddess and the ancestors wouldn't have blessed you with the amount of magic they did if they didn't think you could handle it."

"Goddesses." A small smile pulled at her lips, and she turned toward her brother. "I'm blessed by *two* Goddesses, dear brother."

Xander rolled his eyes and gave her a loving shove as Ser Aeron sidled up to them, a small smile on his face and a piece of parchment in his hand. "Seems we have a visitor."

Auraelia furrowed her brows in confusion, took the small slip from his outstretched hand, and smiled.

Chapter Seven

Auraelia

"Lady Aesira!" Auraelia beamed at the woman standing in the throne room, deep in conversation with Ser Aeron.

Aesira turned and beamed right back, her smile bright as the moon against her dark skin. "Your Majesty," she said as she bowed her head.

As the two women embraced, a little more tension ebbed away from Auraelia. Aesira had been one of her mother's oldest and dearest friends and was like a second mother to her. Having her there, in Emerald, was like having a piece of her mother back.

But when they pulled apart, Auraelia saw heaviness in her eyes. "What is it? As happy as I am that you are here, you never come unannounced. Is something wrong?"

Aesira's eyes flashed toward her brother before returning to the queen. "I assume you know of Davina trying to infiltrate the other courts? Of her attempting to win them over to her side?"

Auraelia nodded, a small v forming between her brows as they drew together.

"Well—"

"The bitch has decided to try her hand at ours." A voice smooth as silk, and one she hadn't heard in far too long, filtered through the space. Effectively cutting off Lady Aesira in the process.

Smiling, Auraelia turned, laughter filling her voice, "Hello, Iridessa."

"Hello, my friend...sorry, *Your Majesty*. It's been a while."

"A while? It's been *ages!*" Piper chimed in from across the room.

Iridessa was Lady Aesira's daughter and next in line as leader of the Court of Opal. She was just as beautiful as her mother, with the same gorgeous mahogany skin and amber eyes—and equally lethal. Having gone through the same rigorous training of their famed warriors, and as far as Auraelia knew, coming out above the rest. Unlike her mother, however, she'd opted to twist her sable hair into locs like her uncle's. Locs that were spiraled into a large bun atop her head, minus the few that hung around her face with tiny gold cuffs clipped around them.

As they all came together, the three women erupted into a fit of laughter. Each tried to talk over the other as they attempted to fit years of catching up into mere minutes. It wasn't until Ser Aeron cleared his throat that they calmed and returned to the issue at hand.

Straightening her shoulders, Auraelia crossed the room back toward where Ser Aeron and his sister stood, her eyes locked on the latter before flicking toward her Commander. "Gather the council. I have a feeling they're going to want to hear this."

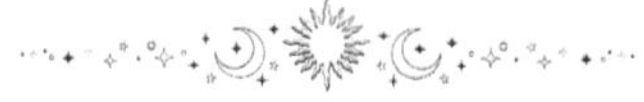

"How many times has she attempted to cross into Opal?" Mister Aramis questioned from where he paced in front of the bay windows of the council chamber.

Both Lady Aesira and Iridessa rolled their eyes, clearly exhausted from explaining this *yet again*.

"*She* has only tried once but has sent others. As you know, our borders are warded and you must be invited to enter them. Try to break through those wards, and well—" a wicked grin spread across Iridessa's face, and a dagger blinked into existence in her palm, "let's just say it won't be a good day for you." Iridessa twirled the blade between her fingers a few times before the weapon blinked out of sight once more.

How in the hell did she do that?

Auraelia's eyes were wide as she stared at where the blade had just been when her friend leaned over and chuckled. "Neat, right? I just figured out how to do it a week ago."

A small smile pulled at Auraelia's lips as she whispered, "You're going to have to show me exactly what kind of magic manifested for you, Dessa."

Auraelia was only a few months older than Iridessa, so it made sense that she was still feeling her way through her new abilities. And just from that one minor demonstration, she could tell it would make her friend even deadlier in combat than she already was.

Seeming to sense Auraelia's thoughts, Iridessa winked, then they returned their focus to the conversation-turned-argument in the room.

"Council, please," Auraelia started, taking a deep breath through her nose before continuing. "Of all the courts in this realm, the one ally that we are certain of is and has always been Opal. I will not stand for you questioning their alliance now."

"But, Your Majesty," Lord Harland rose as he spoke, "the courts are supposed to remain neutral. Be a balance to the realm, you know this."

Before Auraelia could speak, Lady Aesira stood. Her entire being radiated lethality, and as her gaze locked onto Harland's, the man swallowed audibly and returned to his seat. "Her majesty is *quite* aware of the treaty that placed her court as one of the two monarchies in our realm. As I'm sure you're quite aware, I don't give a damn what it says. Davina of Garnet is trying to wage war throughout our realm. I will not stand idly by and remain neutral while she runs amuck through the streets of Ixora."

Auraelia's heart swelled behind her ribs. She knew that Aesira had her back, but hearing it affirmed bolstered her confidence a fraction. Maybe, just maybe, with their help, she could do this. She just had to figure out what *this* was going to entail and how to prevent innumerable, unnecessary deaths.

The meeting continued until the sun began to kiss the horizon, casting the sky in a wash of pinks, purples, and oranges. Auraelia was exhausted, wanting nothing more than a warm meal and her bed...and perhaps a hot bath to relieve the day's stress. But as her council members filed from the room, Aesira and Iridessa stayed behind. Looks of uncertainty swirling in the pools of their amber eyes. When they were finally alone, Auraelia heaved a sigh and turned toward the women. "What is it?"

"We received this about a week ago," Lady Aesira said as she gestured toward her daughter. Dessa nodded, and with a flick of her wrist, a folded piece of parchment appeared between her fingers.

Auraelia's breath caught in her throat as a midnight blue seal stared back at her from between her friend's digits. "How—what?" Words were lost to her. Her brain was a scramble of thoughts and emotions, each warring for dominance.

The two ladies of Opal shared a look before the woman, who was the only mother figure Auraelia had left, stepped forward. Her hand was warm against Auraelia's skin as she grasped her wrist. "He had his captain bring it to us while they picked up necessities for their priestesses from our port."

Auraelia nodded as her eyes tracked back and forth from the letter to the woman before her. "Did you—" Her throat was thick like she had tried to drink molasses, and she had to swallow a few times to clear it away. "Did you read it?"

Both women shook their heads. "It wasn't ours to read, Rae," Iridessa said as she walked over to hand her the note.

Hands shaking, she took the letter, clutching it tightly as Lady Aesira and Iridessa sandwiched her between them in an embrace. When they pulled away, Aesira framed Auraelia's face with her hands. "You may not have trained alongside my warriors, but you *are* one in your own right, Auraelia. You may bend, but you do not break. Do you hear me?" Aesira's eyes narrowed until she nodded, understanding.

Then, after Aesira placed a kiss on Auraelia's forehead and after a quick embrace from Iridessa, the two warrior women excused themselves.

Auraelia walked over to the cushioned bench along the windows when the door clicked shut behind them. The sun's light—not yet extinguished by night's darkness—gave her enough to see by as she peeled open the letter.

Auraelia,

The treaty was broken the moment my father sided with Davina. I don't know if that helps, but I thought you should know.

Yours, always,

D

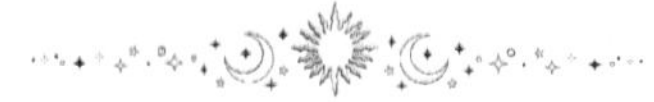

The stone floor was cold beneath her feet, biting through the thin soles of her satin slippers, her nightgown trailing behind her as she made her way down the hall to her bedroom.

What am I doing in the hall?

"Hello, my star."

Her heart pounded in her chest. The voice so familiar, but also...different. Deeper. Rougher. As she turned toward the sound, her face passed a mirror, and she halted.

What the?

It was her face, only...not. Aquamarine eyes shone back at her while a plait of chestnut brown draped over her shoulder and fell to her waist. She raised a hand to caress her cheek, feeling warmth seep through the touch. Real. This was...real?

A chuckle came from her left, from the man who spoke only moments ago. Only now, he had moved to stand behind her. His warm hands slid along her waist, his calluses rough against the smooth silk of her nightgown, as he rested his chin on her shoulder. "I'd look at myself every time I passed a mirror, too, if I looked as stunning as you."

Auraelia's eyes...no, not her eyes, someone else's...turned toward the man in the mirror. He looked like Daemon. Goddess, he was almost a spitting image. Piercing green eyes locked onto the blues in the mirror, and that same damned smirk pulled on his lips. But despite the similarities, he was different. He had no beard, and his hair was lighter and longer, brushing his shoulders as he leaned into her. It was like she was living through a memory or a dream, only one that wasn't wholly hers. And one she had no control over.

The woman in the mirror's mouth quirked up into a small smile, and she melted into the man's touch. "What are you doing here, Killian?"

Killian? That name...was so familiar. Brushing against her mind like a lover's caress or a long-forgotten memory.

Killian smiled as he trailed his nose up the woman's neck. "It's a...diplomatic visit."

The woman hummed in response, her head lolling to the side to give him better access.

His breath was hot against her ear, sending chills down her spine. "I need you, Astraea."

A sharp rap at the door ripped her from the dream, and she sat up abruptly. The movement sloshed water over the edge of her tub to pool on the floor. Her bath had long since chilled, and her skin pebbled as her subconscious faded into her consciousness.

A dream...it was just a dream. Wasn't it?

Auraelia took a series of deep breaths to still her racing heart.

"Rae? You okay in there?" Piper's honeyed voice filtered through the door.

"Yeah, I'm fine. Just...I guess I fell asleep."

"Okay, your dinner is here if you're ready."

"Thanks, Piper. I'll be out in a minute."

When Auraelia entered the sitting room, she found Piper lounging on one of the settees, holding a book above her face. "You know there are easier ways to read, right?" she asked with a laugh.

Piper closed her book around a finger and sat up. "Yeah, and it started off that way. I just kind of *sunk* down the cushions." She shrugged, then gestured toward the table. "Food's over there. It's tomato soup with basil and toasted bread with garlic, butter, and cheese. Liza has been trying new recipes again."

They both laughed, but as Auraelia removed the cloche and the room filled with the warm fragrance of roasted garlic and herbs, her laugh quickly turned into a moan.

"Just wait until you try it." Piper quipped before returning to her book.

They fell into a contented silence as Auraelia ate. But as the silence drug on, her thoughts drifted back to her dream.

"Hey, Piper?" Her friend tilted her head back over the arm of the settee, looking at her expectantly from upside-down. "Want to hear something weird?"

Piper's eyes widened as she practically flung herself from the cushions and leaped across the space. "Is that rhetorical? Because you know that the answer will always be 'yes'."

With an amused shake of her head, Auraelia began to weave together the story from her dream. When she finished, her friend's face turned contemplative.

"You said their names were 'Killian' and 'Astraea'?"

Auraelia nodded, her head cocked to the side, confusion written across her features.

Piper tore off a piece of Auraelia's bread, and before popping into her mouth said, "Aren't those the names of the people who signed The Treaty of Rosewood? Like, your great, great, great, however many greats, grandmother? And Daemon's, however many greats, grandfather?"

As Piper's words swirled around her brain, little pieces began to click into place. The striking similarities between not only her and the woman in the mirror but also between Killian and Daemon. But why was she dreaming of something that may have happened centuries ago? And why did it feel more like a memory than a dream? It didn't make any sense.

Unfortunately, she didn't have long to contemplate that new information. For the second time that night, Auraelia was pulled from her mind back to the world around her as yet another knock sounded at the door.

Chapter Eight

Auraelia

The guard at her door had been wide-eyed and white as a sheet like he'd seen a ghost strolling the castle halls. After taking the parchment from his trembling fingers and reading the scrawling script across its ivory surface, Auraelia immediately turned toward her bedchamber, her magic coursing frantically beneath the surface of her skin.

A man at the gates is requesting an audience with Her Majesty.

That was it. No other details, no name or court affiliation. It was late; who in their right mind would show up and request an audience at this hour?

Needing to dress quickly, Auraelia threw on a simple pair of pants, a tunic, and an overdress that laced across her torso, taking the place of a corset. After strapping her dagger to her thigh, she laced up her boots and headed out the door of her suite, Piper hot on her heels.

"Learn to fight and run in dresses and heels, but always choose ease when you have the choice. Choose pants, and keep your weapons close." The lesson that Aesira had drilled into her for as long as she could remember filled her head, and she was grateful for it as she walked into her throne room. Aesira and Iridessa stood like sentinels at the base of the dais while Ser Aeron and Xander framed the sides of the throne.

Her mother was never one to use this room except for formal occasions, but that wasn't the case here. Not knowing who would walk through the doors, Auraelia wanted to make sure she had as much of an advantage as she could achieve on short notice, using the dais as a vantage point. The stones within her throne calmed and channeled the magic that coiled in her veins like vipers ready to strike.

As Auraelia settled into the seat of the throne, the emeralds responded immediately, warming to her touch as she ran her fingers across them. She took a deep breath, spooling her magic into her core. Then she straightened her shoulders, nodded toward the guards at the door, and let the air in her lungs loose as Xander's shield glided around the dais, protecting her and the people she loved.

A man, tall and lithe, strolled into the room, dressed much too formally for the late hour. There was not a stitch out of place on his onyx jacket, and his boots were shined to the point of reflection, but the grape-sized, blood-red garnet that adorned his ring finger caught Auraelia's attention.

"Who are you?" she asked, using every ounce of calm to keep her voice steady; the emeralds within the stone illuminated as her magic pulsed through them.

"I'm Lord Caius of the Court of Garnet, Your Majesty." Caius bowed with a flourish, and when he rose, a feline smile appeared on his lips. "We saw each other...briefly, on that fateful night so many months ago."

"The snow." The words were spoken through clenched teeth. It wasn't a question, merely a confirmation that she understood who he was.

Auraelia's gaze narrowed as she took him in.

He was an attractive man. Flawless ivory skin stretched over strong cheekbones and a chiseled jaw. His eyes were winter blue and framed by dark lashes despite his shoulder-length hair being white as freshly fallen snow.

"Am I to assume you're another cousin I was unaware of?" Venom dripped from every word. Secrets, so many secrets. And more were popping up every day.

Caius chuckled. "No, Your Majesty, I am not your cousin."

"But you look so much like *her.*" She couldn't mask the sneer that tugged on her lips.

A knowing smile spread across Caius' face. "Characteristics that are common among our court, but I assure you, we are of no relation. I am the emissary for the Court of Garnet and the lover to your enemy."

"*Lover*? You're Davina's lover?" Disbelief filled her tone as she stared down at the man. Not at the fact that Davina would choose him, but that he would choose *her.*

"I am. Which is one of the reasons why I am here."

Auraelia relaxed a fraction, but her eyes narrowed as she leaned back against her throne, her head propped up on a fist. "How did you get here?"

A knowing smile pulled at his lips. "By horse, of course, and it's quite a long journey from Garnet. But as I'm sure you're aware, your brother has placed some quite impressive wards around this place. Wards that even *I* would have trouble breaking through. But seeing as I am here as a friendly face and not as a foe, I chose the safer route."

"Why come here, knowing that I could have had you killed on the spot?" She didn't like the Cheshire smile that spread across his face. "What is it you want, *exactly*?"

"I want *your boy* out of the way. And since you're in love with him, at least, I assume you're still in love with him; I suspect you'll help me."

Lightning simmered at her fingertips as her anger began to rise. "Why would I help you?"

"Because, Your Majesty, I'm the only one who can help *you.* You see, I know Davina. I know how she thinks. What makes her tick."

"What makes you think that I would believe a single word that falls from your lips?"

The smile on his face grew, and the room fell eerily silent as Caius stared into the depths of her eyes. His crystalline blues burrowing into the stormy grays of her own. But it was Aesira who shattered the silence. "He speaks the truth."

All heads whipped toward the warrior who still stood at the bottom of the dais, her unwavering gaze locked onto the emissary from Garnet.

"Lady Aesira?" A million questions filled Auraelia's mind as her eyes flicked between Aesira and Caius.

Caius' smile only broadened as he returned the warrior's stare. "So it's true, then? The great warrior leader from Opal is a truth seeker."

Iridessa stiffened, a blade appearing in her hand from thin air. "Watch it, snake," she hissed between clenched teeth, Xander's shield rippling as he reinforced it around their group.

"Enough." Auraelia's voice boomed throughout the room. "That's enough. I will consider your proposal, but do not hold your breath."

Caius dipped into a low bow, then rose with a cocky smirk on his face. "When you've decided to be smart about this and see me as an asset, use this." He pulled a box from his coat pocket and opened it. Sitting on a velvet pillow the color of obsidian was a jagged, clear stone.

"What is that?" Auraelia asked as she leaned forward a fraction.

"It's clear quartz, but it's been spelled with my magic. *When* you decide you want my help, simply pull it from the box, grasp it in your hand, and think my name."

Great, another magic stone. What could possibly go wrong?

Auraelia stood, lightning wrapping around her arms as she descended the steps of the dais. When she reached the end, Aesira stepped up beside her. "He speaks the truth, but I still don't know if this is a good idea." Her voice was barely a whisper, words meant only for her ears.

Auraelia paused, then after a deep breath, said, "Drop the shield, Xander."

"Your Majesty—" he began to object, but Auraelia looked over her shoulder and repeated the order.

"Drop. The. Shield." Each word was enunciated. The last thing she needed was to look weak in front of Caius, and Xander questioning her did exactly that.

It took more time than she would have liked, but Xander did as she bid, and she cautiously closed the distance between herself and the emissary. "*If* I choose to trust you, and *if* I decide to accept your offer of assistance, what is it that you get out of this?"

His wicked grin appeared once more. "Oh, Your Majesty. That's for me to know, and for you to find out." Then he winked and, in a flurry of snow, vanished.

The box with the stone rested at Auraelia's feet. "That son of a bitch."

So much for the wards.

Chapter Nine

Daemon

A thin, swirling blanket of fog coated the ground of the gardens outside the castle, covering what was left of the decorations from the previous night's solstice celebration. The sun had just begun to rise, the golden streams of light stretching across the horizon, framing her body in an ethereal glow. The sight made his heart falter.

Auraelia? What is she doing here?

He took hasty steps toward her, the mist around his feet dissipating with each step. But as he reached her, something was...off.

Different.

Her hair was a rich golden brown instead of her usual honey-blonde waves, and her waist was slimmer. But when she turned his way and her eyes locked onto his, that same pull came from the center of his chest. The same intrinsic feeling he got whenever he was in Auraelia's presence. She inhaled sharply, and the minute sound wrapped around his heart. She had Auraelia's face, but her eyes, Goddess, her eyes were the color of aqua sea glass and something about that resonated within his soul.

The need *to reach out and caress her cheek was immeasurable, but his hands remained limp at his sides. Like he had no control over them. "What are you doing out here, Astraea?"*

The words had come from his lips, but...Astraea? The name tickled the recesses of his mind, but he couldn't quite place it.

She smiled and turned her face toward the growing sunrise. "I thought it was quite obvious, Killian." She chuckled, and his heart picked up pace. She'd called him Killian. That wasn't his name...was it?

"I thought the sunrise in Lyndaria was beautiful, but here? Goddess. The greatest artist in all of Ixora couldn't capture the colors painting the sky. The way the stars linger until the last possible moment. It's just—" she cut herself off, awe and wonder sweeping across the delicate lines of her face. "What are you *doing out here?" she asked, her gaze still locked on the rising sun.*

One corner of his mouth tilted upward. "I'm taking in the beautiful view."

When she turned his way, her eyes met his once more, and her face flushed. His gaze hadn't strayed from her face for even a fraction of a second.

A cool breeze drifted through the garden, counteracting the warmth from the rising sun while it stirred the remaining fog around their feet. She held his gaze for moments that seemed to last a lifetime, and Goddess, did he want that. Wanted to stare into those pools of crystal blue until the Goddess Narissa called him to Arcelia.

That realization. That feeling *had a sense of knowing settling over him. This wasn't a dream.*

This was a memory.

One from a life lived long ago.

Daemon shot up straight in his bed, his skin slick with sweat. The remnants of reliving a memory long forgotten spiraled through his mind, along with the words of his Goddess.

Yours is a love that has been destined for over five hundred years.

He scrubbed his hands over his face before running one through his damp hair. It felt so real. Like it had happened the day before, not centuries ago. But the question that plagued his mind was *why*? Why was he dreaming of a life long ago? Of a love that never got to be?

Throwing the sheets off his legs, Daemon stalked into his bathing chamber, praying that a cold shower would help clear his head. He needed to get back to Lyndaria. Every fiber of his being demanded it. His magic hadn't stilled in the weeks since he'd left. Lashing against the hold he kept on it, like it could free itself from his veins and find its way back to *her*. Even if Auraelia was determined to have nothing to do with him, with *them*, he needed to find a way to convince her otherwise.

But there were things he needed to attend to in Kalmeera first. And with winter solstice a few days away, Davina had finally returned to the Court of Garnet to celebrate with her people. Giving him the perfect opportunity to slip away—hopefully without her notice.

Daemon stepped into the shower, letting the cool water cascade over his body for a few minutes before switching the temperature to something warmer. After washing quickly, he dressed and headed out to meet his sister—Yvaine—and Aiden in the city.

Since Davina began making her presence known in Kalmeera, it seemed a large gray cloud loomed overhead. The sun didn't shine quite as brightly, and there was a preternatural chill in the air like she'd brought the climate of Garnet with her. Even the colors of the flora didn't seem as bright, and the sounds of the island had been muted to a dull whisper. Like the birds were afraid to sing their songs.

Daemon walked slowly through his city, taking in the unnatural quiet around him. The way his people seemed to walk with their heads down and a hunch to their backs. As if they were trying to make themselves smaller.

What the fuck happened while I was gone?

He hadn't been in Lunaria any longer than usual, but when he'd returned, he'd been in meeting after meeting and tiptoeing around in an attempt to avoid his *betrothed.* Goddess, he hated that word. Hated that it related to someone he despised more than he thought possible. Unfortunately, this was the first time he was free to wander the city unencumbered by the weight of the match his father made behind his back.

Yvaine and Aiden flanked either side as they strolled through the streets. "How long has it been this way?" Daemon asked as they turned down the street that led to Auntie Jodie's bakery. He hadn't been since he'd returned from Lyndaria after Auraelia sent him away. The memories of being there with her were too painful to relive, but months had passed, and it wasn't fair to the elderly woman.

"Been like what, exactly?" Yvaine asked, the anger she held evident in her voice.

Daemon stopped walking and turned toward his sister. He wasn't in the mood for her attitude. "Yvaine." Her name was clipped, and she narrowed her eyes at him in response.

"It's been like this since *she* showed up. It started as this eerie feeling in the city, then the air began to cool...which was just strange. But then father let her roam...unaccompanied."

Daemon's head canted to the side and he crossed his arms, his impatience growing as he waited for his sister to continue. But it was Aiden who filled the silence. "This isn't even the worst of it, D. The market?" His friend blew out a breath. "I've never seen it so...empty."

"Empty? What do you mean 'empty'?" Worry and anger surged within him. Kalmeera's marketplace was one of the main sources of commerce for his court. It was the largest in all of Ixora. And hearing that was no longer the case had his pulse racing.

Yvaine shook her head in dismay. "It's easier to just show you. We'll head there after you see Auntie. She's been asking about you and—" She cut herself off, a look of apology filling her gaze.

Auraelia. Jodie had been asking about him and Auraelia.

Daemon took a deep breath, then turned and headed toward the small white fence surrounding the yard. It wasn't long before the smell of freshly baked goods filled his nose, and memories squeezed his heart. He could still see the nervous look on Auraelia's face when Jodie hinted about her being queen of the Sapphire Isles. Could feel the racing beat of her heart as she slid down his body when he'd helped her off Yvaine's horse. Still saw the way her eyes sparkled like stardust when she realized he'd asked the older woman to make her favorite pastry and heard the sultry lilt of her voice as she teased him about it shortly after. *"Daemon Alexander, do you* like *me?"* Goddess, that had been a gross understatement.

Taking a deep breath, Daemon pushed his way through the gate. He hadn't taken more than a few steps before the door to the bakery flew open, and he was greeted by Auntie Jodie's smiling face. Her salt and pepper hair was pulled into a tight bun at the nape of her neck, and there was a streak of flour across her forehead, the powder a sharp contrast against her umber skin. Her smile was bright and warm but worry swirled in the depths of her eyes. When she pulled him into her embrace, Daemon nearly collapsed under the weight of his emotions.

It was the hug a mother would give her child. One he hadn't sought out from his own mother since everything had come crumbling down. He'd barely even spoken to the queen since he'd returned from Lyndaria. That hug and the love that radiated from it mended a tiny part of his fractured soul. Daemon let Auntie Jodie's warmth seep into him. Let it bandage the fissures that threatened to open into a gaping chasm.

When they finally pulled apart, her eyes were lined in silver, but she quickly blinked away the tears. "Come on now. I have bread in the oven, and if you make me burn it, I'll have your hide. Prince or not." The normalcy that came from hearing the curt tone of her voice brought a small smile to his face. Daemon shook his head with a chuckle and followed the plump woman inside, Yvaine and Aiden close on his heels.

The warmth of the bakery cut through the unnatural chill that permeated the air outside, and he watched as Jodie flitted about her kitchen. He and Yvaine spent a lot of time with Auntie Jodie when they were younger. They had been her 'unofficial taste testers' while their parents performed royal duties in the city. But he and his sister hadn't been there *together* in... Goddess, it had been years.

Memories of those times surfaced. Of him rolling out dough with a rolling pin almost as long as he was tall, Yvaine helping mix the ingredients together, covering both of them with flour. The memories were almost strong enough to counteract the hurt from the ones he had with Auraelia. Almost, but not quite.

They stayed for a while, listening while Jodie prattled on about the gossip in town. But when the conversation shifted to Davina, Daemon stiffened.

"What are you planning on doing about *her*?" Jodie asked, the sneer on her face showing exactly how she felt about the woman.

Aiden and Yvaine exchanged a look before their gazes fell upon him. Pinching the bridge of his nose, Daemon blew out an exasperated breath. "Auntie—"

"Don't you *'Auntie'* me, boy. And don't you dare sit there and tell me that you're going to go along with it. She's running this city into the ground, and it won't be long before the court falls, too."

Daemon's eyes snapped up to Auntie Jodie's. The moss green of his locking onto the soft browns of hers.

"You haven't seen it yet, have you?" she asked, disbelief filling her gaze.

"We're heading to the market as soon as we leave here, Auntie," Yvaine interjected.

Jodie's gaze flicked between the three of them, her eyes narrowing before she gave them a quick nod. "Off you get, then. Don't sit there yammering on with me; there are more important things to deal with than visiting my old self." She dusted her hands off on her apron and turned back toward the kitchen.

Yvaine and Aiden headed for the door but stopped when Daemon hadn't followed. "I'll be right there, just...give me a minute?" They both nodded, then slipped through the door of the bakery.

Auntie Jodie was busy wiping off her already spotless counter, and Daemon gently wrapped his hands around her wrinkled ones.

She sighed heavily, her shoulders sagging under an invisible weight. "You can't—" She stopped mid-sentence like she couldn't force the words to form on her tongue.

Daemon squeezed her hands gently, and her gaze moved to meet his. "I know. And I won't. I promise." He held her gaze a moment longer, hoping that she saw everything he couldn't say aloud in his eyes. When she nodded, he gently kissed her brow and headed toward the door.

Chapter Ten

Daemon

"Where is everyone?" Daemon whispered through clenched teeth.

Empty wasn't the right word to describe Kalmeera's marketplace. Desolate would have been much more accurate. The stalls that lined the streets were nearly barren. The walkways were devoid of people, and trash and debris littered the ground.

This wasn't the Kalmeera Daemon knew. Not the one that he would lay down his life for. Davina's influence on his court had caused this, and in turn, something dark began to build inside of him.

Daemon walked down the street that usually held vendors from every corner of Ixora. Tents, typically full of gems or wares from other courts, stood empty with their tables overturned. The only vendors who *were* present were those from the Court of Pearl and a few from Topaz. Even Kalmeera's own merchants were absent.

Interesting.

Yvaine and Aiden were close on his heels as they slowly crept through the chaos covering the ground. Neither answered his question until they were far enough away from prying eyes and listening ears. He hated that he no longer trusted the ones who resided inside his court. But he also knew that there were some that had been influenced, or whose loyalty had been bought, by Davina.

"As I said earlier, *father–*" Yvaine said his name like a curse, "let her roam around unaccompanied. Evidently, on one of her little outings, she came here. Announced herself as the new princess and future queen—not just of the Sapphire Isles, but of all Ixora—and then closed the market. Only the courts and people who have aligned with her are allowed to sell at the market now."

Daemon's shadows spilled from the tips of his fingers as his rage grew.

"That's not all, D," Aiden said, clasping the prince's shoulder. "She tried to throw the ones who questioned her in the dungeons."

"*What?!*" he seethed. His shadows wrapped around his arms like serpents, the darkness that fed his magic filling his vision as his breath came in harsh inhales. How dare she throw *his* people in the dungeon. She had no right. Betrothed to the heir or not, these were not her people. They would never *be* her people if he had any say about it.

"D?" Aiden's voice was wary.

Yvaine stepped into his line of sight, her brows furrowed as her eyes trailed over his body. "Daemon, they're fine. No one is in the dungeon... You—you need to calm yourself."

He couldn't think, couldn't *breathe*, around the anger that was coiling through him.

Yvaine gripped one of his shoulders, then his chin in her other hand, forcing his gaze to hers. Worry laced the vibrant greens of her eyes before sheer determination replaced the emotion.

Streams of blue that reminded him of the bioluminescence in the tunnels leading into the city gradually penetrated the moss green of her iris'. Then, ever so slowly, a sweet melody seeped into his mind. Lulling the anger that had wrapped itself so tightly around his insides to sleep. It was like the breeze whispering through the trees or a mother's lullaby.

Calm.

He felt...calm.

The melody continued for a few moments before it slowly faded away, taking the black that had crept into his vision. Daemon closed his eyes and shook his head lightly. "Damn it, Yvaine. You promised."

"Yeah, well, promises don't mean shit when your brother is turning into a giant, swirling shadow and looks like he's about to obliterate everything in his path."

Daemon focused on his breathing, and when he opened his eyes, he saw how wide Aiden's had become.

"Holy shit." Awe filled his friend's voice as his eyes anxiously flitted between the siblings. "Yvaine is a fucking *siren*?! How did I never know this?" Aiden's words were barely above a whisper, and there was no way that anyone down the street had overheard, but still...it made Daemon's spine stiffen.

Yvaine's shoulders drooped as she threw her head back and rolled her eyes. When she finally met Aiden's gaze, hers was hard. "Yes. And you're going to keep that to yourself, understood? The last thing I need, that *we need*, is you-know-who finding that out and attempting to manipulate me. Or use it against Daemon."

Aiden nodded, his eyes still wide.

Sirens were rare. It is so rare, in fact, that the only text on them and their abilities was written centuries ago, and the last *known* siren was around during the War of Rosewood. Very few knew of his sister's abilities, and Daemon was determined to keep it that way.

With his magic back under control, he turned toward his sister. "Thanks, sis. I know you don't like doing it, just as much as I don't like you doing it *to me*."

Yvaine shook her head and lightly pushed his shoulder. "Couldn't have you going on a rampage through what was left of the market, now could I?"

Her tone was playful, but there was an undercurrent of worry. She'd never seen his magic out of control like that. And it seemed to be happening more frequently as of late. Not even his week at the sanctuary had helped. His magic seemed to be settled only when he was with Auraelia.

Daemon shook his head to clear the turbulent thoughts from his mind. It wasn't something he could figure out standing on a cluttered street.

By the time they made their way toward the castle again, the sun had begun its slow descent in the sky, painting the tall white towers surrounding his home in vibrant shades of orange. The trio had been silent for the most part on their return trip, each seemingly lost in their own thoughts. But after seeing Auntie Jodie and then the market, Daemon knew he had put off a certain confrontation long enough.

Once at the bridge that led onto the castle grounds, Daemon turned toward his sister and Aiden. He hadn't even parted his lips to speak when Yvaine squeezed his hand in hers and nodded. How she knew, he would never understand. But he gave her a weak smile, then let his shadows consume him.

Daemon found his mother sitting on a bench beneath the plumeria trees that edged the courtyard of the rear gardens. The same ones that he'd sat under with Auraelia after he'd taken her to Azure Falls. The thought had the muscles in his chest constricting, and he rubbed at his sternum in an attempt to alleviate some of the tension.

He approached on foot, making sure to step on fallen twigs to alert her to his presence.

"Mother." His voice was gruff, and even he could hear the accusatory tone laced within it.

Queen Avyanna tensed but then forced herself to relax before looking up from the tome in her lap to meet his gaze. "Hello, my son."

The air seemed to still as a tense silence settled between them. Like the wind itself was waiting with bated breath over who would break first.

It was Queen Avyanna who did so. Sighing into the silence before gesturing to the empty seat on the bench. "Would you like to sit? Or will you just stand there in silence, brooding over me?"

Daemon exhaled sharply through his nose, then sat, keeping his gaze locked onto the horizon as the sun continued to set. "Did you know?"

"Did I know what, Daemon? You need to be clearer."

A wry laugh escaped, and he shook his head. "Did you *know* about Davina? About her plans? Did you know that Father had trapped me in a marriage while also knowing how I felt about Auraelia? Did you know that before or after you tried to help me find a solution?" Daemon ran his hands roughly through his hair and stood from the bench. Whipping around to face his mother and the shocked expression that marred her features. "Was that *clear* enough for you, Mother? Do you understand the question *now*?"

Queen Avyanna's eyes were wide as she stared back at her son. No doubt his hair was sticking out all over the place from the manic way his hands had run through it, but he didn't care. He wanted answers. *Needed* them, and he'd been avoiding this conversation for long enough.

His mother swallowed audibly, then looked down to where her hands were clasped in her lap, resting over the now-closed tome whose cover read *The War and Treaty of Rosewood*. He knew that book. He had read it so many times when he was attempting to find a solution to be with Auraelia that he was sure he could recite it backward.

Queen Avyanna cleared her throat but kept her eyes downcast. "I believe you were quite clear in your inquiries, Daemon." When she finally looked up to meet his eyes, the cornflower blue of her own were brighter than usual as tears lined their rims. "I didn't know about Davina. Not at first. I didn't know anything until *after* your father agreed to her terms." She took a deep, shaky breath, then continued. "But, Daemon. I had no idea what she had planned for solstice. I–I'm so sorry."

Daemon stared down at his mother, and though he was still furious, he could feel the ice around his heart toward her begin to melt away. "Did Father know about her plan for Queen Adelina?"

He believed her when she said she hadn't any idea. He knew that if she had, she wouldn't have gone to solstice and probably would have tried to forbid him from doing so as well. But he had to know if his father knew.

"I...I haven't talked to your father more than necessary since we came back. I've even moved into the Queen's suite. But if I had to guess, I would assume so—yes."

Daemon turned away from his mother, his magic surging under the surface as his fists clenched at his sides. Somewhere in the recesses of his mind, he'd known the answer. It had everything to do with how he'd acted after the Lyndarian queen died. *"It's not our business, son,"* King Evander had said that after the queen collapsed to the ground, his grip on Daemon's arm was hard as he tried to keep him from going to Auraelia.

He had to have known. There was no other explanation.

Daemon turned back to where his mother sat on the bench, wringing her hands in her lap. Closing the small distance between them, he kneeled in front of the queen. She raised her eyes to his when he clasped her trembling hands in his to still the movement.

"I'm going to Lyndaria," he said matter-of-factly. He didn't want to leave any room for argument, and the acceptance in his mother's eyes said that she understood, but her words solidified it.

"May the Goddess protect and guide you, my son. And may *she* welcome you."

Queen Avyanna placed a chaste kiss on his brow, and then he stood and headed toward his chambers.

There was a lot to do and not a lot of time to do it.

Chapter Eleven

Auraelia

Walking down the stone hallway to her rooms, Auraelia heaved a sigh. She was exhausted after a morning spent talking in circles with her council and hours of training in the afternoon. Pushing open the door to her suite, she grimaced. She hated how her tunic and trousers clung to her sweat-slicked skin despite winter's lower temperatures. She wanted—*needed*, if the pounding in her head was any indication—food and a hot shower.

Mister Aramis hadn't had any new information regarding her cousin's movements. What he did have was confirmation that the Court of Pearl was leaning in Davina's direction. The thought of another court siding with her cousin made her stomach roil and her head throb in time with her pulse.

Auraelia pressed her fingers into her temples to try and alleviate the ache. *Food, shower, sleep.*

The sound of the door latching into place echoed through the silence of her chambers. The quiet she once craved after endless hours of royal duties had become something she sought to avoid. She hated the sound of silence. She hated that it gave her too much space to think and *feel* the things she had fought so hard to escape.

She took a deep breath in an attempt to steady her mind and, instead, was greeted with the scent of sandalwood. Sure that her tired, aching mind was playing tricks on her, she closed her eyes and leaned against the door. Breathing in the familiar scent, she let it wash over her and calm the rough sea of her soul.

"Hello, Auraelia."

Her eyes snapped open at the sound of her name, her hand naturally reaching for the emerald dagger she kept strapped to her thigh. She saw no one as she glanced around her sitting area, but there, standing in the shadowed doorway that led into her bedchamber, was Daemon. It hit her then. He'd said her name. Her *real* name. And that realization sent a sharp pain to the center of her chest, making her tense.

His arms were crossed at his chest, and he looked completely at ease as he leaned against the frame. "I'd understand if you felt the need for that," his eyes drifted down to where her hand was gripped around the hilt of her dagger. "But I'd really rather not get stabbed tonight."

Daemon pushed off the doorframe and stepped into the dim light of the sitting area. Goddess, he was gorgeous. His trousers hugged his legs like they had been formed around them, and the laces across the top of his tunic were left loose, exposing the intricate lines of his tattoos. Auraelia drank in the sight of him. Her memory had certainly not done him the justice he deserved, and a familiar heat began to swell in her chest the longer her eyes lingered.

Pulling her gaze away, she released the grip on her blade and pushed away from the door. She needed to get a grip. Needed to focus and find out *why he* was in Lyndaria, let alone in her chambers.

"You're not even going to speak to me?" he asked as he slowly closed the distance between them.

Auraelia straightened her spine as she walked across her suite, counting in her head to keep her emotions in check. He was barely near her, and her magic was already responding to his proximity. Warming and swirling beneath the surface.

"What are you doing here?" Her tone was icy, even to her own ears, but she couldn't take it back now. Within the blink of an eye, he was on her, having shadow-walked the distance between them. His hand was loose but firm around her throat as he pressed her against the nearest wall, and her heart pounded in her chest. But it wasn't fear that elicited the response. It was never of fear, not when it came to *him*.

His thumb idly traced circles around where her pulse thrummed in her neck, sandalwood and the salty ocean air enveloping her senses as he pressed his body against hers. "That wasn't a very nice greeting. I'm wounded," he teased. That damned smirk that made her knees weak, tugging on one side of his mouth.

Fuck.

"I seriously doubt that." Auraelia rolled her eyes, and when they landed on his once more, she immediately regretted that choice. His smirk had morphed into a wicked smile that promised all manners of depravity, and memories of his hand slapping her ass every time she'd done it in the past trickled back into her mind.

Taking a deep breath to try and steady her racing heart and cool the flush that now warmed her cheeks, she asked again, "What are you doing here, Daemon?" Only this time, the ice had melted, and her words had turned breathy.

Shit.

"I *need* you." His voice was a low rumble in his throat as he dragged out the words, and a flood of heat settled in her core.

It wasn't just the way he'd said it or the way his body was pressed against hers. It was the fact that he'd used the same phrase from her dream. The one that had seemed like more of a memory than her subconscious spinning stories. And if it was, that meant they were the same words his ancestor had spoken to hers.

And something about it just seemed...*right.*

Despite everything in her soul telling her that she needed him, too. Needed to *be* with him. Despite the way her magic called to his. There was still a small part of her, one that was louder than the rest, that told her she couldn't. Not until her cousin was handled. Not until he was no longer connected to *her*.

"We—" she swallowed thickly, "We can't."

A sly smile pulled across his lips. "I promise you, we can."

Auraelia's eyes locked onto Daemon's, the gold within them turning molten as it slowly engulfed the green. Between the desire in his eyes, the heat of his body seeping into her own, and the promise of his words, it was a struggle to keep from squeezing her thighs together.

"Daemon—" though it was low, her voice betrayed her. Want bled into her tone, and the slight dilation of his pupils proved that he'd heard it.

His smile grew, his hold on her throat tightened, and he somehow managed to press further into her. "Just sex, Auraelia."

Again, he'd used her given name. And again, it was like a stab directly to her heart, but she couldn't blame him. He was doing as she asked and not calling her *my star*. But she had to admit that she missed hearing it. Missed the way her heart would kick up a notch every time he said it.

Taking a deep breath through her nose, she asked, "Just sex?"

His smile grew into something sinister as he wedged his thigh between hers. When he applied pressure right where she needed it, she couldn't help the whimper that escaped.

"Yes, just sex. Unless you have a counteroffer?" Smug satisfaction dripped from every word as his other hand slowly slid up her torso. Even with her tunic and corset separating their skin, she could feel the heat of his touch as he grazed the side of her breast.

Auraelia opened her mouth to protest—though at the moment, she wasn't quite sure why—but the feel of Daemon brushing his nose across her cheek made her falter.

"Tell me you hate me if it will make it easier. Curse me from here to Arcelia; I don't care. But you need this just as badly as I do. I know you do." Daemon's leg began to move between hers. Adding delicious friction to the steady pressure he'd provided. "I feel it in the way your pulse flutters in your neck. See it in the swirls of your eyes. You can't hide your desire from me, Auraelia. Say yes, and I will make you come until you forget your own name." He nipped at the tender flesh of her ear. "Just say yes."

His whispered words sent shivers throughout her body. He was right. She did need this. Goddess, did she need this. Between her ever-growing magic, the stress over an impending war, and pent-up frustration—regardless of how much training or self-pleasuring she did—she was wound tighter than a top.

She needed a release.

She needed *him*—in more ways than she cared to evaluate at that moment.

Daemon loosened his hold on her throat as he pulled away to look her in the eyes.

Just sex...she could do that, couldn't she? Every fiber of her being begged her to relent. To give into the delicious temptation of the man in front of her. Even her magic vibrated beneath her skin, pushing against the hold she kept on it.

Auraelia took a deep breath and locked her gaze on his. "Yes."

That wicked grin spread across his face once more before he shook his head and tsked at her. "You know better than that. Tell me how much you *need me*."

Letting a sly smile of her own tilt up her lips, Auraelia snaked her arm between them and palmed the hardened ridge in his pants. "I believe it was *you* who said you needed *me*."

Daemon groaned, his eyes rolling to the back of his head as his hand tightened around her throat once more. "You're going to regret that, Princess."

A rush went through her at his tone, and her smile turned devilish. "It's Your Majesty—" she said, tightening her hold on his cock as she slowly ran her hand along his length, "And somehow I doubt that."

A growl rumbled deep in Daemon's throat, and his mouth was on hers a second later. There was nothing soft or gentle about the way he kissed her. It was hard and bruising as their tongues battled for purchase.

Releasing her throat, Daemon slid his hands down her sides until he reached her thighs. Keeping her pressed against the wall, he lifted her from the floor, and Auraelia wrapped her legs around his waist. The move had him pressing his hips into hers, his erection hard against her center.

His fingers dug into the flesh of her ass as he ground into her, and she moaned against his lips as his hands slid closer to her core. Auraelia tugged at Daemon's shirt to free it from his pants, but with their close proximity and position, it wouldn't budge.

A disgruntled moan worked its way up her throat. She needed more. Needed to feel the heat of his skin beneath her fingers.

Twisting her hands into the silky strands of his hair, Auraelia tugged his head back. "Are you going to fuck me or not?" Pure, unadulterated lust filled her tone, and a mischievous grin stretched across Daemon's lips in response.

"As you wish, *Your Majesty.*"

Daemon's hold was firm as he fused his mouth back to hers and turned away from the wall. Maneuvering his way through the room, successfully side-stepping the furniture in the sitting area until he made it to the small dining space.

Magic sent the few items that graced the table's surface crashing to the floor—though she wasn't sure if it had been his or hers—and there was primal hunger in his eyes as he laid her out on its surface. Between the table and how he looked at her, it felt like she was his own personal feast, and he was trying to figure out where he wanted to start.

"Don't. Move." Each word was enunciated, and his eyes locked on hers as he waited for her to acknowledge the command.

Auraelia pulled her lower lip between her teeth and nodded. When he cocked his head to the side, she nearly rolled her eyes. Goddess, the way this man demanded control was both a turn-on and infuriating. But her desire to let someone else take the reins, to let someone else make the decisions for once, overpowered her need to retain that control.

Auraelia locked her gaze onto Daemon's and let a coy smile form on her lips. "I won't move."

His eyes narrowed a fraction before he let them trail down her body, raking across every dip and curve like it was the first time he'd seen them. His hands followed the path of his gaze, and her magic followed his fingers, warming her skin from within and sending a flood of heat between her legs.

When she moved to press them together, Daemon's hands shifted to her inner thighs and pulled them further apart. "Something you want, *Princess*?"

"I *want* the thing you promised."

Daemon's hands slid up her legs, skirting where she longed for his touch before traveling back down the outside of her thighs.

Fucking hell. She'd nearly forgotten how much he loved to tease, and it had been so long since she'd been touched that it wouldn't take much to tip her over the edge.

Daemon continued the movements, each pass bringing his hands closer and closer to the ache at her center. So lost in the feel of him, she hadn't noticed when he'd palmed the hilt of her dagger and gently pulled it from its sheath.

"I hope you're not fond of this corset."

Her brows furrowed, and before she could comprehend what his words meant, he was sliding the blade between her tunic and corset, slicing through the fabric. "What the—"

The anger that had begun to form was quickly doused as wet heat covered her nipple. Her gasp quickly turned into a moan as he sucked the peak through her shirt, and his hand finally met the junction of her thighs. Heat licked up her spine at the sensation, and her eyes rolled to the back of her head. Every move of his fingers and draw against her breast sent her spiraling.

Daemon's teeth grazed the tip of her nipple as he pulled his mouth away, his gaze burning into her own. "One piece of clothing down..."

He slid her dagger back into its sheath, then deftly undid the straps that secured it to her thigh and placed it on the table. Removing his fingers from between her legs, he stood upright, a small smile tugging on his lips.

Auraelia groaned at the loss of his touch, then pushed onto her elbows. "What?"

Daemon quirked a brow at her movements. "I do believe I told you not to move."

She narrowed her eyes, but before she could respond, he continued. "It's nothing, really. I just remembered another time when your boots and pants were in my way."

Waves of heat rolled through her as his gaze seared into hers. "Yes, well. If memory serves, it didn't seem like *too* much of an issue."

The air became heavy as tension built between them. Neither of them moved to the other.

Auraelia let her gaze travel down his body. Taking in the way that his tunic fit the wide set of his shoulders, the way his pants hugged every contour of his legs, and the erection between them. Her eyes lingered on that ridge as memories of the way it felt to have him plunging into her swirled through her mind. Slowly, she lifted her gaze back up his frame as she swept her tongue over her bottom lip. But when her eyes met his once more, she pulled it between her teeth.

Daemon's nostrils flared as he stared down at her like it was taking everything he had not to rip every stitch of clothing from her body. And, Goddess, did she want him to act on that feeling. The taut silence seemed to drag on for ages, but he snapped the thread with one word.

"*Mine.*"

She'd worry about the implications of that word later, but the way he said it? It was more growl than a word, and she felt it through every one of her nerve endings. The hair on the back of her neck stood on end as something deep within her soul clicked into place.

Chapter Twelve

Auraelia

Just sex? Who was she kidding?

It never was, and never *would* be, just sex with them.

It was always claiming and being claimed, and tonight was no different.

They came together like lightning striking the ground. Hard, fast, and potentially devastating.

His lips devoured hers as he lifted her from the table and shadow-walked them to her bed chamber, tossing her unceremoniously onto her mattress. Auraelia watched as Daemon pulled his tunic over his head. Drinking in the sight of him as he exposed every glorious inch of skin and the intricate art that covered his chest and arms.

After kicking off his boots, he quickly unlaced and removed each of hers before moving on to her pants, flicking the button open with a twist of his fingers before yanking them down and off her legs.

He hadn't even given the air time to kiss her bare flesh before he dropped to his knees, pushed the thin fabric of her panties to the side, and licked up her center. Her head fell back as her hands gripped the fabric beneath her body, her hips rocking against the motions of his tongue.

"Fuck, Princess. Do you know how good you taste?" Heat burned in his gaze as he stared up at her from between her thighs, and the magic coursing through her veins responded. Wrapping around her limbs in bright ribbons of light.

Daemon caught sight of her lightning, and the way it reflected off the gold in his eyes made her breath hitch. He didn't even give her anxiety time to take root as a smug smile graced his lips. "I'm not scared of you, or your magic, Auraelia. You could kill me right here and now, and I would die a happy man."

His words were like honey dripping from his lips, and the ease with which he spoke them sent her heart skittering.

Threading her fingers through his hair, she pushed his head back down. "Less talk. More tongue." It didn't matter that she loved the words that slipped from his lips. She needed action, not words.

The more he talked, the more her thoughts spiraled, and her heart wanted to join the equation. And that was a complication she didn't need right now. What she *needed* was the sweet release that his mouth promised.

Desire flared in his eyes as he slid her panties down her legs with achingly slow movements. Returning to his spot between her thighs, Daemon ran his tongue up her slit before his signature smirk overtook his mouth. "Say please, *Princess.*"

His fingers drifted over the opening of her pussy, gathering her arousal before gently swirling the tips around her clit. She groaned as he repeated the motion, her frustration growing with every swipe.

"It's Your Majesty," she said through clenched teeth. With her fingers still tangled in his hair, she pushed him back toward where she was aching for him. "And, *please.*"

He slowly ran his tongue up her center, his eyes never straying from hers. "No need to beg, Auraelia. I'd gladly stay here all night."

Her jaw dropped at his audacity, but it was quickly followed by a moan as he latched onto her clit. Sucking it hard into his mouth and flicking that tiny bundle of nerves with his tongue.

It wasn't long before he added his hands to the equation. Two fingers thrust in and out of her, curling forward and stroking her inner walls just the way she liked.

Auraelia's hand fell away from his head, trading his silky, blue-black strands for the deep teal of her sheets. Within a few strokes of his tongue, he had her back bowing off the bed with an impending orgasm.

As the buildup to her release grew, the hold on her magic waned, and her lightning flickered before glowing an incandescent white around her. Terror began to creep in, taking over the pleasure that was filling her body. But it was never given time to escalate further than a passing thought as Daemon released the hold on his own magic, letting it mingle with hers.

Cool ribbons of shadow, flecked with shimmering stars, began to tangle and braid with her lightning, a delicate dance of light and dark swirling along her skin.

Daemon's fingers never ceased, but he lifted his head long enough to draw her focus. "Let *go*, Auraelia. I've got you."

Dropping his head back between her thighs, his tongue lashed at her clit with renewed vigor as his fingers continued to work her core. And when she came, it was as if the world ceased to exist.

White light filled her vision as her release rocked through her body, and magic pulsed out of her in uncontrolled waves. Wind swirled through her chambers, throwing open the windows. Rain fell through the open panes in sheets as thunder crashed in the sky, and she could feel the heat from her lightning as it crackled along her skin.

It wasn't until her orgasm subsided and Daemon finally ceased his ministrations that Auraelia was able to get a grip on her powers. But as she looked around her chambers, instead of the destruction she had been expecting, she was met with a dome of sparkling, and *sparking*, darkness.

It was almost exactly like the cocoon of stars Daemon had created in Kalmeera from what seemed like lifetimes ago. Only this time, streaks of lightning shot across the star-flecked sky.

Awe swept through Auraelia.

Awe, at the fact that she'd just released the most magic at one time since...she quickly stopped that train of thought. She didn't want to go there. Not now.

But mainly, awe that her magic seemed to purr in response to Daemon's. How they seemed to coexist in a natural sense of harmony. Light and dark, neither able to exist without the other.

Auraelia removed her gaze from the mix of magics around her and returned it to Daemon. He was still kneeling at the foot of the bed, but he had a cocky grin on his face.

"What?" she asked with a slight bite to her tone.

Chuckling, Daemon stood, wiping the evidence of her release from his face before sticking those same fingers into his mouth. Auraelia watched as his hands fell to his waistband. Waited as he slowly unfastened the buttons that kept his length pinned behind the fabric.

"You're quite bratty tonight, Princess." Her breath turned ragged as he pushed his pants off his hips, letting them fall to the floor before stepping out of them and slowly crawling over her. His gaze was locked onto hers as he said, "I kind of like it."

Auraelia wrapped her arms around his neck as he hooked his hands beneath her hips and pulled her onto his lap, positioning her above the tip of his cock. Hesitancy swirled in his eyes as he said, "If you want this to stop—"

Slipping her hand between their bodies, she gripped him tightly in her palm. "I want you to fuck me until I forget my name, your name, and that this is probably a terrible idea." She slowly worked her hand up and down his length, relishing the way his jaw tightened as he tried to give her this little bit of control. "I want you to use me, Daemon. I don't want control."

A wicked grin graced his mouth, but something in his eyes said he understood what she meant. Knew what she *needed*.

"As you wish, Your Majesty." Daemon knocked her hand out of the way, wrapped an arm around her waist, and slammed into her. Fully seating himself in one stroke. Auraelia cried out at the sensation, her back bowing as her head fell back. Only his arm banded around her back kept her from collapsing.

"Take off your shirt, Princess. Let me see you."

Daemon slowed his thrusts long enough for Auraelia to pull her tunic over her head and toss it to the floor. Then, using his shoulders for leverage, she began riding his cock like it was the last thing she would do. Meeting him stroke for stroke with every rise and fall of her hips.

His hands immediately palmed her heavy globes, massaging each before bringing them to his mouth, making sure to lavish each in equal measure.

Auraelia's fingers dug into his back, no doubt leaving marks as she dragged her hands down the hard, muscled panes. Daemon's answering groan spurred her on as she ground against him, his pelvis adding the perfect amount of friction to her clit.

His thrusts became hard and fast. His grip on her ass was bruising.

This.

This is what she needed.

No sweet words. No delicate touches or whispered promises of a better tomorrow.

Just sweat-slicked skin and pleasure.

Auraelia felt her release growing again, but Daemon pulled out before it could go much further. Flipping her onto her stomach, he pressed her flat into the mattress. His body covered hers as his cock slipped back between her legs and through her slick center.

With her legs pressed together, she felt fuller. Felt him *deeper*.

She turned her face to the side, her hair sticking to her cheek. When she pinched her eyes closed, Daemon swept her hair away and wrapped it around a fist. "Eyes open, Princess."

Something in his tone compelled her to comply, and once she did, Daemon peeled away from her back and into a sitting position. "I want you to watch me fuck you, Auraelia. I want you to see how beautiful you are when you're thoroughly and completely ruined by me."

Her response came out as a squeak as he yanked her hips back into his, pulling her back into his lap as he knelt on the bed. He slid an arm up her torso, his hand wrapping around her neck as he helped her into a sitting position. When she looked straight ahead, she was looking into the mirror on her vanity.

It was across the room but close enough to see the sheen on their bodies. To see the desire and possession in Daemon's eyes.

From this angle, she could see *everything*.

Book Cover by *Moonpress* | *www.moonpress.co*

Illustrations by Jessica Hoffa via Canva

First edition 2024

ISBN E-Book: 979-8-9884142-3-0

ISBN Hardcover: 979-8-9884142-5-4

ISBN Paperback: 979-8-9884142-4-7

She could see every slide of his cock as he thrust in and out of her.

Could watch as one set of fingers swirled her clit, and the other wrapped around her throat like a choker. It was erotic in a way she never imagined.

"Goddess, you take my cock like such a good girl. Such a pretty pussy, all wet and needy for me."

The filth of his words, coupled with the scene in the mirror, had her trembling as her orgasm built once more. The gasp that had begun to slip through her lips was cut off by the tightening of Daemon's hand on her throat.

Not sure what to do with her hands, Auraelia locked eyes with Daemon in the mirror and began to play with her breasts. Tweaking her nipples in time with his thrusts.

Daemon's deep chuckle vibrated through her entire body. "I think you like watching yourself. Do you like watching me fuck you, Princess?"

He loosened his hold just enough for her to say, "*Yes*." It came out as more of a moan than an actual word, but it was the triumphant smile on his face that caught her attention.

"Good. Because I want you to watch yourself come."

He held her gaze in the mirror as his fingers worked her clit faster, and his thrusts became deeper.

The closer her release, the more erratic her magic became. Lightning spiraled up her arms and onto Daemon's, but he didn't stop. Didn't slow.

He didn't even seem to notice.

Warmth spread throughout her body, followed closely by the tingling sensation in her extremities and the flutter of her pussy walls.

Close. She was so close.

Seeming to sense that, Daemon picked up his pace. His hand tightened around her throat, restricting her blood flow until black began to swim in her vision. But just as she was about to beg for a reprieve, Daemon released his hold on her throat as he whispered, "Come for me, Princess."

Pure bliss swept through her, rocking her to her very core as she watched her body get hit with wave upon wave of pleasure.

He kept his arms wrapped around her as he continued to pursue his own pleasure. Driving into her with so much force that she was sure he would fuck her off the bed. But once he found his release, they collapsed, limbs still entwined and breathing heavy, as their souls returned to their bodies.

The next morning came far too quickly. Or perhaps not quickly enough, depending on how Auraelia chose to look at it.

Her night with Daemon had been amazing. They'd both found their pleasure...multiple times. But now that the morning light crept through the windows and the winter morning chill had set in, so did reality.

Auraelia slipped from between the sheets and pulled on her robe, trying to be as careful and quiet as possible so as to not wake Daemon.

After managing to successfully slip out of her suite without disturbing him, she crept down the hall toward Piper's chambers. It was early, but she also knew her friend was usually up with the sun.

Auraelia knocked softly on the door but tried again when there was no response. When there was still no answer, she softly called out, "Piper, I know you're awake. Answer the door, it's important."

The sound of hurried steps and hushed whispers filtered through the thick wood before the sound of a latch being lifted echoed through the silent corridor.

"Hey, Rae. Sorry, I just woke up. Everything alright?"

Despite her words, Auraelia knew better. She knew that the flush on her friend's cheeks and the muss of her hair were not due to sleep. "*Sleep*, huh?" she asked as she quirked a brow.

The sound of shuffling feet through the suite beyond the door had Piper's eyes flicking to the side before returning to center. "I–uh."

Auraelia chuckled and shook her head. "Oh, we have *a lot* to talk about later. But am I to assume that whoever is in *your* room is the same reason someone is currently in *mine*?"

Piper's eyes widened as she looked everywhere but at Auraelia's face.

"I see. Well, tell him I said hello and that we *all* have much to discuss." Nodding to her friend, Auraelia turned on her heel and returned to her chambers.

She couldn't put the day's problems off any longer. And one of those problems was currently naked in her bed.

Chapter Thirteen

Daemon

Daemon watched through cracked lids as Auraelia attempted to sneak back into her chambers undetected. The truth was, he'd woken as soon as she stirred. But knowing he had to tread carefully, he'd remained still with his eyes closed. Their night together had been beyond anything he could have imagined, and he wanted more of that. He was relatively sure that she did, too, but he also knew that this was a dangerous game they were playing.

Knew that she wouldn't budge on being together without a damn good reason to throw her current logic out the window. So instead, he'd be what she needed at the moment.

A distraction.

"If you're sneaking off in the early light of the morning, I guess I didn't do as good of a job as I thought I had." He kept his tone light, teasing her the way he knew brought out her feisty side. When her face whipped toward him, he let his lips lift into the smirk that drove her crazy. "Maybe I should try again. Clearly, I need the practice."

Auraelia's eyes widened, and she wrapped the ends of her robe tighter around her frame. "I don't think that's necessary."

"Are you sure? I don't mind." Daemon slipped from the bed and slowly made his way toward her, relishing the way her gaze morphed from annoyance to lust-filled hunger as it swept down his frame. The way it stopped and lingered on his semi-hard cock.

Her tongue swept across her bottom lip before she dragged the plump flesh between her teeth. He wasn't even sure if she knew she was doing it, but it made his cock twitch in anticipation all the same.

When her eyes finally found his again, a flush colored her cheeks, and she quickly turned away.

That just won't do.

Summoning the shadows, Daemon moved within them until he was directly behind her. Wrapping his arms around her waist, he nuzzled into her neck, breathing in the ever-present aroma of lavender and the lingering scent of sex. "Come back to bed, Princess. It's barely dawn."

He trailed kisses up the column of her neck, and her head lolled to the side. Her body melted into his for the briefest of moments before she straightened and peeled his arms from around her. "Daemon—" the reproach in her tone was a dagger to his heart. "We can't."

"So you said last night. And yet, we very much *did.*" He reached for her again, but she stepped out of his grasp.

Auraelia turned toward him, the stormy grays of her eyes swirling with so many emotions it made his heart ache. But the one that shone the brightest was *pain*.

Goddess, he would do anything to take that pain away. To take away the hurt that followed her like a heavy cloud blocking the sun's rays. But he couldn't unless she let him, and right now, she didn't seem to see that as an option.

Dropping her gaze to the floor, she released a heavy breath. "We did. And it was wonderful, but it was—"

"Don't you dare say it was a mistake, Auraelia."

She brought her gaze to his, her mouth opening and closing a few times before she nodded and took another step away. Silence filled the room as they stared at each other. It seemed that if they weren't fighting or fucking, there wasn't much to say anymore.

Daemon donned the mask that she wanted to see. Let the nonchalance he didn't feel shine through the smirk that tilted up one corner of his lips. "It was just sex, remember? No mistakes were made."

Auraelia seemed to mull over his words, then a shy smile tugged at her lips. "Thank you."

"You have nothing to thank me for, Princess."

Daemon turned away from her and strolled across the room to where his clothes were strewn across the floor. "So," he said, pausing as he pulled on his trousers. "What's the plan for today?"

Auraelia had walked into her closet while he dressed but poked her head out at his question, her brows raised in confusion. "Excuse me?"

"What's the plan for today?"

Stepping back into the main area of her room, she leaned against the entrance to her closet, arms crossed over her chest. "Surely you're not planning on *staying*?"

Daemon shrugged and pulled his tunic over his head. "Would that be so bad?" He winked, and her eyes widened. He could see the wheels turning in her mind as she processed what he said and all of the reasons she was bound to come up with as to why he shouldn't. Before she could give those asinine reasons a voice, he continued. "We brought things to trade and sell in your market, so we will be here for a few days. Ours—" he paused, strangling the anger that threatened to surface, "let's just say it's not doing well at the moment."

Understanding flashed in her eyes, and he knew he didn't need to say more. The unspoken name of whom was responsible, filling in the spaces of words left unsaid.

Auraelia nodded, then returned to her closet to dress. When she emerged once more, Daemon's breath caught in his throat. Rich chocolate leather hugged the luscious curves of her legs, and the tunic she wore was the color of her eyes, making them shine brightly beneath the dark fringe of her lashes.

He didn't bother masking the way his gaze traveled over her body. The way it lingered on the swell of her breasts as they rose and fell with every breath over the matching leather corset that cinched her waist.

Auraelia cleared her throat, promptly pulling him out of his lustful stupor. "My eyes are up here, Daemon."

Slowly, he met her gaze. Her lips were set into a thin line. One hip jutted out to the side as she crossed her arms—which only brought more attention to her breasts. But there was also a hunger in her eyes—one that matched his own. "I'm quite aware, Princess."

He let the static build between them. He wanted her to make the first move, to act on the thoughts so clearly written all over her face.

Auraelia dropped her arms, her walls seeming to fall with them. But just as she made to move toward him, a knock sounded at the main door to the suite. And just like that, he watched the walls build back up again.

Son of a bitch.

Auraelia ran her hands down her sides, smoothing wrinkles that weren't there, then fixed him with a hard stare. "Stay here."

Daemon smirked at the authority in her tone. *So bossy.* "I have nowhere else I'd rather be, *Your Majesty.*" There was a teasing lilt to the latter part of his statement, but he meant every word.

Her eyes narrowed a fraction, but with a curt nod, she skirted around him as she made her way into the sitting area of her suite, closing the door to her bedchamber behind her.

Daemon perched on the edge of her bed and ran a hand through his hair before scrubbing it down his face.

By the time the door opened once more, he had just finished pulling on his second boot. "Crisis averted?" he asked as he leaned back onto his elbows.

Auraelia rolled her eyes, and his balls tightened.

Completely ignoring his question, she countered with one of her own. "So what's your plan? Or did you intend to spend your entire trip here, in my bed?"

The sass that filled her tone turned him on more than it probably should have, and he wanted nothing more than to strip her down and turn her ass red as he drove into her. But that would have to wait. "You make that sound like a bad plan. Sounds pretty good to me, especially if you're in it with me."

Auraelia groaned in frustration, then turned on her heel, mumbling, *"You're insufferable,"* under her breath.

The laugh that tumbled out of his mouth was full and loud, and it stopped her in her tracks. He paused for a moment, shocked that he'd actually *laughed*. He hadn't done that in months and the realization had him starting all over again.

When he finally calmed, he smiled at her. "I think I'm quite delightful."

Annoyance colored her features, but there was a smile in her eyes as she scoffed, "Of course you do."

Sighing, she gestured to the table in her makeshift dining area. The memory of her spread out on that same table the night before had his blood heating, and he briefly wondered how mad she would be if he did it again.

Auraelia's voice carried across the space, once again pulling him from his fantasies. "Piper brought breakfast if you're hungry."

So that's *who was at the door.*

Daemon stood and followed her into the main area of her suite. The smell of fresh coffee and baked goods filled the space and made his mouth water.

Auraelia sat in one of the chairs and poured the dark, bitter liquid into two mugs. He had just reached for his cup when she pulled the silver cloche off the tray, and a small smile formed as he took in the contents. Chocolate croissants, enough for *two*, were piled onto the tray, their tops a flakey golden brown.

I knew I liked Piper.

Taking the seat opposite Auraelia, Daemon picked up one of the pastries and took a bite. The slight bitterness of the dark chocolate sang sweetly with the salty butter of the crust.

"Goddess, these are better than I remember," he said around the moan that rumbled up his throat.

Auraelia chuckled, then took a sip of her coffee. "Is Auntie Jodie not making them for you anymore?" Her hands paused halfway back to the table, as something like shock flashed across her eyes. As if she hadn't meant to say the words out loud.

Not wanting to let her thoughts spin, Daemon quickly answered, "She is. But nothing compares to the original."

Her eyes met his, and her cheeks flushed under his gaze. No doubt remembering the first time they'd shared the delicacy under the trees by the training pitch, just as he had been. He'd never get tired of that. Of seeing the way her body reacted to him despite how hard she tried to fight it.

Daemon knew he had his work cut out for him when it came to Auraelia but seeing her fall back into the ease they once had with each other gave him hope—even when she would erect her walls right after she realized it. He was determined to find the chink in her armor that would let him back in. When he did, he would never let her go again.

They ate in semi-comfortable silence, but once Auraelia finished, she cleared her throat and stood from the table. "I uh—I have somewhere I need to be."

"Oh?" he asked, curiosity filling his tone. When she didn't respond, he filled the silence. "Care to share?"

"Not really." Auraelia reached over to where her dagger was still lying on the tabletop and strapped it to her thigh.

"Well, shit, Princess. If you need that, maybe I should tag along." Daemon wiped his hands on a napkin and stood.

"I don't *need* you to come with me," she spat, her tone colder than the air outside. Her hands shook as she attempted to buckle the leather straps around her leg, and her breathing slowly became more and more ragged.

Taking the two steps to get to her, Daemon knelt at her feet and stilled her trembling fingers. "Here, let me."

Auraelia slowly pulled her hands from his grasp, and he immediately felt the loss. Every time they touched it was like an electric current running through him. Like her magic threaded itself into his own veins.

Daemon finished fastening the buckles and ensured her dagger was securely seated within its sheath. When he stood, her eyes were still downcast to where he had been kneeling.

Slipping a finger beneath her chin, he brought her gaze to his. "Where are you going that's got you so frazzled, Auraelia?" She opened her mouth, and he could already hear the lie that was about to slip from her lips. "Don't lie to me, Princess. I can read you better than I can read the stars in the sky. *Where* are you going?"

Auraelia blew out a breath, her eyes closing as resolve settled into her features. "I'm going to the dungeons...to see Kyra."

Kyra? She hasn't been dealt with yet?

"Auraelia—"

She opened her eyes at the sound of her name, fierce determination coursing through them as streaks of peridot streamed across the gray. "Don't."

Daemon dropped his hand but held her gaze. "I'm not trying to stop you. But I don't think this is something you should do by yourself."

"What makes you think I'm going by myself?"

Daemon quirked a brow. "What did I *just* tell you?"

"Ugh, *fine.* Yes, I was going to go by myself."

"Was?"

"Daemon, you may be able to read me, but I can read you, too. We both know that you'd follow me whether I wanted you to or not."

She wasn't wrong, and the fact that she called him out on it made him smile. "Good. Now that we have that understanding, lead the way."

Auraelia didn't budge. Instead, she crossed her arms and raised her brows. "And how, pray tell, are we going to explain your presence when your *fiancée* murdered my mother?"

Daemon barely suppressed the flinch that resulted from her words. Pasting a smile on his face, he took a step forward, closing the already small space between them. "Let me worry about that."

Chapter Fourteen

Daemon

Using the shadows to conceal him from sight, Daemon followed Auraelia through the castle and down the spiral staircase that led into the dungeons, the temperature dropping the further down they traveled.

He'd been down there once with Xander while Auraelia had been in her catatonic state after her mother's murder. He'd tried to help the prince question the maid, but all they'd received was bone-chilling laughter instead of answers.

After what felt like eons of silence, and he was certain that no one was near, Daemon stripped away the darkness surrounding him and asked, "Why hasn't she been dealt with yet?"

Auraelia stopped two stairs down and took a deep breath. "I don't want you to think of me as weak—"

Descending the steps between them, Daemon gently grasped her arm and turned her toward him. "I would never think that, Auraelia."

She held his gaze for a moment, then nodded and continued. "I haven't been down here since...since we put her in her cell. I couldn't bring myself to face her. And I—" she stopped mid-sentence, worry lacing the delicate lines of her face.

"And you didn't want to repeat what happened in the ballroom?"

When she nodded, his heart sank.

"I'm just still so *angry*. And my magic has been...well, you saw. I can't always control it. I don't want to kill someone in the name of revenge or in general. I just...I don't want to be like *her*."

"Like Kyra?" he asked, though he was pretty sure she wasn't who Auraelia was referencing.

"Kyra. Davina. They're one and the same, aren't they? Davina may not have been the one to actually poison my mother, but she was the reason behind it. She's just as much at fault as Kyra is."

Deciding to risk the small amount of progress they'd made and praying that she wouldn't flinch away from him, Daemon cupped her cheek. She leaned into his touch without hesitation, and his heart damn nearly jumped out of his chest. "You're not Kyra, Auraelia. And you sure as hell aren't Davina. You're one of the strongest people that I have ever met. Don't let anyone make you think otherwise."

Tears lined her eyes as her gaze flicked over his face. When they landed on his lips, the need to pull her into his arms, to kiss her until she forgot everything that troubled her, was nearly crippling.

A lone tear slowly trailed down her cheek, and her eyes fluttered closed as he gently swept it away.

Daemon took a step closer, his body close enough to feel the heat radiating off her but far enough away that she didn't feel caged in.

Her hands landed on his chest, curling into the fabric of his tunic, her voice quavering as she spoke. "Daemon, I—"

Brushing his thumb across her cheek, he whispered, "I know."

He didn't need her to say anything; he just *knew.* Knew the words she refused to let loose. Knew that her mind was a scramble of mixed emotions and warring thoughts.

But he also knew—or at least *hoped*—that she needed *him* as badly as he needed *her*.

He wasn't sure if she was pulling him, or if their bodies intrinsically moved toward each other from the draw that neither could deny. But just as his lips were a breath away from hers, shouting, followed by a crash, came from the bottom of the stairs and sent them shooting apart.

Their gazes clashed for a second, and then Auraelia sprinted down the remaining steps.

"Shit." Daemon pulled the shadows to conceal himself once more and hurried after her. When he hit the bottom of the stairs, Auraelia stood in front of Kyra's cell, ribbons of lightning and wind wrapping around her arms in defense of their master as a lone, bone-chilling laugh echoed throughout the chamber.

A solitary guard stood against the far wall, a tray of food splattered against the floor at his feet.

"Leave us." Auraelia's tone matched the chill in the air, sending a shiver down his spine.

"Your Majesty—" the guard sputtered, stepping toward his queen.

"Leave. Us," she demanded, her eyes never straying from the woman before her.

The man's face blanched, but he quickly bowed and hurried from the room.

"Finally got the nerve to come see me, *Your Majesty*?" Though Kyra's voice was sickly sweet, there was an undercurrent of hatred that laced every word.

Auraelia took a deep breath and tightened the hold on her magic, the fiery light dimming until it was nothing more than a memory.

Sticking to the shadows, Daemon skirted along the wall until he was behind Auraelia, keeping a watchful eye on the figure behind the bars.

Kyra was lounging on the threadbare cot of her cell like she hadn't a care in the world. Her formerly blonde hair was matted and a dungy shade of brown. Her clothes were tattered and worn. But there was a ferocity in her gaze as she locked onto the new queen.

Auraelia casually strolled over to where a simple wooden chair sat at a small table and dragged it across the stone floor, placing it directly in front of the cell door.

Daemon's eyes grew wide, and he had to clench his fists to keep from dragging her back out of harm's way. It was fucking risky sitting that close to the clearly deranged woman. But there was nothing he could do but watch.

Auraelia sat, stretched her legs out in front of her, and clasped her hands across her stomach, matching the carefree demeanor of her prisoner. "I thought you might like some better company, seeing as you didn't seem to care for your guard's." Auraelia gestured over her shoulder to where Kyra had thrown her tray.

A crazed smile stretched across the woman's face as she canted her head to the side, studying Auraelia in a way that made even Daemon uncomfortable. "And you thought it wise to be *alone* with me? Are you planning on finishing what you started all those months ago?"

Something about the way she said "alone" made him wary, and he cautiously took a step forward.

Auraelia, however, didn't seem to notice—or didn't care.

"No, Kyra. Unlike you, I don't relish the idea of *murder*. And unlike *you*, I don't have someone pulling my strings. But I am curious why you decided to commit such an egregious act of treason. Were we unkind to you? Did we treat you horribly? If you chose to strike against the people who cared for you, we must have."

"Cared for me? You think you *cared* for me?" Kyra stood from her cot and took the few steps to the bars of her cell, bringing her directly in front of Auraelia.

Daemon straightened, his shadows pooling at his fingers, ready to strike down any threat that should arise. But Auraelia merely stared at her, complete indifference radiating from every fiber of her being.

"I think—" she paused, standing to meet Kyra's gaze head-on. "I think that you killed the woman who gave you a home. Who trusted you and gave you a safe place to land after a hard day. Who filled your belly and your pockets daily. But I also *know* that you murdered my mother. Whether it was at my cousin's behest or not, you still did it. And that's the only thing that I *need* to know. What I *want* to know is why. *Why* did you kill my mother?"

"Because your mother never should have been queen!" Kyra shrieked as she lunged toward Auraelia. Only, instead of reaching what she sought, her hands hit a wall of crackling lightning laced with shadows.

Kyra quickly withdrew her hand, drawing it close to her chest as she laughed, the sound grating against Daemon's ears. "I was wondering when your watchdog would slink out of the shadows. Hello, *Prince.*"

Daemon dropped the shadows cloaking his form and stepped forward. "How did you know that I was here?"

A mad grin spread across Kyra's face. "I may not be royalty, and I may only be a lowly maid, but that doesn't mean I don't have gifts of my own. I can sense magic in others. It glows like a halo around them. And yours, dear Prince, shone through your shadows like a full moon on a cloudless night. I do wonder what your betrothed would say if she knew you were standing here right now." Her laughter pealed through the chamber, bouncing off the walls around them.

Daemon noticed the change in Auraelia's demeanor a split second before it happened. Saw the way her spine straightened and her head cocked to the side. The same thing happened before she pulled the air from Kyra's lungs in the middle of the ballroom. Only this time, she didn't even need to move, her hands hanging limply at her sides.

Kyra's laugh turned into gasping breaths as Auraelia slowly siphoned the air from her lungs.

"I asked you a question." Auraelia's voice was eerily calm, and Daemon took a hesitant step toward her.

"Auraelia—"

"I'm not going to kill her, Daemon. But she needs to understand that I'm not going to play her games." Auraelia released her magical grip, and Kyra sputtered as she tried to drag air back into her lungs.

"You bi—"

Auraelia squatted down to where Kyra was crumpled against the bars, cutting off her air supply again. "That wasn't very nice. I asked you a question. *Why* did you kill my mother?"

Daemon stood in silence as he watched the interaction play out. He didn't want to interfere, but everything about it felt *wrong*. There was no emotion in Auraelia's voice. Not even anger. It was as if she turned it all off to deal with the woman in front of her.

When Kyra's face began to turn purple, Auraelia returned the air to her lungs for the second time.

Kyra was on her hands and knees on the cold stone floor, tears streaming down her face from her struggle to breathe. Glaring up at Auraelia through her lashes, she sneered as she spoke. "Because Davina should be on the throne, and your mother was in the way. So now there's one less obstacle, and I can't wait to see how she deals with *you.*"

"You're originally from Garnet, aren't you?" Daemon asked as he stepped closer to Auraelia, every bit of him screaming to guard and protect her—not that she needed him to.

Kyra pushed back onto her heels and met his gaze. "Well, well. The dog is smarter than he looks."

Auraelia stiffened at his side. He needed to get her out of there. She was teetering close to her breaking point, and it seemed Kyra was itching to push her over the edge. To see how far she could press her before she snapped.

Daemon placed his hand on the small of Auraelia's back and turned his attention to her. "We should go."

Auraelia's eyes were still locked onto Kyra as she inhaled deeply, holding her breath for a few moments before she released it and nodded.

As they turned to leave, Kyra chuckled. "Do send my best to *my* queen. I look forward to seeing her on the throne."

Auraelia stopped mid-stride and sent a streak of lightning straight through its center without glancing toward the cell.

Kyra's scream echoed throughout the chamber as the iron tang of blood filled his nostrils.

Daemon pulled Auraelia into his arms, but just before they were engulfed in the shadows, she hollered over her shoulder, "You should take care of that. I hear infections can be deadly when not tended to."

"Do you want to talk about it?" Daemon asked as the shadows stripped away from them back in Auraelia's chambers.

"Talk about what, exactly?" Auraelia turned and walked toward the small selection of liquors tucked into one of her bookcases. "Do you want one?"

"Uh, sure. But, Auraelia, we should talk about what just happened."

"Daemon—" She took a sip of the amber liquid in her glass, then turned toward him. "There's not much to talk about. You were there. You heard what she said."

"I did. But I also saw how she baited you. She was *trying* to get a reaction out of you."

"You think I don't know that?" Her voice was as calm as if they were merely discussing the weather. "I said that I wouldn't kill her, and I didn't."

"You shot her with a bolt of lightning."

"It barely grazed her."

"Auraelia."

"*Daemon.*"

Her tone was playful, and he couldn't help the small smile that formed in response.

Crossing the room, Auraelia handed him a glass of whiskey, then disappeared into her bedchamber. When she returned to the sitting area, a piece of parchment was in her hands.

"What's that?"

She cut him a glance and held her finger over her lips as she made her way to the suite's main door, opening it just enough to pass the note to the guard standing outside and to give them instructions, but not enough for them to peer inside.

When the door closed behind her, and she'd turned toward him again, he asked, "Okay, *now* do you want to tell me what that was?"

A sly smirk pulled on her lips as she strolled back toward her glass on the shelf, patting him on the chest as she passed. "You'll see."

"You're in a surprisingly calm mood."

"Quite the contrary, actually. I'm *pissed* off." Thunder boomed through the sky outside, accentuating the words. "And I think it's time we let the council in on the things *we* know."

"We? You want *me* in the council meeting? What happened to no one knowing I was here?" Daemon quirked a brow and took a sip from his glass. The soft burn of the liquid giving way to the sweet taste of honey.

Auraelia shrugged. "If you're here, you might as well be useful."

Her words nearly made him choke on his whiskey. Coughing to clear his throat, he asked, "Excuse me?"

There was a knock at the door before their conversation could go any further.

"Could you get that?" she asked, a mischievous light shining in her eyes.

Daemon narrowed his gaze and slowly backed toward the door. "Why do I feel like you're setting me up?"

A giggle—an actual giggle—escaped from Auraelia as she watched him and shrugged.

She's definitely up to something.

Daemon cautiously opened the door, and standing on the other side was Xander.

The prince looked him up and down before sighing and pushing his way into the suite. "Where's Auraelia?"

"Nice to see you again, too," Daemon scoffed.

Xander crossed the space to his sister. "Rae, what's going on?"

"You'll see," she said before taking another sip from her glass. "Do you want one? I have a feeling you're going to need it."

"Tell me what's going on," her brother repeated.

"Xander, grab a drink and sit down."

Not even a minute had passed before there was another knock on the door. Glancing at Auraelia, who nodded in confirmation, Daemon blew out a breath.

Only, when he opened it this time, he was met with the exasperated face of Piper.

"Are we in trouble?" she asked as she stepped around him and into the suite.

"No, you're not in trouble. Though we do have some *things* to talk about. But that's not why I asked you all here." Auraelia gestured to the open seats in her sitting area. "Have a seat; we have a lot to discuss." Glancing around the room, a puzzled look stretched over her features before her gaze landed back on Daemon. "Where's Aiden?"

"He's on the ship, why?" Daemon responded, crossing the room to sit on one of the couches.

"He's on the—" Auraelia stopped, her eyes narrowing in on her friend. When Piper's cheeks flushed, Auraelia's brows shot up to her hairline, her mouth dropping open before she promptly shut it.

"Can someone clue me in, please?" Xander exclaimed as he threw himself down into one of the armchairs.

Auraelia pulled her gaze from Piper and turned it toward her brother. "Xander, *breathe*." Once everyone was seated, Auraelia drained the contents of her glass and began. "I want Daemon and Aiden present at the council meeting today."

"You want to do *what*?" Xander asked, disbelief filling his tone as confusion marred his features.

"I believe she said she wanted Daemon and Aiden at the council meeting today," Piper chimed in, one brow winging up as she focused on her friend.

"I heard what she said, Piper. I just don't understand *why* she said it."

"Because they're the ones with information on Davina. And *I* certainly can't tell them without them bombarding me with questions on *how* I came by the information." All eyes were trained on Auraelia as she spoke, but before anyone could interject, she continued. "Look, we haven't met with Aiden in over a month. He could have new information to share. They're both here. And I think it's time that the council learned what we know."

"Rae, I'm not disagreeing with you, but I have to ask. What brought this on?" Piper's gaze flicked between Daemon and Auraelia as worry lines etched into her forehead.

Leaning back on the couch, Daemon let a smirk take over his lips. "You want to tell them, Princess? Or should I?"

"What's he talking about, Rae?" Xander asked as he narrowed his gaze on his sister.

The look Auraelia gave him was one of sheer annoyance, but she huffed out a breath and explained. "I went to see Kyra today. And before you go off on your tangent about how *I should have let you know, you shouldn't have gone by yourself.* You're not my keeper, and I didn't go alone."

"Rae—"

"Xander, I mean it. I don't want to hear it. Daemon went with me, and look," she gestured to her body, "I'm in one piece."

Daemon chuckled from his spot on the couch and muttered, "Kyra can't really say the same."

"What the fuck is *that* supposed to mean?" Xander asked, turning his wide-eyed gaze to Daemon.

"Ask your sister."

"Goddess, dammit, Daemon. Would you *stop*?"

Xander scrubbed his hand down his face and groaned. "Rae, what happened in the damn dungeon?"

Auraelia blew out a short breath through her nose. "I *may* have shot Kyra with a bolt of lightning—"

"You *killed* her?" Piper asked, surprise filling her tone as her eyebrows attempted to merge with her hairline.

"No, I didn't kill her. It grazed her leg. Maybe now she will think twice about how she speaks to me."

Xander and Piper sat in shocked silence, their eyes wide as they stared at their Queen.

"It was more than a graze, and I think you're leaving out some details, Princess."

"*Fuck,* Daemon. Shut. *Up*."

When Xander's and Piper's gazes didn't falter, Auraelia threw her hands up and sighed. "Okay, fine. I also siphoned her air...twice." She turned a hardened glare at Daemon. "Happy now?"

"Extremely." Daemon raised his glass to her and winked.

He may have hated watching Kyra bait her, but being the one to bring out the fire that had been extinguished all those months ago was quickly becoming his favorite hobby.

Slumping down into his chair, Xander dug his fingers into his temples. "I think I'll take that drink now."

The group fell into a tense silence while Auraelia poured everyone a glass of whiskey. When she returned, her gaze fell on Daemon. "How quickly can you get word to Aiden?"

A mischievous smile stretched across his lips. "Drop the wards, and I'll have him here in a few seconds."

Auraelia nodded and turned to her brother, who had just downed the entirety of his glass. "Xander?"

"Yeah, I'm on it."

Sitting up straight in his chair, Xander tilted his head side to side and placed his glass on the table before turning toward Daemon. "I'm going to drop them for *one* minute. Is that enough time for you to get there and back?"

Daemon stood from the couch and nodded.

"Rae, I need a piece of parchment and your dagger."

Auraelia scrunched her brow but got the items and handed them to her brother. Slicing the blade across his palm, Xander dipped his fingers into the swelling crimson liquid and scrawled a symbol onto the parchment. "You have one minute before I destroy this rune, and then they're back up. I suggest you go."

Daemon flicked his gaze from the bloody parchment to the prince, then gathered his shadows and left for his ship.

Chapter Fifteen

Auraelia

Daemon was barely gone for thirty seconds before reappearing, swathed in shadows with a grumbling Aiden.

"Fuck, D. I had a winning hand! You know how hard it is to beat Neese at poker?"

"Quit your griping. You can finish the game later," Daemon said with a chuckle.

Aiden scoffed and pushed away, mumbling, "You know she's going to look at my cards."

"You sound like a child who got their toy taken away, Aiden." Piper quipped from where she was perched on the couch, sipping her drink with an amused smile.

Aiden groaned as he looked around the room. "Oh, look. The gang's all here...*why* is the gang all here?"

"You'll see," Auraelia sing-songed.

"Is that your favorite phrase today, Princess?"

Auraelia glowered at Daemon. "Xander, please escort the prince and emissary into the council chambers. I need to talk to Piper for a minute."

Xander's eyes widened slightly as he glanced between the two women, nervousness etched in every line on his face. Piper's was a mirror of Xander's as they held each other's gaze.

When her friend gave a slight shrug, he peeled himself from the chair and headed toward the door that opened into the hall leading to the council room. "Gentlemen."

Daemon cast her a confused look but followed Xander with Aiden close at his heels.

"Would someone *please* explain what's going on?" Aiden pleaded.

"Come on, Aiden," Daemon clapped him on the back. "I'll fill you in on the way."

With the sound of the latch clicking into place, Auraelia turned toward her friend. "Who was in your room this morning?" she asked as nonchalantly as possible.

"What are you talking about?" Piper asked, her gaze averted as a flush slowly crept across her cheeks.

"*Piper.*"

After a few moments of silence, her friend sighed. "Xander," she mumbled, almost too low for Auraelia to hear.

"You slept with my brother?" Auraelia exclaimed, gaping at her best friend.

"What? No!" Piper's gaze shot to her friend, eyes wide as she frantically waved her hand from side to side.

"When I came to your room this morning, you definitely had sex hair. *And* you just admitted that it was Xander in your rooms." Excitement bled out of every word. Her brother had finally done it. Had finally gotten the nerve to go after the one girl who had managed to hold his attention for longer than one night.

"I did *not* sleep with Xander."

"Uh-huh. Explain then." Auraelia sat sideways on the couch facing her friend, her arm draped casually over the back, head resting on her fist, as she waited for the answer.

Piper blew out an exasperated breath. "We were just talking. I asked him to come to my suite to hang out, and I *may* have convinced him to drop the wards for a minute...a *precise* minute, to be exact." Her lips tilted up into a cheeky grin.

"You're the reason Daemon was in my room? But how did you even know he was here? Did Xander know that's why you were asking him to drop the wards?"

"I saw it." Piper casually shrugged one shoulder, then continued. "And Rae, before you get mad at me, you *needed* to see him. And if the way *you looked* coming to my room this morning says anything, it's that you didn't mind the surprise. And, no. He didn't."

"That's beside the point, Piper. And it still doesn't explain why my brother was in your room this *morning*."

"Well, we started drinking. Then drinking turned to talking and more drinking, and eventually, we both fell asleep. He *may* have kissed me at some point, but he ran out so fast after you left this morning that I'm starting to think it was a fever dream."

"Okay...but do you *want* him to kiss you?"

"Rae—"

"Don't *Rae* me. Answer the question."

Piper sighed and dropped her head onto the back of the couch. "Yes, okay. Are you happy now? But he's your *brother*."

"Okay, and?"

"We can't. It's too weird."

"You most certainly can! I give my blessing. Hell, I'll throw a party if you both finally get your heads out of your asses." Piper's gaze narrowed in on her friend, but before she could retort, Auraelia continued. "Look, Piper. Don't be an idiot. If you like Xander, go for it. I promise the feeling is mutual."

"Why can't I be an idiot? *You're* being an idiot."

Auraelia dropped her gaze to her lap and let out a heavy breath. "Yeah, well. I have my reasons."

"Your reasons for being an idiot are idiotic, Rae. You love him."

"I know. But we can't. Not right now."

Piper sat up and grasped Auraelia's hand in hers. "You *can*. You're choosing not to. You're *choosing* to hurt when the person who makes you whole is right on the other side of that door."

Auraelia turned toward the large oak door that led to the council chambers, her heartbeat quickening as the pull to be near Daemon grew. The ache in her chest had ebbed since he'd been there, his presence slowly filling the cracks that she'd caused in her own heart.

"It's okay to find light in the dark, Auraelia. Let him in. Let him be your light."

Turning back toward her friend, Auraelia chuckled. "That's pretty ironic since he, quite literally, manipulates *shadows*."

The women fell into a fit of laughter, which resulted in tears rolling down their cheeks. It had been so long since Auraelia had been able to laugh. Grief and despair followed her around like the storm clouds she commanded, blocking out every ray of sunlight that tried to pry its way through the darkness and bring even a smidgeon of light back into her life. But ever since Daemon popped back into view, small beams of warmth had managed to cut through the bleakness that shrouded her, slowly mending the tattered pieces of her soul.

When they finally calmed, Auraelia pulled her friend in for a hug and whispered, "It's okay for you to do the same, Piper." Pulling away, she locked gazes with her friend. "Don't be me, okay? Don't miss out on something that's right in front of you."

Piper's shoulders dropped, her head tilting slightly to the side as her gaze softened. "I won't if you promise to find some happiness yourself."

A quiet smile lifted the corners of Auraelia's lips as she gave her friend another squeeze. "I'll try. Now come on, we need to be in there before the council shows up."

Pushing up from the couch, they made their way through the door and down the hall. Auraelia's nerves stood on end as anxiety began to settle in her chest.

Here goes nothing.

"What are *they* doing here?" Lord Harland demanded, face frozen with disdain, his body immobile in the large double doorway that led into the council chambers.

The rest of the council members filled the space behind him, their expressions ranging from shock to anger as they took in the two newcomers.

Auraelia leaned back casually in her chair, elbows resting on the arms with her hands steepled in front of her face. "Have a seat." She kept her tone calm despite the trickling of static up her spine.

This has to work.

The council filed into the room, their wary gazes trained on the prince and emissary from the Sapphire Isles. When they were all finally seated, Auraelia leaned forward and began. "Prince Daemon and Lord Aiden are here to provide information regarding my cousin."

"Your Majesty," Mister Aramis interjected. "Surely you don't believe they are here in good faith? He's *engaged* to that...that *woman*."

Auraelia cut a sharp glance at her emissary, "I am *aware* of the situation, Mister Aramis." Slowly rotating her gaze through the rest of her council, she continued. "I do not *need* the reminder, as the entire encounter where that information came to light is emblazoned in my memory. What I *do* need is for all of you to listen. I would not bring them into this chamber without just cause, and I would appreciate it if you would give me just a modicum of trust."

Every member of her council's eyes went wide. From her Mistress of Coin—Lady Ophelia, to her Master at Arms—Master Demir. With his usually stoic expression, even Lord Harland couldn't mask the shock radiating across his face.

"Now, shall we begin?" Settling back into her chair, Auraelia turned toward Daemon, who sat to her right. "Prince Daemon, would you please explain what you know about Davina?"

A small smile graced his lips as he met her gaze and nodded. "What would you like to know?"

"Everything."

The council squirmed in their seats as Daemon relayed the information he had. He spoke of the turmoil throughout his kingdom and the upheaval that Davina had already caused to his court. Going into grave detail over the destruction she'd caused on the Sapphire Isles' marketplace, Daemon broke down the impact it had on their economy and how that would inevitably affect the rest of Ixora.

As he went on, she watched the expressions on her council's faces shift from wary glances to ones of shock and anger. But it wasn't until Daemon spoke of his personal experience with Davina's abilities that the others seated around the table found their voices.

"Blood magic? She has *blood* magic?" Master Demir questioned, his bushy charcoal brows pushing up his forehead, forming deep-set wrinkles in his tanned brow. He was one of the more senior council members but wasn't old by any stretch of the imagination. Though only in his fourth decade of life, time spent in the sun and working alongside his family in the blacksmith's shop darkened and aged his skin, making him appear older than he actually was.

"It appears so," Daemon responded. "Though I'm not entirely sure of the extent of her abilities, what I *have experienced* isn't something to take lightly."

It was Lady Ophelia who spoke next, her eyes trained on where her hands rested in her lap. "Nothing about blood magic should be taken lightly. It's dark and unruly and can corrupt the wielder if they're not careful."

Every pair of eyes shifted to the Mistress of Coin as they waited with bated breath for her to continue.

Lifting her gaze from her lap to the detailed map of Ixora that was etched into the tabletop, she continued. "I don't know much, just bits and pieces I picked up when I was younger. People tend not to notice when a child is nearby; if they do, they never consider that they're listening."

She fell silent for a moment, but when her eyes met Auraelia's, clarity swirled in the chocolate-brown depths of her irises. "Your Majesty, if I'm not mistaken, I believe there are some tomes on blood magic in the archives. I haven't read them myself, but I know that your mother did. I remember seeing them on her bedside table not too long ago."

Auraelia glanced toward Xander, his confused expression no doubt matching her own, before turning back toward her Mistress of Coin and asking, "Why would my mother be interested in blood magic, Lady Ophelia?"

Her question was met with a look of sympathy and a slight shake of the head. "I'm not sure. She never said, and I never thought to ask. I'm sorry."

As the room fell silent once more, Auraelia's thoughts began to spin around yet *another* secret that her mother had kept. Why was she looking into blood magic? Did she think it was something she may have had to face one day? And if so, why didn't she share that with Auraelia? Surely, if her mother thought Davina was going to be a real threat, she would have informed her...right?

Auraelia slowly released a breath through her nose.

Too many secrets. Her mother kept too many secrets.

Every time Auraelia felt that she finally found the last one, another reared its ugly head like an unwanted weed in a garden.

"You're awfully quiet over there, Ser Aeron." The nasally sound of Lord Harland's voice broke the quiet of the room. "What do *you* have to say to all of this?"

Ser Aeron was sitting to Xander's left, his brows furrowed as his eyes traced over the map like he was calculating the most advantageous point of strike in a battle.

"Ser Aeron?" Auraelia prodded, attempting to pull him from whatever thoughts kept him from the conversation at hand.

When his amber gaze met hers, he said, "I have trained your armies to fight. I have trained them to handle the worst conditions imaginable. To live with little to no food and still be battle-ready. But no amount of training will save them from blood magic, Your Majesty. This is a war that *warriors* can't win."

The stress he put on the word "warrior" gave Auraelia a sinking feeling, and the way his gaze bore into hers made it feel like a stone had settled into the pit of her stomach.

Caius.

No one—outside of people who had been present—knew of Caius' visit to the Court of Emerald. They hadn't told the council, and Auraelia had intended to keep it that way. She had decided against using his help, sure that they could win the war if it came to a battlefield.

But with all of the information they'd gathered, coupled with the intense gaze of her army commander, that seemed to no longer be an option. If brute force couldn't fight and win this war, they would have to rely on magic. Which meant that she would need to use the one weapon in her arsenal that Davina supposedly didn't know about.

Auraelia stood from her seat and released a steadying breath. Calming her frantic thoughts before addressing her council. "I believe that is enough for today. It seems I have some reading to do. Mister Aramis, if you would please reach out to your contacts in the Court of Topaz to see if they have any idea which direction Lady Orna and Lady Blyana are leaning in this war, I would greatly appreciate it. Master Demir, please meet with Ser Aeron so that we can ensure that our army has what they need in regard to weaponry and armor. I want to ensure we are thoroughly prepared when the need arises. Lord Harland. Lady Ophelia. Has anything changed regarding finances, the harvest, or food supply for our people?"

"No, Your Majesty. Everything is still as it should be," Lord Harland replied.

"Good. Now, if you would, please excuse me."

As if it were a performance, every council member stood and bowed in a synchronized motion, then began to file out of the room. All except for Ser Aeron, who halted at the door.

"You're going to use him, aren't you?" he asked as he turned his head over his shoulder.

"I'm going to see what he has to say, and we will go from there. But I currently don't see any other way out of this. Do you?"

Ser Aeron shook his head gravely, then walked away, pulling the door closed behind him.

"You're going to use *who*, Auraelia?" Daemon asked, his brow scrunched in confusion.

Ignoring his question, Auraelia walked to where Piper was sitting on the bench seat by the windows. "Do you think you could preoccupy Xander and Aiden for a bit?" she asked in a hushed tone.

Piper canted her head to the side, her eyes narrowing slightly as they searched Auraelia's face—like if she looked hard enough, she could see the meaning behind her words or read her mind.

Letting out an exasperated breath, Auraelia held out her hand. "Go ahead. What do you see?"

Over the last few months, Piper had been working on progressing her abilities. She spent hours practicing calling visions of the future to her and attempted to replay scenes of the past. Though she had vastly improved, it still helped when she made contact with the person whose life she was trying to glean.

Piper nodded and grasped Auraelia's hand, closing her eyes briefly before opening them to the wide, vacant stare that always accompanied her visions.

Fragments of what Piper saw filtered into Auraelia's mind as she allowed bits and pieces to flow between them. Flashes of a smile. Stars dancing in crystal clear waters. A cloudless winter night sky, with a nearly full moon shining against the velvety black backdrop.

As the images faded and life came back to Piper's eyes, a small smile tilted up the corners of her lips. "It's a little *cold* for a swim," she whispered, winking at Auraelia as she rose from the bench. Auraelia curled her lips inward, stifling the chuckle that tried to break through. The inner workings of her best friend's mind never ceased to amaze and amuse her.

"Come on, boys, let's go find some food. Aiden, looks like you're staying here tonight, so your game with Raneese will have to wait a little longer."

Piper strolled toward the door, patting Daemon on the chest as she passed him. "Have *fun*."

The confused look on his face was priceless as his head swiveled from Piper's retreating form back to Auraelia. When the door latched, he faced her fully and asked, "What was that about?"

Walking over to where he stood next to the table, she grinned. "I'd like to show you something first."

"Oh?"

Nodding, Auraelia gently laced her fingers with his. Warmth filled her veins, her magic stirring in response to his touch. But beneath that familiar heat was a subtle cool caress. Like she was toeing the line between standing in the shade of a tree and the rays of the sun.

Daemon's hand tightened around hers, excitement and confusion clashing together in the vibrant greens of his eyes. "I–I can *feel you*."

"You can feel me?" she asked, her heart galloping in her chest like a wild stallion.

Nodding, Daemon pulled her to him. With their entwined hands pressed between their chests, she could feel the thunderous pace of his heart where it hammered behind its cage. "It's like sunlight in my veins. Warm and welcoming."

Bringing her hand up to his lips, he placed a chaste kiss on her knuckles. As they held each other's gaze, it was as if time stalled around them. It could have been mere seconds or minutes that passed before the world seemed to begin spinning once more.

"What did you want to show me, Auraelia?"

A broad smile stretched across her face as she looked up at him. "You'll see."

Daemon smiled in return, his chuckle rumbling in his chest as he shook his head. "I do believe that is your favorite phrase today, Princess."

Releasing his hand, Auraelia wrapped both arms around his waist and rested her head on his chest. Daemon stood stock still for a fraction of a second, the embrace seeming to catch him off guard before his arms encircled her shoulders, and they were engulfed in shadows.

Chapter Sixteen

Daemon

As his shadows slipped away, the chill of the winter air kissed his cheeks while the last remaining fragments of sunlight rained down, bathing them in the soft, peachy glow of dusk.

"Where are we?" Daemon asked as he scanned his new surroundings.

Spindly trees, with bark flaking off their trunks, stood in rows before him, their branches nearly bare as the last remaining leaves and flowers refused to fall.

Auraelia unraveled herself from his embrace and linked her fingers through his, tugging him forward as she made her way toward the grove of trees. "If I told you, it wouldn't be a surprise."

"I guess that's your alternative version of '*you'll see*'?" Daemon asked, shaking his head as a chuckle rumbled up his throat.

"You could say that. Now, come on."

Auraelia led him through the neat lines of trees, weaving her way so effortlessly that he was certain she could navigate the area with her eyes closed. A smile tugged on his lips as he followed her blindly, the memory of her doing much of the same when they'd first met spinning through his mind.

When they reached the end of the grove, a large willow—still full of life despite the dropping temperatures—stood in their path. Daemon's eyes widened as he took in the massive tree, its branches stretching wide in all directions.

Auraelia squeezed his hand gently, then disentangled their fingers and walked up to the ancient tree—because how could a tree as grand as that be anything but. Daemon watched the way her hands moved gracefully over the vines. The way they swayed in the soft breeze that followed the trail of her fingers before they were drawn aside as if by an invisible cord to reveal a narrow path that had been worn down to bare dirt.

Maintaining the magic that held the curtain of flora aside, Auraelia walked back to where he stood and relaced their fingers. "We're almost there."

Following her beneath the canopy of vines, Daemon's breath caught in his throat as he took in the sight around him. The light around them dimmed as Auraelia released her hold on the vines, and the limbs above were so dense that the waning light could barely penetrate through them. Floating above their heads were the tiny, flickering lights of fireflies—like the stars had fallen toward the ground, only to be caught in the willow to dance and glow in the growing darkness.

When they reached the other side, Auraelia again brushed the vines aside. And as they stepped out from under them, Daemon was once more in awe.

A crystal clear lake, which he could only describe as a smaller version of Azure Falls, glistened beneath the last bits of daylight. The pastel pinks, purples, and oranges that painted the sky reflected perfectly in the water's glass-like surface.

Bright, spring-green grass lined the edge of the water in front of him, while on the opposite side was a forest of trees so dense that he could scarcely see between them.

"What do you think?" Auraelia's voice was barely more than a whisper, but the sound seemed to fill the stillness of the space around them nonetheless.

Daemon pulled his gaze away from the beauty surrounding him to find Auraelia looking up at him expectantly, the blue calcite of her eyes flicking over his face as she waited anxiously for his answer.

Tightening his grip around her hand, he gently pulled her into his arms. Relief flooded his veins when she went willingly, her body fitting against his like she was always meant to be there. "It's beautiful. Is this Nefeli Lake?"

Auraelia nodded, a shy smile tilting up the corners of her mouth. "Would you like to sit?"

Daemon dipped his head in acquiescence and reluctantly released her, gesturing for her to lead the way.

She brought him to where the water broke gently against the golden shore, the sand warm beneath him as he leaned back onto his hands and dug his fingers into the soft grains of the beach. It was like a piece of the Sapphire Isles had been dropped into Lyndaria. And the fact that Auraelia had found it and claimed it as her own brought a smile to his lips.

Auraelia sat to his left, unlacing her boots and placing them off to the side before rolling the hem of her pants and stretching her legs to where the lake lapped against the shore. The delicate ripples came close enough to kiss her toes.

Turning his face toward the sky, Daemon asked, "So, are you going to tell me who you were talking about with Ser Aeron?"

The breath she took was audible, long and deep, as she pulled her legs up to her chest and protectively wrapped her arms around them before turning her head toward him and resting her cheek on her knees. "Do you know who Lord Caius is?"

The name sounded familiar, but he couldn't quite place it. It was like peering through a thick fog, knowing something was on the other side but unable to see it. Sitting upright, Daemon dusted off his hands and turned to give her his full attention. "I'm not sure that I do."

Auraelia met his gaze as she seemed to mull over his words, then turned her face back toward the water. "He's the emissary for the Court of Garnet."

Daemon let the silence linger and let her work through how much information she wanted to share with him. After a few minutes passed, and she hadn't continued, the worry that she wouldn't began to niggle at his mind. But just as he opened his mouth to speak, she started again.

"He also says he's Davina's lover."

Shock shot straight through him.

Davina has a lover?

"Evidently," she scoffed, a smile evident in her voice.

He hadn't meant to say that out loud, but he was glad he wasn't the only one who seemed surprised by that information. As beautiful as her outside may be, her insides were as rotten as the decaying leaves underfoot in winter.

Daemon took a deep breath and turned his gaze to where the sun was slowly sinking beyond the trees, the stars gradually flickering to life against the darkening sky.

"He came to Emerald," she said as she absentmindedly traced shapes into the sand. "Showed up at the front gates in the middle of the night and requested an audience with me."

"You'll have to give me more than that, Princess. Why did the emissary from Garnet want an audience with you?"

Her shrug was so slight that he would have missed it if he hadn't been so attuned to her.

"He said that he wanted to *help* me."

"You're the one person standing in Davina's way of the throne. And if he's her lover like he claims, why would he want to help you?" Daemon grabbed her hand in an attempt to pull her focus from the shapes in the sand and back to him and the conversation at hand. Her gaze merely shifted to the sky above.

"I asked something similar. He didn't really give much of an answer; he just said that he wanted you out of the way and that he was the only one who could help me. I guess he's not overly fond of her conquest to dominate and take over Ixora. And before you ask, he didn't tell me what he would get out of this. He was very tight-lipped about everything."

Daemon furrowed his brows. Nothing about this made sense. Why would the emissary from the Court of Garnet want to help Auraelia? Surely, it's not as simple as not wanting him to marry Davina. It couldn't be. There had to be something else behind it, and they needed to figure out what that was before Auraelia even considered making a deal with him.

"How do you propose getting in touch with Caius without Davina knowing?" he asked, laying back on the bank with his hands clasped behind his head.

Auraelia followed suit, laying down on her side with her head propped up on her hand, her elbow digging into the sand while she looked down at him. "He gave me a crystal. You know how much I *love* magical stones," she jested, poking him in the ribs as she finished.

He knew she meant it as a joke, but his chuckle died as quickly as it had come as he thought back to the sapphire necklace that she'd returned. He carried it with him since that day—a continuous weight and reminder in his pocket.

Seeming to sense the shift in his mood, Auraelia leaned over and cupped his cheek in her hand, turning his face toward her. "I'm sorry. That...that wasn't very kind. I loved that necklace, Daemon. I just—"

Her gaze fell to the sand as she pulled her lower lip between her teeth. Shifting slightly, Daemon slipped his finger beneath her chin and gently directed her gaze back toward his.

Her eyes softened. "I just couldn't handle the reminder of everything I'd lost."

"You didn't lose me, Auraelia. You sent me away; there's a difference. But I'm right here, and I'm not going anywhere."

Tears rimmed her eyes as she searched his face, her mouth falling open slightly as the words she clearly wanted to say remained unspoken between them.

Daemon rolled fully onto his side to face her. "I mean it, Auraelia. I'm *yours* whether you can admit that you want me or not. I'm not going anywhere, and it doesn't matter how often you try to send me away, I will *always* come back for you. We belong together, and sooner or later, when you're ready to accept that, I will be right here waiting."

Auraelia squeezed her eyes closed, forcing a tear to escape from her lashes and roll down her cheek. As he wiped it away, her eyes fluttered open, and he watched as her softened gaze turned into one of fierce determination, and the walls rose around her heart. Though not as thick as they had been over the last few months, the fact that she was so sure that she needed them around him was a slap to the face. But he took a deep breath and let it go...for now. He couldn't force her to face what was between them; it would only push her further away, and that was the opposite of what he wanted. And if the Goddess Narissa was to be believed, it was the opposite of what Ixora needed.

"Caius said that he would give us all of the inside information on Davina. What she's like. What makes her tick. The ins and outs of her abilities."

"Well, isn't that convenient." It came out harsher than he intended, and the slight recoil from Auraelia had him reaching for her hand. "I'm sorry. I just meant that it's awfully convenient that the emissary from the court currently trying to overthrow you and demolish my own court would want to give you *exactly* what you need to bring down the threat. It doesn't sit right."

When she sighed, it seemed to be weighed down with every worry on her mind. "You think I haven't thought about that? You think I haven't asked myself a hundred times *why* he would be willing to help me? I know it doesn't make sense, but it's the only real lead I have to work with right now. And I... I'd like your support in pursuing that avenue."

"Auraelia, you're a queen. You don't need the support of a prince."

"I'm not asking you as a prince, Daemon. I'm asking you as someone I lo—trust. This affects you and your people just as much as mine."

Daemon couldn't help the way his lips pulled up at the corners. She almost slipped.

Almost.

That little hint of the word she refused to say before she switched to 'trust' gave him more hope than it probably should have, but he couldn't help it.

Progress.

"You want my support, Princess? You have it."

A smile took over her lips, lighting up her face despite the fact that dusk had turned into nightfall. The stars shone like diamonds overhead, but even their light was diminished compared to the stardust dancing in Auraelia's eyes.

Daemon fell back onto his back, staring up at the dark sky as the sounds of crickets and the trickling of water over rocks as it flowed into the lake filled in the silence that was settling between them. Then, for the second time that day, Auraelia surprised him by laying her head on his chest and gazing up at the stars with him.

His heart slammed against his ribs like a blacksmith hammering out the steel of a sword.

As time passed, the once slightly awkward silence became comfortable. It was just...easy. Lying there together, just staring up at the sky. He hadn't even realized that he'd started running his hands through the loose strands of her hair that were fanned across his chest. Auraelia was quiet, her breathing so even that Daemon thought she'd fallen asleep. But when a star shot across the sky with a tail of pink-hued light trailing behind it, she gasped and sat up abruptly, eyes wide as she kept them pointed toward the sky.

"Did you see that?" she asked, awe lacing every word.

Daemon chuckled, then pushed up onto his elbows. "I did. It was quite pretty."

"Pretty? It was *magical.*" Prying her eyes away from where the shooting star had once been, a delicate flush colored her cheeks as she met his gaze. "Do you know what a shooting star means? Here, I mean. In Lyndaria."

When he shook his head, she continued. "It's said that when a star shoots across the sky in the presence of a...a couple... it's the Goddess Rhayne smiling down on them and sending them her blessing."

Her flush deepened as she finished her story, and Daemon couldn't help the wide smile that took over his lips. "Oh, *really*?"

He'd known that both Rhayne and Narissa blessed their relationship. Knew that they were soulmates and destined to be together, in this life and every other. But Auraelia seeing that sign and having her *acknowledge* it and explain what it meant, gave him yet another piece of hope.

Auraelia's face was now the color of a winter berry, and she could scarcely hold his gaze, her flush deepening every time they locked eyes.

When a frosty breeze blew across the lake, sending a shiver down both their spines, Daemon stood and extended his hand toward her. "Would you like to head back?"

Grabbing her boots, she slipped her hand into his, the warmth of her magic tangling with his as soon as their skin connected.

After helping her to her feet, Daemon stepped into her frame and lifted her chin, forcing her gaze up to his face. "Thank you for letting me in, Auraelia. It means more than you know."

Her answering smile was incandescent, and then, before he knew what was happening, she pushed onto her toes and pressed her lips to his. When she pulled away, a sheepish smile was on her lips, and her face was flushed once more. "I never should have shut you out to begin with."

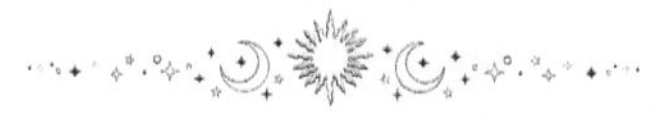

"Killian, what are you doing here?" Astraea asked, her arched brows drawing together at the center.

Another dream, it's just another dream.

She was slightly older in this one than she had been in the others. Her chestnut hair was no longer glossy but instead held a dull sheen, like life was draining the color from it. Daemon closed the distance between himself and Astraea, his legs moving of their own accord. When he was in front of her, his hands cupped her cheeks, and his lips met hers in a hungry desperation.

When she didn't move in response, he felt his heart sink. But the moment passed faster than it lingered, and it wasn't long before her hands were tangled in his hair, and she was pulling him with her through a previously closed door.

Pressing her against the wall, he slid his hands down her sides and lifted her from the floor, her legs wrapping around his waist on instinct.

But when she cupped his face in her hands, the cold bite of metal met his cheek, and he pulled away, letting her body slowly slide down his until her feet hit the floor.

"You're engaged." The words came from his mouth, but he knew it wasn't him who spoke them.

"Killian, you knew this was going to happen. You're married, *for goddess' sake, and you're going to criticize me about being engaged?"*

Slowly, Daemon's gaze trailed down to his left hand where a woven band of metal encircled his finger, then over to where a delicate band of silver sat on Astraea's, topped with an aquamarine stone that matched the color of her eyes.

It wasn't his life, but there was no mistaking the crushing grief that filled his chest. Or the heartbreak that he was all too familiar with.

Killian ran his hands through his hair, gripping the strands tightly at the roots before releasing them. "It's not fair!" he shouted through gritted teeth. "You're mine, *Astraea! We both know it! Fuck, anyone who sees us together knows it! It doesn't matter how hard we try to hide it or how careful we are; it's as clear as day when we're together."*

Astraea twirled her engagement ring around her finger, her eyes downcast as she said, "I know, which is why we can't see each other anymore."

Killian quickly closed the gap that had formed between them and grasped her shoulders, his voice cracking as he pleaded with her. "Don't say that. You can't mean it. I can't live without you, my star. Please, don't do this."

Tears began to stream down her face, her eyes rimmed in red when they finally met his. "I don't want to. Goddess, how I wish I could run away and just be *with you, but we can't, Killian. We can't. Our people, all of Ixora, have been through enough as it is. We can't uproot the peace that was just instilled. It would be selfish."*

Daemon could feel the tears filling Killian's eyes. Could feel their warmth as they slipped down his cheeks. "I wish I had never signed that damned treaty."

Astraea nodded, her lip trembling as she said, "So do I, my love. So do I."

It was nearly daybreak when the sound of Auraelia muttering in her sleep pulled Daemon from his dream. He could still feel the ache in his chest from the heartbreak he'd just relived. Heartbreak that was bound to repeat itself if he couldn't break through to her.

As she began to toss and turn, Daemon gently shook her shoulder. "Auraelia. Auraelia, you're dreaming. Wake up."

When she still didn't stir, her eyes pinched tightly closed as her dream continued, he tried a different approach. Sending a quick prayer to the Goddesses of Arcelia that it wouldn't backfire on him, Daemon pulled her into his arms and whispered, "My star, it's just a dream. Come back to me."

He placed a gentle kiss on her brow, and slowly, her body relaxed into his. Her face was pressed into his chest, and he began to run his fingers in featherlight touches along her spine.

A contented sigh slipped between her lips as she nuzzled into him. "I missed that."

Her voice was still full of sleep, but his heart leaped in his chest as she pressed her body closer to his, looping her leg over his.

"Missed what, exactly?"

"Missed hearing you call me 'my star'. It hurt every time you said Auraelia, but it hurt more to hear that. I didn't feel like I deserved it anymore. That you deserved more—deserved better."

"And now?" Daemon asked, hope filling his chest.

She still seemed to be half asleep, but he'd take her uninhibited thoughts over the ones she constantly turned over in her head, any day. When she didn't answer, he nudged her gently. "Auraelia?"

"Hmmm?"

Daemon chuckled and changed the subject. "What were you dreaming about?"

His question seemed to bring her further into consciousness. Pulling out of his arms, Auraelia slowly pushed up on the bed into a kneeling position and wiped the sleep from her eyes, yawning as she said, "It—um. It was nothing."

Daemon matched her position, his knees brushing against hers as he tilted her chin up so that he could look her in the eyes. "It wasn't nothing, Auraelia. I'm pretty sure I know exactly what it was."

"You do?" she asked, raising her brow as her head canted to the side.

"I'm going to go out on a limb and say that you've been having strange dreams. Ones that feel more like memories. Am I close?"

Her eyes widened at his words, her head slowly bobbing up and down in confirmation.

"I have them, too. I *just* had one, actually, and if I'm being honest, it wasn't too pleasant of a memory."

"*Memory*? I thought it was just a dream."

Daemon shook his head and took her hands in his. "They're memories, Auraelia. Ones from five hundred years ago, when our ancestors were...*involved*. Do you want to talk about what happened?"

When she nodded, Daemon waited patiently for her to continue.

"I—*she* was in the ballroom here in the castle. People were all around, everyone watching the man in front of her. It was an engagement party. He'd just asked her to marry him, and she'd said yes." Auraelia's nose wrinkled as if she were the one marrying the man in her dream, and the thought was repulsive. Which when he thought about it, in a way, she *had* married that man.

"Anyway," she continued after blowing out a breath. "Shortly after she said yes, she excused herself from the party. I could feel everything she did, and everything about it felt *wrong*. She didn't want to marry him but felt like she had to for her people. Then, as she was walking down the hall toward her chambers, a man...Killian...appeared from the shadows.

"He kissed her, and I remember her being shocked that he was there. He wasn't supposed to be; she didn't *want* him there to see her get engaged. Told him to stay away. But as soon as his lips were on hers, everything felt right. Like the stars aligned, and everything was as it should be."

At the small smile on her lips, Daemon interrupted her story. "I think I know how the rest went."

"Really? How?"

Daemon stroked her cheek, his gaze soft as he stared into the swirling storm of her eyes. "Because mine started where Killian showed up in yours."

Auraelia's eyes widened, and he could see the wheels spinning in her mind, trying to piece together—and make sense of—everything that had just happened. Her brow was scrunched in confusion, her head shaking slowly from side to side as she tried to process everything. "But—*why*? How? That doesn't make any sense."

"Doesn't it?" he asked, imploring her to see beyond the surface to the meaning behind the memories. He wanted her to come to the realization on her own. Didn't want to burden her with yet another secret. But, then again, it was another secret being kept from her, and he hated that it was one *he* was keeping.

When she didn't answer, Daemon released a breath. "Auraelia—"

He'd barely gotten her name past his lips when there was a pounding on the door outside her suite, both of their heads swiving toward the noise. Before Auraelia could voice them to enter, Piper barreled into the room. Her eyes were wide, and she breathed heavily as she leaned against the doorframe.

"Your Majesty. Auraelia—" she said between pants. "I'm so sorry, but we've got to go. Davina is going to attack the city."

Chapter Seventeen

Auraelia

Shooting up from where she was kneeling on the bed, Auraelia sprinted to her closet and grabbed whatever garments she could get her hands on. While she slipped into her leather trousers, she could hear Daemon scrambling around her chambers, trying to ready himself as well—all while Piper explained her vision.

There wasn't much to go on, and the details seemed to change or become fuzzy with each retelling. What remained the same was the flames rising into the pastel sky of dawn. The screams of citizens as they tried to save whomever and whatever they could, and then there was Davina.

Her eyes near the color of obsidian as she wreaked havoc on the unsuspecting citizens of Lyndaria, their bodies crumbling beneath her magic.

As Auraelia stepped out of her closet—her second boot haphazardly laced and the ties on her corset hanging open—Piper rushed to her side.

"Good goddess, Rae. Fix *that*." She gestured to the laces across Auraelia's bust. "I'll fix your boots. Daemon, grab her dagger from the table and her emerald necklace from the top drawer of her vanity." She tacked on without losing her focus. "I swear you would fall apart without me."

When Daemon returned with the requested items, Piper had just finished fixing Auraelia's boots.

Kneeling at her feet, Daemon strapped the dagger around her thigh, the emerald blade warming as soon as it came into contact with her leg, even through the thick leather of the sheath.

A mixture of emotions swirled in his eyes as he stood, and as much as she wanted to, she didn't have time to dissect them. However, when she looked down to see the emerald necklace he'd given her when she was in Kalmeera, she could have easily guessed what they were.

Swallowing audibly, Auraelia turned and swept her hair from her neck. The chain was cool against her skin, but everywhere Daemon's fingers touched was scorching.

Focus, Auraelia.

When she turned around, Daemon's eyes bounced from the pendant to her face. Before she could say anything, could explain why she'd kept one and not the other, Piper's sharp intake of breath pulled her attention.

Snapping her gaze to her friend, she watched as Piper's eyes stared vacantly into the void of her vision. When clarity came back to her hazel orbs, Auraelia rushed to her side and grasped her hands. "What is it?"

Piper's eyes were still wide, terror coursing through them as her head rotated from side to side as if she couldn't believe what she'd just seen.

Dropping her friend's hands in favor of cupping her face, she demanded, "Show me."

Heaving a heavy sigh, Piper nodded, and Auraelia could feel it the moment her friend dropped the barrier between them. Piper's magic flowed freely through Auraelia's veins, filling her mind with images of death and destruction.

As the wall between them rose once more, lightning crackled between Auraelia's fingers, and she spun around, piercing Daemon with a hard stare. "We're leaving. *Now.*"

Every nerve ending stood on end as her magic coursed through her body. Not even the cool caress from Daemon's shadows as they swirled around them, transporting them to the outskirts of the city, could lessen the fire that filled her veins.

Their feet had barely touched the ground before the sound of screams pierced the air, and the smell of smoke filled her nostrils. The sound of men, women, and children overpowering the flames that crackled as the fires burned through the wisteria and gardens that covered Lyndaria.

Launching into a sprint, Auraelia threw everything she could into her magic, pulling the water from the clouds in the sky until they turned from fluffy and pink to heavy and gray.

Thunder rolled as she reached the city line, the sound of her citizens in peril piercing her ears and stabbing her heart.

Daemon was right on her heels as they wove their way to the harbor. It was where Piper's visions continuously placed Davina, and where Xander had ridden out to intercept their cousin while Piper alerted Auraelia. But with the chaos cluttering the streets, it was hard to determine where she was going.

Pausing for a moment, Auraelia looked around to try and get her bearings. Nothing was as it should have been. Roads were blocked by debris. Most of her people were crying and screaming in the streets, while others attempted to control the chaos—issuing orders and directions to keep the flames from spreading.

Panic began to surge in her chest, working its way up her throat and stealing the air from her lungs.

One. Two. Three—

She only made it to three before the familiar feel of Daemon's arms wrapping around her pushed her anxiety back down.

"Breathe, Auraelia," he whispered in her ear. "Focus on where you need to be, and let my magic take you there."

"Daemon, I don't have time—"

He kept her back to his front but tightened his arms around her. "You have time to take a second and breathe. You're not going to be any good to your people if you're running around like a crazed person. They need you focused. Let me *help* you."

Taking a deep breath, Auraelia closed her eyes and let her mind go to where she needed to be. She pictured the ships rocking gently in their ports, the waves lapping against their hulls and the docks.

When she opened her eyes again, Daemon's shadows faded away to reveal not only the harbor but also her cousin's back.

"*Davina!*" Auraelia yelled as she pulled out of Daemon's embrace, using the wind in her control to project her voice over the crackle and pop of the fire.

With all the grace of a feline, Davina turned. There was a menacing smile on her face as her head slowly tilted to the side. "Hello, *cousin.* Come to play?"

Auraelia stiffened, and thunder clapped in the sky, drowning out the sizzle and hiss of water droplets falling onto the flames as the clouds released their heavy burdens.

The sound made Davina jolt where she stood, but that shock was short-lived.

"I've come to send you back where you belong," Auraelia shouted. Bands of lightning wrapped around her extremities, cocooning her in incandescent light, while wind swirled around her in a protective barrier. It wasn't until Daemon's shadows joined the mix that Davina seemed to even notice his presence.

Tsking as she shook her head from side to side, her gaze narrowed in on where he stood behind Auraelia. "Daemon, Daemon, Daemon. Did you really think that you could come here and I wouldn't know? That even here in Lyndaria, I wouldn't have little birds relaying your every move?"

Auraelia felt—more than saw—him step up to her side. His body was poised for battle as his magic spilled from his fingers, pooling into swirls of shadows at their feet. She could sense the rigidity in his muscles as if they were her own, as if they had become so attuned to each other that they had become one.

The deep tenor of Daemon's voice cut through the chaos around them as he answered Davina. "I am not yours to keep tabs on."

"Our engagement would say otherwise, *my love.*"

Auraelia knew that she called him that to get under her skin. *Knew* that Davina was doing it to see how she would react. Despite the rational side of her mind telling her not to, she couldn't help the possessive rage that overpowered her rational thought.

The cresting glow of morning faded away as light, brighter than the sun itself, filled her vision. She could feel the static crackling in the air, the way her hair floated around her like she was suspended in water, as her magic spilled out of her. And as she spoke, the words more of a growl than anything else, the ground began to rumble beneath her feet.

"Get the *fuck* out of my court."

The heat from her lightning was a warm embrace as it flared and coalesced in her hands, glowing like the evening star as it swirled into an orb of fiery light. But as she took aim at Davina, her cousin's feline smile shifted into something much more sinister.

"I wouldn't do that if I were you, dear cousin," Davina chided. "You see, if you did, poor Xander here wouldn't live to see tomorrow."

Auraelia's blood ran cold as Davina stepped to the side.

There, on his hands and knees, with blood gushing from his nose, mouth, and ears, was Xander. How she'd gotten past his shield, she didn't know. But seeing her brother crumpled on the ground sent flashes of her mother's death to the forefront of her mind.

"You'll find, cousin, that I have many talents. Ones that not even your dear Prince Daemon has knowledge of. Did you really think that you could beat me?" Davina began slowly walking toward Auraelia as she spoke. "That you could sneak around *trying* to get information about me without my knowledge? Seems I gave you more credit than you were due."

Auraelia's thoughts began to race. She needed to get Xander out of there. Needed to get him to Ser Aeron so that he could be healed. But *how*?

With Davina steadily approaching, there was no way for her to communicate with Daemon. No way to ask him to save her brother, or beg him to leave her there and save the last remaining member of her family.

A familiar cool caress slithered along her spine as if he had heard her thoughts. A simple acknowledgment that he knew what she needed without her having to say a single word.

When Davina was far enough away from Xander, Auraelia sucked in as much air as she could into her lungs, and as she exhaled, she whispered, "*Now.*"

Before she could even blink, Daemon was gone, his shadows devouring his form only to release him next to her brother. Then, within the next second, they had both vanished. She wasn't sure how far Daemon could shadow-walk or how far away Xander needed to be before the effects of Davina's magic subsided, but at that moment, all she cared about was that they were both away from the bitch standing before her.

Davina's head swiveled from Auraelia to the bloody mess where Xander once was, and when she turned back, she loosed a blood-curdling scream as she charged forward.

But Auraelia was ready.

Charged with rage and the need for vengeance, she released the hold she had on her magic. Wind and rain assaulted Davina from all sides while the quaking ground threw her off balance—but still, she persisted, fighting through everything Auraelia threw her way.

With her lightning once again swirling in the palm of her hand, Auraelia took aim as time seemed to slow to a crawl.

Red.

All she could see was red.

Crimson like the blood that poured from her brother's face.

Hatred and rage led the charge in her need for retribution against the person who had irrevocably altered her life. For the one who facilitated the murder of her mother and threatened to destroy all that she loved. Who was trying to destroy the *one* she loved.

Daemon.

One thought of him, and the red clouds began to part, leaving room for clarity and her earlier words to shine through. *I don't want to be like her.*

Taking a deep breath, Auraelia spooled some of her magic back into her veins.

I'm not a murderer, but I will *fight for what I love.*

Davina's magic slammed into Auraelia, ice filling her veins and stealing the breath from her lungs, her assault faltering as her muscles turned rigid.

No, this can't be happening.

Auraelia reached deep within her well of power. Let the fire in her veins melt away the ice that was determined to take root. When Davina was only an arm's length away, she took her shot. Lunging forward, she gripped her by the arms and let her lightning course through Davina's veins.

Her eyes shot wide with a mix of fear and anger, her mouth left gaping as Auraelia's magic assaulted her system.

"I said, get *out* of my court. And if I ever see you again, it will not be my blood that is being washed away in the rain."

Davina staggered backward as Auraelia released her grip, her nostrils flaring in her rage. But when she tried to lift her arm toward Auraelia, she cried out in pain. Burns the shape of Auraelia's hands, with trails of what looked like lightning streaking out from them, marked each of her arms.

There was a small part of her that was sorry for the burns she'd inflicted; she'd never been the one to intentionally hurt someone. But as she watched the blood slowly seep from Davina's ears, just like they had Xander's, that small part died.

"Leave, Davina. I won't tell you again."

Cringing, Davina reached into her tunic and pulled out a clear crystal attached to a chain. One that looked strikingly familiar to the one stowed away in a box in her chambers.

She watched as Davina gripped the stone in her hand, then disappeared into a flurry of snow.

Fucking Caius.

After a few deep breaths to calm her pounding heart, Auraelia pulled back what remained of her magic. But as the clouds began to disperse, and the clear blue winter sky was once more overhead, the devastation that Davina had brought to Lyndaria was glaring.

Every step she took through the city made her want to break down and cry.

Almost every home was destroyed, or at the very least, uninhabitable. Black scorch marks covered every visible surface. Windows had been blown out either from the heat or from the flames themselves, and some homes were gone altogether.

The gardens and wisteria were nothing but ash, mixing with the debris and rubble that covered the streets.

And her *people.*

Everywhere she looked, her people were crying. Tears streaming down their soot-covered faces, leaving flesh-toned tracks in their wake.

Children cried out for their mothers or fathers.

Women roamed the streets, calling out for missing loved ones, while men scoured the rubble.

No one noticed who was among them. And with that thought, Auraelia knelt down in the street and wept.

Wept for her mother and for the healing of her brother.

Cried for her people, the lost, and those who had lost someone.

She stayed there for a few moments and just let herself *feel*.

Let all of the pain and grief and sorrow wash over her like violent waves in a storm. Let it soak into her soul and erode away the stone that she'd built around her heart.

Enough.

She'd been closed off from pain for long enough. She needed to heal so that she could help her people heal.

Wiping her nose on her sleeve, Auraelia stood, took a deep breath, then headed to the nearest group of people and got to work.

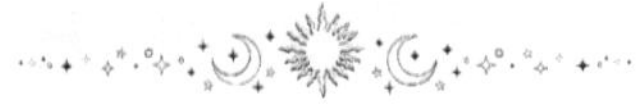

She'd been there for hours, digging through rubble, searching for people, and praying to the Goddess Rhayne that the ones they found would be safe.

But those prayers fell on deaf ears.

Body after body, pile after pile, hope that they would find *someone* alive dwindled away.

When she'd found Piper amongst the throngs of people clambering for answers, relief flooded her chest. After pulling her into an embrace and making sure that she was okay, Auraelia sent her back to the castle for food, water, and any other supplies she could find. And she'd come back with more than Auraelia could have ever asked for.

Not only had she brought food and water, but she'd brought carts full of tools and helping hands. Chef Liza and her entire kitchen staff set up a makeshift kitchen and began cooking hot meals for everyone. Guards piled people into carts and brought them to the castle for hot showers and clean clothes. Though they extended the offer of a warm place to sleep with a roof over their heads, most declined, opting to stay in the provided tents so that they could be close to what was once their home.

It was nearing midday when Piper finally pulled Auraelia away, forcing her to take a break.

"You need to rest, Rae," she whispered as she shoved a canteen into Auraelia's hands.

Sighing, Auraelia lifted it to her parched mouth. She'd meant to take only a sip to appease her friend, but as the cool water hit her lips, thirst gripped her throat, and she began to drink deeply.

Only when she had drained the last drops did she reply, "My people need me, Piper. I can't abandon them."

"They won't *have* a queen to abandon them if you run yourself into the ground!" she scolded, placing her hands on her hips as if that would emphasize her statement.

"Piper—"

"No. We're not doing this. You've been out here since before the sun was up, and you were awake before I even came to get you. You *need* to rest." She paused for a moment, her hands dropping as her eyes softened into a pleading gaze. "Please, Rae."

Nodding, Auraelia handed Piper the canteen and stood. Exhaustion slammed into her like lightning striking a tree, causing her knees to buckle and her head to throb.

Piper lunged for her, but before she could get there, an arm—strong and familiar—wrapped around her waist and lifted her from behind her knees. "I've got her."

As she leaned against his chest, Auraelia breathed in the scent of ocean and sandalwood and sighed.

Daemon.

"Where have you been?" she muttered, her body and mind succumbing to the fatigue that was sweeping over her.

"I was with your brother. I didn't think you'd want me to leave him alone."

At the mention of Xander, Auraelia tried to sit up and nearly fell out of Daemon's arms.

"Easy, Princess. I've got you. I'll take you straight to him."

And with that, swirls of sparkling darkness consumed her sight.

Daemon stayed with her while she sat vigil by Xander's bed. He'd gotten him back to the castle and into Ser Aeron's care just in time, and her army commander was certain there would be no permanent damage.

Still, she remained.

From what Daemon had told her when they arrived, Xander had gone unconscious from the pain and blood loss before they'd reached the castle. And he'd been that way ever since.

"Auraelia, you need to sleep." Daemon's soft tone was like a blanket of warmth wrapping around her.

"I don't want him to be alone. I need to be here," she muttered as she squeezed her brother's hand, silently urging him to open his eyes so that she knew he was alright. But not even the loud creaking from the door opening stirred him.

"He won't be alone, Rae. I'll sit with him." The comforting chime of Piper's voice filled the room, but when her friend placed her hand on her shoulder, Auraelia lost it.

Lost the hold she had on the tears she'd been trying to keep at bay.

Lost the ability to stay strong so that her brother saw a smiling face when he finally woke.

Gone.

Every defense she'd built around her heart to keep it from shattering was gone.

Piper's arms wrapped around her shoulders in a tight embrace. "He'll be fine. He's a stubborn ass; he's not going to let a little blood loss beat him."

Though Piper's voice quavered, her words brought a little bit of light into the darkness. When she retracted her arms, Auraelia stood, leaned over to place a kiss on her brother's brow, and whispered, "Don't you dare leave me, Xander. I *need you*. Piper *needs* you. I'll bring you back and kill you all over again if you break my best friend's heart."

When she straightened once more, she turned to Daemon and extended her hand. "Take me to my room?"

Daemon's hand was warm against hers as he laced their fingers together. Pulling her to him, he swept the loose hair from her face and smiled. "I would take you anywhere as long as I got to be with you."

Chapter Eighteen

Daemon

Daemon would never outgrow the feeling of having Auraelia in his arms. As soon as they'd returned to her chambers, Auraelia slumped against him. Her eyes were half-lidded as she attempted to stifle a yawn.

"You need to sleep," he said softly, soothingly as he stroked her hair.

Auraelia groaned and buried her face into his chest, her voice muffled as she spoke. "I am *not* getting into my bed like this. I need to bathe first. But... I'm just so *tired.*"

She couldn't fight the yawn that escaped with the tail end of her statement any more than Daemon could fight the chuckle in his throat. "I can help you if you'd like."

Even with her eyes heavy from exhaustion, there was no mistaking the quizzical look she gave him as she tilted her face up toward his.

Daemon laughed and shook his head. "I have no ulterior motives, Princess. I swear it, by my goddess and yours."

Her eyes narrowed a little more as she contemplated his words, but eventually, they rolled to the back of her head as she nodded.

Helping her to the seat at her vanity, Daemon removed the dagger he'd strapped to her thigh and placed it on the seat next to her. When he moved on to her boots, carefully unlacing each one before setting them aside, Auraelia ran her fingers through his hair.

"You should get on your knees more often."

Her words were slightly slurred from exhaustion, but he could still hear the smile in her voice. And though he knew he shouldn't—and it would undoubtedly backfire on him—he couldn't resist playing along.

Daemon looked up at her through his lashes and let his smirk shine through. "I don't get on my knees for just anyone, Auraelia. But I would gladly make my home at your feet."

Even with the sly smirk on her lips, a rose-colored flush crept across her cheeks, and as he ran his hands up her thighs to her waist, it deepened to a rich crimson.

Daemon held her gaze as he rotated his hands inward to unlace her bodice, her breath hitching as his fingers skimmed her breasts.

Fuck, this was a bad idea.

He had zero intention of taking this further than flirting. Hell, he'd had zero intention *of* flirting. They were both tired, but Auraelia was so far past exhaustion, so far past the ability to give informed consent, that it would feel like he was taking advantage of her if he pushed this too far. And that was something he would *never* do...regardless of how many times she bit her lip—which was becoming more frequent with the more clothing he removed.

When she was down to her undergarments, Daemon gently lifted her from the seat and brought her into her bathroom.

It was bigger than her previous one, and instead of a skylight above the bath, the wall next to it was full of opaque, colored glass, which cast a rainbow of colors across the floor as the sun shone through.

After setting her on a tile next to the tub, he turned on the shower to let the water heat before he helped her into it.

When steam began to roll out over the top of the glass surrounding the stall, Daemon knelt in front of Auraelia and swept the hair from her face. "Do you think you can handle a shower by yourself?"

Sitting up straight, Auraelia fixed him with a hard stare. "I *am* a grown woman. Of course, I can." But when she went to stand, her knees buckled, and she reached out to cling to him. "Okay, I *usually* can."

Daemon chuckled and placed a chaste kiss on the crown of her head. "I'll help you into the shower. Just rinse off as best you can, and then we'll get you into the bath, okay?"

Memories of helping her bathe after her mother's death resurfaced, and he had to fight to keep the smile on his face.

This is different; she's just tired.

It's not the same.

Auraelia nodded and let him help her out of her undergarments and into the shower. Once she was under the streams, he backed away, making sure to give her privacy without being too far away should she need him.

The warm water seemed to rouse her enough to scrub the soot and grime from her skin, the smell of her lavender soap filling the air around him.

He didn't mean to stare but also couldn't help it. There was nothing sexual about it; he just simply liked looking at her. Liked watching the way her muscles flexed as she moved about the shower and the unintentional sensuality in her movements. How she would tilt her face to the water and just let it rain down over her. Like she was letting it cleanse her soul as well as her body.

When she turned around, shock colored her features, like she'd completely forgotten he was there.

"Oh...um...hi," she said meekly, the flush on her cheeks from the heat deepening with her apparent embarrassment.

"Hi, yourself. Do you still want me to run you a bath?" he asked, making sure to keep his eyes on her face.

Auraelia's lips curved inward as she nodded. "I need to wash my hair...but my arms are so sore that I don't know if I can manage."

"I can help you with that once you're in the tub if you'd like?"

A small smile played on her lips, and she nodded.

"Alright, I'll go start the water. You just let me know when you're finished."

The bath was half full by the time Auraelia emerged from the shower, and Daemon had to focus his mind on anything *but* the water rolling down her naked frame as she sashayed her way to the bath—anything to deflate the erection growing in his pants.

The Nevermore.

The Cerulean Sea.

Aiden.

A small shudder ran through him with his last thought, but it did the trick.

Auraelia eyed him curiously as she slipped her hand into his and stepped over the edge of the bath. "Everything alright?"

Nodding, Daemon sat on the tiled edge surrounding three sides of the tub and retrieved the hair wash.

Once Auraelia was settled, Daemon lathered the wash into his hands and began to work it through the strands. When he began to massage her scalp, a contented sigh escaped through her lips, and her eyes fluttered closed.

After rinsing her hair and adding her smoothing lotion, he gently detangled her locks and began to weave them together.

"You know how to braid?" Auraelia asked with a small chuckle.

"I do," he replied with a chuckle of his own.

"Who taught you?"

"When I was younger, back before I learned anything about knots and sails, Yvaine made me learn. She said it was a trait my future wife would appreciate, and if I ever had a daughter, I could do it for her too."

Auraelia sat silently as he finished the plait. When he tied it off, she turned to face him, leaning against the edge where he was sitting. "That's really sweet. And thank you."

"You don't need to thank me, Auraelia. And you think so?"

Resting her head on her propped arms, she nodded.

They sat there for a few moments, rainbows of light dancing across Auraelia's cheeks before her yawn cut through the silence.

"Let's get you to bed, Princess." Daemon slid from where he was perched and grabbed a towel from the shelves lining the wall between the shower and tub.

As he helped her dry off, her exhaustion seemed to creep in once more, her eyelids drooping further as the minutes ticked by.

Scooping her into his arms, Daemon carried her to the bed, then tucked her beneath her blankets. But when he began to walk away, she grabbed his wrist.

"Stay. Please?"

A soft smile tugged at the corner of his lips as he gently stroked her cheek. "I'm not going anywhere, Auraelia. I just need to shower, then I'll be right back."

When she grimaced, Daemon knelt down beside her. "What is it?"

Yawning, Auraelia snuggled deeper into her pillow and pulled the sheets up to her chin. "I don't like when you call me that... it's too *formal*."

"It's your name," he responded with a small laugh.

"You didn't use to call me that."

Auraelia yawned again, and then her breathing evened out, sleep claiming her at last. Daemon stroked her cheek once more before standing and smiling down at her. "As you wish, *my star*."

Auraelia had been asleep for a few hours. Snuggled up against his side with her arm draped over his lap while he sat propped up by pillows against her headboard. Other than the sound of her deep breathing, there was a peaceful stillness around them. But not even that could quiet the thought that spun around relentlessly in his mind.

It was my fault.

Although she hadn't outright said it, Davina was there because of *him*.

Because he thought that with her in the Court of Garnet, he would be able to get away with slipping into Lyndaria unnoticed.

But he was wrong, and he'd never forgive himself for the pain and destruction that his presence had brought to Auraelia and her people.

The one thing that niggled at the back of his mind that he couldn't quite put his finger on was who was the one reporting back to Davina?

Was it someone in his own court? In Auraelia's?

Very few people in Kalmeera knew he was going to Lyndaria, and even fewer knew in Auraelia's court. As far as he was aware, the nobles of the Sapphire Isles believed that he was in Lunaria doing his bi-monthly check-in with the priestesses...which he would eventually have to do.

Taking a deep breath, Daemon looked down at Auraelia's sleeping form.

He'd idly smoothed her hair with his hands the entire time she slept, and the contented smile on her lips brought a small smile to his own.

Peace. She looked at peace, and he had a feeling that she hadn't experienced that in a while. He'd do anything to let her hold on to it, even if it was just in her dreams.

When Daemon thought back over everything that happened down at the harbor, his stomach churned. Seeing Xander on the ground with blood pouring out of his face would be etched into his mind forever. But the crazed look on Davina's face when she realized that his star had outsmarted her to get her brother to safety was priceless.

His star. Goddess, she was impressive. He had no idea what happened on that pier after he'd gotten Xander out—they hadn't had a moment to talk about it—but he knew it had to have been amazing.

He hadn't wanted to leave Auraelia to deal with Davina alone. He'd fully intended to be there with her for the entire fight, fighting by her side—goddess knows she didn't need anyone to fight her battles *for* her, and she would have killed him if he'd tried.

The moment Davina moved out of the way to reveal Xander, he just *knew* what he would need to do. What he would *have to* do so Auraelia could concentrate on getting her cousin out of the city and away from her people.

He couldn't explain it any more than he would have been able to then. All he knew was that it was as if he and Auraelia had become connected in a way that he couldn't describe. That he could read her so well that she wouldn't have to utter a single word. And in the moment, it seemed as if she'd felt it too. She somehow just *knew* that he would understand her when she said '*now*.'

Resting his head back on the headboard, Daemon closed his eyes and breathed deeply.

He needed to apologize to her for—albeit unknowingly—causing her so much grief and pain.

A small moan came from Auraelia as she stirred in his lap—her arms reaching above her head as her legs extended in a long stretch. When he looked down, she was gazing up at him with a sleepy smile on her face.

"Hi."

"Hello, my star. Did you rest?"

Chapter Nineteen

Auraelia

My star.

It'd been so long since she'd heard him call her that it was as if all cognitive abilities had flown out the window. Her brain? Empty.

No thoughts, let alone words, circulated through her mind.

While she stared at him, trying to find *something* to say, a cocky smile tilted up his lips. That one little uptick of his mouth had her thoughts whirling once more.

"I've missed that," she admitted shyly, heat rushing to her face as she broke eye contact.

Daemon gently brushed his fingers across her cheek and down to her chin, tilting it back up so that she would look at him. "So have I."

Her heart pounded in her chest at his words, and butterflies took flight in her stomach as he leaned down and pressed his lips to hers.

Never in all her life would Auraelia believe that two little words would be able to set her world spinning in the right direction. To push it back on its axis from where it had been rotating on its side. And yet, there they were. Nestling into her heart and soul, filling the cracks in one fell swoop.

My star.

When Daemon pulled away, she could feel the heat coloring her cheeks. But when she realized that she was, in fact, still naked, she could only imagine that she looked like a freshly picked strawberry in spring.

Hastily pulling the sheets over her head, Auraelia groaned.

"What?" he asked with a chuckle that gently shook the bed.

"I'm *naked.*"

Daemon attempted to lift the sheets from her face, but Auraelia tightened her grip, causing him to laugh as he spoke. "Trust me, I'm *quite* aware."

Peaking one eye out from under the covers, Auraelia gave him a skeptical look as he continued. "You fell asleep shortly after your head touched the pillow, and I didn't want to wake you just to put on a nightdress. But I promise, I have been the perfect gentleman."

Letting her gaze roam down his frame, she noticed that he was clothed and lying *on top* of her covers. The sight was both comforting and not, all at the same time. She knew he would never do anything without her consent—and goddess knows she was exhausted to the point of delirium, so she wouldn't have been able to give it even if she wanted to—but she also loved the way his body felt curled around her own. It made her feel safe. Comforted...and not so alone.

It was all so confusing, these emotions spinning around in her head. She wanted nothing more than to pull him close and never let him go, but in the same breath, she felt the need to push him away.

To protect not only her heart but his as well.

Slipping the sheets away from her face and tucking them under her arms, Auraelia sat up. "What time is it?" she asked, glancing toward the windows.

The sky was painted in a wash of colors that an artist could only dream of capturing on canvas. Rich oranges and soft purples melded together, creating a beautiful ending to an otherwise horrendous day.

"It's nearly time for dinner," Daemon replied, his voice laden with exhaustion.

Had he not slept while she did?

With her eyes still trained on the window, she felt him stir beside her. His warmth and scent wrapped around her as he moved to sit at her back, followed by his fingers gently running the length of her spine, leaving pebbled flesh in their wake. "I can ask someone to bring you something from the kitchen if you'd like?"

His soft and soothing voice matched his languid movements along her back.

Taking a deep breath, she turned toward him. "No, that's alright. I need to check on my people. Make sure that they have everything that they need for the night."

A singular brow rose on Daemon's gorgeous face. "You want to go back into the city? *Tonight*?"

Shaking her head, Auraelia explained further. "We offered the castle as a safe haven for those in need. Not many accepted, but there were some—most of them mothers with small children."

Daemon's gaze softened as he gently stroked her cheek and nodded. "Then let's get you dressed, and then we'll head down together."

"You...you want to come with me?"

Smiling, he pressed a gentle kiss to her lips and then rested his forehead against hers. When his hands cupped her cheeks, heat filled her body as the magic coursing through her veins seemed to melt beneath his touch. "My beautiful, shining star. I want to be wherever you are. Doing whatever it is that you need me to do. If that's passing out blankets and plates of hot food or reading children stories to give their tired mothers a break, then that's where I will be."

Auraelia's heart swelled in her chest, hammering against the cage that held it captive.

Love.

Goddess, did she love him.

More than she had ever let herself believe. More than she ever thought possible, for fear of crumbling into a heap of devastation. Relief washed through her when she finally let herself acknowledge the extent of her feelings for him. And yet, there was still that tiny voice in the back of her mind that kept whispering...*not yet.*

Every wall of the throne room was lined with cots. Rows upon rows of grieving families with tear-streaked faces and soot-covered clothes.

Overwhelming grief slammed into Auraelia as she stepped into that room, the air heavy with the despair of her people. "This...this isn't enough. They need *more*," she said in a hushed whisper—more to herself than to Daemon, but he'd heard her anyway.

"What more can you do?"

His question was genuine, and when she turned to where he stood at her side, his brow was furrowed as he scanned the room around them.

Looking around her once more, she took note of what had already been provided and what could still be offered. "They need clean clothes and the ability to bathe if they choose to. I need to make sure they all have blankets and pillows. Chef Liza is no doubt exhausted from cooking all day; perhaps we could take over?"

From the corner of her eye, she could see the quizzical look on Daemon's face and turned toward him with one of her own.

"*You* want to cook? Do you know *how* to cook?"

"That's not what I meant," she said with a roll of her eyes. "I merely meant that we could take over passing out plates, refilling water, and the like. But for your information, *Prince*, I do know how to cook a few things. I actually spend as much time in the kitchens as I can." Auraelia shrugged, watching as his eyes widened in surprise before shifting to a softer gaze. One of awe and adoration. One that sent her pulse racing for no reason other than the fact that she could see love shining in the moss green of his eyes. Love for her and everything that she was.

"The more I learn about you, my star, the more in awe I am of you," he whispered as he tucked a stray lock of hair behind her ear, causing heat to rise to her cheeks.

She held his gaze for a moment before turning back toward the rest of the room. No one even seemed to notice she was standing there until she took a few steps, the heels of her boots echoing through the space.

Despite the amount of people that crowded the room, it was nearly silent, save for the quiet whimpers from children that were still barely audible in the silence.

Slowly, she made her way through the lines of beds, making sure she took the time to stop at every one and see to the needs of whoever needed her. Whether it was organizing showers, additional blankets, or simply a shoulder to cry on, she made sure she took on their grief as her own, hoping to leave each of them with a little more hope than they'd had before she moved on to the next.

Daemon was by her side as she visited with each and every person. Was there to aid the elderly when they needed assistance rising from their place or lying down. And when they had finished with the last family, he'd done exactly as he'd suggested in her room. Gathering the children in a far corner, he sat them down and told them tales of his adventures on the sea, his crew, and of Kalmeera.

Auraelia stood off to the side for a while—soaking in the way the children's faces lit up with every story and holding onto every gasp of excitement—before she slipped away to help pass out dinner to everyone.

The serving station had been set up inside the throne room doors, with trays of freshly baked rolls, bowls of roasted potatoes and garden vegetables, and platters piled high with roasted boar and chicken.

She'd never seen so much food, even during solstice celebrations and balls, and she had never been more grateful for the people who resided in her court. For the way they all pulled together in a time of crisis, making sure that their own were taken care of before they took the time to care for themselves.

Despite the horrid day that was coming to an end and the long way that she and her people still had to go to overcome what had happened—and what was surely to come—Auraelia smiled. For the first time since the crown had been placed on her head, she was happy that she was queen. Because she was the queen of people who *cared.* Who loved beyond themselves.

As she stepped behind the banquet table, Liza raised her brows in Auraelia's direction and crossed her arms. "What do you think you're doing, Your Majesty?"

Liza had been the head chef at the castle for longer than Auraelia had been alive. The wrinkles on her round, ivory face told the stories of a life well-lived, and the gold band around her finger told of a love that withstood the years. Her once auburn hair was now white with faint streaks of strawberry blonde and forever twisted into a knot on top of her head. And though she was hard as stone when it came to her kitchen, making sure that everything and everyone was where they should be, she had always had a soft spot for Auraelia...except when she was where Liza didn't think she should be—like now.

"I'm helping," Auraelia said with a small smile as she grabbed a spare apron and tied it around her waist.

"Your Majesty—"

"Liza, you've been cooking *all day.* First here, then down in the city, and now here again. I know you're exhausted—"

"I am n—"

"Yes, you are. You fuss at every person in your kitchen for leaning on the counters, and now look at you." Auraelia gestured to where her chef was leaning against the banquet table. "You're tired. Let me help, *please.*"

Liza straightened and grumbled under her breath before handing Auraelia a serving spoon. "One scoop of potatoes and veggies. After everyone has been served, if there is anything left, they may return for more. Understood?"

Chuckling, Auraelia nodded. "Yes, ma'am."

The line went by quickly, and by the time everyone had been served, Auraelia's stomach was growling.

Liza cut her a stern look. "You didn't eat before you came down here, did you?"

Curling her lips inward, Auraelia made to look anywhere *but* at the harsh glare coming from her head chef.

"*Auraelia Rose*!"

Shit.

"Getting into trouble, Princess?" Daemon's voice sent a wave of heat down her spine and flooding into her cheeks.

"You!" Liza pointed an accusing finger at Daemon, her hard gaze turning from Auraelia to him. "Why didn't you make sure she ate before coming down here?"

Daemon's eyes widened, his gaze flicking between the plump woman and Auraelia. "Uh...excuse me?"

"She hasn't eaten! I'm not even sure she's eaten at all today. Have you?" Liza's eyes cut back to Auraelia as she finished speaking.

Feeling like a child being reprimanded for stealing chocolate from the kitchens—which she was quite familiar with—Auraelia gave a grim smile. "I was...busy?"

"I swear by the Goddess." Liza threw her hands up in exasperation, then rubbed her temples before turning back toward Daemon. "If you don't get some damn food in her, I don't care if you're a prince; I'm going to come after *you*. Because evidently, *she* can't be trusted to eat when she's supposed to." The last of her tirade was spat directly at Auraelia, and she cringed.

Auraelia had seen Liza angry before—and it was a scary sight to behold—but it had never been directed at her.

Daemon, however, seemed to be struggling to contain a laugh as he responded to the woman. "I will ensure she eats. You have my word." He gave her a low bow, then grabbed two plates from the stack at the end of the table and proceeded to load them up with a little bit of everything that remained. When he finished, he smiled at Auraelia. "I'll be in the hall whenever you're ready to go." Shooting her a wink, he turned on his heel.

Once he was out of earshot, Liza slowly turned toward Auraelia with a knowing smile on her face.

"What?"

"Nothing...*Princess.*"

"Liza."

"Don't '*Liza*' me. He seems like a good one. He's easy on the eyes, too."

"*Liza!*"

"I may be old, Auraelia. But I'm not blind."

Shaking her head, Auraelia untied her apron and placed it into the chef's outstretched hand. "Off to bed with you, Liza. And take the morning off."

"The morning off? Have you lost your mind?"

"We have plenty of pastries and fruit to go around. You're taking the morning off. That's an order."

Groaning, Liza conceded and pulled Auraelia in for a hug. "Take care of yourself, Your Majesty. We would be lost without you." Tears lined the chef's eyes when they pulled apart, but she blinked them away and gave Auraelia a stiff nod. "Now, off with you before your stomach wakes the kiddies."

Shaking her head with a chuckle, Auraelia stepped from behind the table and headed to where Daemon was waiting for her.

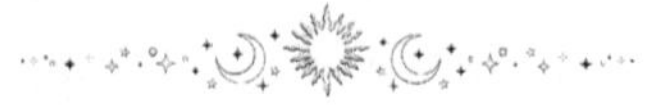

"Goddess, that woman knows how to cook," Daemon exclaimed as he leaned back in his chair and swiped a napkin across his mouth.

"That she does."

When silence fell between them, Daemon reached over and grasped her hand. "What is it?"

"I'd like to go see Xander. I know they will let me know if there are any changes, but—" Her words were cut short by a knock at the door.

Straightening in her seat, Auraelia gave Daemon a look of confusion and then called for whomever it was to enter. When Ser Aeron stepped into the room, all of the air rushed out of her lungs as dread set in, and every horrible thought she could imagine played on a loop in her mind.

Xander is dead.

Davina is back.

We lost more people.

Seeming to sense where her mind had gone, Daemon gave her hand a reassuring squeeze. When she still hadn't found her voice, he asked, "What can we do for you, Commander?"

The relationship between Ser Aeron and Daemon had always been a tense one. Her commander didn't seem to trust him—or at least, he didn't seem to trust him with *her.* But there was now an understanding in his eyes as he met Daemon's before averting his gaze back to Auraelia.

"Your Majesty, your brother is awake. And he's asking for you."

Auraelia had never gotten out of a chair faster in her life, reaching for Daemon with a pleading look in her eyes. She didn't want to waste time sprinting through the halls. She wanted to see her brother, and she wanted to see him *now.*

Her heart was pounding in her chest as Daemon pulled her into his arms.

Xander was awake.

As his shadows swirled around them, he placed a kiss on the crown of her head and whispered, “Breathe, my star.”

Chapter Twenty

Auraelia

The hall outside of Xander's suite was bright and warm, but the dark wood of his door seemed larger than usual. It felt ominous, and she couldn't bring herself to open it. Not as her anxiety took hold, and thoughts like '*what if he's not actually okay?*' took root.

She stared at the handle as the sound of her pulse thrummed in her ears, her breath turning into quick and shallow pants.

Daemon's hand was warm as it slid around her waist, pulling her back against him. "Deep breaths, Auraelia. He's awake. You only need to open the door to see for yourself."

Auraelia shook her head, her vision blurring as tears lined her eyes. "I—I can't. I can't lose him, Daemon."

"You haven't lost him, my star. You *saved* him."

When she still didn't move, Daemon pressed a kiss to her temple and tightened his hold. "Do you want me to open it?"

Nodding faintly, Daemon reached out and turned the knob, pushing the door open slowly.

The sound of Xander's voice filtered out into the hallway, and Auraelia's heart leaped into her throat. Then she heard him laugh, and tears began to stream down her face.

He's okay.

"You ready?" Daemon asked softly.

Wiping her tears, she nodded, hating the way her hands trembled as he slipped his arms from around her. Daemon laced his fingers with hers and brought her hand to his lips, a deep-seated understanding in his eyes as he looked at her.

Taking a deep breath, she hesitantly stepped through the doorway.

Xander's suite was a similar size and layout to her old bedroom. Same floor-to-ceiling windows and bookshelves. Only instead of varying shades of blue, there were browns and ambers. And where she had plush, velvet seating, he had worn, buttery soft leather.

Gently, she pushed the door to his bedchamber open, and what she saw made her heart want to burst out of her chest.

Piper was leaning on the bed, her hands wrapped around one of Xander's, and the look in her brother's eyes was one she knew all too well. It was one she saw in Daemon's every time he looked at her. Even when they argued, behind the annoyance or the anger was a longing that even the blind could see—and she had tried to be blind to it for too long.

Deciding that seeing her brother alive and well was enough, Auraelia attempted to back out the door. But when the floor creaked beneath her foot, Xander's attention turned her way.

"It must be bad if the Queen is coming to my sick bed," he joked. His voice was low and scratchy, but it was strong and calmed the tumult of her mind.

"Yes, well, I have to ensure everyone in my court is cared for. And it seems like you're getting the best of the best." Auraelia jested in return.

Piper flushed at her comment, and when she slowly withdrew her hands from Xander's, Auraelia watched his smile falter.

"I'll uh...leave you two to talk," Piper said to Auraelia before turning back to Xander and whispering something too low for her to hear.

When her friend crossed the room, Auraelia gently grabbed her hand. "You don't need to leave. Please stay."

"No, it's fine. You and Xander need to talk, and I need to eat anyway. You think Liza has anything leftover from dinner?"

"Trust me, there's plenty. She outdid herself," Daemon said as he stepped in behind Auraelia.

Piper's stomach rumbled as if on cue, and she excused herself. But Auraelia didn't miss the sorrow in Xander's eyes as he watched her best friend walk away.

Once the door to the suite was closed, Auraelia stalked across the room to her brother. The closer she got, the less she could hold back the tears threatening to spill over since she stepped foot in his room. "Don't you *ever* do that to me again!"

"Rae—"

"No. You don't get to do that. You don't get to lay there and tell me you're fine."

"I *am* fine, though."

"You had blood pouring out of your face, Xander! She nearly *killed* you!" The wall holding back her tears shattered and freely streamed down her face. "I could have lost you," her voice cracked under the weight of every emotion that she'd been trying to keep at bay so that she could appear strong to those around her. The grief she felt for her people. The overwhelming fear that she was going to lose her brother. The bone-crippling anxiety over what was to come next. It all bled into every word as she stared down at him. "I *can't* lose you, Xander. I just—I can't."

"Auraelia, I'm right here. I'm okay."

"But you weren't. I thought I lost you, just like—" She let her words trail off. No one in that room needed her to finish that sentence, and neither she nor Xander needed to relive that trauma.

Crumpling into the chair at his bedside, Auraelia grabbed his hand and, through her tears, fixed him with a hard stare. "*Promise* you won't ever do that again."

Xander gave her a small scoff. "You know I can't do that." When her eyes narrowed on him, he shook his head and continued. "I *can* promise that I won't go alone and will be better prepared in the future. But, Auraelia, these are my people, too. I couldn't just sit by and do nothing. Not while she laid waste to the city and murdered innocent people."

Auraelia nodded. Of course, she understood. Knew she couldn't blame him when she knew full well that she would have done the same—hell, she *did* do the same after Daemon got him to safety. And moreover, she was about to do it again.

She needed to talk to Caius.

Wanted to beat him senseless and demand answers. And she knew Xander wouldn't be happy with what she had in mind.

After a few seconds of silence, Xander cleared his throat. "So you'd bring me back from the dead and kill me all over again?"

Auraelia's brow quirked in confusion. "What?"

"What you said earlier...about Piper? I heard you."

"You did?"

Xander nodded, and a rosy hue colored his cheeks. "I wouldn't do that, you know...hurt Piper. Even without the looming death threat."

She couldn't help but laugh. The fact that he was okay and felt well enough to crack jokes was a balm to her nerves. "I know. Just don't make this a habit, okay? That's a direct order from your Queen."

"Yes, *Your Majesty.*" Sarcasm dripped from every word, and he punctuated it with as much of a mock bow as he could from a prone position and a flourish of his hand.

As their laughter died off and silence filled the room once more, Auraelia tried to solidify her plan to meet with Caius. She just needed somewhere that was safe and discreet. It couldn't be the throne room, and she didn't feel comfortable having him in the council chambers either.

Just as the solution manifested, Xander's voice cracked through the quiet. "What are you thinking so hard about over there?"

"What?"

"You've got that little wrinkle between your brows that you get when you're thinking too hard. What is it?"

Shit.

"Nothing you need to worry about, I've got it handled."

"*Auraelia.*" He ground out her name in the way only an older brother could when they were calling out a sibling on their bullshit.

"I'm *really* getting tired of hearing my name said like that tonight."

"Maybe you should stop doing things that get you in trouble."

Auraelia narrowed her eyes at Daemon before returning her gaze to her brother. "Xander, really. You couldn't come anyway. You're in no condition to leave this room."

"Why would he need to leave the room, Princess?" Daemon asked, pushing away from where he had been leaning against the wall.

Expelling a sharp breath through her nose, Auraelia tried to explain her plan in a manner that wouldn't upset her brother...and failed miserably.

"You want to do *what*?" he yelled as he attempted to sit up.

"Xander, please. Lay back down."

"Like hell am I going to just lay here while you go off and summon that snake."

"What are you going to do? You can barely sit up. Dammit, Xander." Standing, Auraelia gently pushed him back against his pillows. "Lay back down!"

"Daemon, *please* talk some sense into her."

Daemon scoffed and shook his head. "If you think I'm going to have better luck than you on that front, then you really *should* stay in bed."

Groaning, Xander let his head fall back against the pillows. "Why, Rae? Why do you want to meet with him?"

"Because I want to know who Davina's source is. And I need to know how to take her down."

"You really think he's just going to hand that information over?" Xander riposted, raising a skeptical brow.

A cocky grin spread across her face. "I'm not going to give him a choice. I just need you to tell me how to set a trap."

"What are you talking about?" Daemon asked warily.

Pinching his eyes closed, Xander sighed and explained. "There's a way to trap someone with runes. The problem is, you have to ward the entire room, so it traps everyone except for the one who wrote them. And I *assume* you're not going to let her do this by herself...*right*?"

Before Daemon could answer, Auraelia cut in. "But you know how to avoid that."

"Been reading my books, *Your Majesty*?"

"We had the same tutors, Xander. You just happened to pay more attention to runes than I did."

Xander scrubbed his hands down his face. He looked more tired than she'd ever seen him, and she hated that she was pushing him on this, but she needed to know in order for her plan to work.

And it had to work.

"Yes, there is a way to avoid it. You'll need to mark anyone who you want to give the capability of leaving with a rune—"

"Easy enough. Just—"

"Hold on, Rae. It's not that simple. You have to draw it in *your* blood, infuse it with *your* magic, and they have to be willing to accept it. And I've heard it's not a pleasant experience for the receiver."

"You mean I have to—"

"Yes, Rae. You will have to funnel some of your magic into another person."

Dread dripped down her spine.

As quickly as her plan had come together, it slowly began to fall apart around her.

When she'd done that to Davina, it had burned her. Caused veins of lightning to sear into her skin. And the thought of doing that to anyone else, let alone to someone she cared about, made her stomach churn.

"I'll do it."

Auraelia's head whipped toward Daemon, her eyes wide as shock and fear collided. "Daemon, no. I can't do that to you. You didn't see—"

"Didn't see what?" His brows drew together as concern swirled in the mossy green depths of his eyes.

Swallowing audibly, Auraelia's voice quavered as she spoke. "I—After you got Xander to safety, Davina charged at me. And when she got close enough, I grabbed her arms and funneled my magic into her body. It *burned* her."

"Rae." Xander's voice was soft—pitying.

It made her skin crawl.

She didn't want his pity. She did what she needed to do to get Davina to leave and would do it over again if she had to. But that didn't mean that she *wanted* to.

Averting her gaze from Daemon, she focused on her brother instead. She didn't want to see Daemon's face when she explained what happened down in the harbor. Couldn't bear the idea of seeing disappointment in his eyes. "Before she vanished—with the help of Caius, I might add—I saw them...the burns. They looked like streaks of lightning burning down the length of her arms. And where my hands had been were blistered palm prints. I can't—I *won't* do that to Daemon."

She felt his presence at her back and turned as Daemon knelt at her side and folded her hands into his. But instead of the disappointment she had anticipated, there was only understanding. "That was different, Auraelia. You were angry and trying to save your brother and your people and did what you had to." When she opened her mouth to retort, he squeezed her hands. "You won't hurt me. I *trust* you."

Auraelia let his words settle into her heart and mind.

Trust.

Trust was something that was earned. It was something that people had to work to keep. She didn't understand how he could still trust her after everything that she'd put him through. But looking into his eyes, she saw it, and the words from the letters he'd sent all those months ago filtered back into her mind.

I will always come back for you.

I will always love you.

Giving Daemon a slight nod, she turned back toward her brother. "Teach me the runes."

Ser Aeron's brows were drawn together, lips set into a thin line, and arms crossed over his broad chest as he watched Auraelia work her way around the room, drawing runes on the floor every two paces as Xander had instructed. She felt his eyes on her the entire time, and when she finally finished, she stood and met his disapproving glare. "What?" she clipped as Daemon wrapped a bandage around her hand, pressed a soft kiss to her palm, and reminded her to breathe for the hundredth time that day.

"I can't believe you're doing this in a brothel of all places."

"It's not like we could have done it at the castle," she retorted.

Madame Sylvie's was the best solution she could come up with in the limited time she had. It had been untouched by Davina's tirade, was away from the prying eyes of the council, and because she wasn't sure who was betraying her, she needed to keep this meeting between the people she trusted most—which, at that point, also included the Madame of a brothel.

Ser Aeron rolled his eyes, pushed away from the wall, and headed to the bar cart that Vee had set up in the corner.

When they'd arrived, Vee's face had blanched at the sight of the Queen's Commander in her establishment. It had taken a while—and a few tumblers of whatever concoction she kept on the top shelf—to convince her that he wasn't there to arrest or close her down. But once she calmed, she relinquished her office and even took Auraelia's suggestion of closing down for the night. Though she wasn't happy about that, she'd gladly accepted the bag of coins Auraelia had dropped onto the bar.

"Rae, are you *sure* about this?" Piper asked from where she stood nervously in the middle of the room.

"No, not really," she answered honestly. "But it's the only thing that makes sense right now. I need to know what he knows."

Worry lined every inch of her friend's face, and she began to second guess asking her to come along. She *needed* her there for moral support, but she also wanted her there in case she saw something amiss. But if Piper was unsure, she also wouldn't make her stay.

Crossing the room, she took her friend's hands in her own. "Piper, you don't have to stay if you don't want to."

"Nice try, Rae. I'm not leaving you. I haven't seen anything that would suggest this goes awry, but that doesn't mean that it won't."

"Thank you." Tears sprang to her eyes at Piper's unending loyalty. It wasn't because she was the queen and she was her lady, but because they were sisters in every way that mattered. Souls bound together through whatever life decided to throw their way.

"Okay, so how does this work again?" Ser Aeron asked, stretching out his arms and tilting his head side to side like he was getting ready to fight someone.

"The runes have set a perimeter around the room; no one will be allowed in or out without my permission. If you are all willing, I will place a rune on your forearm that will grant you the ability to come and go freely. But, from what Xander said, it's not going to be pleasant. So I understand if you decide not to."

Daemon stepped up first, rolling his sleeve to his elbow to expose the intricate lines of ink that were scrawled along his skin. The idea of possibly marring the beautiful artwork permanently, of causing him any pain or discomfort, made her hands shake and bile rise in her throat, her dinner threatening to make an unwanted reappearance.

When she met his gaze, it was soft and trusting. Like he knew she was spiraling and beginning to doubt herself. "You won't hurt me, my star," he spoke low enough to where only she could hear as he gently unwrapped the bandage from her hand. "I trust you; you just need to trust yourself."

Nodding, Auraelia pulled her dagger from its sheath, wincing as she reopened the cut on her palm. When the blood began to pool, she dipped her finger into the warm, crimson liquid and took a deep breath.

The moment her finger touched Daemon's skin, there was a sharp intake of breath as his muscles contracted, and she almost stopped right then. But when they relaxed, and a soft glow began to illuminate the path that her finger made, she breathed a sigh of relief.

Once the rune was completed, every symbol in the room shone brightly for a brief moment, like they were all connecting to one another, before dimming until all that was left was her blood against the black ink of his arm.

She looked up expectantly at Daemon, searching his face for any sign of pain, but all she saw was awe. "Are you okay?"

"Never better." Daemon pressed a kiss to her cheek, then rolled his wrist around like he was working out a kink and stepped to the side. "Who's next?"

Ser Aeron stepped forward, his arm extended, and sheer determination was in his eyes.

"Are you sure?" she asked tentatively.

He bowed his head to her. "Not a doubt in my mind, Your Majesty."

When she finished with the commander, Auraelia walked over to where Piper was fidgeting on the couch, pulling at her fingers as her foot bounced against the floor. "You don't have to do this."

"I know, but I want to. I *need* to. I need to hear what that bastard has to say." Venom dripped from her words, and Auraelia knew it had more to do with Xander than anything else that had transpired. Straightening her spine, Piper rolled the sleeve of her tunic and extended her arm toward Auraelia.

Taking the seat next to her friend, she gently laid Piper's hand in her lap to repeat the process. Only this time, it was different.

With every movement of her finger across Piper's skin, flashes of memories scrolled through her mind like living portraits. Scenes from when they were girls running through the gardens. Images of training on the pitch together throughout their lives. Of countless nights staying up laughing with each other. It was like reliving her life through Piper's eyes. But then, the visions shifted.

The images were distorted, like staring through ice on a window or trying to peer through fog. She could make out shapes and identify some of the people that danced across her vision. Could recognize the sounds of clashing metal and distant screams. But it all passed by too quickly for her to discern any real information.

When the final line of the rune connected and her mind cleared, she looked up to find Piper's eyes as wide as hers felt.

What in the...

"Did you—?" Piper's words came out in a rush of air.

"What was *that*?"

"I—I'm not sure."

They stayed that way for a few moments, staring openly at each other like they could figure it out if they just stayed still.

She could feel the eyes of everyone else in the room digging holes into her spine, but she didn't care. They finally broke eye contact only when Ser Aeron cleared his throat. "Shall we?"

Pushing up from the couch, Auraelia walked over to the desk where she had placed the box of crystals Caius had given her.

Here goes nothing.

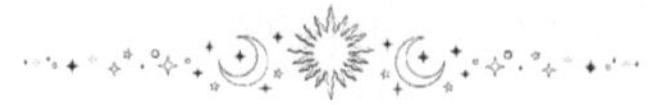

"Where is he?" Auraelia seethed as she paced the room. It had been hours since she'd summoned him with the crystals, and she didn't understand what was taking so long.

Did she do it wrong?

Were the runes keeping him from entering?

Auraelia ran over every instruction that Xander had given her. She'd done it right. Followed every step, down to the last detail. When she thought over what Caius had said about the crystals, it should have worked. He'd said all she had to do was hold them and think his name, and he would come. So why wasn't he here?

"Auraelia—"

"Don't tell me to breathe, Daemon. I *am* breathing."

"My star," his voice was level. Steady, like the soothing sound of water trickling downstream. "Your fingers are sparking. I need you to calm down."

She hadn't even noticed that her magic was seeping out at her fingertips. When she looked down at her hands, she saw tiny blips of light flickering in the deep green that colored the tips of her fingers—green that had progressed past her first knuckle after her altercation with Davina.

"I'm sorry, I hadn't realized." Curling her hands into fists, Auraelia forced air into her lungs, holding it until her anger began to subside. When she let it out, the hair on the back of her neck stood on end as an eerie feeling settled into her bones.

"Well, this certainly is a welcome party, I must say." Caius' voice filled the stillness in the air, and Auraelia whipped around to find him lounging on the couch near the fireplace.

"Where the hell have you been?" she yelled, thankful for the fact that no one was in the brothel to hear her.

"I may have given you the ability to call on me, Your Majesty. But I am not at your beck and call. I had...*things* I needed to take care of first."

"What kind of '*things*'?" As Auraelia crossed her arms over her chest, she felt Daemon's presence at her back. A gentle reminder that he was there for her and a reminder for the emissary from Garnet that she was not alone.

"Glad to see the happy couple back together." When no one moved, Caius let out a disgruntled sigh and sat up—wincing slightly as he did so. He gestured to the chairs across from him and said, "You might as well get comfortable; I have a feeling we might be here for a while."

Once everyone was gathered around—Auraelia directly across from Caius with Daemon standing at her side, Piper in the chair next to hers, and Ser Aeron closing out the circle at the end—Caius began to spin his tale.

"How well do you know your history, Your Majesty?"

"As well as any other Ixorian, I would assume. Why?"

"And the history of the Goddesses? How well do you know that?"

"Would you get to whatever point you're trying to make?" Daemon's voice was cold and demanding, and she could feel his growing frustration as if it were her own.

"Very well. In the stories, long before Ixora came to be, the twin Goddesses—Morana and Esmeray—were cast out from Arcelia for creating blood magic. Esmeray worked with the lighter side of their magic. Always helping others and using her power to heal and mend. But Morana was drawn to the darker side, using it to seek revenge on those who she considered wrong, and eventually, she attempted to use it to overturn the peace in their realm. Though Esmeray denounced her use of blood magic because they were twins—and bound in ways more than by the blood coursing through their veins—the Goddess Rhayne, with the help of the others, cast them out of Arcelia and sent them to reign over the moon. Esmeray and her bright white light guide from the face of the moon, shining down on those who wish for her guidance. While her sister clings to the darkness, to the side of the moon that is only seen once every twenty-nine days."

"Thanks for the lesson, but is there a *point* to your rambling?" Piper demanded, her irritation evident.

Sighing, Caius continued. "Though they are twins, they can be worshiped separately. And Davina worships Morana."

"Why should I care who my cousin worships?"

"You should care, Your Majesty. Because Davina is her most devout subject. And when the moon is new, and darkness fills the sky, *that* is when she is at her strongest."

Auraelia tried to read between Caius' words, but endless questions filled those holes, leaving her more confused than when this all started.

"Goddess, I hate when people speak in riddles. Speak *plainly*, Caius. What does Davina worshiping Morana have to do with me? With this war between us?"

Caius leaned forward, resting his elbows on his knees while his eyes bore into Auraelia's. "How much do you know about blood magic, Your Majesty?"

"Again with the fucking questions," Piper mumbled under her breath as she fidgeted in her chair, clearly over the way this conversation was going.

Caius shifted his gaze to Piper. Though his words were soft, they were spoken through clenched teeth. "There is a *reason* for my questions, Lady. I need to know what your Queen knows so I don't waste my breath explaining things that are already known. Now." He turned back to Auraelia. "Answer the question, please."

"I don't know much if I'm honest. It's not something that is spoken of here. Or if it is, it's in hushed tones or behind closed doors. Why?"

"And blood binding?"

"I've never heard of it."

Reaching for the collar of his tunic, Caius unlaced the ties before pulling it down to expose his chest. There, sitting right over his heart, was a rune. It looked like a brand on his skin, and Auraelia couldn't help her sharp intake of breath.

"What is that?" she asked, hesitantly reaching forward before pulling her hand away.

"*This* is what Davina does to those that she 'loves.' This is what a blood bond looks like." He paused for a moment and refastened his tunic. "When she was first beginning to practice blood magic, she discovered a way to bind her life to someone else. At the time, we were very much in love and couldn't imagine spending our days without the other—"

"And now?" Daemon asked as his hand came to rest on Auraelia's shoulder.

"Now?" Caius scoffed, his eyes flicking up to Daemon. "Now, it's a burden I don't want to bear. A weight on my soul that I can't remove."

The room fell silent as Caius' admission settled around them.

"What exactly *is* a blood bond?" The deep tone of Ser Aeron's voice reverberated through the room.

"It means, Commander, that my life is bound to Davina's. What happens to her happens to me. Take pain, for example." Caius winced as he leaned back against the couch, his gaze honing in on Auraelia. "Though it's not as severe, any pain she feels, I get the *privilege* of experiencing it as well."

Auraelia's eyes widened, scanning over every inch of the emissary's body before settling back on his face. It couldn't be...could it? Had her magic affected him, too?

Daemon's voice cut through her rampant thoughts, demanding proof of what Caius had said. Her heart stuttered in her chest. No one other than Daemon and Xander knew what happened in the harbor. But if what Caius said was true, then the extent of the damage she'd inflicted on Davina would be present on him as well. The idea of seeing it on someone she hadn't intended it for made her head spin.

The corner of Caius' mouth lifted into a menacing smile, his eyes still locked onto Auraelia's as he began to remove his shirt. When he slid his arms free of the fabric, Auraelia's hand flew to her mouth, silencing the gasp that slipped through her lips.

Stark white lines trailed down both of his arms, originating from two clearly defined palm-shaped imprints on his upper arms.

Auraelia stood, her gaze flicking over the marks on his arms, as she took a hesitant step forward, closing the distance between herself and Caius. When she finally met his gaze, he seemed to read the question in her eyes and inclined his head, extending his arm out toward her.

Starting where they ended on his hand, Auraelia's fingers hovered over the marks cascading down his arms, afraid to touch them. To feel the damage that she'd unknowingly caused. When she reached her handprint on his shoulder, she noticed faint lines that shot out over his chest, stopping mere inches from the blood bond rune—like it had kept her magic from penetrating his heart.

"I didn't know—" She shook her head slowly. She hadn't meant to do *this.* Not to him.

"Would it have kept you from doing it if you had?"

His question surprised her. Would it have kept her from harming Davina if she'd known?

It didn't take long for the answer to become clear, and as she steeled her spine, she met his gaze. "No, Caius. It wouldn't have changed anything. It changes nothing."

She'd expected anger, perhaps even sadness, in response to her honesty. Instead, she received a devilish smile that made his eyes sparkle with mischief. "Good."

"Good? What do you mean '*good*'?" Daemon questioned as he came to Auraelia's side, his brows pinched together.

Sighing, Caius pulled his arms away and grabbed his shirt from where he'd tossed it onto the couch. After slipping it over his head, he said, "That's good because I want this to end. I'm tired of being her plaything. Tired of taking her hits. She's not the woman I fell in love with, the one with whom I agreed to enter this stupid bond. I don't know *who* she is anymore. And she won't let me go."

"Why not just sever the bond?" Piper asked.

The laugh that emanated from Caius was one of pure disbelief. "You think I haven't *tried*? The only way to sever a blood bond is death. Either mine or hers."

"So, if we kill you, she'll die too? Easy enough. Rae, do you want to? Or shall I have that honor?" Piper stood then, a menacing smile on her face as she stalked toward Caius.

Auraelia had known Piper her whole life, and she'd never heard her speak that way—she didn't have a mean bone in her body. The only time she lifted a blade was during training. But she also knew that Piper would do anything for those she loved, consequences be damned. After seeing her friend with her brother and the tears trailing down her face as she slipped from Xander's room, she recognized the venom in Piper's voice for what it was. She was well acquainted with it because that same rage filled Auraelia whenever she thought of anything happening to the ones she loved. Her family, her people. Daemon. They were all pieces of her heart, of her soul, and she'd be damned if she let anything else happen to them.

"If only it were that easy," Caius said with a scoff.

"Explain, and do it quickly before I try it her way." Auraelia seethed, her magic warming in her veins, begging to be released. She was over him talking in circles, over this conversation and how everything he said brought more questions than it did answers.

"If you kill me, all that would do would infuriate Davina. She'd feel it; it would probably weaken her for a while, but it wouldn't kill her."

"And if we kill her?" Auraelia countered.

"*If* you kill Davina, and that's a large if, then I will be free."

"Would you die?"

Caius shrugged nonchalantly as if they were discussing what canapes to have at a party. "Perhaps. But either way, I'd be free. If I die, I am no longer able to bend to her will. If she dies and I live, the same applies."

Auraelia narrowed her gaze, searching his face for any clues as to whether he was telling the truth or spinning a web of lies. What she saw was resolve.

He'd resolved himself to the idea of dying. Saw it as the only way out of the situation that he was in, and a part of her pitied him.

"So, what do you say, Your Majesty? Now that you know more about what and who you're up against."

Auraelia tilted her head slightly. "Before we go any further, I have one more question."

Caius raised his brows in surprise. "Go on."

"Who is Davina's informant?"

A slow, easy grin spread across his face. "Look to your own court, Your Majesty. Not all are as loyal as they seem."

Anger, red-hot and searing, burned through Auraelia's veins. Her magic bleeding out of her as lightning began to spark at her fingers.

"*Who*?" she demanded, her teeth clenched so tightly that she could hear them grinding against each other.

"Remove the runes holding me here, and I'll tell you."

Shock hit her like a slap to the face. "You knew?"

"Of course," he taunted. "Those may be considered organic magic here in Emerald, but in Garnet...well, that's where blood magic begins."

Keeping her gaze narrowed on Caius, she reached down and squeezed Daemon's hand. "Do it."

"Auraelia—"

"Daemon, please. There is a bowl of water on the desk with a rag in it. Just swipe it across the rune in front of the door."

Daemon expelled a heavy breath but released her hand and did as she asked. As soon as the symbol was broken, a wave of magic swept through the room, severing the connection between each of the runes.

Caius' smile grew, and it seemed full of relief when he sighed. Like the runes had been a heavy weight on his shoulders, and once they were nullified, he was able to breathe freely. "Well, this has been fun, but I must get back before she notices I'm gone."

"*Caius*." Auraelia's voice was firm with warning, her lightning wrapping around her limbs like ribbons. Like hell, she would let him slip away without giving her an answer.

Unphased, he bowed. "Until next time, *My Queen*."

Snow swirled around him, the cold sizzling against the anger that heated her skin. But before he was fully gone, a cold breeze swept past her ear, bringing with it the answer to her question.

"Lord Harland."

That son of a bitch.

Chapter Twenty-One

Daemon

"Lord Harland?" Ser Aeron growled, shock and rage bringing his already baritone voice down another octave.

It had surprised Daemon just as much as everyone else in the room to hear that name fall from Caius' lips, but they still didn't know *why*. And he couldn't decide what irked him more—the fact that someone Auraelia trusted was betraying her or that the one who provided the information conveniently left without so much as an explanation.

Auraelia snatched the bowl and rag from the desk where he had left it and began scrubbing vigorously at the floor.

Her anger was palpable.

Sparks of lightning lit up the deep emerald coloring of her fingertips as a breeze began to lick against the back of his neck.

"My star—"

"Don't." Auraelia stopped scrubbing and heaved a heavy breath. "I don't want to talk about it right now. I just want to get this clean so Vee doesn't kill me and go home before I do something I'll regret later."

Daemon slowly walked over to where she was crouched just past the door and knelt at her side. "Let me help?"

She turned her head and met his gaze, but it was like she was seeing straight through him. Her mind undoubtedly swirling through everything that they had learned that night, trying to make sense of it. Trying to find a way through the maze of information that had just been laid at her feet.

He gently pulled the rag from her hand and, with the other, brushed the stray strand of hair that had fallen from her braid behind her ear. Her eyes fluttered closed as she leaned into his touch, and a small sigh escaped from her lips.

"We'll figure this out. *Together*," he whispered, and she nodded.

Pressing a kiss to her brow, Daemon stood and turned to where Ser Aeron and Piper still stood in the small sitting area. "Care to lend a hand?"

The trip back to Emerald Castle was nearly silent, save for the sound of the horse's hooves pounding against the dirt below. Each of them seemed lost in their own trails of thought, but none were as far away from the present as Auraelia.

Her back was near straight in the saddle, the hood of her cloak thrown back by the wind from the pace they set. Her hands were clenched so tightly around the reins of her gorgeous mare that if he could see beneath her gloves, he was sure they would be white. Daemon watched her the whole way back, but her eyes stayed straight ahead, never once glancing toward him or the others.

When they arrived at the stables, she dismounted and passed the reins off to the stablehand. Only then did she turn and finally meet Daemon's gaze.

Her eyes flicked over his face like she would somehow find whatever answers she was looking for there. When her stormy-gray gaze finally met his, he let a tendril of his magic slip between his fingers, reaching out toward her until it wrapped around her hand.

He knew the moment she felt it.

A small contented sigh slipped between her lips, her eyes briefly fluttering closed as her shoulders eased away from her ears.

Daemon made his way toward her after passing off his borrowed horse—a chocolate stallion with white star marks flecked across his flank like a constellation that Xander had aptly named Orion.

He heard Piper say something about going to check on Xander and filling him in, though he didn't believe that for a second since it was the middle of the night, and what they learned could wait until morning, but he kept his thoughts to himself. Ser Aeron muttered something, but his words fell on deaf ears.

His entire world was wrapped around the woman in front of him.

She was his priority.

And the only words he wanted to hear were the ones that came out of *her* mouth.

"Walk with me?" Daemon asked, gently pulling a glove from her hand before lacing their fingers together.

Auraelia nodded, then led them away from the stables and toward the bench at the edge of the training pitch. It was the same one they'd sat at what felt like eons ago when the world was simpler, and the only thing that stood in their way was a piece of parchment signed over five hundred years ago.

Their walk was quiet—the only sound coming from the cold winter breeze that rustled through the naked branches of the trees—but he didn't mind. He knew her mind was a jumble of thoughts, and he didn't want to pressure her into talking before she was ready. Knew she needed to work through it on her own first before she said it aloud.

So he kept silent and let her lean against him as they walked.

Soaked in the feeling of her skin against his and the way his magic seemed to reach out for hers.

As they crossed the pitch, Daemon tilted his head toward the sky. The stars sparkled like diamonds overhead, the moon shining brightly against the velvety backdrop of night.

The longer he looked, the more pieces from earlier in the night fell into place.

When the moon is new and darkness fills the sky, that is when Davina is at her strongest.

Daemon knew the moon cycle like the back of his hand. As a sailor, he had to. But that also meant they had less than a month before Davina would undoubtedly attack.

"Fifteen days," he muttered toward the sky.

"What did you say?" Auraelia stopped in her tracks, pulling him to an abrupt halt as well.

Releasing a heavy breath, Daemon turned toward her. "Fifteen days."

"What's in fifteen days, Daemon?"

"Caius said that when the moon is new, that's when Davina is at her strongest."

Auraelia quirked a brow, her head tilted slightly as confusion marred her features.

"The cycle of the moon takes approximately twenty-nine days. That," he said, gesturing toward the sky, "is the full moon at its peak. Which means we have about fifteen days until the new moon rises."

She stared at him for a long moment, her brows forming a v between them. But when his words began to make sense, the confusion there mere moments ago shifted into a fiery rage.

"I'm going to kill him." Auraelia yanked her hand from his and began to storm back toward the stables.

"Auraelia, wait."

"I'm going to *kill* him!" she screamed, her words echoing into the darkness.

Pulling on the shadows that filled the night, Daemon summoned a barrier around Auraelia, stopping her in her tracks long enough for him to shadow-walk to her.

"Let go of me!" she screeched as Daemon wrapped his arms around her, pinning hers to her sides.

"No." He kept his tone even, but when heat began to lick against his arms where ribbons of lightning began to spiral along hers, he let out a curse. "Stop fighting me, Auraelia."

Willing his shadows to obey, he did the only thing he could think of. His magic swirled around them, cocooning them in darkness while she struggled against his hold.

Only when they landed in her rooms did he release her.

Auraelia whirled on him, fire burning in her gaze as she pushed against his chest. "Why did you do that!" Her voice shrill as she yelled at him.

"What were you planning on doing, Auraelia? Ride all the way to Garnet?"

"Garnet?" she scoffed, releasing the clasps of her cloak and tossing it onto a nearby chair. "No, I'm going to kill that treasonous bastard who sold out my court to the person trying to destroy it!"

"My star—"

"Don't." She pointed an accusing finger at him, her lips pursed as rage flared in her eyes.

"Alright, *Princess*. Do you really think it's a good idea to go barging into a Lord's estate in the middle of the night to *murder* him?" His tone was toeing the line between calm and frustration. He didn't want to fight about this, but he needed her to see reason.

"No, but am I expected to just let him live?" she spat back.

Daemon stared at her for a moment, then lifted his lips into a smirk. "Yes."

"Yes?" she asked incredulously.

"That's exactly what you do, Princess."

"*What?* You want me to just let it go?"

Daemon shook his head, then stalked toward her, slowly closing the distance between them. "No, my star. Let him think that he's one step ahead. Let him run his mouth to Davina. *Feed* him information, then let him fall flat on his face."

Auraelia's eyes narrowed, then widened as his words sank in.

When Daemon was but a breath away, he cupped her face between his palms and let his lips brush against hers as he spoke. "Let him think he's on the winning side. And when you're the one to come out on top—because you will, I will be sure of that—not only will I not stand in your way, I'll even hand you the blade."

The moment he pressed his lips to hers, she softened, her hands gripping his waist and pulling him closer to her body. A soft moan vibrated from her lips into his, but the moment he made to draw her closer, her spine straightened, and she pulled away.

Auraelia gently pried his hands from her face and stepped away. Her eyes were downcast as she spoke. "You should go home."

Daemon dropped her hands and widened the space between them. He couldn't breathe. Couldn't think. It was like she'd ripped his heart straight from his chest. "What?"

She took a steadying breath, then slowly raised her eyes to meet his. "You need to go home, Daemon."

All the calm he'd been trying to maintain dissipated, anger and confusion promptly taking their place as he stared at the woman who seemed bound and determined to do everything alone.

"Don't do this. *Please*, my star. Don't do this. Not again." Disbelief clung to every word, his stomach twisting into knots.

Auraelia wrapped her arms around herself, eyes falling to the floor once more. "Daemon, please. I—" her voice trailed off like she couldn't find the words she needed to say.

"No. I know you think you need to do this on your own, but you don't. Let me be there for you," he pleaded. When she still refused to look at him, Daemon angrily ran his hands through his hair, pulling on the strands until pain shot through him. He paced the floor a few times, then whirled on her. "Look at me, dammit!"

Gradually, she lifted her gaze toward him, the pain in her eyes piercing through his shattering heart. She was more than anything he'd ever wanted or needed, and he'd be damned if he let her push him away again. Let her throw what they had away.

Dropping his hands, he strode across the floor toward her. He didn't care if he woke the entire castle; she was going to listen to what he had to say. "I know you love me, so stop *fighting* me! Stop pushing me away!" Daemon cupped her face in his hands, forcing her to look him in the eyes where tears threatened to spill over. "This? Us? We've been written in the stars for centuries—our souls bound together, destined to scour the realm until they could find each other again. But even without that, without fate deciding that we were meant to be, I want *you*. We have a chance to be happy together, Auraelia. Stop fighting it. *Please.*"

Auraelia eased his hands from his face, her voice barely a whisper as she dropped her gaze to his chest. "I can't."

"No, you can. You just won't." His voice was sharp as a blade. When she pulled her hands from his and took a step away, it was like a boulder dropped into the pit of his stomach. Like she couldn't stand breathing the same air he did. "Why, Auraelia? Tell me why the fuck you are *choosing* to do this to us. Not just to me but to *us.* I fucking deserve that much."

Auraelia's eyes shot to his as she screamed, "I'm doing this *because* I love you, Daemon. Fuck!" Turning away from him, she looked up toward the ceiling.

When her gaze met his once more, tears lined her eyes. Regret and devastation swirled in her blue-gray orbs as she stared him down, her nostrils flaring as she tried to rein in her emotions.

She closed her eyes and ran her hands down her face, holding them over her mouth for a moment like she was praying before she continued, her voice still raised and shaking with every word. "Don't you understand?"

Glassy eyes met his once more, her voice softer as she continued. "I would bring this realm to its knees. Burn it to the ground until all that was left was ash and cinder if it meant keeping you safe. Keeping you *here* by my side. But I can't do that." Tears streamed down her cheeks, but when Daemon reached for her, she held her hand out, took a step back, and shook her head. "I can't think straight when you're here. But I can barely *breathe* when you're not. I have to think about my people, *your* people, and the whole of Ixora. I will *not* allow this realm to fall into her hands. I don't care whether we're written in the stars or in the sand. I will not lose you. I *can't* lose you... It would break me."

They stared at each other for what felt like hours, though it had only been seconds.

He heard every word she said, but the one thing that played on repeat through his mind were those three little words he'd been dying to hear. The ones that kickstarted his heart into a gallop.

She loves me.

He'd known it to be true, but knowing and hearing were two very different things.

Daemon closed the space between them before Auraelia could even blink. Cupping her face in his hands, he gently wiped away the tears that continued falling. "I heard everything that you said, I did. But, Auraelia—" he paused, resting his forehead against hers. "I'm not going to ask you to say it again. Not because I don't want to hear it—I want to hear it every day of my goddess damned life—but because I've been waiting for so long to hear it that even though you've said it while frustrated with me and this whole situation, it's still the sweetest sound I've ever heard. And I need you to know, my beautiful, shining star, that I love you, too. More than there are stars in the sky, and it runs deeper than the depths of the sea. I need you more than I need air in my lungs. I am yours. In this life, the next, and whatever may lay beyond that. I am irrevocably in love with you."

A choked sob slipped through Auraelia's lips as she pushed up on her toes, her lips soft and forgiving beneath his.

Daemon let his hands fall from her face in favor of encircling her waist. Her body melted into his. Her hands snaked up his chest to wrap around his neck, fingers delving into the hair at his nape.

The kiss was unlike any they'd shared before.

It wasn't rushed.

There was no frantic pulling of clothes or fumbling fingers.

It was like coming up for air.

Like stepping into the sunshine after days of rain.

When they finally parted, Auraelia looked up at him, and the world faded away until all that remained was her.

Love shone in the bright gray swirls of her eyes.

There was no mask.

No hiding.

It was pure and unfettered, and it was all for him.

"Take me to bed?" she asked, her voice barely above a whisper.

Daemon lifted her behind her knees, his lips melding against hers as he carried her into the bedchamber. After kicking the door behind them, he set her back on her feet, his hands finding her face again. He searched her gaze as his thumb swept idly across her cheeks. "I know I said I wouldn't ask—"

"I love you, Daemon Alexander. I have for a long time, and I'm sorry I didn't tell you sooner." It was a whisper across his lips but felt like fire in his veins. Igniting every inch of his body.

Daemon rested his brow against hers, breathing in the ever-present scent of lavender and something else that was intrinsically *her*. "And I love you, Auraelia Rose."

He kissed her lips deeply, slowly working his way across her jaw and neck. When he reached the junction at her shoulder, he lifted his head. "May I?" he asked, his fingers playing with the laces of her corset.

Auraelia slowly bobbed her head, a coquettish grin on her face as one corner of her bottom lip disappeared between her teeth.

Daemon had to suppress the groan attempting to work its way up his throat. The thoughts that swam through his head with that one little movement would make even the goddess of love blush.

He took his time, gently tugging on the strings until they gave way and he could push it from her shoulders. He relished every hitch in her breath as his hands brushed against her. Savored the way love and lust filled her eyes and bore into his.

After her corset was on the floor, Auraelia reached for the ties on his tunic. "Can I?"

"You can do whatever you want, my love. I am yours to command." Her cheeks pinkened at his endearment, and he couldn't help the smile that pulled at his lips. They'd been through hell to get to this point and still had more to overcome. But this, right now, was all that mattered.

Auraelia slowly loosened the neck of his tunic, then trailed her hands down his chest to his waistband. Her eyes stayed locked onto his as she gently pulled the shirt from his pants, sliding her hands beneath it before lifting it over his head. Her hands were like a brand on his skin, marking every inch of him as hers.

With his shirt gone, her fingers skimmed across the lines of his tattoos, then the indents in his abs, his muscles jumping with every pass.

"My turn," Daemon growled as he gripped her hips, walking her back until her knees hit the end of the bed. He peeled the sheer linen tunic from her body, added it to the growing pile on the floor, and then gently pushed her down onto the mattress. He let his eyes travel down her body. Taking in the way her chest rose and fell with every breath she took. The way her nipples stiffened into peaks, and her skin pebbled under his gaze.

She was utter perfection.

Stepping between her legs, he leaned forward and kissed her softly before pushing her down onto the mattress and trailing featherlight kisses down her body. His hands skimmed her sides while his lips kept to the line down her torso, using every grain of willpower he possessed not to stray to where her breasts heaved with every breath. Auraelia's hands lazily ran through his hair as he worked his way down, soft whimpers falling from her lips the closer he got to her center.

Kneeling at her feet, Daemon pressed a kiss to the ties between her hips, then pulled away, smirking as Auraelia let out a disgruntled groan and pushed onto her elbows.

His eyes locked onto hers as he made quick work of her boots, unstrapped the dagger from her thigh, then slowly peeled the leather down her legs.

A beautiful rosy hue colored her cheeks and radiated down her neck as he slowly kissed his way back up. Delicately pressing his lips to the inside of her ankle, the back of her knee, and the inside of her thigh before switching to the other side.

"*Daemon*," she mewled. "*Please.* I need you."

"What do you need, my star? Tell me what you want, and will scour the realm to make sure you have it." Daemon hovered over her center, his breath coasting over the fabric that kept her from being completely bare before him.

Auraelia stared down her body, her gaze full of so much love that his heart clenched in his chest. "*You*. I just need you."

As much as he wanted to drag this out, to tease her until she was writhing beneath him and begging for his touch...when she looked at him like that? Every thought and plan was thrown to the wayside, and all that existed was her.

Hooking his fingers beneath the straps on her hips, he slowly slid the fabric down her legs and tossed it on the floor.

Her pussy was gloriously pink and glistening with her arousal, the little bundle of nerves at the apex swollen and begging to be touched. Daemon leaned forward and ran the flat of his tongue up Auraelia's center, groaning as she completely engulfed his senses.

The salty-sweet tang of her on his tongue.

Her arousal, mixed with the lavender on her skin, filled his nose.

The feel of her silky smooth skin beneath his hands and the low moans that slipped past her lips filled his ears.

He could have died right then and gone a happy man.

Daemon sucked her clit into his mouth, and her hands instantly flew to his head. Gripping the strands in an attempt to hold him where he was. When he slipped two fingers into her slick center, her hips bucked against him, and he smiled.

He would never tire of feeling her unravel for him. Of the way her walls clenched around his digits when he stroked the sensitive ridges that lined the front wall of her pussy.

"Be a good girl and come on my tongue, Princess," he muttered against her.

Auraelia's hips began to rock against him as he flicked his tongue against her clit, his fingers pumping in and out of her in tandem with her movements.

When her walls began to flutter, he picked up the pace of his fingers and sucked hard on her clit. Her breathing became erratic, her hands tightening against his scalp as her orgasm edged closer. It wasn't long before she clamped down on his fingers, her legs locking around his head as he licked her long and slow. Her hips continued to rock against him, drawing out her release until finally it subsided and her muscles relaxed, her hand slipping from its hold in his hair and her legs falling to the side.

Daemon removed his fingers and ran his tongue over her once more before crawling out from between her legs. Through half-lidded eyes, she met his gaze and watched as he swiped the evidence of her release from his chin with his thumb and sucked it clean.

As he kicked off his boots and removed his pants, her eyes slowly trailed down his body, and every nerve ending sparked to life, his magic purring in his veins.

Daemon slowly made his way up her body. Every kiss he planted on her skin sent a wave of anticipation through him. They'd fucked countless times, but this was different. This was more than giving and receiving pleasure from another person.

This was deeper.

Emotions and feelings were all out in the open, and there was no way to bottle them up again. And it made everything more intense.

Auraelia closed the distance between their lips, her hands framing his face, before slowly traveling down his body. Every muscle contracted and relaxed as her fingers skimmed across them like she was mapping out every contour. But then her hand wrapped around his cock, stroking him with the perfect amount of pressure from root to tip. The groan that rumbled in his chest was primal as he rocked his hips into her hold.

Every fiber of his being told him to claim her and mark her so that the world knew she was his. To have her mark him in much the same way.

"My star," he ground out, his eyes clenched closed.

Auraelia tightened her grip, twisting her hand slightly as she reached the tip. "I need you, Daemon. I need to feel you inside me. *Please.*"

His eyes shot open as she slowly guided him to her entrance. Rubbing the swollen head along her slit as her legs wrapped around his waist, her heels hooking into his ass in an attempt to pull him closer.

Rocking forward, Daemon slid his cock against her slick center, the head rubbing against her clit and causing her breath to hitch. "As much as I love it, you'll never have to beg me, my star." Daemon slid into her in one swift movement, bottoming out inside her with a groan. "Fuck, Princess."

Auraelia's nails raked down his back as he began to rock into her. The world slowed to a crawl around him. Every push and pull of his hips sent a wave of pleasure through his body, and it had nothing to do with sex and everything to do with *her*. With the way her eyes shone up at him with adoration and love. The way her lips parted as he slowly brought her to the edge of release.

The moment he pushed her hands above her head and locked their fingers together, her magic slipped her hold and began to spiral around their hands. It was warm, like a lover's caress against his skin, and his magic responded in kind, braiding around the ribbons of lightning until they were twisted into a singular rope.

He felt her, then.

The tumult of emotions that crashed through her and mimicked his own.

It was as if their souls were melding together.

Like the fact that she'd finally admitted her feelings broke down some invisible wall between them, giving him unfettered access to every part of her.

Auraelia's eyes were glassy as they met his, tears spilling over as she gazed up at him. "I—I *see* you. All of you." A small choked laugh escaped her lips, her eyes lighting up as she smiled.

Daemon pressed his lips to hers, tears mingling with the ones trailing down her face. "I've always seen you, my star. But now it's like a fog has lifted, and I can see more clearly."

Their kiss turned from soft and languid to hungry and demanding. Daemon released Auraelia's hands, and they instantly tangled in his hair, holding his mouth to hers. Their magic still hung in the air, wrapping around them in a mixture of light and dark, and every caress against his skin spurred him on.

His hips drove into hers, the sounds of their bodies filling the air. Auraelia's sweet moans slipped into his mouth.

Breaking their kiss, Daemon slung her legs over his shoulders and lifted her hips so that he could sink deeper and hit that spot that made her writhe.

"*Fuck, Daemon*," she keened, her eyes rolling to the back of her head.

"That's it, beautiful. You take my cock so well," he crooned as he increased his pace and began to rub his thumb in fervent circles on her clit. "Do you want to come, my star?"

Auraelia nodded, mumbling a string of *yeses* as her head bowed backward against the bed. Tingles began in the base of his spine, his balls heavy as his release loomed on the horizon.

"Who do you belong to, Auraelia?" Her eyes shot toward his, heat flaring in their depths as they latched onto him. "Say it, Princess. Tell me you're mine." Daemon continued his punishing pace as he waited for her to answer.

"You, Daemon. I belong to you. I'm yours," she said between pants, her eyes never straying from his.

Leaning forward, he sandwiched her legs between their sweat-slicked bodies, and Auraelia gasped as he sank even deeper. "Give me what's mine, Auraelia. Pull me over the edge with you."

As if his words were a command on her body, the walls of her pussy fluttered around him before clamping down. Her mouth opened in a silent scream, her head thrown back, and her eyes closed. The tingling in Daemon's spine intensified, his balls tightening as he continued to pump into her, prolonging her release as he dove head-first into his own.

His cock throbbed as he came inside her, his vision blackening with its intensity. Auraelia's pussy still pulsed around him as he slowly rocked his hips into hers, drawing out every drop of pleasure.

Only when her muscles relaxed did he ease out of her, a mixture of both their releases seeping out and trailing down her ass.

Daemon carefully unfolded Auraelia's legs. As he pulled her body against his own, she curved against him, her body nestling perfectly against his. Using his shadows, Daemon gently pulled the sheets over their bodies and pressed a kiss to her shoulder. "I love you, my star."

A contented sigh slipped through Auraelia's lips as she snuggled deeper into the covers and him, bringing his arm to run parallel to her chest. She clung to it and kissed the back of his hand. "And I love you."

As her breathing evened out, the air leaving her lips and tickling the hair on his arm, Daemon pulled her as close as he possibly could, then closed his eyes and let sleep wash over him.

Chapter Twenty-Two

Caius

The trip back to Garnet had taken longer than he had anticipated. The residual weight of the blood runes that Queen Auraelia had placed around that room was still a heavy blanket over him, slowly draining his strength until that connection had been severed.

He'd underestimated the new queen. Never thought for a moment that she would get entangled in blood magic. It didn't matter that drawing blood runes was the most basic of skills when learning the art. Her magic was *strong*, and he'd felt the weight of it settle upon his shoulders as soon as he'd manifested in that room.

His body ached. Between the draining effects of using his own magic, coupled with what Auraelia had done, and Davina's injuries' impact on his own body, he was exhausted.

The frigid air beyond the Onyx mountains kissed his cheeks as his feet finally touched down on familiar territory, and the sound of snow crunched beneath his boots as he walked the rest of the way toward the imposing structure of Bloodstone Castle.

Having been carved straight from the mountainside, its tall walls were pitch black—a stark contrast against the glistening white powder that settled upon its spires and coated the ground around it. Ground into the stone, however, were fragments of garnets. Their color was so rich and deep that they were barely noticeable until the sun's rays shone down and illuminated the gems, giving the illusion that blood dripped down the castle's walls.

Caius inhaled the crisp air deep into his lungs. Let it lift the last fragments of magic from Auraelia's runes from his skin and recharge the flurry of ice and snow that coursed through his veins, then let it carry him the rest of the way into the castle.

Sweltering heat slammed into him as soon as he stepped foot inside, beads of sweat instantly coating his brow.

Heads moved on a swivel around him, servants dipping into low bows before scurrying away to finish whatever task had been handed to them. It hadn't always been this way. The people in their court used to be happy, laugh, and smile. But that wasn't the case any longer. And he hated it.

Hated that they feared him just because of whom he was blood-bonded. Hated the fact that Davina had caused everyone in their court to turn against him, against *them*, in her tirade against her cousin. Torturing anyone who dared cross her.

It was madness.

Caius had just turned down the hall toward his room when a strangling grip squeezed around his heart, sucking the air from his lungs and causing his knees to buckle.

"*Davina,*" he ground out through clenched teeth. He staggered, letting the wall hold him up until his ability to breathe returned and his legs were stable once more. Once the effect had fully subsided, he pushed off and continued toward his room.

She could wait. He needed to change, needed to sleep so that he could regain the strength that she'd taken from him when she'd fallen at the hands of her cousin. He'd warned her not to attack Auraelia's sleepy little city, but once again, she didn't listen.

He got all of two steps down the hall when the sensation returned, stronger and more insistent than the previous. "Fuck," he groaned, clutching where his heart seemed to be trying to burst from his chest. Warm liquid trailed down his upper lip and he hastily swiped it away, his hand painted in the deep crimson that was his blood.

Pulling on his remaining strength, Caius let his magic bring him to the person he had once loved but had come to despise.

Davina was prone in her bed, her eyes heavy with exhaustion, and each of her arms wrapped in bandages from shoulder to fingertip. Snow packs had been settled along the bandages, dripping steadily onto the floor beneath her bed. He just looked at her for a moment, his heart squeezing in his chest for an entirely different reason now than it had mere moments ago.

She looked calm and almost like the girl he remembered from their youth. The one who had pleaded with him to bind their lives together so they would never have to be apart. Whose eyes shone with love and mirth every time she laughed or danced. Who used to sneak out of the castle at night to stand beneath the flurries as they danced through the air and gazed up at the stars with hope in her heart.

But then her eyelids fluttered open, and her crimson gaze landed on him—hard and unmoving—and he remembered exactly why he'd chosen to turn to Auraelia. Why he'd decided that the possibility of death was more bearable than a life standing at Davina's side.

The girl he once knew was gone.

Her heart had turned colder than the ice surrounding their home, and he was *done.*

"What do you want, Davina?" he asked, trying to keep the rage from his voice and the sneer from his lips.

Ice that didn't bow to his will seized his heart, filling his veins. "Is that any way to speak to the lady of this court? To the future queen of all of Ixora?"

"My apologies, *Your Majesty*," he ground out through the pain that sliced through him. It didn't matter how often she used her magic against him; it never got her the results she wanted, which only hurt him more in the long run.

Davina released her grip over his blood and fixed him with a hard glare. "Where have you been? I've been calling for you for hours. You know how I hate using my magic against you, Caius. Why do you make me do it?"

"I didn't realize I had any control over you, Davina."

"Don't be snide. Where were you?" Her voice was weak, like every word had been drug over hot coals, searing her vocal chords with the strain.

"I was checking the borders. After you attacked your cousin, I wanted to be sure that our people would be safe from retaliation."

Davina let out a strangled laugh that quickly shifted into a cough. "Don't be ridiculous, she's *weak*. She doesn't have it in her to attack another court."

Silence hung heavy in the air, prickling at the back of his neck as he waited anxiously for what would happen next, never knowing which way her mood would swing.

Surprise struck him when her eyes softened a fraction as she stared at him, the stormy gray that looked so similar to her cousin's seeping through the crimson. "Have you seen my mother?" she croaked.

He hadn't, but he also didn't need to.

Davina's mother was dying, and the moment she found out, Davina forced her mother into a blood bond in an attempt to save her life. But all that it had done was put her into a state of stasis. Unable to do anything on her own and prolonging a life that was supposed to have ended long ago. And if what their bond had done to him was in any way similar to what had been inflicted on her mother, there was no possibility in his mind that she was all right.

"I have. She's dying, Davina." The rage that he'd been so determined to keep locked down exploded from him like a geyser. "You're killing her—killing *me*!" he yelled, his lips pulling into a snarl as he took a few steps forward before thinking better of it. He couldn't get too close. Couldn't risk her figuring out where he'd actually been. "Two people you swore that you loved, that meant more to you than anything in this world, and you're killing us!"

Davina's eyes shot wide, their coloring a red so deep it was almost black, as she glared at him. Caius ripped his tunic from his body, revealing the proof of what he spoke. "*This* is what you're doing to us. We feel *everything* that you do. Every joy, every pain, *everything*. Remember?" He couldn't stop the anger that lit every word. He'd had it. He didn't want to do this anymore. *Couldn't* do this anymore.

"I didn't do that, *she* did!"

"You attacked her fucking city, Davina! Murdered innocent people, innocent *children*! What did you think she was going to do? Roll over and let you take it? You need to stop this petty vendetta over something that happened before either of you were born. It's not *her* fault that your grandfather chose her mother over yours."

"No."

"No?"

"I will not stop until she bows to me or is dead beneath my boot. She doesn't deserve to wear that crown."

"And you think that you do?" Caius scoffed, shaking his head in disbelief as he stared down at a wide-eyed Davina. He would regret having this altercation with her, of that he was sure. She didn't take kindly to anyone disagreeing with her, and they always paid for it dearly.

When Davina didn't say anything, he turned on his heel and stalked toward the door, speaking loud enough that his voice would carry without having to turn his head. "I don't know who you are anymore, Davina."

Chapter Twenty-Three

Auraelia

Sunlight filtered into the room, its rays a gentle caress on her face, pulling her from the first restful sleep she'd had in months. Auraelia smiled to herself as memories of the night before flitted through her mind.

Sex with Daemon had always been amazing, but what happened the previous night was beyond anything she'd ever experienced. It was as if her senses had been opened wide, and she saw the world in color for the first time. She felt every sensation, every emotion, that Daemon had as if it had been her own, which only heightened the experience.

It was intimate.

Overwhelming in all the best ways.

World-shattering clarity that she never imagined would be possible if it hadn't been for him.

Auraelia stretched, the smile on her lips spreading wide across her face, causing her cheeks to ache. There was a glorious, lingering tenderness between her thighs and a delicious warmth that seeped into her spine. As she relaxed, Daemon's strong arm wrapped around her waist and pulled her closer, his face nuzzling into the space between her shoulder blades.

"Good morning, my star," he mumbled as he trailed his lips along her spine and across her shoulders.

Auraelia hummed in response, then rotated around until she was facing him. "Good morning, my love."

Daemon let out a self-satisfied hum as he pressed his lips to hers. "Say it again."

Chuckling, Auraelia closed the small space he'd created between their lips, kissing him softly as she ran her fingers through the sleep-mussed hair that had fallen across his brow. "Daemon—"

At the sound of his name, Daemon groaned and buried his head in her cleavage, pulling her closer as he mumbled, "That's you're '*we need to talk*' voice, and it's far too early for that, Princess."

Hooking her leg over his hips, Auraelia pulled his head back so that he was forced to look at her. She stared into his eyes, taking in the rich swirls of mossy green and the bright golden bursts in their centers.

Goddess, I love this man.

She pressed a kiss to the tip of his nose. "That's because we *do need* to talk. I meant what I said last night; you need to go back to Kalmeera."

Daemon rolled away slightly, his head falling back against the pillows as he pulled his arm from around her torso and pinched the bridge of his nose. "Are you at least going to give me a *reason* for this asinine idea? I don't want to leave you. Not after everythi—"

Auraelia gently placed her finger over his lips, silencing his words in the process. "You're not *leaving me*, Daemon. But you need to make sure that your people are protected. Need to prepare them for what is coming."

Letting out a resigned sigh, Daemon gripped her waist and rotated until she was on top of him, her legs straddling his hips, her center settling directly over his hardening length. A ripple of desire swept through her, landing squarely between her thighs as she slowly rocked against him.

"*My star*," he growled through clenched teeth. "Don't start something that you don't intend on finishing."

Auraelia planted her palms on his chest and slowly rolled her hips. "I fully intend on *finishing*, my love. But not until after we talk."

Daemon's eyes slid closed, the muscle in his jaw ticking as he clenched his teeth together, his hold tightening as he slowly guided her along his length. "Talk fast."

"Go home to Kalmeera. Prepare your people however you can, and then come back to me."

The muscle in his jaw continued to jump as his teeth grated against each other—clearly at war with himself over what he knew was the right thing to do and what he *wanted* to do. Holding his gaze, Auraelia didn't bother trying to hide the sly smirk that tugged on one corner of her mouth as she slowly increased her pace, and the groan that rumbled up his chest was like music to her ears. She'd never tire of the effect she had on him. Of the way he always seemed to toe the line between restraint and wanting to bury himself so deep within her that they didn't know where one of them started and the other ended.

It may have been wrong to use that against him, but if it was the only way he would agree, she'd use every weapon in her arsenal.

"*Daemon*." His name sounded like a plea on her lips as she steadily rocked against him.

"Fuck, Princess. If I agree, will you stop torturing me and let me slip inside that slick cunt of yours?"

Auraelia leaned down far enough that her words were a whisper against his lips. "Only one way to find out."

"Fucking, hell. *Fine*. I'll go, but I *am* coming back."

His lips were soft and demanding beneath hers. Tugging his bottom one between her teeth, she slid her hand between their bodies and wrapped it around his cock. A thrill of excitement shot through her as it jumped against her palm, and she slowly positioned it at her entrance. "You better."

As soon as the last syllable left her lips, she slid down his length. He filled her so completely that all of the air in her lungs escaped in a rush.

Daemon's grip on her hips was near bruising, but she didn't care.

She wanted his marks.

Wanted to see the evidence of him on her skin after he left.

For every downward slide, Daemon thrust up into her, the sound of their bodies coming together mixed with the grunts and moans that fell from their lips. It was a symphony of lust and love, and she never wanted it to end.

Daemon's hand slid from her hip to where the steady pulse pounded between her thighs. The delicious friction from his relentless circles sped up the rate at which her orgasm would crash into her. But as soon as her walls began to flutter around him, he stopped, and she couldn't have suppressed the disgruntled sound that came out of her mouth if she'd tried. "Nooo, why'd you stop?"

Daemon thrust up into her once more, then held her hips down against his. "Your pleasure belongs to me, my star. And if you're sending me away, I plan to lead you to the edge of bliss and drag you back again as many times as I see fit."

Auraelia attempted to rock against him, searching for the friction that would bring her what she sought, but his grip was firm. Deciding on a different tactic, she slid a finger down his abs, watching as his muscles responded to her touch and savoring the quick intake of breath through his lips. "So, you're punishing me for asking you to take care of your people?" she asked, a singular brow hiking up to her hairline.

"You could say that." Daemon's thumb began swirling against her once more. "But you and I both know that you *like* my punishments. So be a good girl, and ride my cock."

When she didn't move, his brows furrowed, and his thumb stilled. "*Auraelia*."

The way he ground out her name made her skin pebble with anticipation, but the only movement on her body was her lips tilting up into a mischievous smile. "What are you going to do, Daemon?"

Fire flared in his eyes, and before she could even register what was happening, she was on her back, wrists pinned above her head with sparkling shadows, and Daemon's face a breath away from her own.

"Is that a challenge, Princess?" Daemon slammed into her, stealing the air from her lungs. When her response was nothing but a whimper, he did it again. "You're *mine*, Auraelia. Every bit of you. Every breath. Every beat of your heart. Every drop of pleasure. It all belongs to *me*."

Auraelia nodded emphatically as a scorching heat flared in her veins, his words igniting a fire in her soul and sending her magic into a frenzy. There was no denying it—not anymore.

"Say it, Auraelia."

"Yours, Daemon. I'm yours." Her words were stilted with every thrust of his hips, the ferocity with which he claimed her body, sliding her further down the bed. If this was the consequence for disobeying him...well, maybe there wasn't a point in *obeying* him.

Daemon's threats of edging were far from empty. He brought her to the precipice of ecstasy more times than she could count, and each time was more harsh than the last.

She was a writhing, whimpering mess by the time he promised to let her come. Only instead of him denying her, the loud knock on the door to the suite pulled her out of the moment.

"Shit," she exclaimed, wriggling beneath Daemon to try and free her wrists.

"Ignore them, Princess. They'll go away." Daemon pulled out and flipped her onto her stomach, pressing her top half into the mattress but keeping her hips raised.

The person outside her door knocked again, but it was quickly forgotten as his tongue sent waves of wicked bliss through her center. Eager for more, she pressed her hips back into his mouth, but as quickly as his tongue appeared, it vanished, leaving her exposed and unsated.

Auraelia whined, her pussy throbbing with the need for release. "Daemon, *plea—*"

The plea was left half-spoken as Daemon sunk into her, stealing her words and causing her eyes to roll back in her head. His pace was punishing. His fingers were relentless as they began circling her clit once more. But at the feel of his thumb pressing into the tight ring of her ass, her entire body went rigid.

Daemon slowed his pace. "Breathe, my star."

She took slow, calculated breaths, her muscles relaxing as he slowly eased his thumb into her. When he began picking up his pace again, it felt like she was burning alive.

Sweet flames of ecstasy consumed her in their blaze.

"Fuck, Princess. You're such a fucking good girl. Look how beautiful you are when you're so full of me."

Words were nonexistent in her brain. The world around her was nothing but a blur of shadows and stars. Every synapse firing and focusing on the pleasure that Daemon was pulling from her body. She was so close. Teetering on the edge with one leg extended over the cliff, ready to fall head first into the pleasure that Daemon had promised and always delivered. But just as she was about to fall, the faint sound of her door opening pierced through the veil of bliss, pulling her back from the cliff's edge.

"Rae?" Piper hollered from the sitting room of her suite, her footsteps closing in on the door to Auraelia's bedchamber.

"Goddessdamnit." Auraelia groaned into the mattress, trying once again to pull away.

Daemon's arm tightened around her waist. A wave of sparkling, velvet shadows slammed against her bedroom door as he growled, "I'm not finished with you, Princess. You're not leaving this room until you're screaming my name as you come all over my cock. Now come for me. Give me what's mine, and tell your Lady exactly what she's interrupting."

Daemon's pace picked up once more, his thumb and fingers matching the momentum he'd set, steadily working her back toward the cliff she was dying to fall over. Tingles cascaded through her extremities, and her walls began to flutter, but as soon as he pinched her clit between his fingers, she was done. Auraelia screamed his name as her hands dug into the sheets beneath her, stars exploding through her vision.

She hadn't even begun to recover when Daemon slipped his thumb from her and pulled her up so that she was leaning against his chest. Thrusting up into her as his fingers continued their relentless ministrations on her clit, sending her careening back over the cliff.

She'd never come so hard in her life. Wave after wave of pleasure crashed through her as Daemon followed her over, her name a muffled groan as he buried his head in her neck.

He rocked into her a few more times, peppering her shoulder and neck with kisses as they both came down from their high.

Auraelia reached behind her and wrapped her arm around his head, threading her fingers through his hair and pulling him forward as she turned to kiss him. Their lips were a breath away when Piper's voice rang out into the space.

"I can come back if you want. But Rae, Xander is asking for you."

"Goddess," Auraelia mumbled under her breath, pinching her eyes closed. "Give us a few minutes, Piper," she hollered back to her friend.

"Sure thing! I'll be over...uh... I'll see you there."

Auraelia listened to the sound of her friend's retreat, and as the door to the suite clicked closed, she couldn't help the laugh that tumbled out of her mouth.

"You both have some serious boundary issues, you know that, right?" Daemon asked as he rested his forehead on her shoulder.

"Hush, you. Come on, we need to get dressed."

Daemon groaned as he slipped out of her and fell onto his back, his arm slung over his eyes. Turning, Auraelia crawled over to him, her hair skimming his chest and causing his skin to pebble.

"I'm going to shower." She waited until he peeked out from under his arm. "If you're a good boy and get up, maybe I'll let you join me."

Fire blazed in his eyes, a mischievous smile tugging on his lips. "Trust me, Princess. I'm *up*, alright."

Auraelia squealed as Daemon reached for her, and she hurriedly skittered off the bed, heading for her bathing chamber.

She should have been focusing on so much—her brother's healing, her people rebuilding, the impending war with her cousin—but she wanted to stay in her blissful bubble with Daemon a little longer.

She had just turned the water on when Daemon's heavy steps filled the room, and his arms snaked around her waist. He twisted her around, his lips crashing into hers as he slowly backed her beneath the streams of water that had barely begun to warm.

"Have I been a good boy, Princess?"

Auraelia smirked against his lips and slid her hand down his body until she found what she sought. "There's nothing *'boy'* about you, my love." She tightened her grip and slowly worked his length.

"Damn right."

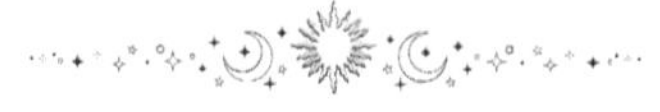

It had been another hour before they finally made it to Xander's rooms, but the immense relief she felt when she saw him walking around his sitting area—well, it was more *pacing* than walking—was a weight off her shoulders.

He was well and truly alright.

"Where the fuck have you been?" Xander barked once the door was closed behind them.

"They were...*preoccupied*, Xan." Piper chimed, her lips folding in on themselves as she attempted to stifle a laugh.

"What's that supposed to—" he cut himself off, a flush coloring his cheeks as his eyes flicked between his baby sister and the man who had been warming her bed. Groaning, Xander pinched the bridge of his nose. "You're lucky I don't hate you, Daemon. Or you'd be dead."

"Xander!" Auraelia admonished, but even she couldn't keep the smirk from her lips.

Daemon chuckled and crossed the room with his hand extended toward her brother. "I completely understand. I'd be the same way if my sister liked men."

Xander's gaze hardened slightly as he swept an appraising glance over Daemon, locking their hands together in a grip so tight that their knuckles began to whiten. The air in her lungs froze, and time seemed to still as the two most important men in her life stared each other down. Auraelia didn't *need her* brother's approval, but she wanted it, and *having* it meant more to her than she could express. So relief flooded her veins when his lips tilted into a friendly smile.

"Now that...whatever *that* was...is over, can we talk about what happened last night?" Piper asked from where she sat on one of the couches. She was completely at ease in Xander's space, sitting cross-legged on his couch with her boots left haphazardly on the floor in front of her. As Auraelia looked around the room, little pieces of her best friend stood out like red poppies poking their heads out of a blanket of snow.

It was nothing extreme, just little things that meant Piper spent more time in Xander's suite than she had previously known. Her favorite novel lay open on the small table by the windows next to a set of empty plates. Her cloak and gloves from the night before were draped over an armchair, and there were other little odds and ends scattered around the space leaving a slightly feminine mark on an otherwise masculine room. The sight warmed Auraelia's heart. They deserved each other. Deserved to be happy...she just wished they would get out of their own way and see what was standing right in front of them. Take the leap over the proverbial cliff and fall into the happiness that they both craved. Though having just decided to let *herself* go careening off the same cliff, she couldn't very well blame either of them for being cautious.

Drawing a deep breath, Auraelia took a seat and prepared to fully explain the previous night's events, but Daemon responded before she had the chance to.

"I thought *you* filled him in last night?" The joking lilt to his voice had her head canting to the side, her gaze flicking between her friend and the man perched beside her. When Piper's cheeks flushed slightly, Auraelia widened her eyes at Daemon, but he merely raised his brows and shrugged in response, a sly smirk making its home on his lips.

What the hell did I miss?

Before she could ask the question aloud, Piper answered Daemon's. "I intended to. But—"

"I was asleep," Xander supplied, filling in the remainder of Piper's sentence as they shared a look.

Clearly not buying anything either of them said, Daemon quirked a singular brow, crossing his arms over his chest as he took them in. "You were *asleep*?"

An awkward silence blanketed the room as Auraelia's gaze traveled from one person to the next. She was obviously out of the loop on *something*, but now was not the time to dig into whatever secrets her friend and her brother were trying—and failing—to hide.

"Whatever this," she gestured between her three companions, "is, can wait. We need to figure out what our next steps are."

Piper and Xander visibly relaxed and released a synchronized sigh.

Sinking into one of the chairs that made up the small sitting area, Xander rested his elbows on his knees and steepled his fingers in front of his face, his gaze intent on Auraelia.

The room was silent as she explained what happened at the meeting, and she watched her brother's every reaction to the words she spoke. His lips were set into a thin line, brows drawn so closely together that it seemed they would merge into one if he held them there for any longer. He was her brother, but he was also her advisor. The one who was meant to keep her and her council on the same page. The one who was meant to be level-headed and keep her from making rash decisions. But when she got to the point of no return when she explained that Lord Harland was the one who was supplying the information to their cousin—their enemy—Xander's face flamed in rage, and a wave of his magic pulsed against her skin.

"I'll kill him," Xander growled through clenched teeth, shooting up from his chair and aiming for the door. He managed all of two steps before he collided with a wall of shadow.

"Your sister said the same," Daemon said with an air of ease, his body completely relaxed against the back of the couch next to her. "I talked her out of it. You're welcome."

Xander's gaze hardened on Daemon, his hands balling into fists at his side so tightly she was sure that blood would be dripping onto the floor at any moment. Standing, Auraelia moved between the two men, forcing her brother's attention back to her. "Xander—"

"Rae, he *betrayed* you. He betrayed our court!" The anger in his eyes was sharper than any sword in their armory, but she would rather it be aimed at her than anyone else at the moment.

"I know, but please sit down. We have a plan; just hear us out."

"*We*?" Xander asked incredulously.

"Yes, *we*. Look, Xander. I get it; I do. Daemon had to keep me from murdering him last night because I felt every drop of rage that you feel now. I just need you to hear us...hear *me*...out. And if you still want to murder him?" She shrugged and waved her arm toward the door. "I won't stop you."

She felt Daemon's surprise at her words drifting across her back like a summer breeze. Something extraordinary was happening between them, something she couldn't quite explain. It was more than being attuned to another person. It seemed to be changing the very fabric of her being. Like their souls were two pieces of an unfinished tapestry that was finally being stitched together. Pulling and tugging until the ends met in perfect unison to create a beautiful piece of art.

She pushed the sensation to the back of her mind and focused on her brother.

Xander's eyes narrowed as they bore into her own, but he blew out a short breath, returned to his seat, and gestured for her to continue. "I'm listening."

"We're going to continue on as normal."

"Wha—"

"Let me finish. We're going to act normally. We're not going to let him know that we know what he's done, what he's *doing*."

"You're going to feed him information that you want to get back to Davina. Let him think that he's ahead of you." Daemon supplied as he leaned forward, resting his arms on his thighs.

"Then we're going to let him fall flat on his face." Auraelia let a sinister smile pull at her lips. "And if *she* doesn't take care of him, then we will. He doesn't know that Caius is helping us, and he thinks that we don't know that he is helping Davina. We need to keep it that way."

"So, let me get this straight. We're going to let that snake *stay in* the court?"

"Yes." Auraelia and Daemon said in unison.

"And we're going to feed him false information while trying to organize the army and plan for her attack *without* him catching wind of the actual plan?"

"Exactly."

"Yeah, this can't backfire at all." Xander's head fell back against the worn leather, his eyes pinched closed with obvious frustration.

Taking the seat next to Daemon, Auraelia laced their fingers together. "You're not wrong. It definitely could. But right now, we have somewhat of an upper hand. If we kill him outright, Davina will know that we know, and she may move up her timeline."

"We don't know her timeline as it is, Rae."

"That's not *entirely* true," Daemon said as he gave her hand a reassuring squeeze.

"Come again?"

Auraelia turned toward Daemon and nodded, letting him take the lead since he knew more about moon phases than she did.

"Caius informed us that Davina would be at her strongest during the new moon. That's approximately fourteen days from now, which means we have just around two weeks until she is likely to attack."

"*Two weeks*?!"

"That's the impression that we're under, yes."

Xander scrubbed his hands down his face and groaned. "Okay, so what's the plan then?"

"Well," Auraelia began. "The immediate plan is for Daemon to go back to Kalmeera and prepare his people for what's to come. We don't have much time, so we need to act fast. I was hoping you could show him some wards he could place around the islands."

"I can, but I want to go with him."

"Xander—"

"Rae, let me do this. Not as my sister, but as my Queen. Daemon and his people are important to you, right?"

"Of course, but—"

"Then let me help. I want to be there to make sure they're done properly...no offense." The latter was directed at Daemon, who shrugged in return.

"What if I need you *here*?" A tinge of panic laced her words. Her taking risks or putting herself in imminent danger for the ones she loved was one thing. Letting someone she loved do the same was something else entirely. He'd only *just* begun to heal. She'd only just gotten her brother back from the brink of death. What if something happened? What if Davina attacked the Isles while he was there? *What if...what if...* round and round the thoughts spun, adding unwanted confusion to an already restless situation.

"Auraelia." The way Xander said her name, soft and full of understanding, pulled her from the tumult. She hadn't even realized he'd moved to sit on the table in front of her, his knees bumping against her own. "You don't need me here. You're one of the smartest people I know and have enough magic to protect our people. Piper will be able to see any threats, and I'll place wards around the city before we leave...which is when exactly?" His question was directed at Daemon, but Xander's eyes stayed locked on hers.

"I had planned to leave this evening."

Xander redirected his focus to Daemon, and Auraelia met Piper's wary gaze from over her brother's shoulder—she seemed just as apprehensive of this plan as Auraelia was.

"So it's set then." The finality in Xander's voice pulled her back to the conversation at hand.

"What's set?" she asked.

"Daemon and I will be leaving tomorrow for Kalmeera. After lunch, you and I will head out to place wards around the boundary lines. We'll start at the harbor and work our way out in opposite directions. Once they're all placed, we'll meet back at the harbor and place the final rune in the center of the city."

"Then what?"

"Then, dear sister, *you're* going to seal them. With me leaving, they would hold better if you did them. Not to mention that your magic packs more punch than mine."

Auraelia's face blanched and she clenched her fist around the cut on her palm that still throbbed. The thought of drawing more blood for *more* runes made her head spin.

Seeming to sense where her thoughts were headed, Xander let out a light chuckle. "No more blood runes, Rae. Promise...well...kind of." When she quirked a questioning brow, he walked across the room to grab a roll of parchment and a satchel from one of his shelves.

With practiced fingers, he unrolled the map of Lyndaria, spreading it out on the table between them. Magic swept across her skin as Xander extended a shield around them and began. "We need to construct and bury runes at all of the compass points out of emerald shards." As he spoke, he pulled emeralds the size of robin's eggs from the leather pouch and placed them to the north, south, east, and west of the Court of Emerald.

"Then, at the halfway points between, we will bury a singular emerald." He added, placing pebble-sized stones on the corresponding map markers. "Once all of them are in position, we will convene in the center of the city and place a final emerald marker here." He placed another stone in the city's center, then leaned away from the map and waited until Auraelia met his gaze. His eyes bore into hers with sharp intensity, like if he stared hard enough he could force her to understand the gravity of his next words. "From there, you'll need to funnel your magic into the stones. It will branch out to all the other points and connect them like a giant shield. But Rae, it's going to take a lot of power to create a shield that large. I'm not sure how deep your well of magic is; I'm not even sure if you are yet. So, I need you to promise me that you will stop if you feel yourself draining or even remotely close to the end of your abilities. We can find another way."

Auraelia's mouth popped open, her mind reeling as it attempted to process through what she'd just heard. Xander was right. She had no idea how deep the well of her power stretched. Hadn't had the chance to find out, even with Ser Aeron making her dig deeper into the seemingly endless chasm that held her magic every time they trained. But this? This was different.

This was a potentially deadly unknown that rocked her to her core. But it was also the only way she *knew* would protect her people from any more attacks. And if that meant draining her magic down to its last dregs, meant weakening herself and putting herself in danger for the safety of her people, then that's what she would do.

"Xander—"

"Rae, promise me. I won't show you the runes unless you do. That's my line in the sand. I know you want to protect our people, but it's my job to protect *you.* Even if it's from yourself."

Auraelia let out a resigned sigh, her eyes falling back to the stones on the map. Letting them wander over how the inky lines within them seemed to swirl and move through the gems like rivers, dividing them into segments. Each of them is home to both light and dark as if they needed to embody the chaos of the world around them.

"I promise." The lie was sour on her tongue, and the look on Daemon's face, as her gaze drifted to his, said that he knew. Knew that she would say whatever her brother needed to hear, regardless of the consequences. Understanding shone in his eyes, but behind it was sadness. It sat on her heart like a boulder, growing heavier with every second that she held his gaze. She knew he wouldn't try to change her mind, but a small part of her still wished that he would.

Over the next hour, Xander sketched out the runes they would need to make and the order in which to place the shards. It was simple enough, made mostly of straight lines that connected together at a series of points to create sharp angles.

When Xander was confident that Auraelia understood what to do—and the correct order to do everything in—they left the secure space of his suite to gather the necessary materials.

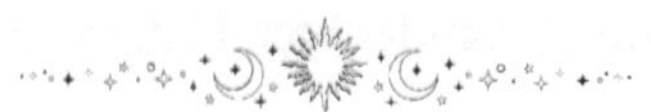

The treasury was located across the castle in the Queen's wing and heavily guarded, not by physical guards but by ancient magic that was more powerful than what protected the archives. But what stopped Auraelia in her tracks was the door leading inside. It was a massive expanse of oak and gold artistry.

The wood was stained a deep brown, and the ornamental gold swirls that decorated the door accented the natural swirls in the wood. It was the most ornate entrance in the castle, and no one other than a privileged few ever got to see it.

Pressing her finger to the sharpened point of an emerald shard that protruded above the knob like the needle of a spinning wheel, Auraelia let the blood pool and drip onto the runes that were carved into the floor in front of the massive oak and gold door. The magic that sealed the entrance vibrated against her skin as the drops of crimson trickled into the delicate carvings, spreading out between the stones and staining the runes. The air seemed to still around her as she waited...and waited. It was as if the wards were scrutinizing her. Judging her worthiness of entering despite the fact that she was the only one capable of opening the door.

Seconds felt like minutes.

Minutes like hours.

But when the runes flared a brilliant blue, its edges tipped in a bright shade of green, the gears and mechanisms that held the lock in place began to creak. The sound of metal grinding together after years of misuse filled the silent corridor.

"Fuck, it's about time." Xander breathed, the tone filled with relief.

Nodding, Auraelia waited until the sound of groaning metal ceased, then stepped forward and pushed the doors open.

Sconces flared to life, cerulean flames dancing along the walls and illuminating the scene in front of her. It was unlike anything she'd ever seen. Rows upon rows of floor-to-ceiling shelves covered in emeralds of every shape, size, and color lined the center of the room and seemed to stretch further than the castle itself. There were satchels—presumably filled with gold or silver—piled in the corners, and rolls of parchment shoved haphazardly into open spaces, their edges pristine with none of the telltale signs of age.

Magic.

There was no other explanation for it. That room had been constructed from pure magic, and it slammed into her like a battering ram as soon as she stepped foot across the threshold.

Ancient power buzzed along her skin, and her magic responded in kind. Purring against the caress as it turned languid in her veins like it was saying hello to an old friend. Auraelia looked down at her hands—fully expecting to see them glowing with the amount of power that was suddenly rushing through her—only to find her stained fingers shimmering in the flame's glow.

The sound of a sharp intake of breath from behind her pulled her focus, and as she turned toward the sound, she saw Daemon—eyes wide as he stared at his own hands, turning them back and forth like he would find something new marking his skin.

When he finally met her gaze, his eyes were wide with awe and shining like twin suns in a crystal clear sky. They were stunning, and she could have melted in the heat of his gaze...if it hadn't been for the sound of a cough coming from the entryway.

"I hate to interrupt. But, Rae, we can't get in." Xander called from the doorway.

Shifting her focus, she met her brother's questioning gaze with one of her own. "What do you mean you can't get in?"

Rolling his eyes, Xander attempted to step over the runes and through the opening. But instead of landing on the opposite side, his foot collided with a wall of golden light, one that flared brightly at the contact, then dimmed back into nothing as he pulled his foot away.

An eerily familiar warmth washed over Auraelia as a honeyed voice slipped into her mind. "*Only those destined as rulers of this kingdom are welcomed into these chambers.*"

The voice may have faded, but the words lingered. It made sense why *she* had been allowed entrance...but Daemon? Her gaze slid to where he stood to the right of the door, his eyes just as wide as hers felt. Had he heard it, too?

"He did, young queen. Though I speak directly to you now."

"Who are you?" she muttered to herself, her eyes flying around the room looking for the voice inside her head.

"I am the soul of Emerald. I am the heart of her people. I am you.*"*

Auraelia shook her head. She hated riddles, and that one made about as much sense as hugging a rabid animal.

A soft chuckle reverberated in her skull. *"Think with your heart, Auraelia.* Listen *to my voice. In your heart of hearts, you know who I am. You know my voice as well as you know your own."*

"Auraelia? Is everything alright?" Daemon asked, his brows furrowed as he took hesitant steps toward her.

Closing her eyes, Auraelia breathed deeply.

I am the soul of Emerald.

I am the heart of her people.

I am you.

Me?

Clarity blossomed as countless dreams flooded her mind. Ones from years ago, from *lifetimes* ago, unfurled in her mind one right after the other.

It couldn't be.

"And yet, it is. Hello, Auraelia. It's nice to finally meet you."

Chapter Twenty-Four

Auraelia

"Auraelia! Wait up!" Daemon yelled from behind her.

After her—albeit brief—conversation with the *dead* first queen of the Court of Emerald, Auraelia gathered the stones needed for their runes and left the treasury faster than she imagined possible. As she skirted past them in the hall, she hadn't said anything to anyone. She hadn't even bothered to make sure the treasury doors were closed as she attempted to run from the sound of Astraea's voice, their soundless conversation ringing in her mind like a bell's peal.

Why was Daemon allowed entrance?

"You know the answer to that question, young queen. You simply refuse to acknowledge it. Even after everything you've realized, everything you've let yourself accept, and everything you've begun to feel, *you still deny the obvious in front of you."*

And what is that?

"That you and the young prince are destined for one another, just as his ancestor and I were. But as I said, you knew that already. Stop running from it, Auraelia. Let fate guide you, and let his love catch you. Your souls

are bonded together, and the more you accept it, the sooner *you accept it...the stronger you* both *will become. Don't squander this. I am you, but you don't need to be me."*

So lost in her thoughts, she hadn't realized that she had reached the stables—or that Daemon had shadow-walked in front of her until she ran into his broad chest. His hands settled on the sides of her face as she peered up at him, his eyes swirling with worry and concern.

"What happened in that room, Auraelia?"

As she opened her mouth to respond, Xander and Piper reached the stables. "Damn, Rae. Where's the fire?" Xander asked from behind Daemon.

Auraelia cupped Daemon's cheek like he held hers, releasing a heavy breath, whispering loud enough for only his ears. "Later, my love. I'll tell you everything later." His brows furrowed as his eyes roamed over her features, but after a few moments, he nodded in acquiescence and pressed his brow to hers.

"Promise?"

"With all of my heart."

After pressing a brief kiss to his lips, Auraelia pulled from Daemon's embrace and faced her brother. "Let's get this over with, shall we?"

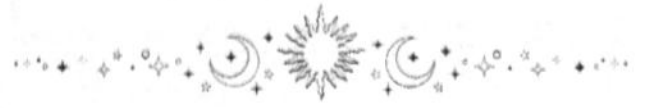

The air was crisp, the wind chilling, as they stood in the low tide at the center of Lyndaria's harbor. Winter had fully and unnaturally settled into Emerald. Frost crept along the edge of windows and blanketed the ever-moist ropes along the piers. The normally crystal clear skies were shrouded in depressing gray clouds, promising colder weather to come.

It was an omen. One that Auraelia felt deep within her bones. Like the weather itself was trying to warn her of what was looming on the horizon.

"Ready?" Xander asked as he brushed the sand from his palms.

Nodding, Auraelia held out one of the brown leather satchels that she'd filled with emerald stones and shards. Taking the bag from her hand, Xander carefully laid the first rune in the hole he'd just finished digging. When he finished and the mark was buried, he stood and held out a slip of parchment with the rune sketched on its surface. "Be safe, but be precise, Rae. One stone out of place, and this won't work."

"The same goes for you both, as well. We'll meet you back here and head into the city's center together." Xander and Piper nodded in unison, then wrapped her in a tight embrace before heading off to where their horses waited.

As she watched her brother and best friend ride off toward their first point, Daemon stepped up to her side and linked his fingers with hers, silently letting her know that he was ready whenever she was—and not just to place runes around her kingdom.

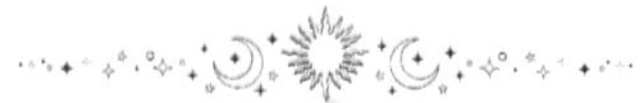

By the time Auraelia and Daemon reached their first mark, tension clung to the air like static. Silence reigned between them as she struggled to find the words that would accurately explain the thoughts warring in her head.

By the second mark, the one where she would have to construct the rune's shape in shards, it was so thick it felt like she'd been draped in a heavy, wet blanket.

And still, Daemon never pressed. Never pushed or prodded for information or let her ever-present silence get to him. He just let her...*be.* Let her find her own way, patiently waiting for the moment she would be willing to let him in.

Daemon dismounted first, unstrapping the shovel from where it had been secured on the saddle bag and tossing it to the ground before offering his hand to assist Auraelia from Jasira.

She'd never tire of the feel of his hands on her waist or the gentle way he let her slide down his body until her feet were firmly planted on the ground, setting every point of contact ablaze. He held her like he was afraid she would slip through his fingers.

After tucking a strand of wind-blown hair behind her ear and pressing a kiss to her lips, Daemon asked, "You ready?"

Auraelia nodded, pushing up on her toes to capture his lips once more before turning out of his grasp and heading toward the edge of the Amber Woods.

She knew these woods like the back of her hand. Had traveled through them countless times and knew which direction would inevitably lead her to Nefeli Lake. But there was a quiet stillness to them that set the hair on the back of her neck on end. Even in the dead of winter, birds still perched on the naked branches and sang their songs. Small animals still scurried along the blanket of leaves on the ground, rustling them beneath their tiny paws. But this? This kind of quiet warned of danger and had Auraelia scanning her surroundings. Looking for anything out of place. Releasing the hold on her magic, she let it spool down to her fingers, heat blossoming at the tips where her lightning settled beneath the surface.

"What is it?" Daemon asked when they stopped in a small clearing between the trees.

"I'm not sure. It just feels...like someone is watching us."

Daemon dropped the shovel, his eyes widening as the gold of his irises expanded until it engulfed the mossy green. Shadows spilled from his hands, reaching beyond the trunks and slithering like snakes along their roots as if they were searching for whatever lurked beyond what their eyes could see.

Pulling in a deep breath, Auraelia pushed the air into a sphere around them, guarding them from all sides. "I don't like this," she muttered beneath her breath.

"Nor do I." Tension radiated off of Daemon in waves as he reached down for the discarded shovel, his eyes swiveling around the forest as his shadows continued to snake between the trees. "We need to get this done and move on."

Nodding once in agreement, Auraelia kept her eyes on the trees as Daemon began to dig.

There has to be a better way, she thought as the blade of the shovel pierced the cold, hardened ground. Dipping into her magic, she searched for that part of her she hadn't yet explored. The one that connected her to the ground beneath her feet and caused it to shake, wondering if she could tug that thread and manipulate it into pulling the earth forward instead of pushing energy out.

Auraelia visualized her magic, threads winding deep within her, diving into the depths of who she was. Saw the vibrant golden glow of her lightning, the wispy blue that represented her connection to the air, and the smokey gray of the storm, all woven together in a tight braid. But as she began to pull them apart, a delicate line the color of the richest earth was nestled in the center; its presence was barely noticeable amongst the effervescent threads surrounding it. Mentally wrapping it around her fingers, Auraelia gently gave it a tug.

At first, nothing seemed to happen, the ground remaining stagnant below her feet. But after another pull, a slow, steady rumble coursed through the ground, settling within the shallow hole that Daemon had made.

"What the—" Daemon muttered, his words cut short as he staggered back a step.

Auraelia dug her magic into the ground, severing its connection with the surrounding earth and forming it into a solid mass in her mind. But just as she was about to lift it from the hole, Daemon stiffened at her side.

"Auraelia." Her name was a ground-out warning, Daemon's shadows thickening at his fingers before pooling around his feet. "We have company."

She heard it then. The crunch of dried leaves and the snap of a branch underfoot.

Auraelia released her grip on the earth, her head swinging to her right as someone stepped between the trees. Dressed in deep browns, making it easy for them to blend into their surroundings, they slowly made their way to the edge of the clearing, their cloak shrouding any distinguishing features.

"A little far from the safety of your castle, aren't you, false queen?" The tone was distinctly male—deep and full of arrogance.

"I'd watch what you say if I were you," Daemon said with a chuckle, his magic pulsing through the air, clearly amused with the audacity the man exuded.

"And whom do I have the pleasure of receiving insults from?" Auraelia asked, her head canting to the side with annoyance.

The stranger tossed back their hood to reveal a mop of auburn hair, sun-kissed skin, and eyes the color of cinnamon that matched the freckles peppered over their face. When those eyes met Auraelia's, he smiled, and the malice behind it sent a chill down her spine.

"I'm simply a messenger." He shrugged, pushing off the tree to take a step toward them.

"And what is the message you need to deliver, *mister...?*" Auraelia hedged, keeping her arms loose at her sides as he continued to take cautious steps forward. There was a good twenty yards between them, but that didn't mean he needed to be any closer to inflict damage. Magic? No magic? Assassin? She knew nothing of this man. Knew nothing of his intentions.

His head shifted from side to side like he was contemplating the answer he wanted to give before finally settling on one. "My name is of no consequence."

"And your message? Is that also of no consequence?" Daemon asked, mirth filling his words. His tone might have been placid, but Auraelia could tell how on edge he was. She could *feel* his worry and agitation as they mingled with her own.

The man tsked. "My message is this. The Court of Pearl stands firmly behind the rightful queen of this realm, Lady Davina of the Court of Garnet."

"If that's what you came all this way to say, then I'm sorry you wasted your time. We were already aware of where Lady Levena and Lord Kaemon stood. So if that's all—"

His laugh cut Auraelia off, echoing through the silence and ricocheting off of the trees. "Oh, *Your Majesty*," he spat her title like it tasted bitter on his tongue. "That's not the only message we have for you."

"We?"

The world seemed to have slowed to a crawl as cloaked figure after cloaked figure stepped beyond the tree line, dressed like the man in front of her. "You see, the message was this. Infiltrate the castle and take your life to head off the unnecessary bloodshed. We really must thank you for making this easier on us."

Auraelia's eyes rotated between each assailant, taking a quick assessment of any potential weaknesses as Ser Aeron had taught her. Mentally marking who would be easiest to subdue and who would live to see the sunset. She and Daemon were outnumbered six to two, but like hell would she let someone else do Davina's dirty work.

A small smile ticked up one side of her lips as she watched a blade slip from the original man's sleeve and into his awaiting hand before he hurled it toward her. Her heart pounded in her ears as adrenaline pumped through her veins, sending jolts of energy down her spine as her brain settled into the calm that came from years of honing her combat skills. Thunder boomed through the sky as her magic responded to the threats, making her anger palpable as heavy winds knocked the knife to the ground. Drawing her dagger from her thigh, Auraelia glanced toward Daemon as he unsheathed his sword, a vicious smile on his face.

In the next heartbeat, they moved, meeting the advancing assailants head-on.

Metal clanged against metal as Daemon parried one of the assassins. Bone crunched beneath Auraelia's fist as she uppercut into one of their noses, followed by a bellow of pain as her blade slashed across their belly.

As she spun to engage in another attack, a blade sliced across her shoulder, blood trickling down her arm and staining her tunic crimson. Before she could get her bearings, a broad man grabbed her from behind, pulling her arms behind her back until she was sure her shoulders would dislocate, and pressed a blade to her throat.

"I'm going to enjoy this," he whispered against her ear as the blade sliced into the delicate skin of her throat.

Pain coursed through her, but the cry that left her lips was one of pure rage. Diving into her well of power, Auraelia let her lightning wrap around her. Let it sear through fabric, skin, and sinew. Let it burn until the man's arms fell away, and he collapsed into a charred heap on the ground.

Breathing heavily, Auraelia whirled around and picked up her dagger, channeling her lightning through the emeralds as she launched it at a man across the clearing who was charging at Daemon's back. Relief flooded her system as her dagger struck true, the man collapsing to the ground as Daemon turned toward him. His eyes met hers for a brief second before he shifted his attention back toward the remaining assailant.

Daemon had cut down two men while she'd handled her own, but as he raised his blade to the final one, she hurled a gust of wind toward him and knocked it from his hand. "Not that one."

Bruised and coated in blood, Auraelia began to cross the clearing. "I am *sick* of people coming after me, and what's *mine.*" Auraelia seethed as she stalked toward the man, her lightning a living thing as it twined around her, crackling along her skin. "*I* am the rightful Queen of this realm, and I have a message of my own."

The last man standing was the original messenger, the one who'd promised to deliver her death to Davina. His eyes blew wide as a bolt of lightning landed right in front of his foot, and Auraelia smiled as he attempted to back away, only to slam into a wall of Daemon's shadows.

Her steps were slow—calculated—as she closed the distance between herself and the supposed assassin. When she reached him, she leaned into his space. Sweat beaded on his brow, and she wasn't sure if it was fear, or that she was close enough that he could feel the heat radiating from her magic. It turned out to be the former, his swallow audible as the smell of ammonia filled her nostrils, and the once swaggering male turned into a whimpering mess.

The laugh that bubbled up Auraelia's throat was anything but kind as she met his gaze. As she leashed some of her own magic, Daemon's snaked up the man's legs and down his arms, binding him to the mass of shadows at his back.

"I want you to give your mistress a message. Can you do that?" Her tone was sickly sweet even to her own ears, but she was done. Tired of always looking over her shoulder. Tired of playing nice when everyone around her fought dirty. The time for fighting fair was over, and it was time to send a message of her own, even if it stained her soul.

When the man nodded, she continued. "Tell your Lord and Lady you were unsuccessful in delivering your whole message. That the next time they decide to send me a message, I will *gladly* accept it from them in person." She laid her hand flat against his sternum. "Tell them to let Davina know that her cousin is done playing these games." Heat began to swell in her palm, a gentle glow emanating around the whole of her hand. "And tell them, *all* of them, that anyone who tries to take or harm what is *mine* will meet an immediate end."

Auraelia released the hold on her magic and let it flow out of her hand, burning through the fabric covering the man's chest and down to his skin, his screams filling the silence of the forest.

Daemon released the shadow binds as Auraelia pulled away, and the man collapsed to the ground. She slowly knelt next to him. "Tell Davina I'm ready. That her fear tactics do not work here. She can send as many assassins as she wants; I will not run. I will not bow. If she wants my crown and my kingdom, she will have to pry it from my cold, dead hands. Tell her I will see her on the battlefield, and my rage will be the last thing her eyes see of this world. After all, only one of us will be walking off that field, and I fully intend on it being *me*. Do you think you can do that?"

Tears ran down his face as he met her gaze and nodded.

"Good." Auraelia stood as the man fell unconscious and turned on her heel, meeting Daemon's knowing stare. A wave of emotions washed through her as she held it, both hers and his.

He closed the distance between them in one stride and cupped her cheeks. "Are you alright?" he asked, his eyes scanning from top to toe. When they landed on the harsh red line across her neck and blood stain on her shoulder, his nostrils flared, his gaze snapping to the last remaining assailant before flicking back to her.

"I will be." It was the only honest answer she could give. As the adrenaline wore off, her mind began to race. The one thing she never wanted was to be like her cousin...and now? The sound of her dagger sinking into the man's spine would echo through her mind for days, but the sound of their screams as she cut down each man would haunt her nightmares.

"Hey," Daemon's soothing voice cut through the impending storm in her mind, his thumb stroking gently across her cheek. "None of that, alright? You did what you had to, and she needs to know that you're not going to take her actions lying down." Auraelia nodded as Daemon pressed a kiss to her brow, his body still riddled with tension. "What do you want to do about that?" he asked, flicking his head toward the unconscious man behind her.

"How far can you shadow-walk?"

A cocky smile pulled across Daemon's face, and she couldn't help but smile in return. "I can get him to the other side of the Amber Woods. He can walk the rest of the way to Pearl."

It wasn't surprising that Xander and Piper beat them back to the harbor, and a breath of relief escaped when Auraelia saw that they were no worse for wear. The same could not be said when Xander's gaze landed on her.

"Goddess, Rae! What the fuck happened to you?!" Xander's eyes moved rapidly over her, assessing every blood stain with questioning eyes before whirling to glare at Piper. "You didn't *see* this?"

Piper narrowed her gaze at Xander, sucking on a canine before snapping back, "Of course, I fucking saw it. But Daemon was with her, and I also saw her handle it. If I thought for one second that my best friend, our *queen*, was in danger, don't you think that I would have told you? Goddess, Xander, have a little fucking faith."

"Don't blame Piper," Auraelia snapped at her brother. "You wouldn't have been able to reach us in time to help anyway, and it's not even all mine, Xander," she said as she dismounted Jasira.

"*None* of it should be yours. What the hell happened?"

"We were ambushed in the Amber Woods. The Court of Pearl says *hello*." Daemon replied, his voice dripping with sarcasm.

"Goddess help us." Xander groaned, scrubbing his hands down his face before raking them through his hair. "Are you sure you're alright?" His tone was calmer than it had been moments ago, the panic bleeding away to be replaced with concern.

"I'll be fine."

Silence lingered for a heartbeat before he squared his shoulders and gave Auraelia a curt nod. "Alright, we've got one more of these fuckers to do, and then we can go home. Ready?"

Expelling a heavy breath, Auraelia nodded and followed her brother into town.

Devastation clung to every corner of the city, hitting her with a force strong enough to knock her off her feet. As they walked through the streets, Auraelia scanned her surroundings. Lifeless bodies lined the roads, draped in the traditional black cloth of death. The once gorgeous stone homes had been reduced to piles of rubble, and the wisteria burned down to nothing but twigs and charred wood.

She still couldn't believe that this had happened to her people.

As her emotions began to swell to an overwhelming magnitude, Daemon laced his fingers with hers. His strength swam through her veins, calming the storm that raged inside her.

When they reached the center of the city, Xander stared at what had once been a larger-than-life rendition of their Goddess Rhayne but had now been reduced to a pile of stone.

"This may be harder than I anticipated. It's going to take forever to move all of this," Xander said on an exhale.

"Maybe not." Auraelia slipped her hand from Daemon's and dove into her well of power, pulling on that rich brown thread that spooled down into her soul. Let the feel of the earth fill her veins and pull on the ground beneath the rubble.

As the ground began to quiver beneath their feet, Piper staggered, clinging to Xander's arm in an attempt to regain her balance. Then, she quickly righted herself, her face pinched in annoyance. Slowly, the debris fell away, and the soil beneath surfaced, leaving behind a hole large enough to bury the final rune.

"Well, that's new," Xander breathed, his eyes wide as he stared at the upturned ground.

Daemon's pride swelled in her own chest, cool and velvety just like his shadows, and she took a moment to glance his way. The sensation was mirrored in his eyes as he beamed down at her, but it was quickly replaced by something else. Something warm and welcoming that felt like home.

She lost herself in his gaze and the immense outpouring of love that she felt for and from him. Let it ground her as Xander worked to get the last of the runes into place.

"Ready?" Her brother's voice sliced through her, bringing her back to the situation at hand.

Daemon gave her hand a reassuring squeeze, then released her.

Kneeling at the bottom of the rune, Auraelia went to place her hand in the center like she had for every other one but stopped when Xander placed his hand on her shoulder.

"Remember when I said no more blood runes?"

Expelling an exasperated breath, Auraelia hung her head. "You said, 'I promise...kind of.' Is this the 'kind of' part of that statement?"

"It is. Sealing these with your blood will strengthen them. Reinforce them."

Sitting back on her heels, Auraelia turned her face toward the sky, soaking in the peachy tones as the sun made its way to the horizon. She should have known there was a catch. Should have known that more blood would need to be spilled to keep her people safe. But she hadn't realized how much of it would be her own.

Auraelia pulled her dagger from its sheath on her thigh, the emerald blade glowing beneath the sun's rays, her magic humming beneath her skin in recognition. A hiss slipped between her teeth as she dragged the edge across her palm, and she felt a sharp pang of panic in her chest before it quickly disappeared.

Placing her palm down on the rune, Auraelia closed her eyes and let herself sink into her power. Let it spill over like a waterfall, crashing through her blood and into the stones. Blinding light flared beneath her palm and shot out in every direction, a direct line to the runes buried along the lines of her kingdom.

It was working.

"That should be good, Rae," Xander said from behind her, his voice taking on a panicked edge. When she didn't stop, he reached for her shoulder. "Auraelia, stop. You're giving too much."

More. She needed to give more.

Needed to ensure that her people would be safe.

Her strength was waning between the blood loss in the clearing and the energy spent on her magic. The crushing weight of fatigue crashed into her full force as she continued to pump her magic into the runes.

"My star, you need to stop." She felt him next to her, but his voice sounded far away.

"Just...a little...more..." She could feel the end of her magic nearing. Calling to her like a siren's song, beckoning her onward. But when she tried to pull up, to reign in the power flowing out of her in waves, those threads slipped through her fingers, sending her careening toward the bottom with nothing to catch her.

The world around her flared white before black swam across her vision.

The last sound she heard was Daemon calling her name as darkness claimed her.

Chapter Twenty-Five

Daemon

"What the hell happened?" Ser Aeron bellowed as he stormed into Auraelia's suite, his eyes wide as they landed on his queen's limp body.

"I've never seen so much..." Xander's face was white as he stared down at his sister, seemingly unaware of the mass of muscle and anger that was Emerald's Army Commander stalking toward him.

When Xander still didn't answer, Ser Aeron pinned Daemon with a hard stare as he knelt next to the queen. "You! Explain. *Now*!" Effervescent white light radiated from his palms, washing over Auraelia and seeping into her body.

"She expelled too much magic at once. She drained herself."

"You let her *drain* herself?" Ser Aeron's anger was palpable, his hands shaking as he continued to move them over her body.

Chills spider walked down Daemon's spine as the memory of watching Auraelia push herself beyond her limits resurfaced. Of watching the color drain from her face. The way her magic spilled from her in rough waves, dragging her further into her well of power until she couldn't reach the surface. He'd felt her waning. Felt it as she neared the end of her rope, diving headfirst into a burnout.

"Daemon saved her." Piper's voice was small and shaky, her eyes welling with tears as she clung to her friend's hand. "If he hadn't been there… hadn't wrapped her in his shadows…I…I don't know that there would be anything for you to heal."

"Fuck." The commander shook his head in disbelief. "Xander," he snapped, the sharp tone finally pulling the prince from his shock. "Go tell Liza we need fruit, chocolate, and nuts, but don't tell her why. Ask for some of those silly little pastries that Auraelia likes, too." Xander stared at the man for a moment, the war between following orders and staying with his sister swimming across his eyes. "Now!" Ser Aeron demanded.

As Xander fled the room, Ser Aeron took a deep breath before asking, "What of the blood? That didn't come from draining her magic."

Daemon knelt by Auraelia's head at the arm of the settee, stroking the hair from her brow. "She and I were attacked in the Amber Woods. The Court of Pearl sent them."

"They what?"

"Calm down, Commander. You trained your queen well. She took down three of the men and saved my neck in the process. She's stronger than she thinks."

Ser Aeron shook his head, his shoulders sagging as he expelled a heavy sigh and returned his focus to healing his queen.

Silence blanketed the room as the commander worked. Piper's eyes slid closed, her lips moving in what sounded like a whispered prayer as Daemon continued to idly stroke Auraelia's hair.

*Come back to me, my star. Your people need you…*I *need you.*

Hours passed, and still, Auraelia hadn't woken. Her body was unnervingly still next to Daemon's as he watched like a sentinel.

He'd moved her to the bedchamber after Ser Aeron finished healing her body. Gently stripping her of the soiled garments, he wiped away the traces of blood and grime from her skin before redressing her in one of her silk nightdresses. The slices on her throat and shoulder were now nothing but faint pink lines, and the bruises that once colored her skin were nothing but a memory. But healing her mind and replenishing the stores of her magic was beyond even Ser Aeron's capability.

Piper brought dinner to Auraelia's chambers, the hope in her eyes fading when she saw her friend still unconscious and only staying long enough to watch over Auraelia while Daemon showered and ate.

Her presence was replaced by Ser Aeron, then Xander after him, and Daemon watched the pattern repeat, masks of hope slipping into sorrow as their queen's status remained unchanged.

Anxiety prickled in Daemon's chest. His shadows were restless in his veins, longing to reconnect with the fire that once burned brighter than the sun inside Auraelia, but there was no change. As he gazed down at her motionless body, at the delicate lines of her face and the way her lashes fanned out against her cheeks, he couldn't help but notice how fragile she looked. The only thing that brought him hope was that he'd witnessed her strength more times than he could count and in more ways than just physical. His star was a feat to behold, an intricate tapestry of power and resilience that would make lesser beings buckle under the weight of what she'd endured.

Daemon watched each pull of breath into her lungs until exhaustion crept in like the tide, dragging him under until he could no longer force his eyes open.

Though sleep claimed his body, his mind swirled back through every encounter he'd had with the woman who'd stolen his heart without even meaning to. The memory of seeing her across the ballroom. The way his shadows called to her, like a wayward ship finally finding safe harbor. Of the fire in her eyes whenever they met his. That undeniable draw to each other, pulling them together regardless of how either of them fought it. Their souls had been braided together, a thread pulled so taut over the centuries that it seemed that not even death could break it. But that thread had grown limp as Auraelia burned through her power. He'd felt it weaken and begin to fray at the ends, their connection growing weaker with every passing second.

It wasn't until Daemon wrapped her in shadows that it began to tighten again, resolidifying the weakening tether as she collapsed in his arms.

Those shadows now moved frantically in his veins, thrashing against the hold he kept on them and pulling him from his subconscious. Blinking the sleep from his eyes, he looked around the room. The moon had nearly reached its peak, its light showering the room in a silvery glow. His heart jolted in his chest as his gaze shifted back to Auraelia. The rose coloring was returning to her sun-kissed skin, her heart a strong, steady thrum in her chest. But then he *felt* it, the slow trickle of power filling the once near-empty chamber deep within her soul, and it was as if his lungs were finally capable of fully expanding once more.

Gently, Daemon stroked her cheek, his heart hammering in his chest like a stampede of wild horses as he waited for her eyes to open. To be graced with the storm that swirled in their depths. Seconds turned into minutes that felt like hours, but just as he was about to lean back against the headboard, her lashes fluttered, and he was pinned to the spot by incandescent green eyes.

The air around them stirred, static clinging to it and causing the hair on his arms to stand on end. It was as if her magic refused to be contained, swirling through her irises in streaks of champagne lightning, emanating the power held within.

"Hi," she whispered, her voice soft and scratchy.

Relief flooded through him, and it took a moment for him to find his voice, to make sure that it sounded calmer than he felt at that moment. "Hi, yourself. How are you feeling?"

Auraelia pinched her eyes closed, wincing as she attempted to sit up before deciding against it and letting her head fall back against the pillows. "I'm tired and sore. I feel like I—"

"Just drained almost every ounce of power you possessed?"

"Daemon—"

Daemon shook his head and cradled her cheek in his palm. "I know why you did it. I *understand* why you did. But I almost lost you."

"No, you di—"

"Yes, my star, I *did*. I felt you fading. Felt your body growing weaker with every passing second. If I hadn't intervened, I don't know that you'd be here right now."

Auraelia held his gaze, the rich green in her eyes giving way to their natural slate coloring as she slowly controlled her magic. "What of the wards? Do they stand?"

Daemon shook his head with a chuckle. "Of course, you're worried about that right now." When her eyes narrowed on him, he released an exasperated breath and continued. "They do. And from what your brother said, they're stronger than anything he's seen." He paused for a moment, letting the words sink in, but when she opened her mouth to respond, he narrowed his gaze. "You've done all that you can do for now, Auraelia. You've taken care of your people; it's time for you to let me take care of *you*."

Auraelia began to push up from the bed, and Daemon rested a steadying hand on her back, easing her into a sitting position. "Daemon, I can't just sit here."

"You can, and you will. I mean it, Princess. You can't do everything on your own. I know you want to, that you don't want to risk putting anyone else in danger, but you have to let someone help you. So, you can either *let me* help you, or I can tie you to this bed and *make* you." Auraelia turned toward him slowly, her eyes lighting up at his words as her bottom lip disappeared between her teeth. "Oh, no, my star. This would not be the pleasurable kind. If you let me hold the reins for a while, I might make it worth your while."

With a huff of a breath and a roll of her eyes, Auraelia finally acquiesced.

After a quick dinner, Daemon sent a note to Xander while Auraelia showered, letting him know that his sister was awake and doing well. Once she emerged from the bathing chamber, they returned to bed with the tray of food that Ser Aeron sent Xander for.

Auraelia picked at the fruit and nuts while he braided her hair, a contented silence settling over them. When he finished, he pulled her back into his hold, nuzzling into her neck before leaving a trail of kisses along the slender column. "You need to rest, my love," he whispered against her skin.

"From what you've said, I've been *resting* all day." Her words were punctuated with a roll of her hips against his own.

A low chuckle rumbled in his chest. "Insatiable creature."

"Daemon," she whimpered.

"My star, you're still recovering from the day."

"*Please.*" The word was drawn out into a breathy plea, her hips moving in small circles against him. "You said you would make it worth my while, and it will help me sleep."

"You're incorrigible, you know that?"

"Is that a yes, then?"

Daemon hummed as his lips moved along her shoulder, his hand sliding down her side to where the silk of her nightdress had bunched at the top of her thigh. "If I let you come on my hand, will you go to sleep?" His fingers slowly slipped beneath the hem and up over her stomach.

Her head fell against his shoulder, and a groan slipped between her lips. "More, I need more."

Daemon glided his hand down, his pinky fingering the top of her undergarments. "It's my hand or nothing, Princess. How badly do you want to come tonight?" Auraelia whimpered as she rocked her hips forward, searching for the friction she knew he would provide. "Who do you belong to, Auraelia?" he asked as his fingers slipped lower.

"You, I belong to you."

"Who owns your pleasure?"

"You. Daemon, *please.*"

"Don't you ever forget that." Auraelia was dripping by the time he plunged two fingers inside. Every little breathy word that left her lips was a straight shot to his cock. Every moan was a shock to his system. She'd claimed him in ways he didn't know was possible. Saturating his senses until all he knew, all he saw was her.

Auraelia rode his hand while he nipped and licked his way across her neck and shoulder. His other hand held her flush against him, her hips grinding against his in delicious torture. This wasn't how he expected to spend their last night together; he had intended to be buried inside her until the sun came up. But holding her while she came apart for him was more than he could have asked for after the day that she'd had.

When her orgasm finally ripped through her, she'd come with his name on her lips before he devoured it with a kiss. Then, true to her word, she curled up against his chest, her breathing even as she drifted back to sleep.

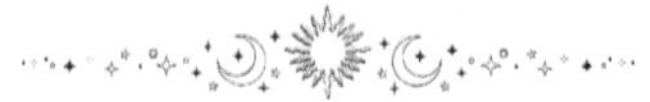

The sun's rays hadn't even begun to peek over the horizon line as Daemon slipped from bed the following morning. Auraelia was still fast asleep, only a mumbled groan slipping from her lips as she reached toward the spot where he'd just been. He hated leaving her—everything about it felt wrong—but he also knew that he needed to. Needed to prepare his people and get his council on the same page.

After dressing as silently as possible, Daemon pressed a kiss to her brow and snuck from her chambers to meet Aiden in the front courtyard of the castle.

"Ready to go?" Aiden asked as soon as he approached.

"I am, but I need you to stay here."

"What? No." Aiden recoiled, his nose scrunching as if he'd smelled something foul as he backed up a step.

"As a friend, I am asking you to stay. But as your prince, I am *telling* you to stay. I need someone I trust here with boots on the ground. I need you to watch after my girl, Aiden."

"Fucking, Goddess." Aiden breathed, running his hand through his neatly combed locks. "Fine."

"Thanks. Now, I've got to go. I'm supposed to be meeting Xander at the stables. Keep her safe, Aiden."

"Not that she needs it," he scoffed.

"She'd certainly agree with your sentiment, but regardless. You're my eyes and ears while I'm in Kalmeera."

"Safe travels, brother."

The men clasped their forearms before pulling each other into a quick embrace.

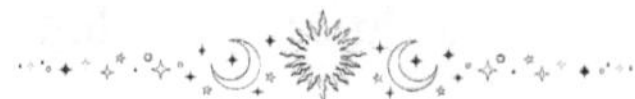

Daemon watched the early morning light dance along the water's surface as The Nevermore pulled out of Lyndaria's harbor.

"You alright over here?" Xander asked as he approached, leaning against the railing on the ship's upper deck.

"It just feels...*wrong*. I can't explain it."

"She'll be fine, Daemon...she has to be."

The latter was barely louder than the beat of a butterfly's wings, but Daemon heard it all the same. *She has to be,* not just for the sake of the realm and all of its inhabitants but for his as well. He couldn't survive a world in which Auraelia didn't exist.

Silence settled between them, and the only sounds around them consisted of the hustle and bustle of the crew combined with the crash of the waves against the hull as Lyndaria faded into the background. It wasn't until the city was no more than a blip on the horizon that Xander spoke once more.

"So, I guess now is as good a time as any."

"For what, exactly?" Daemon asked, crossing his arms as he turned his back to the ocean and directed his full attention to the prince.

"I know you both have feelings for each other, but what exactly are your *intentions* with my sister?"

Something between a sigh and a laugh escaped as Daemon eyed the man to his right. *Feelings for each other?* What they felt for each other went far beyond simple *feelings.* It was soul-altering, bone-deep, and all-consuming. *Feelings* didn't even put a dent into the enormity of what they had, and he decided to say just that. "I don't just have feelings for your sister, Prince Xander. I'm not even sure if love is an adequate term. She consumes me. My thoughts, my soul. Everything I am is hers."

"I see." Xander's head bobbed, his eyes locked onto the way the water crested against the ship. "What about your kingdom?" he finally added after a few beats of silence.

"What do you mean 'what about my kingdom'?"

Sighing, Xander turned toward him and fixed him with stern eyes. "When all of this is over, what happens? Auraelia is already the queen of Emerald, and I don't see her giving that up after fighting so hard to hold on to it. So," he matched Daemon's stance, his brows raised in expectation, "What happens when this is all over? Will you leave your kingdom to be with her in Lyndaria? Will you continue this long-distance arrangement until you're both miserable and resent each other?

What is your *plan*, Daemon? Because I don't want to have to pick up the pieces when this inevitably falls apart."

The bluntness at which he laid it all out was both relieving and unnerving. Had he thought about it? Of course, but it had been pushed to the back of his mind while they focused on the immediate future. They needed to focus on saving the realm before they could figure out what to do about their future together—a future that he fully intended to have.

"Well?" Xander hedged when he'd taken too long to respond.

"Listen, Xander. I don't have all the answers right now. Goddess, I wish that I did, but I don't, and I'm not going to stand here and lie to you and say that I do. I *will* tell you, however, that I would never even dream of asking Auraelia to leave her throne or her people, and I can't abandon my own either. But I refuse to spend my life an ocean away from her. Refuse to reduce what we have down to clandestine meetings and letters. I would give her this realm on a silver platter if she wasn't so determined to save it on her own."

Small crinkles lined the edges of Xander's eyes as a smile crept across his face. "That's all I needed to hear. You both have a lot to figure out; I just hope you can do it before the world goes to shit." Xander clapped his hand on Daemon's shoulder and gave it a tight squeeze before heading below deck.

Chapter Twenty-Six

Auraelia

Sunlight filtered through the windows, bathing her cheeks in a warm glow. A languid smile stretched across her face as the gentle heat lured her from sleep, but as she reached her arm out for Daemon, all she found were cold sheets.

Her heart was heavy as she peeled her eyes open, but instead of the empty space she was expecting, she found the sunlight glittering off something on his pillow.

Wiping the sleep from her eyes, Auraelia pushed onto her elbows and reached for the object. A steady, familiar hum of magic vibrated through her palm, and a sense of calm washed over her. She didn't need to see it to know what it was. The familiar, resonant frequency of the stone nestled within her hand, and the cool, delicate chain told her all she needed to know.

Her sapphire.

Auraelia clutched the gem tightly in her fist and held it against her chest. She'd missed the weight of it sitting between her breasts. Missed the way it brought her a sense of comfort. But most of all, she missed the connection to Daemon that it gave her. An overwhelming wave of emotion barreled into her, causing her hands to shake. Love. Happiness. But the sprinkle of loneliness clenching her heart made her look toward the ceiling and blink rapidly to keep the tears that welled in her eyes from falling.

With a deep, steadying breath, she slowly unclenched her hand and gazed down at the stone. Admiring how the rich, deep blue glittered in the morning light and how Daemon's shadows seemed to swim beneath the surface. Looping the chain around her neck, she relished the familiar feel of its weight as it settled against her chest. Slipping from her bed, Auraelia traversed the short distance to her writing desk and threw open the top, pulling drawer after drawer open until she'd obtained all the needed materials.

Her heart fluttered in her chest like a field of butterflies taking flight, and as her quill glided against the blank parchment, she smiled.

My dearest Daemon,

You left without saying goodbye... again. Can we please not make this a habit? Goddess, I miss you already. Thank you for leaving me this piece of yourself and for giving it back to me after everything I put you through. I don't think I'll ever be able to apologize enough for my transgressions, and even if it takes the rest of my life, I promise that I will make it up to you.

Please be safe.

I'll be waiting for you.

All of my love,

Your Star

P.S. I love you

Folding the parchment into a neat square, Auraelia placed lavender over the opening and pressed her new crest into the wax. It's been so long since she'd written to him that it felt reminiscent of the first time. Her stomach was in knots, and her heart was pounding. Only this time, there was no wondering whether or not he would receive it. Clutching the letter in one hand, the stone in the other, she pictured the man she finally allowed herself to love. The one who stole her breath with every look, every touch. Who filled a hole in her life that she hadn't even been aware was empty until she'd pushed him away, and it emptied once more. Daemon's magic wrapped around her in a familiar caress, and then, within seconds, it and the letter were gone.

After dressing in fighting leathers—the braid Daemon did the night before still miraculously intact—she strapped her dagger to her thigh. She headed into her sitting room, only to be met with Daemon's emissary's discontented, scowling face. "What the hell are you doing here?"

"Fuck, lightning girl, took you long enough to wake up. I've been here since sunrise."

"*Lightning girl*?"

"Well, you told me not to call you Princess, and I'm pretty sure D would have my balls if I called you '*my star,*'" he said Daemon's nickname for her like it left a foul taste in his mouth before shrugging. "So, ipso facto, lightning girl."

"You could just call me Your Majesty. Or, I don't know, here's a crazy idea, you *could* just use my *name*." Auraelia countered, matching his snark with some of her own.

Aiden thought for a second, then shrugged again and pushed up from the settee. "I think I'll stick with lightning girl. I feel like it fits your personality."

Anger coiled in her veins, setting her magic alight, and she tamped it down before she *accidentally* sent a bolt in Aiden's direction. "You still haven't told me why you're here."

"Oh, that." Aiden reached into his coat pocket and pulled out a piece of parchment, twisting it between his fingers before he held it out toward her. "This is for you."

Auraelia all but lunged for the missive between his fingers; its midnight-blue seal was like a beacon to her soul. Prying the wax away, she carefully unfolded the note.

Hello My Star,

I'm sorry I left without saying goodbye, but as always, if I had woken you, I wouldn't have been able to leave.

I'm sure you're wondering why Aiden is still there with you instead of on the ship with your brother and me, and you won't like the answer. I left him there to protect you.

"I don't need protection," she muttered to herself.

Aiden scoffed. "I said as much."

Auraelia shot him a withering stare, then turned her attention back to the letter.

Now, I know you're going to say that you don't need protection, and I know you're quite adept at defending yourself. But this is more for me than it is for you. I need someone I trust to be my eyes and ears while I'm gone. Someone to look out for you even when you don't need it. And regardless of your feelings toward him, he was that for you at one point, too. So, please, for me, try not to kill my best friend and emissary? I know he's a pain in the ass, but he's my pain in the ass, and he has his moments.

Stay safe, Princess. I'll see you soon.

I love you.

Daemon

She read the letter twice before refolding it and tucking it between her breasts next to the sapphire.

"So what was in that thing anyway?" Aiden asked as he pushed onto his tiptoes, his eyes trained on the v of her neckline. It was as if he could see down her shirt, and he would be able to ascertain what was written in the letter.

"He asked me not to kill you, so I *highly* recommend you stop trying to look down my shirt." Auraelia's head canted to the side, her eyes wide as her lips tilted up into an unamused smile.

Throwing his hands up in surrender, Aiden plopped back down onto the settee and propped his feet on the low table in front. "So, what's on the schedule today, Lightning Girl?"

"I swear by the Goddess if you don't stop calling me that, I'm going to use you for target practice."

His eyes widened slightly before an amused grin stretched across his face, making twin dimples appear. "Don't tempt me with a good time, *Your Majesty*. But, really, what's on your schedule today?"

"I have training with my Army Commander and a council meeting; why?"

Pushing up from the couch once more, Aiden gestured toward the door with an over-exaggerated flourish. "Lead the way. Daemon may have shadows, but consider me your personal one."

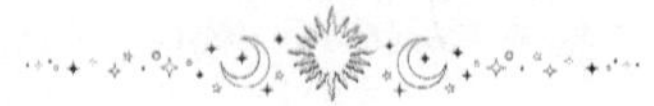

Clang. Her sword reverberated in her hand as she blocked one of Ser Aeron's blows, his broad sword wider and heavier than the short sword she carried, sending shock waves down her arm.

"Again!" he bellowed, his anger palpable as he lunged toward her once more. They'd been at this for hours, the sun now high in the sky, its heat dissolving the chill in the air and causing her wool tunic to stick to her skin. Sweat pooled between her breasts, her palms slick as they held tightly to the hilt of her sword, and she blocked another blow. This session had been more intense—more brutal—than in all the years she'd been training with the warrior from the Court of Opal. Daemon had told her how angry he'd been when he'd found out she'd drained her magic, but now it almost seemed as if he was trying to punish her for it.

Huffing out an aggravated breath, Auraelia parried. Using her advancement as a distraction, she pulled at the thread that tied her magic to the earth, splitting it wide beneath the commander's feet and sending him staggering backward. As Ser Aeron fought to regain his balance, Auraelia knocked his blade from his hand.

"Do you yield?" she asked between heavy breaths, pressing the tip of her sword to the center of his chest.

His eyes narrowed, but a proud smirk pulled across his lips as he took a step back, dropping to a knee as he bowed his head. "I yield, Your Majesty."

Auraelia released a relieved breath, her arm shaking as she dropped it to her side. "Thank the Goddess." Sheathing her sword down her back, she reached out a hand to help Ser Aeron to his feet. "Were you trying to kill me today?"

"I could ask you the same question in regards to the stunt you pulled yesterday," he responded blandly, bending to pick up his discarded weapon.

"It was necessary."

"Nearly *killing* yourself is not necessary, Auraelia. If you have that much of a death wish, I'm sure your cousin would be happy to oblige." Ser Aeron's tone turned icy, his amber eyes pinning her to the spot.

"*Protecting* my people is!" she shot back. She was so tired of people trying to dictate what she did and how she did it. Of them trying to leash the power that coursed through *her* veins. "Whether you deem my actions necessary or not is irrelevant. *I* did what *I* thought was necessary to protect *my* people."

"Auraelia—"

"Don't." Auraelia took a deep, steadying breath, and as she released it, she let her anger flow out with it. "I know that you, Xander, and every other Goddess-blessed person in my life is just trying to help. That you all just want to keep me safe. Hell, that's why Daemon left his watchdog here," she said, throwing a hand over her shoulder to where Aiden was propped against the stone wall. "And I appreciate it, I do. But it's my job to protect *you*. My job is to protect this court and its people. I can't do that if I constantly have someone questioning my every move and decision."

Ser Aeron fell silent for a moment, his eyes pensive as they scanned her face, then nodded in acquiescence. "My only wish is to see you live a long and happy life, Auraelia. It's what your mother would have wanted; it's what your kingdom wants for you." He released a long-suffering sigh and gently gripped her shoulders. "It's what you *deserve*."

A small smile pulled at the corners of her mouth. "And I intend to have exactly that." They stood there for a moment, and Auraelia watched as some of the tension seeped from Ser Aeron's body before asking, "Now, what's next on the torture list for today?" Laughter filled her tone, lifting the heaviness that had fallen over them.

Ser Aeron matched her smile with one of his own and chuckled, the sound deep and warm as he shook his head. When he met her gaze once more, there was a glint of mischief as he gestured toward the targets on the opposite end of the field before canting his head toward Aiden. "How about some target practice?" Auraelia's eyes widened, a small disbelieving laugh bubbling up her throat. "What?" He shrugged. "He's a cocky bastard, and you need to practice bending your abilities around objects, or people, who aren't your target. Two birds, one stone. Just don't hit him, okay?" The smile on Ser Aeron's face broadened, and as if he had heard them, Aiden pushed off the wall, his eyes wide as they flicked between Auraelia and the commander.

"I don't know what you're thinking, but I highly advise against whatever it is."

"It's a good thing you're not my advisor then," she hollered across the pitch.

"Where's Lord Harland?" Auraelia asked as the council members settled into their seats around the table. She'd never known the man to miss a meeting, and now that she knew what he was up to, his absence sent anger prickling down her spine.

"I believe he's ill, Your Majesty." Mister Aramis supplied, briefly meeting her gaze as he shuffled the parchment in front of him into a neat stack.

"I see." Auraelia drummed her fingers along the tabletop. "Well, let's begin then."

Just as the final syllable left her lips, the doors to the council chamber swung open, and a red-nosed, bleary-eyed Lord Harland came staggering in.

"Apologies for my tardiness, Your Majesty." He pulled a handkerchief from his pocket and wiped his nose. "I'm a little under the weather, but the physician is adamant that it is nothing serious, and I should be well soon."

Reigning in the sneer that was beginning to form on her face, Auraelia gave him a placid smile as he sank into his seat. "I'm glad to hear it."

The last thing she wanted to do was inquire about preparations for the impending war with a traitor in her midst, but she had no choice. She had to appear as if everything was fine. That she was oblivious to his treachery and still saw him as one of her trusted court members. Lord Harland nodded his thanks, and she blew out a breath as she turned her attention to Master Demir. "Where are we in regards to the completion of the new armor and weapons for our troops?"

"Right on schedule, Your Majesty."

"Excellent. I would like to see them before they are distributed."

"Of course, Your Majesty." Master Demir responded, bowing his head.

Not willing to give Lord Harland the details on when the equipment would arrive, she shifted her focus to Mister Aramis and changed the subject. "What of the Ladies of Topaz? Have we any new information on where they stand?"

Her emissary gave her a sympathetic smile. "My contacts within the Court of Topaz have no new information, Your Majesty. They say that their Ladies have sequestered themselves."

"I see." The room fell silent, all eyes trained on Auraelia as she came to the only possible conclusion. "Well, if your contacts can't ascertain their stance, I shall ask them myself. Write to Lady Orna and Lady Blyana to let them know their presence is requested at court."

"Ye–yes, Your Majesty," he stammered. Confusion marred his features, but he bowed his head in acknowledgment.

"Oh, and Aramis. Do word it as a request, but make sure they know it is not an option."

All eyes at the table widened, except for Lord Harland, who looked at her with curiosity. Her mother had never demanded anyone appear at court; she'd never had to. And Auraelia had planned to follow in her mother's footsteps, abiding by that same courtesy. She never wanted to reign this way. It wasn't who she was. Wasn't who she wanted to be. But there was no time to placate people's sensibilities. This wasn't the time for anyone to stand in the gray area. War may be coming to her doorstep, but it impacted everyone in the realm, and it was time that the ladies of Topaz faced that fact, whether they were ready to or not.

After the remainder of the council had given their reports, the meeting came to a close, and Auraelia dismissed them from the chambers. Her head was pounding, and she rubbed at her temples in an attempt to alleviate the ache that was determined to take root. Every time Lord Harland so much as breathed too loudly, her magic burned beneath her skin, begging for retribution. The constant effort of tamping down her rage, of making sure that the mask she'd donned stayed firmly in place throughout the entirety of the meeting, had been daunting. Acting as if everything was fine would be harder than she thought.

At the sound of the door creaking open, Auraelia pulled her head from her hands.

"You ready?" Aiden asked, his face a mask of indifference. Nodding, Auraelia pushed up from her chair and gestured toward the door that led from the council room to her chambers. "What, no quippy response?" he asked, crossing the room to meet her at the door.

"Aiden," she huffed out in exasperation, "I don't have the energy for your sarcasm right now."

"Too tired from trying to fry my ass?"

Auraelia scanned him from head to toe. She'd taken Ser Aeron up on his offer of turning Aiden into a live practice dummy, and there was not a single scorch mark on his person or a hair out of place. The exercise had been educational and exhausting, but seeing the terrified look on the emissary's face any time a bolt of lightning curved a little too close for his comfort had made the exhaustion worth it. A Cheshire grin spread across her lips. "Trust me, if I was trying to '*fry your ass,*' I wouldn't have missed."

Turning away, she opened the door and headed toward her chambers, not bothering to see if he'd followed.

Chapter Twenty-Seven

Daemon

The gentle lap of water against the shore did nothing to calm the storm that roiled within him. Daemon looked out over the Cerulean Sea, taking in the glittering water that had always been a home away from home and the thing that always brought him back to Kalmeera.

But home was no longer the city he grew up in, not in the ways that counted.

Home had become long, golden waves of hair. It was the smell of lavender and the warmth of an embrace. It was quiet nights and ones tangled in sheets. Conversations beneath the stars while fireflies danced overhead.

Home was Auraelia.

It had been for longer than he'd realized. The magic in his veins knew the second he laid eyes on her all those months ago. But it hadn't been until the Summer Solstice when she was dressed as a queen of *his* court, that he'd finally begun to understand.

Daemon closed his eyes and let the soft sound of water meeting sand remind him of what he had to lose if this all went awry. He'd lose the home he'd always known and the one that took its place, and he couldn't let either of those happen.

"Is it always this warm?" Xander asked as he lifted his face toward the sun, his words pulling Daemon from the thoughts swirling through his mind since they ported the night before.

"It is a tropical island," Yvaine laughed, shaking her head at the absurdity of the question.

"I've only been here once before, remember?" Xander shot her a sardonic look. "But I guess I was just a little surprised, is all. Even Emerald is unusually cool for this time of year."

"It was damn near freezing when Davina was here," Daemon scoffed, his hand rubbing at his sternum. It was as if the mere thought of her brought back the ice in his veins, stealing the breath from his lungs and causing his chest to ache.

Yvaine placed a gentle hand on his forearm, her eyes soft yet determined as they met his. "She will never set foot on our islands again, D. I'll make sure of it."

Placing his hand over hers, he gave it a reassuring squeeze. "We both will."

"On that note, let's get started," Xander cut in, rounding out their little group into an awkward triangle. "Did you get what you need?"

Nodding, Daemon pulled a dark leather satchel from the bag he'd slung across his body. Having done this in Lyndaria, he knew he'd need sapphires...and a lot of them. The Sapphire Isles may have been islands, but they were large, and more than one needed protecting. After pouring some of the stones into his palm, Daemon looked up to meet the wide eyes of his sister.

"Did you rob the treasury? What the fuck are those for?"

"We need them to strengthen the runes that set the wards," Daemon explained as Xander picked through the gems. "Just pay attention, okay? I'm going to need you to repeat this process on Malaena and Lunaria while I handle things here."

"What do you mean, 'handle things here'?" Yvaine asked, crossing her arms as a singular brow reached toward her hairline.

"I need to prepare the fleet and get the council on board. Unless *you* want to deal with Lord Syrus and his rabble."

Yvaine's hands flew up in surrender. "Nope. Wards on the other islands got it. So how do we do this?" The latter was directed toward Xander, who had walked a short distance away to a where the grass tapered off as it met the sandy bank.

"Come on." Daemon pulled Yvaine along until they reached where Xander knelt in the sand.

"You have to dig a hole deep enough to not be discovered but shallow enough that the magic can penetrate it easily." The crunch of his spade piercing the wet ground mingled with the crash of waves in the distance and the cries of the birds overhead. When he finally finished, Yvaine squatted next to him to examine the hole. "Now—" Xander reached into the pocket he'd deposited the sapphires into, "you have to place the gems in the shape of the rune." Slipping his other hand into the opposite pocket, he pulled out a small sheet of parchment and handed it to Yvaine. "Here, I drew it out for you. It has to be *this* exact shape. It's really simple, just a few lines that have to connect at the right points. Any deviation and the wards will not set." Xander raised a skeptical brow, tapping his finger against the ink scrawled on the parchment. "Do you think you can handle that?"

Yvaine lifted her gaze from the slip in her hand to meet Xander's, and Daemon blew out a breath through pursed lips as he rocked back on his heels.

She hated when people, especially men, spoke to her like a petulant child. She'd been reduced to number two the moment he'd been born. Despite all that she did for their kingdom, she was downgraded to a "pretty woman" by most of the men at court. She'd been undervalued by most of their father's council for the majority of her life, which meant her tolerance for arrogance was below zero.

Daemon watched Xander's eyes widen, his jaw going slack as blue began seeping into Yvaine's eyes. "Vaine," he scolded.

Her hold over Xander's mind continued as her gaze met Daemon's, the bright turquoise engulfing the mossy green that matched his own. "I'm not going to hurt him...just get him a little wet."

A sweet smile graced her mouth, but there was venom behind it. There was a reason few knew of Yvaine's abilities. A siren's song could be a tremendous blessing or a curse, and the line between the two was thinner than a strand of hair.

"Yvaine, let him go. He's trying to help us."

Still in the trance, Xander stood and took clumsy steps toward the water's edge.

"He's got a shitty way of showing it," she scoffed with a roll of her eyes. Her entire demeanor shifted then. Her breath came in slow, calm pulls as the blue began to retreat from her eyes, luring the unsuspecting prince back to where he'd been before fading away into their usual green.

"What the hell was that?" Xander asked, shaking his head before pressing his fingers into his temples.

"Must have gotten overheated," Yvaine supplied dryly, then gestured toward the half-completed rune. "You going to finish that?"

By the time they made it back to the castle, the sun was painting the sky in vibrant oranges and pinks as it slowly sank into the horizon.

Xander excused himself as soon as they'd crossed the bridge, claiming a lack of appetite due to a persistent headache. As soon as he was out of earshot, Daemon turned to his sister. "You really did a number on him, Vaine."

"Weak minds are easier to corrupt, little brother."

"He's not weak-minded. He's worried about his sister and their kingdom. The same as you and me. Give him some grace. He didn't have to come here."

Yvaine sighed, then closed her eyes as a sweet hum rang out through the marble of the castle. Echoing down the halls and through the chambers.

"What are you doing?" Daemon whispered next to her ear, his eyes on a constant swivel to make sure that no one was around them. A siren's song was only meant to be heard by those who were targeted, and the fact that *he* could hear it had his magic coiling beneath the surface.

"Fixing it," she stated matter-of-factly. Her song faded out, the usual sounds of the castle returning to fill the space once more. "There. Prince Xander should be fine in a moment or two."

Daemon blew out an exasperated breath and pinched the bridge of his nose. "Do me a favor? Until I'm positive there are no spies in our court, keep the magic to a minimum? *Please*? The last thing we need is you-know-who finding out what you are capable of."

The fire burned in the depths of Yvaine's eyes—whether from anger or the need for retribution, he wasn't sure—but as she opened her mouth to respond, Sariah rounded the corner.

"Daemon! You're back!" Her arms wound around his neck in a quick embrace before she pulled away, her brows furrowed in confusion. "Wait, *why* are you back? I thought you were going to Ly—" Yvaine elbowed Sariah in the ribs. "*Ow!* What the hell, Yvaine!?"

"The walls have ears, Ri," she hissed through clenched teeth.

A disbelieving chuckle slipped past Daemon's lips before he released the hold on his shadows and whisked them into his suite. The last thing he needed was for his council to catch wind of his whereabouts before he was ready for them to. He needed things in place. Needed to see how deeply his court was entangled with the Court of Garnet before he could begin to unravel the foothold Davina had established. He needed to weed out the vermin that undoubtedly sat at his father's table. And if Davina had established a stronghold in his court, it was going to take more time than he had to demolish it.

"Exactly how many people know where I went?" he seethed, storming across the room to the bar cart. As he poured amber liquid into a glass, he heard someone fall onto one of the leather couches, followed by an exhausted-sounding sigh.

"Mother told me, and I told Ri. No one else knows. Even Father thinks you were on Lunaria, doing your princely duties with the Priestesses."

Daemon downed the contents of his glass, then poured another before turning to face the women sprawled across his sitting area. "You're sure?"

"As sure as the nose on my face, little brother."

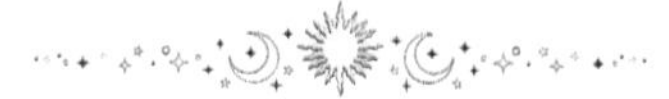

Exhaustion was a heavy blanket as the peachy light of early morning filtered into his room. *It's too fucking early*, he thought, groaning as he grabbed the pillow next to him. The soft scent of lavender saturated his senses as he used it to block out the offending light. Inhaling deeply, he let the familiarity and calm accompanying the scent wash over him. He was just about to drift back to sleep when a startling realization had him shooting up in bed, his eyes scouring the room for the source and coming up empty. Resolved to the fact that his sleep-idle mind was playing tricks on him, Daemon fell back against the pillows, his nose buried into the one that smelled of *her*.

Even through the sleep-induced fog of his mind, it didn't make sense. There was no reason for his pillow to smell like Auraelia. She hadn't been there in months, and even when she had, they'd spent their time in her chambers.

Pulling his face from the silk, Daemon sat up once more and took a more critical look around his room. Everything was in its place—including the curtains that he'd evidently forgotten to draw the night before—and there was no sign of anything that would lead him to believe she was there. And though—logically—that made sense, there was still a pang of hurt in his heart, of longing to be back where she was.

Daemon scrubbed a hand down his face before running his fingers through his hair, deciding to get up for the day instead of stealing a few more hours of sleep. As he moved the sheets aside, a flash of cream and emerald green entered his peripheral before falling to the floor on the opposite side. A singular chuckle escaped, and he shook his head. *Of course.*

Stretching across the bed, Daemon reached down to scoop up the parchment, his thumb skimming the new signet that had been pressed into the wax, subsequently knocking a few of the lavender buds to the floor.

2 days down. I love and miss you. Come back to me soon.
All of my love.
Your Star

It wasn't long. It held no pertinent information. But the words enclosed in that letter meant more to him than anything else.

With a smile firmly in place, Daemon refolded the parchment and placed it in the drawer that held all their other letters. He wanted to get back to Lyndaria by the end of the week, and he needed to set things into motion for that to happen. With renewed determination, he pushed up from the bed and headed into his bathing chamber.

A soft snore greeted him as he stepped into his sitting room, Yvaine and Sariah still prone on his couch from where he'd left them the night prior. With a shake of his head, Daemon crossed the space to his desk and set a summons to the kitchen, asking for breakfast and coffee for three to be brought to his suite.

Within minutes there was a knock at the door. Yvaine groaned and mumbled, "Go away," as she attempted to rotate on the cushions but fell to the floor instead.

"Oh, good. You're up," Daemon said, not even attempting to hide the humor in his voice or his smile as he sipped casually from his mug.

"Why are you in my roo—This isn't my room, is it?"

"Afraid not."

With an aggravated puff of air, she blew away the hair that had fallen in her face, her eyes flicking to the cup in Daemon's hand. "Coffee?"

"Always. There's some for you, too, if you get up."

Begrudgingly pushing up from the floor, Yvaine shuffled to the tray on Daemon's desk. She sidled up next to him by the windows with a cup of coffee in one hand and berries in the other.

"I need you to leave for the islands today," he said without turning in her direction.

"I thought as much." She popped a red berry into her mouth, then took a sip of her coffee. "What are you going to do?"

"I think it's time Father and I had a talk," he answered through clenched teeth, his hand tightening around the bowl of his mug. The thought of having a conversation with the man who'd bargained him off to marry Davina made his stomach turn, but he wanted to...*needed* to understand why.

Yvaine blew out a breath through pursed lips, then raised her cup in salute. "May the Goddess be with him."

Turning toward his sister, Daemon raised his brows in question. "With *him*?"

"Well, yeah. I sure as hell wouldn't want to be on the receiving end of your anger. You're literally grinding your teeth right now at the thought of it; I can see the muscles in your jaw flexing." She blew out a sharp breath through her nose. "Father's not going to stand a chance." She popped another berry into her mouth, chewing thoughtfully. "Just try and keep the shadows under control, okay? No repeats of the marketplace. I won't be here to sing you back into your right mind."

Daemon chuckled. "I'll do my best." After a brief pause, he asked, "Are you going to bring her with you?"

"Who? Ri?" Yvaine's shoulders drooped when he nodded, and she directed her attention back out the windows. The silence drug on as she took leisurely sips from her mug until finally, she said, "I don't know. Things are...complicated right now. We're together, but not *together.* If that makes sense."

"It does," he said, taking a swig from his mug. He knew—better than he would have liked—how true that statement could be. He and Auraelia had only *just* come out on the other side of that situation, and he hated that his sister was suffering from the same. He only feared that Yvaine was holding back, and he didn't know why. "Do you want to talk about it?"

"Not really, no. At least, not right now. There's too much going on to worry about my difficult love life."

"On the contrary, now is the perfect time to focus on it. After all, who knows what tomorrow will bring?" Daemon quirked a brow and bumped his hip against Yvaine's, bringing a small smile to her face.

"You've got it bad, little brother."

"You have *no* idea. Did I tell you that Xander asked me what my intentions were?"

Yvaine's laugh echoed through the room, and she turned to make sure it hadn't woken Sariah, her gaze softening as it fell over the still-sleeping redhead on the couch.

Time stretched on, and they fell into easy conversation over coffee and breakfast pastries. Sariah joined them a while later, and once they were finished, Yvaine excused herself from the room to prepare for the journey ahead.

When Sariah placed her napkin on the table, a sure sign that she was also about to leave, Daemon said, "You know she loves you, don't you?"

A sad smile tugged on the corners of her lips, her gaze falling to her lap before meeting his once more. "I do...but I'm not sure if *she* does." Sariah let out a gentle laugh. "She reminds me of Auraelia, actually. Well...the little bit of her I know from you and Yvaine, anyway."

Daemon smiled at the mention of his star. "Perhaps, in some ways, I can see it. But if that's the case, then the only advice I can give you is to be patient. She'll come around eventually."

"And if she doesn't?"

The sadness in her eyes was reminiscent of the pain he'd become familiar with over the last few months, and his heart ached for his friend. Reaching across the table, Daemon squeezed her hand. "She will. Fate tends to find a way to give us what we need when we least expect it."

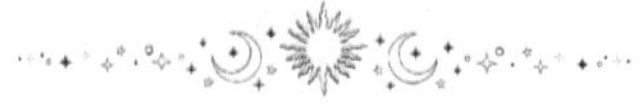

Daemon had hardly stepped foot out of his room when a guard bellowed down the hall, stating that he had something for him. The man's face was flush, sweat beading on his brow, as he handed Daemon the missive. Opening it, he skimmed the contents before balling it into his fist and shadow-walking to the other side of the castle.

"Was a summons really necessary, Father?" he seethed, slamming the parchment down on the desk in front of his father.

"I didn't think you'd come otherwise," King Evander stated flatly, leaning back in his chair with his hand resting over his stomach.

"Well, I'm here now. What do you want?" He'd planned on seeing his father in his own time. Had intended to calm his mind and form coherent thoughts to portray what he wanted to without completely losing his shit. But getting a *summons* to see his own damn father had shredded that last bit of calm and obliterated all thoughts of possibly reconciling with the man who helped give him life.

"Have a seat, Son."

"Son?" he scoffed. "A father wouldn't sell his son to a vile witch in order to save his own skin. But you did. So no, *Father*, I'm not your son. I'm simply someone who shares your blood and will sit on the throne once the Goddesses claim your soul."

"You want to play the victim? So be it. But *I am* still the King, so you will sit. Down."

Daemon's magic swirled around his hands, and he had to consciously pull them back as he begrudgingly sat in one of the deep leather chairs across from his father. "What do you want, *Your Majesty*?"

"It's time you understood the workings of this court. If you want to sit on *my* throne, you will shut your mouth and listen."

"The only thing I want to understand is why you did what you did. Other than that, you have nothing that I want or need."

King Evander let out a patronizing laugh. "I did what I did to save our kingdom. If you can't—"

"You did what you did to save your own ass. It had nothing to do with this kingdom."

"*I am* this kingdom!" he yelled. "The Sapphire Isles would be nothing without me!"

Daemon sat silently as his father's outburst sent him into a coughing fit. Watched as the man scrambled for a handkerchief and tried to hide the dots of crimson that shone like rubies against the crisp white linen.

"You're still dying, aren't you?" he asked, disbelief filling every word.

"I'm fine."

"Last time I checked, coughing up blood wasn't a good sign. How long has that been happening?"

King Evander wiped his mouth and leaned back in his chair, his head falling against the back. "Since the ball."

Daemon couldn't have suppressed the laugh that tumbled out even if he had wanted to. "So, you're telling me that even though you gave her *everything* she wanted, she still didn't hold up her end?"

"Daemon—"

"No. Just be honest for one goddess damned second and tell me *why*."

King Evander let out a heavy sigh and met Daemon's gaze. "I wasn't ready to die. I wasn't ready to leave your mother. Or you, or your sister. It was the only way—"

"Bullshit. There's always another way."

"What would you have had me do, Son? Truthfully. How would the mighty Daemon Alexander, Crowned Prince of the Sapphire Isles, have handled this in the face of death?"

"Did you even *try* to find the person responsible after you found out? After you knew what she'd done to you? Or did you just take it and hand over your son, your heir, your goddess damned *kingdom* to the woman who tried to kill you and, by the looks of it, is succeeding?" The king's silence was all the answer Daemon needed. "You're pathetic." Daemon pushed up from his seat and walked toward the door, halting briefly to turn back toward the king. "I used to want to be just like you. To rule with a steady hand, with a woman I loved and cherished by my side. But now?" He shook his head. "Now, all I see is a sad man who put himself before his kingdom. Before his own flesh and blood. And I want nothing to do with that man. You're unworthy of wearing that crown, and I am ashamed to call you my father."

Chapter Twenty-Eight

Auraelia

Rain fell softly against the window, its gentle pattering the only sound as Auraelia watched the beads of water slide down the misty glass.

It had been four days since Daemon left to go back to Kalmeera, and though she had nothing to do with the weather outside her window, it mirrored the ever-present ache within her chest.

"Are you ready to go, Rae?" Aiden asked softly, as if not wanting to intrude on her thoughts.

Over the last few days, they'd established somewhat of a truce. The snarky comments had dropped to a minimum. He'd finally given up on the *Lightning Girl* moniker when it no longer provoked the response he was evidently looking for and had instead switched to calling her by her normal nickname. They ate meals together—albeit in relative silence. He still followed her around like the shadow he'd deemed himself to be, but the awkwardness of having someone trailing her had abated...somewhat.

She'd even come to appreciate his presence at times.

Aiden always seemed to know when to give her space to think and was there to draw a laugh when she needed it most. If he hadn't been such an ardent asshole to her best friend, she might have even liked him.

Auraelia blew out her breath, the warm air fogging up the glass, then turned to where Aiden stood patiently in the doorway. "I just need to put my boots on and grab my weapons. Can you go down to the stables and ensure the horses are ready, please?" Whether it was the calmness in her tone or the fact that she said 'please,' she wasn't sure, but the surprised look on Aiden's face brought a small smile to her own. "What?"

He shook his head, a matching smile tugging on his lips. "Nothing. Ten minutes, okay?"

Auraelia nodded and turned back toward the window, her fingers absentmindedly sliding the sapphire pendant along its chain in a rhythmic motion.

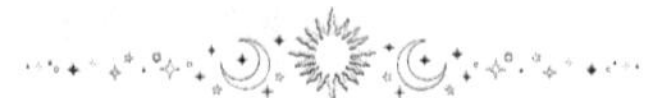

The rain had slowed to a steady drizzle by the time Auraelia made it outside, the droplets bouncing off the shield of air she'd conjured to keep herself dry. They had a long ride to the army's training field, and the last thing she wanted was to make the journey in soaked fighting leathers.

As she crossed the field and the stables came into view, the sound of arguing reached her ears, prompting her to hasten her steps. The closer she got, the more distinctive the voices became, and she stopped in her tracks to let out an annoyed sigh. *Piper and Aiden.*

She managed to keep their interactions to a minimum while Aiden was there, not wanting to be in the middle of whatever was—or wasn't—between them. But the inevitability of them running into each other without her present had finally happened.

Piper had explained why she was annoyed with the man, but Auraelia had assumed that her disdain had waned...and evidently, she had been severely mistaken.

"*Piper—*"

The pleading sound of Aiden's voice made Auraelia stop just outside the door to the stables.

"Why can't you just leave me be!?"

"Please. Just let me explain."

"I don't need your explanation! I don't want it! Goddess. I don't want to play these games with you anymore! Just... Go *home*, Aiden."

Footsteps echoed through the stables, and Auraelia backed up a step as the sound drew closer. When Piper stepped out, her gaze clashed with Auraelia's, and her shoulders dropped in exasperation. "How much of that did you hear?"

Auraelia gave a nonchalant shrug and closed the distance between them. "Are you alright?"

Piper blew out a breath through her nose and briefly turned her face toward the rain. "I'll be fine. I just...I need some air." When her eyes fell to Auraelia's once more, there was a heaviness in her gaze. "Be careful today, okay? And try not to make our soldiers look too bad. Not everyone grew up with one-on-one training from the greatest warrior in the realm." Her lips pulled up at the corners, but the movement didn't reach her eyes, exhaustion clinging to the swirls of green and brown.

"Do you want to come? You seem like you need to blow off some steam."

"Goddess, no." Piper huffed with a small laugh. "I'll be fine, really."

Auraelia hugged her, then released her to go on her way. When she was a few feet away, Auraelia yelled, "I love you!"

Her friend turned, walking backward as she yelled back, "I love you, too! Now go show them who's boss!"

"I think they already know that!" Auraelia retorted with a laugh.

After a blasé shrug, Piper waved and turned back toward the castle, and Auraelia chuckled to herself as she turned to head into the stables.

Aiden was leaning against one of the posts that separated the stalls, his hands tucked into his pants pockets, head hanging in defeat. "That friend of yours is pure fire, you know that?"

Auraelia scoffed as she stroked Jasira's nose. "Are you trying to get burned?"

"I was *trying* to apologize."

"Oh?" Auraelia asked, quirking a brow in his direction.

"Yeah. Come on, you're going to be late." Aiden pushed off the post and grabbed the reins of his borrowed horse, leading the stallion out of the stables.

They traveled in tense silence, the heaviness of Aiden's attempted conversation with Piper hanging like a weight between them.

When Auraelia couldn't take it anymore, she asked, "You doing okay over there?"

Aiden glanced her way, the look in his eyes questioning as he scanned her from head to toe. "How in the goddess are you dry?"

A laugh erupted from deep in her belly, causing it to ache. "I ask about your mental well-being, and you're worried about how I'm *dry*?"

Auraelia's laugh lightened to simple amusement as she pushed the bubble of air that surrounded her out until Aiden was also under its protective dome. When she swirled a warm breeze around him, drying out his soaked clothes, his eyes widened. "Better?" she asked, a knowing smirk on her lips.

"You're an ass, you know that? I could have been *dry* this whole time?!"

She shrugged. "All you had to do was ask."

"Goddess, I don't know how Daemon puts up with you." Laughter filled his tone, and a sense of relief washed over her.

"Can I ask you something?" Auraelia hedged after a few beats of silence.

"Didn't you just?" A cocky smile stretched across his face, and she couldn't help but smile in return.

"Asshole."

"So I've been told." His shoulders slumped slightly, and he let out a long, suffering sigh. "Just ask whatever question has been bugging you since we started this journey."

"I haven't—" He gave her a sardonic look that stopped her rebuttal in its tracks, and she huffed out a breath. "Fine. Why were you such an ass to Piper?"

"Yep. I was waiting for that."

"Well? Can you really blame me? From what she said, you two got all hot and heavy in the library—which I can't unsee, by the way, and my favorite place is now tainted, thank you very much. Then you left, and she never heard from you."

"I thought we were both under the impression it was a one-night thing."

Auraelia cut him a disbelieving glance. "A one-night thing? Is that why you did it *again* after the coronation party?" Aiden's eyes flicked to hers, then back toward the path ahead. "And if so, then why did you rope her back in when we went to Kalmeera?"

"Daemon wasn't kidding; you two really do share everything," Aiden grumbled.

"She's my best friend, Aiden. I may have to drag it out of her at times, but no, we don't keep secrets." Auraelia tugged on Jasira's reins, pulling her to a stop. Once Aiden did the same, she continued. "I've heard her side. Now I want yours."

"Auraelia—"

"If you don't want to tell me, then fine. We can go back to tolerating each other's presence. But I'd really rather not."

Aiden released a heavy sigh. "She deserves more than what I can give."

"You don't get to decide for her, Aiden."

He took a steadying breath. "Did Daemon ever tell you what power I wield?" She shook her head, and he nodded. "I'm an *empath*, Auraelia. I can read people's emotions better than Daemon can read the stars. For instance, right now, you're shocked but also slightly wary—which isn't surprising in the slightest." He huffed out a choked laugh. "There's a reason the Sapphire Isles named an empath as their emissary. I'm able to read the room and help...*guide* negotiations in the preferred direction."

"Can you manipulate people's emotions, too?"

Aiden gave her a wry smile, and a sense of ease washed over her. A lightweight feeling filled her heart, lifting away the heavy cloak of loneliness, longing, and dread for what was to come.

"What in the—are you?"

Aiden nodded sheepishly.

"Stop!" Within a fraction of a second, the heaviness settled back into her heart, pulling her under like being caught beneath a wave. Her breath came in quick, shallow pants as she tried to breathe through the ache that had settled into her chest once more. "What the fuck, Aiden?!"

"You asked," he deadpanned.

"A simple 'yes' or 'no' would have sufficed." A full-body chill ran through her as Aiden chuckled.

"True, but I needed to prove a point."

"Which was?"

"That I *could* have manipulated Piper's emotions in my favor if I wanted to. I could take away her disdain for me in an instant if I chose to."

"But you don't want to?"

"No, Auraelia. I do not want to control a woman's feelings for me. I don't want to control *anyone's* feelings; it's not right. Who am I to say how someone should feel?" Aiden ran a hand through his golden locks, mussing up the perfect coif he always wore. "As an empath, I feel *everything*. From joy to sorrow and everything in between. It's draining. After a while, I struggled to differentiate my emotions and feelings from those around me. So, I just...stopped."

"So, what? You just shoved your feelings down, locked them in a tight little box so you wouldn't have to deal with them?"

"Basically."

"So, what happened with Piper?"

"Piper was supposed to be a one-night thing." A small smile lifted the corners of his lips. "I was drawn to the fire in her eyes and that smart mouth of hers—much like the way Daemon was drawn to you, I'd imagine—and she was fun."

"So what changed?"

His smile faltered, and he sucked on a canine. "I could feel her feelings shifting, and I'm not that guy. I'm the fun guy, the 'let's meet up and fuck' guy, not the 'let's settle down and make babies' guy. And then, when you came to Kalmeera, I could feel Xander's feelings for her. So I backed off. She deserves someone like him. Someone who will put her first. She deserves a man who will settle down. And that's never going to be me."

"You like her."

"It doesn't matter."

"Aiden—"

"Rae, please. Just...let it go, okay? I'm fine with how my life is."

"No, you've accepted how you've *chosen* to live your life."

Aiden scoffed, a soft smile returning to his face. "You're one to talk."

"Hey! I'm learning—growing. And if I can do it, so can you."

"Whatever you say, *Your Majesty*."

"Come on, we're almost there." Auraelia chuckled, pressing her heels into Jasira's sides, urging her into a trot.

When the muddy field came into view, they slowed to a walk, the horses picking their way through the muck.

"Aiden?" Auraelia asked with slight hesitation.

"Yeah?"

"Thanks for telling me."

He met her smile with one of his own and inclined his head toward her. "Thank you for asking."

The smell of food cooking over open flames and the sound of laughter mixing with the squelch of boots in mud made for an interesting backdrop to the meeting she was attempting to have with Ser Aeron and Captain Soren—his first in command.

They stood around a small table, a map of Ixora laid across the top and draping over the sides. Tiny figurines that indicated the number of men they had and the known number that supported Davina were set into tight formation lines on top.

"How are the men doing? How's morale?" she asked, her gaze trained on Captain Soren.

She'd only met the man a handful of times since he rarely came to court, choosing instead to stay with his men in the barracks. Despite that, she trusted him—if only because Ser Aeron did.

"Morale is good, Your Majesty. The men are in good spirits despite the new circumstances."

"*What* new circumstances?" she asked, her voice sharpening.

Captain Soren's gaze shifted to Ser Aeron, who nodded once. "Tell her, Alaric."

The captain expelled a reluctant breath. "We're running low on supplies, ma'am. Food, fresh water. We're getting to the last of it."

Lightning struck just outside of the camp, causing some of the men to yelp in surprise.

"Your Majesty," her commander warned.

Lord fucking Harland.

Reining in the anger that burned in her stomach, Auraelia spoke through clenched teeth. "Lord Harland hasn't said anything about supplies running low. Quite the opposite, actually. He informed me that all was well. When was the last time he insured a drop-off? Did you know?" The latter was directed to Ser Aeron, who shook his head in response.

"General Koa had no knowledge of it, ma'am. I'd been communicating directly with Lord Harland. Though I realize now that I should have informed him sooner."

She almost forgot that out there, immersed among the men who had dedicated their lives to protecting the crown and the people the crown served, Ser Aeron wasn't *just* Ser Aeron. He was Commander General Koa.

Auraelia's fists clenched at her sides, her breath ragged as her anger began to build. "Captain Soren, I will *personally* handle ensuring that our troops get the necessary supplies. If there is anything else, do not hesitate to let me know. Whether directly or through the General."

Captain Soren nodded as he bowed at the waist. Directing her attention back to Ser Aeron, she said, "General Koa, if you would please escort me to the training ring. I'd like to...*observe*."

The smirk he gave her said he knew she didn't want to merely observe—he knew her too well. He knew all of her tells and could probably read her mood about as well as Aiden could—and that was *without* being an empath.

"As you wish, Your Majesty." He bowed, bending at the waist before sweeping his arm toward the opening in the tent. "If you'd follow me."

Aiden followed a few feet behind as they wove their way through tents and around circles of men that had gathered around a fire while they ate their lunch—their conversations stopping, food forgotten, as soon as Auraelia came into view.

There was a flurry of bows and a cacophony of mumbled *Your Majesty*'s before Ser Aeron barked out, "As you were!"

Auraelia met their wide-eye gazes with a smile and a small wave as they slowly returned to whatever they had been doing prior to her showing up. That was one thing she despised about being queen. She hated the formality that followed her everywhere. The bowing, the wide-eyed stares, and the palpable nervousness that came with them. She was a normal woman. She had hopes and dreams like everyone else...there just happened to be a heavy crown resting on her head and an entire kingdom that relied on her.

When they'd reached an empty stretch of path, Auraelia took a quick glance around before whispering, "I knew he was helping her come after me, but coming after his own people? I never thought he'd sink that low."

"It's all strategy, Auraelia. He can't come after you directly, so he's going to try and cut you off below the knees," Aiden cut in, hastening his steps to close the small gap between them.

Ser Aeron nodded, adding, "Depleting the men's resources could have gone in one of two ways. They could have either deserted—which none of my men would ever do, just so we're clear. Or, they would have turned on the crown—which, again, they would never do again."

Auraelia heaved a heavy sigh and pressed her fingers into her temples. "I want him gone. I want him out of my court and dealt with."

"I know. But you know we can't do that yet. You're smarter than he is, Auraelia. Let him think he's taking you apart from the inside while you work around him from the outside. He may be a rat, but you, my dear, are a fox."

"A fox?" Aiden chuffed. "I'd say more like one of Narissa's creatures from the deep. Lurking beneath the surface, lying in wait."

"Fox, sea creature, whatever analogy you want to use, *I* need to blow off some steam before a certain *rat* gets incinerated before it's *convenient,*" she fired back, lifting the hood of her cloak over her head.

Scowling toward the fenced-in training ring where two men grappled shirtless in its center, she asked, "Is that absolutely necessary?"

"No, but it beats having to launder your clothes on a daily basis." Ser Aeron winked, then shouted a call to attention at his men—all of whom promptly stopped what they were doing, their bodies going ramrod straight, arms motionless at their sides, as they waited for orders.

"Men," he began, "we have a special guest with us today. Impress her, and I may save you from having to face her in the ring."

"Is this really such a good idea?" Aiden asked in a hushed whisper.

"*Her,* General?" one man questioned, his bushy brows drawing together at the center.

"Indeed, gentlemen. Unless you're too afraid to take on your Queen." The smile on Ser Aeron's face was one of pure amusement as Auraelia stepped forward and tossed back her hood.

Smiling at the shocked faces before her, she let a kernel of her magic loose. Lightning flickered at her fingertips as she drew her sword from its sheath down her back and spun it over the back of her hand. "So, who's up first?"

Chapter Twenty-Nine

Daemon

In the five days since Daemon arrived in Kalmeera, he'd placed wards, had an—albeit unproductive and more argument than anything—conversation with his father, and helped rebuild some of the market. Out of all the things he knew he'd have to accomplish, having a simple council meeting shouldn't have been the worst. So why did it feel like it was about to become the most grueling task he'd have to complete?

He escorted his mother into the council chamber, helping her into the chair on his left before meeting the suspicious gazes of the men around the room. They all dipped their heads in reverence to him and the queen, but their expressions remained the same.

"What can we help you with, Your Majesty?" Master Calen—the master at arms—asked as he slowly sank into his chair.

"I'm merely here to support my son, Calen," Queen Avyanna explained, smoothing out the non-existent wrinkles in the skirt of her gown before her gaze traveled around the room. "Please, gentlemen. Have a seat."

"Is the king well?" The question was asked over a cacophony of chairs screeching across the stone floor as people took their places around the table.

When everyone had settled, Daemon slid into his seat, his eyes sharpening as he met every man's gaze, *begging* them to challenge him. Then, he lied through his teeth. "He is."

"If the king is well, why are *you* leading this meeting, *Your Highness*?" Lord Cassius questioned, his gaze narrow as it raked down Daemon's frame.

"Because I am the one who *called* this meeting. If you have an issue with that, you're more than welcome to excuse yourself." Daemon replied blandly, unwilling to give the man the reaction he was undoubtedly looking for.

The man was a snake in the grass, always had been. There were multiple advisors on the council, but Cassius was the one who was always whispering in King Evander's ear. The one who always pushed his own agenda with no regard for how it would affect the rest of the kingdom. And he would be the first one to go as soon as Daemon took the throne.

When Lord Cassius didn't move from his seat, his arms crossed over his chest like a disgruntled toddler, Daemon brought the meeting to order. "I've asked you here today to discuss the upcoming war between the Court of Emerald and the Court of Garnet."

"What's there to discuss?" Cassius' son, Lord Syrus, sneered, his thick brows drawing together as he rubbed a hand across his jaw.

The apple certainly hadn't fallen far from the tree. Syrus was just as bad as his father—if not worse. He was born into the title, just as Daemon was, but instead of rising to its challenges, he used it for leverage and to undermine those he found *beneath him*. His nose always seemed perpetually pointed toward the sky, and despite what Daemon's—or Syrus'—father had promised, there wasn't a chance in hell that Syrus was taking Lord Cassius' place on the council.

"What's there to—" Daemon scoffed, disbelief filling every pore as he met the gaze of his father's council. "Surely you're not *actually asking* me that question." When stoney gazes met his, he blew out a breath, fingers tightening on the arms of his chair as his shadows threatened to spill from every pore and demolish the men at the table. His jaw tightened, teeth grinding together as he gritted out, "We are here to decide how many troops we are going to send to Emerald to help—"

"*Emerald*? Why would we help Emerald? Your father—"

"My father has made a grave error in judgment. We will *not* be aligning ourselves with Garnet."

Lord Slater—Aiden's father and the master of ships—cleared his throat. "I don't believe that's your decision to be making, Prince Daemon."

James Slater was like a second father to Daemon. He taught him everything there was to know about ships and sailing the sea, so to hear him side with the Syrus and Cassius was like a punch to the gut.

Daemon pinched his eyes closed for a moment. Taking a deep inhale through his nose, he clenched and unclenched his fists to quell his churning anger, then let it out slowly. "Lord Slater, though I value your input, I did not ask for it. My father made certain promises about *my life*; I'm sure everyone in this room knows why. But I will *not* be subject to his rash decisions and let this realm fall into the wrong hands. If you disagree with my choices—" he swung his arm out wide, "then there's the door. Feel free to make use of it."

Lord Slater's eyes widened, his mouth popping open before closing once more.

"Now, if there are no more objections to my running this meeting. Can we *please* get on with it?"

When there were no further protests, Queen Avyanna gently squeezed his wrist below the table, and some of the tension that had begun to settle between his shoulders ebbed away. "I believe you now have their attention," she whispered, a conspiratorial smile inching across her lips.

The meeting went on for hours. Discussions over what side they should be on—or if they should even be involved at all—escalated into angry arguments that went nowhere. The majority understood—and backed—Daemon's stance, but there was still a handful who pushed back and stood with Lord Cassius and Lord Syrus.

"I don't see why we need to be involved at all." Lord Cassius insisted, running his thick hand over his beard. "If, as you say, you don't want to be subject to your father's *rash decisions*, then why stick your neck out at all? Let the...*women—*" he spat the word out, his lips turned down in a grimace, "handle their own *issues*."

"Their issues—as you so delicately put it—are concerns for the entire realm," Queen Avyanna said coolly, though the whites of her knuckles gave away her true feelings.

"My apologies, Your Majesty. This is a delicate matter, and things must be considered from all sides. I'm sure you understand." Lord Cassius's smile made Daemon's shadows thrash beneath the surface, and his mother gave a terse smile in response.

"I don't see why we don't just claim the land ourselves," Lord Syrus chimed in, popping a nut into his mouth.

"It's not ours to claim, Syrus," Daemon seethed.

"Or maybe *you're* not man enough to take advantage of the situation the Goddess gave you, *Prince.*" A Cheshire smile stretched across his wretched face, and black began seeping into Daemon's vision, shadows slipping through his hold as he took heavy pulls of air into his lungs.

"You may have a seat at this table, Syrus. But that's all it is. A seat. And that's only because your father got it for you. Your words hold no weight here. I suggest you remember that the next time you speak."

A flush began to creep up Syrus' neck, his nostrils flaring as he clenched his jaw. "I am a Lord. I have every right—"

"You may be a Lord, Syrus. But I am a Prince and the next King. You may have inherited your title just as I have, but the difference between you and me is that I also committed my life to earning my title. And in case it slipped your mind, I can also take yours away."

While some of the council's eyes widened—flicking between Daemon and Syrus with curious expressions—others fell to the table, finding anything to focus on other than the storm brewing in the room.

Syrus scoffed, leaning back in his chair as if he hadn't a care in the world as his lip pulled up into a sneer. "Maybe if you started using what's inside that *pretty head* of yours instead of thinking with your dick, we wouldn't be in this situation to begin with. I mean, I get it. Truly, I do." Syrus' lips pulled up into a knowing smile. "I can still feel the way she melted against me as we danced."

Images of Syrus dancing with Auraelia at both the Summer and Fall solstice celebrations burned through his mind. The way his hands constantly dipped too low on her back, the uncomfortable look on her face. It had taken more restraint than he thought he had not to pull her from his arms and even more not to cut the man's hands from his body right then and there. He called on that restraint now as Syrus continued.

"Her body is quite supple, isn't *Prince Daemon*?"

"Watch it." The words came out as a warning growl, but Syrus didn't seem to take the hint. Daemon spent his life learning the ins and outs of politics. How to act during these meetings and keep his composure when people were determined to get a rise out of him. But all of that training meant nothing as the next words spilled from Syrus' lips.

"I'm sure you could seduce her into giving you her kingdom. It's not like that bitch Auraelia is fit to rule anyway."

Black.

Endless, impenetrable darkness enveloped the room before gathering together and slamming Lord Syrus into the nearest wall. Cords of shadow wrapped around his neck, his arms, and his torso, lifting him until his feet dangled over the ground. Choked sounds came from his lips as Daemon appeared in front of him, like a nightmare given flesh.

"How *dare* you." Venom dripped from every word. "How dare you speak her name." Ropes of black slithered up Syrus' body, sliding along his face like they were searching for a place to burrow into. "*Queen* Auraelia has done more for her kingdom since she took the throne than you have in the whole of your miserable life. She's endured the worst of what the world had to throw at her with more grace and dignity than you have in your entire body. And you think that, what?" Daemon's gaze raked down his body, a sneer pulling one side of his lips upward. "That since you're a *man*—and trust me when I say that I use that term lightly—that she's unfit to rule?"

Syrus' face was splotchy, his eyes bulging out from their sockets, lips purpling under the grip Daemon's shadows held on his throat.

"I'm—sorry," he managed through a choked breath.

Daemon's laugh was sinister as he leaned infinitesimally closer. "I don't want your sorry excuse of an apology, you worthless piece of shit." He leaned in further until his lips were a breath away from Syrus' ear, his voice low as he ground out, "I want to hear you choke as I rob your body of air. I want to watch the life leave your eyes. Only then will you be worthy of saying her name, and that's only because you won't be able to."

Voices came from around him, but their sound was muffled by the rage roaring in his ears. He had just begun to tighten the grip around Syrus' neck when the melodic tone of his mother filtered through the fog of fury, shining an incandescent light into the darkness.

"Be still, my son. Release him. He's not worth it."

In all his life, he'd only experienced his mother's ability a handful of times—and it was usually when he wasn't paying attention to his tutors. But as an adult, she'd never infiltrated his mind. Never slipped into his thoughts. She viewed it as an invasion of privacy, and that respect for Daemon's personal boundaries always brought her the truth she sought without having to pull it from his mind.

"*Mother—*" Daemon internally growled, his eyes staying locked on the man before him.

"I know. But he's not worth the trouble this will undoubtedly bring you. Let him go."

Daemon huffed a disgruntled breath and yanked his shadows back into himself, sending Syrus crumbling to the floor.

"What is wrong with you?!" Lord Cassius bellowed as he rushed to his son's side.

"Lord Cassius, Lord Syrus, you are hereby dismissed from your positions on this council." Daemon's voice was calm and detached, his hands sliding into his pockets as he stared down at the two men.

"You can't do that!" Syrus screeched from the floor, eyes wide with panic as he rubbed the column of his throat.

"He can." The deep timbre of his father's voice filled the chamber, reverberating off the walls and silencing the protests that had begun to arise from the other members of the council.

"Your Majesty, surely you can't mean—" Lord Cassius stammered.

"You heard your prince. Now get that whimpering mess you call a man off my floor, and remove yourselves immediately. You are both dismissed, Cassius." The finality in King Evander's tone seemed to shake Lord Cassius to the core—his eyes narrowed into slits, his face turning cherry red as he yanked his son from the floor and practically dragged him out of the room.

Tension settled over the space, heavy like black clouds before a storm. "Does anyone else have anything that they would like to say?" King Evander asked, a singular brow rising in question.

What remained of the council shook their heads slowly before they all dropped to a knee with their heads bowed. It was Lord Slater who broke the silence. "No, Your Majesty. We are here to serve you."

"You want to serve me? Listen to what my son has to say. His is the only voice that matters when I am not present." The king turned toward Daemon. There was a heaviness of guilt in his gaze and a softness to his voice as he said, "And sometimes, even when I am, his is the voice of reason." Turning back to address the council more directly, he asked, "Is that understood?"

A chorus of "Yes, Your Majesty" filled the room, their gazes still downcast toward the floor.

"Let today be a lesson to you all. This war is coming, and we *will* be on the right side of it. You're dismissed."

The sound of feet scuffling across the floor filled the space as the men of the council rose and slipped out the door, but Daemon's gaze was trained on his father. He hadn't spoken to—or seen—him since their argument a few days ago, and the *last* thing he'd expected was for him to barge in and have his back.

After everyone aside from his mother and father left, and as the door closed behind Lord Slater, Daemon's brows pulled together as a tangled web of emotions ran rampant through him. He was grateful that his father had stepped in, but it didn't make sense after the conversation they'd had. Nothing seemed to make sense anymore.

Daemon scrubbed a hand down his face and blew out a short breath. "What was *that* about?" he asked, unable to keep the sharpness from his tone.

"Daemon—" His mother's tone was full of reproach, but his father held out a hand and gave her a gentle nod.

"It's okay, Avyanna. He has every right to be upset with me."

"*Upset*? You attempted to upheave my entire life with no regard to how it would affect me, this kingdom, or the realm!"

"You're right."

Shock slammed into him like a tidal wave, and Daemon couldn't help the recoil from the words. "*What*?"

"I said, you're right, son, about everything. I shouldn't have let her manipulate me. Shouldn't have agreed to that asinine marriage. I struck when I should have stayed my hand. If I had known—" King Evander blew out a breath and sank into one of the chairs surrounding the table. "If I had known it would have escalated to...to *that*. If I had known she was planning to kill Queen Adelina sooner, I would have done something to stop it. Turns out I didn't know much at all, and for that, I am immensely sorry."

"As much as I appreciate your words, Father. It's not me who needs to hear them." Daemon took a hesitant step forward and rested his hands on the back of a chair.

"I can't change what I've done, Daemon. But please allow me to help remedy it. Tell me what you need me to do, what you need our kingdom to do, and I will ensure it is done."

"How do I know you won't run back to Davina and tell her everything that we have planned?"

As if speaking her name had summoned it, King Evander launched into a coughing fit. Queen Avyanna knelt at his side, pulling his handkerchief from his pocket and handing it to him as she rubbed soothing circles along his back. When the coughs finally subsided, his father pulled the fabric away, the white linen once again painted in crimson.

"You may not trust my motives, son. But trust me on one thing. That bitch deserves to have the wrath of the Goddess rained down on her, and if I can put even the smallest hitch in her plan, well?" A cocky smile pulled across his blood-stained lips. "Then I can die with a shred of my soul intact."

"Father—"

"I thought I wasn't your father anymore?" His smirk grew a fraction before another cough wracked his body. "Listen, Daemon. You're going to be king one day, and that day may come sooner than we ever thought. And though I wish you wouldn't, if you choose to stay mad at me and keep me at arm's length, I would understand. But give a dying man his last wish?"

"Evander," Queen Avyanna whimpered, her eyes turning glassy as she stared at her husband.

Daemon held his father's gaze; the green of his eyes—once so similar to his own—were losing their vibrancy. Losing the fire that had always swirled in their depths. But there was also a glimpse of the man he once knew. The one Daemon thought he'd lost after his father bartered his only son to save his own skin.

Losing a shuddered breath, Daemon nodded. "Together, then?"

"Until the very end."

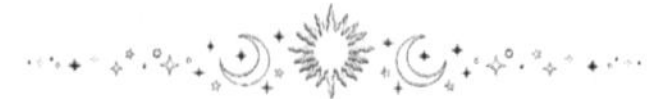

The sun's rays beat down against the harbor, sinking through the sweat-soaked linen of Daemon's tunic and bathing him in a burning heat. Yet still, he worked. The rope slid through his hands in rhythmic motions as he completed the intricate loops and twists of the knot he was working on. He'd just pulled it taut when the sound of light steps and the swish of fabric reached his ears.

"Hey, little brother," Yvaine trilled as she got closer, the chime of her bracelets ringing through the air as she waved in his direction.

Daemon stood and brought a hand to his brow to block out the blinding reflection of the sunlight bouncing off the water's surface. "Back already?" he asked, a small smile pulling on his lips.

"It's been four days, D." He shrugged nonchalantly, and Yvaine's mouth popped open. "Don't be an ass!"

A light chuckle rumbled in his chest as he closed the distance and embraced his sister.

"Ew, D. You're gross." She squirmed in his arms before giving up and wrapping her own around his waist. "I knew you missed me," she said smugly.

"Always, Vaine." He released his hold and eyed her curiously. "So, how'd it go?"

"Can't even give me a second to breathe first?" When Daemon gave her a bland look in response, she rolled her eyes and huffed out a breath. "Fine. Everything went well. Both Malaena and Lunaria are warded as instructed, and the Priestess' added additional ones around the temple as well."

"They added *more*? What? The nine-thousand steps that strip away your magic wasn't enough?"

"Evidently not." She shrugged, then poked her head around Daemon's frame. "You about done out here?"

"Just finished up, why?"

"Come on, I want to know what I missed while I was gone." Yvaine looped her arm through Daemon's and pulled him toward the end of the pier. "From the hushed whispers around court, you lost your cool in a council meeting. I thought we talked about that?"

"No, we talked about me not '*losing my cool*' on Father. Which I didn't do...kind of."

Yvaine let out an exasperated breath, her head falling back. "Come on. We can talk about all the messy details once we're back in your suite...but after food. I haven't eaten since I got home and am *famished.*"

An amused chuckle slipped between his lips. Then, pulling the shadows around them, he walked them back into his chambers.

Once the food had been consumed, Yvaine flopped onto his couch, her feet dangling over one of the arms. "So, tell me what happened."

Daemon let out a heavy breath, then recounted the events, watching as Yvaine's reactions shifted from shock and anger to the largest Cheshire grin he'd ever seen.

"Yes!" she exclaimed, bouncing in her seat like a kid who was about to get chocolate for dinner. "I've been *dying* for someone to bring those assholes down a notch."

"It wasn't my finest moment, but watching the blood drain from Syrus' face? It was worth it."

"I still can't believe Father stepped in. Lord Cassius has been in his ear for decades."

"Surprised me too, believe me." Daemon paused, taking a deep swig from his water glass. "Do you think he meant what he said? About helping put an end to this mess?"

Yvaine didn't answer immediately. Instead, she pushed up from the couch and walked toward the windows, pulling aside the sheer white fabric to gaze out over the harbor and city. "From what you've said, I think it's safe to believe him. But I don't know that I would fully trust him yet."

Daemon stood and met Yvaine at the window, taking in the views of the city he loved. The way the setting sun's light shone through the houses, casting the streets in a rainbow of colors. How the warm tangerine glow of the setting sun colored the sails of their ships, blending them into the skyline.

The silence lingered for a while as they watched the sun slowly sink into the sky, the clouds shifting to pastels from their normal crisp white.

"I need you to do something for me, Yvaine." She turned toward him, her brows furrowed as she waited for an explanation. "I need you to stay here while the world goes to shit."

"*Excuse me*?"

Daemon met her hardening gaze with a pleading one. "Please, Yvaine. I need you here."

"Over my dead body am I staying here while the realm erupts into chaos."

"Vaine—"

"No, Daemon. And don't pull that *I outrank you* bullshit either. You cannot *leave* me here. I can help; you know that I can."

"Of course, I know you can, but our people need someone here to protect them."

"Mother sure as shit isn't going to ride into battle. So, why should I stay?"

"Because I can't lose you, Yvaine."

"D—"

"No. Listen to me, okay? If something happens, and I don't make it back—"

"Don't you *dare* go there, Daemon Alexander." Angry tears lined her eyes, her lip trembling slightly as she pulled them into a tight line.

"*If* I don't make it back," he stressed, grasping her hands in his. "You are the best chance that our kingdom has. Hell, you're probably the best bet even if I do," he said with a nervous laugh.

Yvaine took a steadying breath, her eyes closing briefly before opening and piercing him with a hardened gaze. "Be that as it may, little brother. I'm not standing idly by while everyone I love fights for what they believe in. I am an asset. And if I have to sneak or sing my way onto a damn boat, I will."

"*Please*, don't—"

She canted her head in disbelief. "Would you tell Auraelia to stay out of it?"

"I uh—no. I wouldn't. Not that she would listen to me if I had." He palmed the back of his neck.

"So why try to force me to?"

"You're my sister, Yvaine. I don't want any harm to come to you."

"She's the love of your life, Daemon! She is the one you would bring the world to its knees for. Being your sister doesn't even compare. Though I appreciate your concern, and goddess, do I love you for it, little brother. But I am a grown woman. And much like the woman you love, I will make my own decisions for my own life."

Daemon stared at her for a moment, her reasoning swirling through his mind as his conversation with Sariah trickled back in. *Sariah was right; she really is so much like Auraelia.*

Tonguing a canine, Daemon nodded in acquiescence. "Alright, sis. You win."

Yvaine's eyes narrowed slightly, and she reached out her hand. "Bind it. I want your binding word that you will not try to keep me from the battlefield."

Daemon gave her a wry smile and clasped her forearm, her long, delicate fingers wrapped around his in return. "You sure you want to do this?" he asked, his brows rising. Magically binding a promise wasn't something to take lightly. Though it wasn't as serious as a blood bond, it still held weight, braiding the participant's magic together until the promise was fulfilled...or broken. It's said that when a bonded promise is broken, it would drive the offender mad. Cause their goddess-gifted magic to turn on them, destroying their minds, bodies, and souls. Though Daemon had never heard of someone breaking the commitment, he certainly wasn't going to be the first.

When she gave him a curt nod, he blew out a steadying breath and recited the binding spell. "I, Daemon Alexander, Crown Prince of the Sapphire Isle, do so swear that I will not inhibit Princess Yvaine Cordelia, firstborn of the Sapphire Isles, from participating in the upcoming conflict with the Court of Garnet." After a brief pause, he added, "Unless her life is in imminent danger." Yvaine's mouth opened to protest, but Daemon narrowed his gaze. He'd let her help win this war, but there wasn't a chance in hell that he would let her fall at someone's hand.

Yvaine released a resigned sigh and said her lines to complete the ritual. "I, Princess Yvaine Cordelia, firstborn of the Sapphire Isles, hereby accept Prince Daemon Alexander, Crown Prince of the Sapphire Isles' binding promise."

A surge of magic flowed between them, and warmth washed over him. It was like stepping into the surf heated by the sun's rays all day. Sliding along his shadows in languid movements like a calm tide. It twisted and twined with his magic, braiding them together in an intricate knot before settling and ebbing away—a kernel of Yvaine's magic nestling into his, sealing the promise and binding him to his word.

As they released each other, a loud knock sounded at the door. Crossing the room, Daemon pulled open the door to the same flush-faced guard who had brought him his father's summons. *You've got to be kidding me.* Snatching the missive from the man, he closed the door with more force than necessary and flipped the parchment over. Only, instead of his father's cobalt blue seal, pearlescent wax with twin-crossed swords pressed into it stared up at him.

Not wasting any time, Daemon broke the seal and opened the letter.

Prince Daemon,

Come to Opal.

Lady Aesira

"Fuck." Within a few words, his entire plan shifted. He'd planned on returning to Lyndaria—to Auraelia—the next day. But now? He couldn't just ignore the summons. If Lady Aesira needed him to come to Opal, it meant that something was wrong.

"What is it?" Yvaine asked, closing the distance between them.

Daemon passed over the note and ran his fingers through his hair.

"Shit," she hissed under her breath. "What do you think it's about?"

"I don't know. But I know I need to find out."

Chapter Thirty

Auraelia

Dark clouds loomed overhead, casting the city in a dreary gray and bringing a coolness to the air. Auraelia stood on the harbor's edge, arms folded protectively over her chest, hand clutched around her sapphire. The steady warmth of the stone and the pulse of Daemon's magic brought her a semblance of comfort as the wind bit through the wool and leather of her clothes, billowing her cloak out behind her. She didn't know how long she'd been standing there—just watching the ships bob on the water as sailors scurried about their duties—and it wasn't until she felt a familiar presence at her back that she pulled her gaze from the horizon.

"He's not coming back today, is he?" Aiden asked stoically, his gaze trained out over the water just as hers had been.

She shook her head slightly. "No. I got a note from him this morning. Lady Aesira needs him in Opal, though he's not sure why."

Aiden met her gaze, sympathy filling his honey-colored eyes. "He'll be back, Rae. You know he would be here if he could."

"I do, but the closer the new moon gets, the more anxious I become. I don't want this war, but I also can't stand by and let her ruin the realm." Auraelia blew out a heavy breath, her gaze returning to the water for a few moments before saying, "Come on, I don't want to keep Demir waiting."

Aiden turned halfway, his arm extended out toward where their horses were tied off. "After you."

As much as she missed Daemon and wanted him by her side, there was too much to do, and she was running out of time. Auraelia pulled the hood of her cloak over her head and gave the harbor one last longing look before turning away.

The Blacksmith Quarter was across the city, and as they rode through the streets, hope slithered into Auraelia's heart. Her people had been working tirelessly over the last week. They'd removed most of the debris from the streets, some areas had begun to rebuild, and tiny gardens had been replanted, bringing life and color back to the bleakness that seeped into their very foundation.

Each smiling face brought a lightness to her heart, and she met them all with one of her own.

This.

These people.

They were the reason she would meet her cousin on the battlefield. Not her mother's death. Not the attempt at stealing Daemon away. Not Caius' need to be free of her. Sure, she wanted Davina to pay for what she'd done, but *her people* were the only reason she needed to storm into battle. The only one that mattered.

Smoke billowed out of a chimney as they arrived at Master Demir's workshop. Heat seeped from the open work area, bringing with it the smell of a crackling fire and the clang of a hammer as it beat metal into submission against an anvil.

"Master Demir?" Auraelia called out tentatively as she stepped into the space.

The hammer met steel once more before the blacksmith straightened, surprise coloring his features as his brows pushed upward and he met Auraelia's gaze. "Your Majesty!"

He was covered in soot, his apron smooth and black from the years of work he put into his trade. He quickly bent at the waist, then straightened, placing his hammer on the nearest table before palming the back of his neck. "I'm sorry, I didn't see you there. I tend to get lost in my work."

Auraelia chuckled softly, then took another step inside. "It's quite alright. I didn't want to startle you and risk you mistaking your hand for the blade." Her eyes flicked to the darkened metal that was lying across the workspace. "May I?"

"Of course. It is yours, after all."

"Mine?" she asked excitedly. She'd commissioned him to make her a special blade, but she'd also stressed that the men in her army were top priority and hadn't been sure if he would have had time to complete it before the new moon. But as Auraelia took measured steps across the floor, watching as the firelight caught and danced along the inlay, her breath caught in her throat.

"Now, it's not quite finished, Your Majesty—"

Master Demir's words faded into the background as she ran her fingers along the still-warm steel. It was beautiful. The blade was thin but strong, and even with the black coating the metal, she could still make out the intricate scrollwork etched into the top where it would join the hilt. But down the center, laid into the core of the blade itself, was a long shard of emerald; the deep, rich hue glowing beneath the orange of the fire, bringing out the delicate veins that ran through the stone.

"It's made to the same specifications as your current short sword, so it should fit within the same sheath, should you choose to carry one and not the other. But I will have a separate sheath for it as well so that you can wear one at your hip if you need to carry both."

"It's stunning," she whispered, still so enraptured with the craftsmanship that she hadn't noticed that Aiden and Master Demir had closed the distance.

A faint flush colored Demir's cheeks when she met his gaze, but he cleared his throat and looked away, gesturing toward the back of the shop. "The new armor and weaponry are in the back if you'd like to see them."

She pulled her gaze from the blade and nodded, following in Master Demir's wake with Aiden close at her heels.

Auraelia ran the tips of her fingers along the smooth leaves of her mother's peony bushes. A few seemed to cling to the idea of what they used to be, but the once colorful shrubs had been reduced to darkened hues of green and brown without a bud in sight. Letting out a breath, Auraelia sat on one of the stone benches and tilted her face toward the sky, the sun's rays finally penetrating the dark clouds.

The sound of heavy, booted steps crunching on the gravel pulled her attention, but she kept her face upturned. "What is it?" she asked as the guard stopped a few feet away.

"Lady Blyana has arrived, Your Majesty."

"*Just* Lady Blyana?" Auraelia dropped her gaze to her guard, his throat bobbing around a swallow.

"Yes, Your Majesty." He seemed nervous, though she wasn't sure why. Perhaps it was because he was new; maybe it was due to the slight sharpness of her tone. Either way, she gave him a small smile, hoping to put him a little at ease.

"Thank you. Would you escort her out here, please?"

Some of the tension seemed to evaporate as he released a breath, his shoulders relaxing slightly. With a quick bow, the man retreated back to the castle, and she turned her face back skyward.

It wasn't long before the footsteps walking toward her filled her ears again, and Auraelia straightened, smoothing her braid over one shoulder.

"Your Majesty." There was a wariness to Lady Blyana's tone, and she dropped into a curtsey before approaching. "May I?" she asked, gesturing to the empty space on the bench.

Nodding, Auraelia tilted her face back toward the sky, her voice wistful as she said, "This was once my mother's garden. Peonies dotted every inch of these bushes, and my mother cared for them all. She hardly ever let the groundskeepers touch them."

Blyana shifted in her seat. "What happened to them?"

"They died with her," Auraelia stated flatly, shifting her gaze to the woman next to her.

"Queen Auraelia...I—" She stumbled over her words, her face paling. "I'm not sure what to say."

"I don't need you to say anything. My mother's death was not your doing." Auraelia let the silence linger for a few moments before steering the conversation in a new direction. She'd specifically asked that *both ladies* from Topaz come to court, and the fact that only one had shown was slightly concerning. "How is Lady Orna? My emissary says that the two of you have sequestered yourselves in your manor? I hope everything is well."

A small, tentative smile pulled at Blyana's lips. "She is well, but..."

"But, what?" Auraelia asked when her hesitation lasted longer than a breath.

"We're expecting, Your Majesty. That's why she didn't join me on the journey here."

A pang of guilt shot through Auraelia's chest, the anger she once held ebbing away as excitement took its place. "A *baby*?" she exclaimed, reaching over to grasp Blyana's hands in her own.

Lady Blyana nodded, her excitement palpable. "It's still early; she's only a few months along. But pregnancy sickness has been taking its toll. She can barely keep food down. It's why...why we haven't responded to your missives, Your Majesty. I've been so focused on keeping her comfortable that nearly everything else has fallen to the wayside."

Auraelia understood to an extent. She knew how hard pregnancies could be on a woman's body and could only imagine how the excitement would overshadow everything else, but there was a war coming, and she still needed answers. Clearing her throat, Auraelia squeezed Blyana's hands before releasing them. "I'm happy for you both; truly, I am. And I wish that I didn't have to push this on you when you have so much to be excited about. But war is coming, and I need to know where you and your court stand."

"I...I can't put Orna in harm's way, Your Majesty."

"I'm not asking you to. I would *never* ask you to put your wife's or your unborn child's life on the line. But that doesn't mean that your court isn't a part of what's coming."

Lady Blyana nodded, but there was a sadness in her eyes as they met Auraelia's. "My court is yours to command if that is what you choose to do." There was a 'but' that hung between them, and Auraelia waited as Lady Blyana gathered her thoughts. "But maybe we can be a safe haven for those seeking refuge?"

"A safe haven?"

A small smile tugged at her lips as she nodded. "We could open our borders to those who want to escape the brutalness of the war. Women, children, the elderly. Whomever you decide. I would see to their care personally. And we have the resources to feed them since Lord Harland stopped ship—*ments*." The word was broken into two, Blyana's expression twisting into a mix of confusion and concern when Auraelia's eyes shot wide, her fists clenching in her lap. "Are you alright, Your Majesty?"

Thunder boomed overhead as storm clouds rolled before the sun, blacking it out again. "What do you *mean* Lord Harland stopped shipments?"

"He sent a missive—"

"How long ago?" Auraelia demanded.

"About a week. Is everything alright?" Lady Blyana's brows drew together as she searched Auraelia's face.

Lightning crackled between the clouds, lighting up the sky with white light tinged in blue. "No, Lady Blyana. Everything is *not all right*."

Auraelia took a deep breath in through her nose and held it until her lungs screamed. There was nothing she could do—not yet anyway—and if he'd sent a missive to the Court of Topaz under the guise that the order had come from her? She blew out the air in her lungs and drew in a ragged breath. The crimes Lord Harland committed were mounting by the day, and she wasn't sure how long she could let this continue before her anger took over.

"Your Majesty?" Lady Blyana hedged. There was a slight tremor in her hand as she grasped Auraelia's.

Auraelia closed her eyes and released a shaky breath. "Lady Blyana, I appreciate and accept your offer of refuge. Please, make yourself at home. We've set up a suite for you in the castle's east wing. Once you're settled, please see my emissary to finalize the necessary details to set this plan into motion, and I will meet with you both later. If you'd please excuse me, I have another matter that I need to attend to." Auraelia rose, and Blyana followed suit, dipping into a curtsey before Auraelia turned and stalked up the path back to the castle.

Beneath the tightly coiled anger was a question that niggled at the back of her mind. If Lord Harland stopped the shipment of supplies, where were the money and resources designated for the exchange going?

Stopping as she reached the doors, Auraelia turned toward the same guard who had escorted Lady Blyana to the gardens. "Find Lady Ophelia and bring her to the council chambers. *Now.*"

His eyes widened a fraction before controlling his expression and bending at the waist. Not bothering to wait and see if he did as he was told, Auraelia continued on her way, her boots clicking on the stone floor as she hastened her steps.

"Your Majesty, I had no idea," Lady Ophelia repeated for what, Auraelia was sure, was the hundredth time since she'd entered the council chambers.

"Then where is it?!" she seethed, throwing her arms out wide before slamming them on the table as she stared down her Mistress of Coin. Auraelia's temples throbbed, her headache escalating into a migraine as her magic burned beneath her skin, begging to be released. Taking a ragged breath, she tightened her hold on her power. Internally, she grabbed the threads in both hands and shoved them deep down until it was just a steady thrum in her veins.

Lady Ophelia's face paled, her mouth opening and closing like a fish out of water as she seemed to search for a plausible answer. "I gave the money to Lord Harland; he's responsible for the shipments, Your Majesty. Always has been. I'm not sure what happened."

Her jaw ached from how tightly she was clenching her teeth. Everything always came back to *him*. He'd wormed his way into every facet of her court. Tried to take her down from within, and she'd just been *letting him*.

Let him continue to wreak havoc.

Allowed him to spin lies in her name to hide the atrocities that he had been committing.

Enough was enough.

Daemon told her to let him be. To let him believe that he was getting away with it. And though he may have been right in the beginning, there was no way she could let it continue. She needed to do *something*.

"Lady Ophelia, please meet with Lady Blyana and Mister Aramis in the east wing to remedy this situation. You're dismissed."

Ophelia's eyes widened as she hastily pushed back her chair and sank into a low curtsey before hurrying from the room.

Slowly, like a bead of water sliding down a glass, her magic began to flood her veins. Sweltering heat filled her body as her lightning raged beneath the surface. She may not be able to take out the man responsible, but the next best thing was only a few floors below. She hadn't had the courage to do what needed to be done when her mother had been murdered.

Hadn't been willing to sink to that level.

But this was war.

An example needed to be made.

If that meant blackening a part of her soul, then so be it.

Auraelia slammed her fists onto the table, then stormed down the hall between the council chambers and her suite, throwing open the door with enough force that it ricocheted off of the wall. When she stepped inside, she was met with the concerned gazes of Aiden and Piper.

"You're really going to go through with it, then?" Piper asked, her gaze hardening as it met Auraelia's.

"I am. Maybe then Lord Harland will understand that I'm not some meek little girl that will just let him take apart my court piece by piece."

"You're sure this is the path you want to take, Rae?" Aiden asked as he took a hesitant step forward, careful to keep an arm's length between himself and Piper.

"Do you see another way? Do *you*?" The latter was directed back to Piper, whose eyes went vacant and hazy for a moment before she blew out a resigned breath and shook her head.

"I didn't think so. You don't need to be a part of it. But I'm *tired* of people underestimating me. It's time to send a message. To Lord

Harland. Davina. Goddess, to all of Ixora at this point, because I can't be sure who is on my side and who is just waiting for me to fall."

"So what's the plan, Lightning Girl?" Aiden asked, a sly smile taking over his face.

Auraelia met his smile with a menacing one. "I think it's time I paid Kyra a visit."

"Is it always this fucking cold down here?" Aiden snapped, rubbing his hands together as he trailed closely behind Auraelia, his breath visible with every exhale.

Despite the thick wool of her tunic and cloak, the chill surrounding them as they descended toward the dungeon had Auraelia's skin pebbling, the flames in the sconces that illuminated the path doing nothing to ward off the icy bite to the air.

"Not typically. But then again, we don't tend to house prisoners, and it *is* winter," Piper retorted, her tone as cold as the air around them.

Aiden began muttering incoherently under his breath, and Auraelia rolled her eyes. She didn't have the bandwidth to deal with their squabbling. She needed to stay focused on the task at hand. Pulling on the shimmering blue thread representing her connection to the air around them, she pushed her magic out until a sphere of warmth surrounded them.

"Better?" she asked sardonically.

"Much," Aiden replied, a tad too cheery for her liking.

She was about to *kill* someone, and he was happy as a clam because he was no longer cold. With an exasperated huff, Auraelia quickened her pace down the steps.

She hadn't been down there since she came with Daemon, and the flashes of his hands on her in the stairwell, the heat of his body as he stood protectively behind her while she confronted the woman responsible for murdering her mother, sat like a heavy stone in the pit of her stomach.

She wanted him there with her.

He was her grounding force. Had been since they first met. Though she hadn't realized how much of a role he'd played in her life then, she now felt his absence like she would a missing limb. Without him there to keep her mind off of the rage and revenge that filled her, she wasn't sure *what* she would be capable of…or how far she would dive into the darkest parts of herself.

The door to the dungeon was slightly ajar as they came to the bottom of the steps, a cold breeze seeping through the crack and cutting through the warmth her magic provided.

An eerie silence met them as she cautiously pushed the door open, the hair on the back of her neck standing on end, her magic coiling tightly as if it was waiting to be unleashed.

Much to her surprise—and *annoyance*—there was no guard present, but Kyra was still in her cell, sitting on her cot with her back propped up against the wall.

Auraelia halted in the shadowed doorway for a moment to assess the woman beyond. Kyra was so still that she seemed lifeless. Her hair was a matted mess, her clothes dingier than they had been the last time she'd seen her, and there was a distinct stain on her clothing from where

Auraelia had struck her. Only the faint puff of air coming from between her lips signaled that she was still alive.

A pang of guilt shot through her heart with the sight, but it faded away as a choked, sinister laugh trickled out from the cell.

"Finally, come to finish what you started? Or are you going to run away again, like the scared little girl you are?" Kyra's eyes were closed, her voice hoarse, and the harsh rasp sent her into a cough that seemed to overtake her whole body.

Stealing her spine and adopting an air of nonchalance that she didn't feel, Auraelia closed the distance to the cell. "I see you didn't heed my advice," she said, gesturing to the festering wound on Kyra's leg.

A menacing smile tugged on Kyra's lips as she cracked her eyes open and peered at Auraelia. "Your healers must have lost their way to my cell."

Auraelia shrugged and sat in the chair that was still sitting where she'd left it. "Must have."

"So—" Kyra winced as she pushed away from the wall to adjust herself. "Is this it then? Am I to finally meet the Goddesses in Arcelia?"

Auraelia's chuckle was dark as her gaze clashed with Kyra's. "I think you and I both know you won't meet the Goddesses in Arcelia. You'll be lucky if the Goddess Keres claims your soul for the underrealm."

Kyra let out another choked laugh. "And what about you, *Your Majesty*? How black will your soul be once this is all over?"

Auraelia clenched her jaw, every muscle in her body drawing taut as she struggled to maintain some semblance of control. She knew that Kyra was going to push her. Had thought that their last encounter had been enough of a lesson to prepare her. But she'd been wrong.

One look at the smug smile beginning to stretch across Kyra's face had cracked her carefully placed mask, and her rage manifested tenfold.

Heat began to flood her veins, white light creeping into her vision as sparks lit the ends of her fingers. Everything that she'd been suppressing rushed to the surface.

Hate.

Pure, unfettered, and blinding hatred for the people who insisted on uprooting her life.

Lord Harland. Davina. Lady Lavena, Lord Kaemon of Pearl, and the assassins they'd sent to kill her.

But tangled within it was also hatred that she'd thought she'd squashed months ago. Hatred for her mother. For how she'd kept Auraelia in the dark all these years. For the secrets she'd refused to share that inevitably led to her death.

That realization fueled her rage into a living, breathing thing. The air around them stirred, and from her periphery, she could see Piper and Aiden stiffen where they stood just inside the doorway.

Blocking out the anxious gazes on their faces, Auraelia focused on the woman who'd set this all into motion. The one who would receive the brunt of the rage she'd kept bottled up for far too long. "I will turn my soul the color of the blackest night if it means keeping my people safe."

Kyra shifted then, turning her body to face Auraelia as a Cheshire grin spread across her lips. "Then we are one and the same."

"I am *nothing* like you."

Auraelia released the hold on her magic. Let it flow out of her in controlled waves and delve into Kyra, her lightning lighting up the dark cell. Kyra's screams bounced off the walls, echoing through the small chamber until Auraelia pulled the air from her lungs to smother the sound. Kyra's body convulsed so violently that she flung herself from her cot, her head landing with a loud crack against the stone floor.

She could feel the life beginning to leave Kyra's body.

Could feel her heart slam against her ribs as it attempted to pump blood to her dying limbs. Felt Kyra's lungs scream for the air Auraelia continued to deny them.

It was a rush like no other.

The feeling of holding someone's life in your hands. Of being the one to either grant them the gift of life or snuff out the light in their eyes.

Auraelia fed into that feeling, letting it build and grow until it nearly consumed her. The magic in her veins flooded every pore, and she poured it into the writhing woman in front of her.

She no longer cared what happened to her soul.

She no longer cared for anything other than the euphoria from delving into her darkest parts. From the feeling that seeking retribution gave her.

She was on the brink of fully succumbing to that alluring darkness when a ghost of a voice filtered into her mind.

You're not Kyra, Auraelia. And you sure as hell aren't Davina. You're one of the strongest people that I have ever met.

As if Daemon had been standing right beside her, the silky cadence of his voice wrapped around her like the shadows he commanded, luring her away from the nothingness that called her name. A welcome sense of calm washed over her, smoothing the rough edges of her soul and clearing the blinding rage that coursed in her veins. It was like being bathed in sunshine, and realization took its place as the darkness ebbed away.

Aiden.

Auraelia spooled her magic back into herself and collapsed into the chair. She hadn't even realized she'd risen from it until her legs gave out from under her.

Staring into the cell, Auraelia's stomach roiled. She thought she'd feel relief. Thought that ending Kyra's life would have brought her some semblance of peace. But as she looked at the lifeless body in front of her—at the way Kyra's limbs were broken and splayed in different directions, smoke rising in delicate swirls from the way her lightning had wreaked havoc on her body—she felt nothing but hopelessness.

She hadn't just killed her; she'd obliterated her.

Panicked voices surrounded her, but they all sounded like they were underwater—muffled and muted to the point of being unrecognizable. Auraelia pulled her gaze from the lifeless body on the other side of the cell bars and stared down at where her hands were trembling in her lap. To the darkened green stain on the tips that had grown past her second knuckle, and she couldn't help but wonder if they now mirrored her soul.

Auraelia squeezed her eyes shut, attempting to block out the image of Kyra's battered body, but it was emblazoned in her mind; her screams were a nightmare's echo.

She kept them closed despite feeling someone pulling the chair away from the cell. She kept them clenched when she felt warm, callused hands wrapped around her own. And even still, when a wash of calm settled over her and a warm, hesitant voice filled her ears.

"*Rae*?" When she didn't answer, the grip on her hands tightened to the point of pain, and the voice spoke again. "Come on, lightning girl. Talk to me. You alright?"

Auraelia let out a huff of a laugh as Aiden's voice finally permeated the fog clouding her mind. "I thought I told you not to call me that?"

His laugh seemed to be one of relief, and he loosened his grip on her hands. "You did, but I think the moniker fits. That was some power back there. Are you alright?"

As she cracked her eyes, she realized that not only had she been pulled away from the cell, but Aiden had turned her chair away from the devastation she'd caused. She met his honeyed gaze before letting hers travel to meet the glassy eyes of Piper, who was squatting by her side. When she met Aiden once more, she released a heavy sigh.

"Honestly? No, I'm not. I never intended for it to go that far."

"She got what she deserved," Aiden said with conviction.

"Did she? Or is what I did no better than what she did to my mother? What Davina did to my people and is planning to do to the realm?"

"Rae," Piper's hands replaced Aiden's, and Auraelia shifted her attention to her best friend. The tears in her hazel eyes made the green outshine the golden brown hues, and Auraelia latched onto them as she listened. "Kyra and Davina attacked your family and your people *unprovoked.* What you just did? No one can fault you for that reaction. And I hate to say it, but this isn't the only time you're going to have to do that. War is coming. *People are going to die.* There's no avoiding that, no matter how hard we might try."

Auraelia held Piper's gaze, then nodded. She knew Piper was right. Knew that not everyone could be—or should be—saved. But that didn't mean she shouldn't do everything in her power to save the ones she could. Taking a deep breath, Auraelia pulled her hands from Piper's and pushed up from the chair. Her knees buckled, and she was immensely grateful when Aiden wrapped his arm around her waist.

"You need to eat, Sparky."

Auraelia's eyebrows shot upward as she swiveled her head toward Aiden. "*Sparky*?"

"No, you're right. Lightning Girl fits better."

Auraelia shook her head and let out a small laugh. Knowing everything she did about Aiden, it shouldn't have surprised her that he'd try to lighten the mood with ill-placed humor. "Whatever you say, Blondie."

"Blondie?" Aiden gasped. "You wound me, Your Majesty."

Auraelia chuckled at their exchange and leaned into Aiden as he carefully maneuvered her around the chair and toward the door.

When they reached the threshold, Auraelia paused as an idea sprung to mind. Killing Kyra was meant to send a message, and letting her body rot in the dungeon or in the ground wouldn't do that. She pulled away from Aiden for a moment to meet his gaze head-on. "How discreetly do you think you could get her body to the border?"

"To the...border? Which border?" he asked hesitantly.

Auraelia didn't think a person's eyes could get as wide as Aiden's had become, shock etching every feature on his face as she said, "Garnet's."

Chapter Thirty-One

Caius

The air was crisp, the snow falling in delicate flurries around him as Caius trudged across the white expanse to the Onyx Mountains. The missive from Auraelia hadn't said much, but it had said enough that he'd jumped out of bed and threw on the first thing his hands made contact with in his wardrobe.

I left you something at the border at the foot of the Onyx Mountains. Consider it a gift from me to my cousin. A reminder of what she started and what I intend to finish.

-A

He still wasn't sure how she'd manipulated the crystals to send him something when that wasn't their intended purpose, but the blatant malevolence in her words had piqued his interest.

The Onyx Mountains marked the border between the Court of Emerald and the Court of Garnet, but the actual boundary line was on Emerald's side.

As he approached the foot of the mountains, Caius summoned the wintery air around him and moved within it until his feet touched down just outside of Emerald territory. Darkness clung to the area like a heavy blanket, making it hard to make out one shape from another, but the distinct smell of charred flesh filled his nostrils and churned his stomach.

Begrudgingly, he followed the foul smell until he came upon a person-sized roll of fabric dusted in a light layer of snow.

Squatting next to the emerald-toned wrapping, Caius carefully pulled back one of the loose ends. The stench hit him with full force, and he had to turn away as his dinner threatened to reappear.

What the fuck?

Swallowing down the bile that had risen in his throat, Caius turned back around to examine what appeared to be a body. The skin was black in some places, the lips cracked and bloody, but there was no mistaking the blonde hair that peeked through the grime and glimmered beneath the moonlight.

Kyra.

Shock rattled through him as he stared down at the lifeless corpse. He'd seen what Auraelia had done to Davina and had felt it to an extent on his own body. He'd heard what she and Daemon had done to the Court of Pearl's assassins.

But this?

This was an entirely new level that he'd never expected Auraelia to surpass. In the few conversations he'd had with her and from the observation missions that Davina had sent him on over the years, never in his wildest dreams had he thought that Auraelia held this level of viciousness within her.

But as he looked over Kyra's body, he knew, without a doubt, that Auraelia now held a darkness within her—one that could rival Davina's if she gave herself over to it.

Slowly, his shock turned to excitement, and a smile pulled up the corners of his lips.

Maybe she actually *could* do this.

Perhaps Davina would actually fall.

Clinging to that thought with everything he had, Caius placed the fabric back over Kyra's face and brought her back to Garnet.

Chapter Thirty-Two

Daemon

The sun's rays beat down on the Court of Opal, the heat seeping through Daemon's clothes and causing a pool of sweat to form at the base of his spine. The only saving grace was the cool breeze that blew in from off the water. Stripping off his leather jacket, Daemon closed his eyes and took a steadying breath as the wind cooled his skin, and Raneese guided the Nevermore into the harbor.

It had taken two days to get to Opal's main city—Lilura—from Kalmeera, meaning there were only three days until the new moon.

Three days until the realm fell into chaos and Auraelia met her cousin on the battlefield.

And it would take two of those days for the return trip to Lyndaria.

Daemon's grip tightened on the railing, his magic raging against the hold he kept on it. He needed to meet with Lady Aesira as soon as possible so that they could be on their way. Time was precious, and it seemed to slip through his fingers like the sand reaching as far as the eye could see.

The sound of Raneese calling out orders to their men pulled Daemon from the spiral his mind was attempting to dive into, and he scrubbed a hand down his face before running his fingers through his hair.

"Neese," he called out. Her gaze swung away from the bustle on deck to meet his, and she closed the distance within a few strides, coming to stand by his side with an expectant look on her face. "I need to see Aesira, but I need you to make sure that the crew is ready to go as soon as Xander and I get back." She huffed out a sardonic laugh, curls bouncing around her as she lightly shook her head from side to side, eyes surely kissing the back of her skull with how hard she'd rolled them. "I mean it, Neese. No one leaves the ship."

Raneese rubbed her forefinger and thumb across her brows and released an exasperated breath, her annoyance as clear as the sky above them. They'd had this conversation countless times over the last two days, but the pit in Daemon's stomach was growing by the second. He needed confirmation one more time. Needed to hear her relay it back, if only to soothe the nerves that pricked down his spine.

Letting out a resigned sigh, she said, "I know, D. As soon as I see you, we'll pull the lines, then shove off as soon as your boots hit the deck. I've got this." Her gaze was stern, locking onto his, *daring* him to question her again. When he finally let out a breath and nodded, the corner of her lips tilted upward. "Now, go do what you need to do so that we can get you back to your girl so you can quit bugging me."

Daemon let out an amused scoff and matched her grin with one of his own. "Bugging you, *huh*?"

"Absolutely. You've been a walking storm cloud ever since we left Lyndaria ten days ago. And have been up my ass, reminding me over and *over again* how today needs to go over the last two."

"Sorry, Neese," he said with a chuckle.

Raneese pursed her lips and shook her head, clearly fighting the smile still lingering.

"Daemon!" Xander shouted from the deck. "Let's go!"

"Impatient bastard," Daemon laughed.

Raneese's laugh filled the air. "No more than *you*. Go on. I've got the ship and the crew handled."

"You always do." Daemon smirked, pushed away from the railing, and shadow-walked to where Xander was waiting.

They made their way down the gangplank in silence and into the bustling port where sailors and merchants scurried about, none bothering to cast them a second glance.

When they reached the end of the harbor, Daemon asked, "You want to get there the fast way or go the long way?"

"The fast way, obviously. What kind of quest—" Xander's eyes widened, his head whipping toward Daemon. "Oh, *fuck* no. I saw what *that* did to Piper; I'm not about to let that happen to me when we're short on time."

Daemon couldn't help the laugh that tumbled from his throat. "You said you wanted the fast way. And as you said, we're short on time, so..."

"Fuck. No." Xander enunciated each word.

Shrugging, Daemon took a step back. "Suit yourself. I guess I'll see you there."

"Wait." Xander let out an aggravated sigh and scrubbed both hands down his face with a groan before tilting his head to both sides. "I don't have to *hold you* like my sister does, do I?" His lips pulled down into a sneer, and Daemon chuckled.

"No, that's purely because I like the feeling of her in my arms."

"Goddess," Xander mumbled, pinching the bridge of his nose.

Closing the distance he'd placed between them, Daemon quirked a brow and shrugged nonchalantly. "You asked. Now, are you ready?"

"Fuck," Xander said on a groan. "Yeah, I guess."

Daemon placed his hand on Xander's shoulder, and despite the limited amount of time they had and the anxiety over what was to come, he couldn't keep the laugh from his tone as he said, "Just remember to breathe."

"Wha—"

Xander's words were cut off as his shadows wrapped around them. When they dissipated, Xander staggered a step but maintained his footing as he pressed two fingers into both temples.

"You alright?" Daemon asked, his brows raised as he watched Xander work through the effects of shadow-walking for the first time.

"How in the goddess does Auraelia put up with that?" Xander groaned, dropping his hands to his knees as he drew in long, steady breaths.

Chuckling, Daemon slapped him on the back. "Deep breaths, Xander. We're here."

Standing upright once more, Xander's cheeks puffed out as he expelled a stream of air through pursed lips. "Let's go."

Guards stood like statues on either side of the arch, which served as the only entrance and exit into the Court of Opal's military compound. They nodded toward Daemon, acknowledging his presence and letting him know they could enter with a simple drop of their chins.

As they stepped under the arch, Xander's sharp intake of breath was audible, and Daemon cut him a glance out of the corner of his eye. "Never been here before?"

"No. Not once." His eyes were wide as he took in the sights around him, and it reminded Daemon of the first time he'd seen the home of the greatest warriors in Ixora.

The Court of Opal wasn't like the other courts. They didn't have grand manors or extravagant castles. They built the home for the head of their court in the center of their training facility. It was like a city within a city; the only thing separating it from the rest of the population was the barely six-foot-tall wall erected around it.

Buildings of all shapes and sizes were lined in neat rows, each of them set apart by the personal touches added by their inhabitants. Canopies of the richest purples and brightest blues extended out over doorways, and plants dotted a few of the windowsills. Towering trees created little, shaded oases amidst the copper-colored sand that coated the ground. Lush green grass sprouted around their trunks but didn't dare to grow beyond the shade the tree provided.

As they made their way through the compound, the sound of warriors training reached Daemon's ears. Mixed in with the sound of swords crashing together was the distinct sound of flesh hitting flesh. And as the training field came into view—which was more sand than it was field—Xander halted in his tracks, eyes roving over the sight in front of them.

"I knew they were well trained, but I never expected *this*." Xander gestured to the scene in front of them and let out a low whistle. "If his skills were solely the byproduct of being a member of the academy here, it's no wonder my mother wanted Ser Aeron to train Auraelia and me."

The pitch was sectioned off into four different areas: sparring, weapon and combat training, physical training—which included an obstacle course—and finally, magic-wielding.

"I'm pretty sure that Ser Aeron still holds the 'greatest warrior in all of Ixora' title, even after all of these years," Daemon said with reverence. He had immense respect for Emerald's Army Commander, especially after seeing the way Auraelia handled herself in training all those months ago. Ser Aeron didn't treat her like a fragile flower; he seemed to treat her like any other warrior, which would come in handy in the coming days.

Xander began rattling off different observations he'd made, but his words faded into the background as the hairs on the back of Daemon's neck stood on end, his shadows swirling, seeming to sense something he couldn't.

"I take great offense to that statement, Prince Daemon. Shall we see how you fair against me in the ring?" The voice was warm and smoother than silk, but there was an underlying deadliness to it that Daemon recognized immediately.

Lady Iridessa.

Seeming to come to the same conclusion, Xander smirked, rolling his eyes as he shook his head and turned around. "Dessa, I wouldn't enter the ring with you if both of your hands were tied behind your back and you were blindfolded. And that was *before* you went through the Warrior Academy."

A menacing smile tugged on her lips, her eyes sparkling with a mischief that reminded him of Auraelia. "It's *Inara's Warrior* Academy, and I didn't ask you; I asked *him*." She tilted her head in Daemon's direction, her grin growing as she raked her eyes down his frame.

"Don't even think about it, Daemon. She doesn't fight fair."

Iridessa scoffed, her hand flying to her chest in feigned innocence. "I do, too." When Xander raised his brows in challenge, she narrowed her eyes. "It was one time, Xander. And long enough ago that you should have gotten over it by now."

"Once was enough."

Daemon's gaze shifted between them, a singular brow arched as he attempted to follow their conversation.

Seeming to notice his confusion, Iridessa turned his way with an exasperated sigh. "When we were kids, Xander and I got into a...*scuffle*."

"*Scuffle*? She hit me with a metal tray because I took the last chocolate croissant," Xander deadpanned.

"Can't say I wouldn't have done the same," Daemon replied with a laugh.

"Oh, fuck off."

Iridessa snickered, then looped her arm through Daemon's. "Come on, I was sent to retrieve you. Mother and Father are waiting."

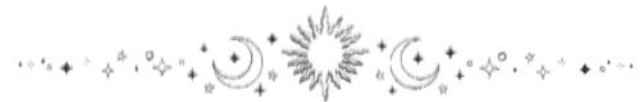

"When did this begin again?" Daemon asked, his eyes trained on the map Lord Arlo had rolled out over the tabletop. They'd been staring at the damned thing for at least an hour, trying to figure out the best course of action, and all that resulted was them talking in circles.

"Pearl's forces have been steadily lining up at the border over the last day or so. We'd heard whispers of them gathering their troops to move out, which is when I sent you that missive." Lady Aesira was sitting in the chair at the head of the table, her chin perched on threaded fingers as she, too, tried to make sense of their situation.

"We know that Davina won't move until she does whatever fucking blood ritual bullshit she's planning, and that's still three days away," Xander said with an exaggerated wave of his hand, pacing the length of the room once more before returning to the table. "So why would Pearl be assembling their forces *now*?"

"That's what we still don't know." Lord Arlo's deep timbre rumbled through the room as he stood sentinel by his wife's side, his hand resting reassuringly on her shoulder.

"What do you need from me?" Daemon asked.

"At this moment? I need you to get this information to Auraelia. But we may need assistance when the time comes. We've caught wind of their numbers, and though we are unmatched when it comes to combat, I'd still like to tip the odds in our favor."

Daemon scanned the map and the tiny figurines that dotted its surface, each one representing fifty soldiers. From their information, the Court of Pearl's forces seemed to be evenly matched in numbers to Opal's. But even with that, there was no way for them to match the efficiency that Lady Aesira's warriors fought with. Their accuracy was unmatched, and every movement was graceful, precise, and deadly.

Finally peeling his eyes from the lines of the map, Daemon met the hard gazes of the lord and lady of Opal. "I will send word to my Father and tell him to send half of the fleet here. They should be here in two days' time."

"Your *father*?" Lady Aesira seethed, her eyes wide as she clenched her jaw.

Daemon recoiled at the venom that laced her words. He'd briefly forgotten the relationship between the two courts and the women who led them. It was well known that Lady Aesira and the former Queen of Emerald had been close, so close that the Court of Opal sent its best warrior to train her children—a fact that Daemon was more grateful for than ever as the war drew closer.

"Lady Aesira, I know that my father is likely the last person you'd seek help from, but he wants to see Davina fall just as much as we do."

"Oh? And what gave you that impression? Him signing away your life?"

Daemon blew out a breath. There was only one way that he could potentially change her mind to the point where she would accept his father's help...he just hoped it would be enough. "He's dying, Lady Aesira. Months ago, Davina orchestrated someone to poison my father in low doses over time." Aesira's eyes narrowed, but he continued. "Sometime before the Fall Solstice Ball, she presented him with the antidote and the conditions that came with it. He didn't think. All he knew was that he didn't want to die—didn't want to leave my mother. Since then, he's fallen ill again. Only it's worse this time. He knows he may not live to see the end of this war, but he wants to help."

The room fell silent, Daemon's words hanging in the air like a swinging pendulum.

Lady Aesira looked to her husband, who cupped her cheek, then bent to rest his brow on hers. When he pulled away, she blew out a resigned breath and met Daemon's gaze.

"Send the message to your father, then get your ass back to Lyndaria. So help me, Prince Daemon, if Auraelia falls, I will find *you* at fault. And there won't be a Goddess in all of Arcelia who would be able to save you."

Even with the seriousness in her tone—and the accusatory finger pointed in his direction—Daemon let his smirk shine. "I wouldn't have it any other way."

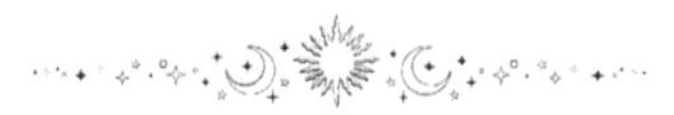

Auraelia

"Just set the tables up on the far wall," Auraelia called out as a group of men carried them into the ballroom. She hadn't stepped foot in this area of the castle since that fateful night. She'd kept the room sealed off, not wanting the physical reminder of when her entire life was turned upside-down—her nightmares haunted her enough. Months passed, and it still hadn't seemed to right itself, and it didn't seem like it would until the conflict with her cousin was over.

Taking a deep breath through her nose, Auraelia let her gaze slowly trail across the space. The windows were still blown out from when her magic had taken on a life of its own, but their glass had finally been removed from the marble floors, the late afternoon sun shining through the empty panes. The once beautiful crystal chandeliers were nearly bare but had been outfitted with new lights so that they functioned once more. The flowers wrapped around the columns had long since died and were replaced by twisting vines. Tables lined the walls and were slowly being filled with the food they could spare and tankards for the ale that Madame Sylvie promised as a thank-you for getting her ladies to safety in the Court of Topaz.

It was all starting to come together.

Ever so slowly, life was being brought back to the room that held so many harsh memories, and a hesitant smile began to tilt up the corners of her mouth.

"Planning your victory party already?" Daemon's husky tone washed over her body, bathing her in a warmth that seemed to have seeped away the moment he left Lyndaria's shores.

His name was nothing more than a breath on her lips, her heart racing into a gallop in her chest as she whirled around and met the mossy green of his eyes. The cheeky grin on his face did nothing to dim the adoration there or the love that she felt deep in the very fabric of her being. Her magic ignited beneath her skin, moving languidly through her veins like liquid fire and pushing against her hold as if it were trying to reach for him.

"Hello, my star."

In one stride, Auraelia leaped into his arms, hers wrapping around his neck as her fingers found their way into his hair. She could feel his smile as she pressed her lips to his, his arms tightening around her waist, and he held her against him.

Home.

No other word could accurately explain the feeling of being wrapped in his embrace. The way his heart always seemed to beat in synchrony with her own. How their magic seemed to seep from one and into the other, swirling and weaving together in a tapestry to form a beautiful mural.

"I've missed you," Auraelia whispered, pressing her brow to Daemon's, their breaths mingling together in their shared space.

"You have no idea," he sighed, his tone reverent as he lowered her back to the ground and pressed a chaste kiss to her brow. His hold on her loosened, but his arms remained wrapped around her as if he couldn't bear the thought of letting her go. They shared a smile as he gently ran his thumb across her cheek, and then he looked over her shoulder and around the ballroom. "So, are you?"

"Am I what?"

"Planning your victory party," he said with a laugh, his eyes sparkling as they met hers once more.

Auraelia scrunched her nose. "It's more of a '*the realm is about to erupt into chaos, so we might as well celebrate life as we know it before it implodes'* party."

Daemon tried to suppress his smile as he let out a muffled chuckle, tonguing a canine as he nodded his head. "Do you need any help?"

"No, *we've* got it. She's been having me do all of her *dirty work.*" Aiden's honeyed voice echoed through the room, briefly pulling Daemon's gaze from her own.

"Do I even *want* to know what he's implying?" Daemon raised a brow with his question, and Auraelia's lips turned inward. "*Auraelia*, what does he mean?"

"I'd like the answer to that question as well." Auraelia leaned around Daemon to see her brother propped against the threshold. "Hey, Rae," Xander said with a smile.

She could feel the flush creeping up her neck and into her cheeks. "Now is not the time or place for that particular conversation."

"Oh?" Xander's brow quirked as he pushed off the doorframe and closed the distance to where she was standing with Daemon.

Reluctantly pulling out of Daemon's embrace, she turned to cut Aiden a glare. "Damn it, blondie."

"*Blondie*?" Daemon's surprise was evident in his tone, his eyes flicking between Auraelia and Aiden.

"Don't look at me, ask lightning girl."

"*Lightning girl*?!" The confusion on Daemon and Xander's faces had Auraelia choking on a laugh that grew into an explosion of hysterics as Daemon asked, "What the fuck did we miss in the last twelve days?"

"A whole hell of a lot, D. A *whole* hell of a lot," Aiden said with a smile, mischief shining in his honey-colored gaze as he waggled his brows in her direction.

Auraelia rolled her eyes but returned his smile before returning to Daemon, slipping her hand into his. "Come on, I'll fill you in while we get ready."

"You killed Kyra?" Daemon asked as he pulled his trousers over his hips.

After they'd gotten back to her chambers, clothes had been ripped and flung to opposite corners of the room, their bodies colliding like a wave crashing against the shore in a storm. They'd spent more time remapping each other's bodies and drawing out their pleasure than they had talking. But they'd reluctantly pulled apart when the sun began to kiss the horizon, the last remnants of light bathing her room in a warm tangerine glow, and Auraelia finally told him everything.

"That's putting it mildly, don't you think?" she asked with a sheepish smile. She'd gone into more detail than was necessary, but as soon as she began, the words seemed to tumble from her lips like water spilling over a cliff.

"Are you alright?" he asked, his warm, callused hands sliding up and down her arms in a comforting rhythm.

"More so now than I had been. Aiden's been helping me, even after I made him bring her body to the border."

"Auraelia." Daemon pinched the bridge of his nose and expelled a ragged breath. "Are you trying to piss her off?"

She opened her mouth to respond, but the way Daemon's eyes snapped to hers—a little *v* appearing between his brows—made her stop.

"What do you *mean*, Aiden's been helping you? Helping you *how*?"

"Jealous?" she asked with a chuckle.

"*Auraelia.*"

She palmed his cheek and gave him a small smile. "He told me." Daemon's brows pinched further together. "I know he's an empath, Daemon. After I...*eviscerated*...Kyra, he numbed what I was feeling." Daemon's eyes shot wide, and she shook her head, a silent request to let her finish. "Slowly, over the next day or so, he let the weight of what I did settle back into me. Let me work through my feelings in small, manageable doses. He's a great friend; I can see why he's your right-hand man." A small smile played on Auraelia's lips as she watched her words sink in.

His eyes softened, and he brought a hand up to cover the one on his cheek. He leaned into it for a brief moment before he twisted his head to press a kiss on her palm. "Thank you for giving him a chance."

"And for not killing him?" she asked jokingly.

Daemon snickered and pressed his lips to her palm once more. "That, too, my star. That, too."

Chapter Thirty-Three

Auraelia

The party was in full swing when Auraelia and Daemon made their way to the ballroom. Music filled the space, mingling in the air with trills of laughter and the clink of glasses as people reveled in the calm before the impending storm. Auraelia's heart clenched in her chest—an ache radiating down into her very soul—as she stopped in the doorway to watch her people.

How many of them would live to see the sunrise in two days' time? Would they survive to see their loved ones grow into the people they were destined to be? Make it through to have children at all?

Would *she*?

She was as prepared as she could be. Trained until her muscles screamed for a break and her magic dimmed in her veins. But still, there was a lingering thought in the back of her mind. Would she be the one who walked off the battlefield victorious? Or would Davina come out on top, finally achieving the goal she'd set out to obtain by prying Auraelia's kingdom from her grasp?

Daemon's hand tightened around her own, and it was as if she could finally take in a full breath. She turned her face his way, and the love in his eyes sent flutters through her stomach. But then he smiled that crooked smile that always made her knees weak, and those flutters grew wings. The way he could read her body and sense every time she began to spiral into the darkest corners of her mind would never cease to amaze her. The way he always seemed to know just what to do or say to pull her back from that ledge. He'd always been able to read her, but as they grew closer, as their magic and souls seemed to meld together, it was as if a piece of him had seeped into her very being, giving him unfettered access to everything she was.

"Breathe, my love. They know what is to come and what they are fighting for."

"That doesn't make this any easier," she whispered, turning her gaze back toward the people gathered.

"I know, but I also know that they would gladly die for you and your reign. As would I." Auraelia's gaze snapped to his, and his smirk shifted into a smile full of warmth. "Come on. Tomorrow will come soon enough, and I want to enjoy this night with you."

Daemon tugged on her hand, gently guiding her further into the ballroom and the revelry around them, and she couldn't help but return his smile. As they neared the center of the room, he pulled her flush to his body, his arm snaking around the small of her back as he pressed a kiss to her brow. "Dance with me?"

Auraelia tilted her face toward his, watching his eyes flick between her own as if he worried she would deny him that simple request. A soft smile pulled up the corners of her lips as she cupped his cheek in her hand. "Until the stars fall from the heavens."

It wasn't until Auraelia stepped out into the garden for a moment of fresh, cool air that she realized how much time had passed. Stars filled the sky, twinkling against the velvety darkness that blanketed overhead with the absence of the moon.

A heaviness began to settle in her chest as reality attempted to creep in, but as she inhaled the crisp winter air, she pushed it down and smiled. Time sped by, seconds ticking into minutes and hours, and there was no stopping it—regardless of how much she wished to. But that night hadn't been measured in the minutes that made up so many of her days. She measured it in the laughter that still echoed through the ballroom and filtered out the empty windowpanes. In the twirls around the dance floor wrapped in Daemon's arms, and the drinks and stories that had been shared with her people.

Auraelia took a steadying breath as she stared into the moonless sky, its implications settling into her bones as resignation made its home in her soul. Dalia—the Goddess of Fate—had already decided how the battle would end. She'd decided who would walk away from the field victorious. And though Auraelia didn't know—or understand—the reasons why, she had no choice but to accept the path that had been laid before her...she just hoped that the goddess was on her side.

The air grew colder the longer she stood outside the ballroom, but she stayed. She let herself get lost in the formation of the stars, sought out the clusters that Daemon had shown her, and allowed her mind to wander. She'd just found the ones that made the shape of an archer when she sensed Daemon behind her. She kept her face tilted toward the sky and smiled as his arms wrapped around her torso. She leaned back into his touch.

"Find what you're looking for, my star?" His breath was hot against her neck, his lips soft as he trailed a line of kisses down the column of her throat.

"I think it found me."

She felt him smile as he pressed another kiss to her neck before gently turning her to face him. "Do you think they'll miss us if we escape for a little while?"

Auraelia quirked a brow, her head canting slightly as she searched his face in the dim light that filtered out of the ballroom. "Escape to where?"

Daemon's mischievous grin was infectious, and she couldn't help but return it. He pulled her to him, and shadows whisked them away into the night.

When the shadows dissipated, Auraelia's brows pinched as she took in the familiar line of trees. "Nefeli Lake?"

Daemon's arms slipped from around her, his hand sliding into hers as he guided her through the trees. "While I was in Kalmeera, I did some digging in the archives for any information that may be helpful in the battle against Davina. And though I didn't find anything that would help you or us, I did find something interesting."

"Oh?" Auraelia asked, intrigued—but also slightly confused—as to where this conversation could possibly be going and what it had to do with the lake. When the silence lingered, she let out a small laugh. "Care to share what that discovery was?"

"Patience, my star." He replied, laughing when she groaned in disapproval. "It's worth the wait, I promise."

When they arrived at the willow, Auraelia sent a wisp of magic to pull the vines aside and let Daemon guide her through them and to the bank on the other side. Fireflies danced in the tall grass surrounding the lake, and the stars were a shimmering reflection on the water's still surface.

They sat in silence, staring up at the stars that twinkled overhead, but when it lingered too long, Auraelia turned toward him. "Daemon—"

"When you brought me here the first time, I remember my first thought being that it looked like a piece of my home had been dropped into yours. And at the time, it seemed far-fetched and nonsensical. But, when I was in the archives, I found a box full of journals and letters." Daemon pulled his gaze from the stars and turned toward her, grasping her hands. "Journals and letters from Killian and Astraea."

Auraelia's heart leaped into her throat, her eyes flicking frantically between his as she waited for him to continue.

"Those dreams we've been having? They truly are memories, Auraelia. And this place?" He released one of her hands to gesture around them. "This was a gift from Killian to Astraea."

"I—I don't understand."

Daemon pulled her into his lap and cupped her face between his hands. "I don't know how he did it, he didn't say in the journal entry I read, but somehow he got a piece of the Sapphire Isles to Lyndaria. He gave her a piece of his home, of *him*, after she became engaged."

"But, he was married... wasn't he?"

"He was." He nodded gravely. "But it seems that he was still holding onto some shred of hope that they could be together. That if she wasn't married, he could still have her."

Auraelia tracked his movement as he dropped her hand and reached into his vest pocket. When he pulled out an aged piece of parchment, her breath caught in her throat.

"Here. It might make more sense if you read it for yourself. I think it's a draft of the letter he sent to her."

She didn't understand why her hands were trembling as she gently took the paper from Daemon. Tears were already welling in her eyes as she thought back to the pain she'd endured in her dreams. Pain that had felt so real...because it had been. She'd been *reliving* a love that had ended in heartbreak.

She unfolded the parchment with gentle fingers, smoothing out the creases before running her finger along the one jagged edge from where Daemon had pulled it from its binding. The writing seemed rushed; some of the lines had been crossed out, and there appeared to be tear stains where the ink had run.

Closing her eyes for a brief moment, Auraelia inhaled deeply, letting it out slowly as she read the first line on the page.

My dearest Astraea,

~~Please don't do this. Don't marry him.~~

Today is your wedding day, and I find my head and my heart battling for what I am to do. My head says this is the way it was meant to be. That this treaty between our two kingdoms is what is best for the realm. That it must stand for the betterment of our people.

But my heart? Oh, my star, my heart rages in my chest with the absurdity of it all. How could the Goddesses put you in my life only for Dalia to decide we weren't meant to be?

~~How could she be so cruel to punish us for my father's wrongdoings? That's what this is, isn't it?~~

My heart, my mind, my body all yearn to be near you. To be in your light, to hear your laugh, and see your smile. My magic rebels against me with every moment I am not in your presence.

~~This cruel twist of fate has left me hollow, leaving me to resent my people—my place on this throne. And though I know you don't want that for me, I can't help but feel like my life is of no consequence if you are not by my side.~~

But as I am a man of pride and conviction, I cannot leave my people, nor ask you to leave yours. Which leads me to this. Upon my last visit to Lyndaria, I left a piece of me behind. In an open space beyond your beloved lavender field, behind the willow we loved so much, is a lake crafted from the Azure Falls in Kalmeera. Visit it, my star, and it will flourish as our love did. And as long as you hold love for me in your heart, that place will live on.

I know that we cannot be, that fate dealt us a hand neither of us could win.

But at least I could give you a place all your own to remember me. To remember what we had.

I love you, Astraea. More than there are stars in the sky or words could ever convey. You own every inch of my heart. Consume every corner of my mind and soul.

Perhaps in another life, we can get the ending we deserve.

Yours, forever more.
Killian

Tears streamed down Auraelia's face.

Tears for the love that was lost lifetimes ago and for the love that had been renewed between herself and Daemon.

Carefully, she refolded the parchment and handed it back to him. "How—how could she just let him go?" Her voice quavered as she spoke, and he gently wiped away the tears that continued to fall.

"She did what she thought was best for her people; they both did."

His words struck a chord, like a bolt of lightning straight to her heart. She'd done the same thing. Repeated a history that had been lost or unknown for centuries.

"I'm so sorry, Daemon. I—"

"Have nothing to be sorry for, my star." His finger slid beneath her chin, and he tilted her face up toward his. "You did what you thought was best for your people; I cannot blame you for that. You also *came back* to me. You let me in, and for that, I will be forever grateful."

My star.

Suddenly, his nickname for her held more weight than it previously had. They'd unknowingly followed in their ancestor's footsteps. Step by step, history had begun to repeat itself; she just hoped their ending wouldn't be the same.

"Daemon—"

"I love you, Auraelia. Even if the stars fall from the sky. Even if the world is cinders around us, I will always love you."

A sob caught in her throat. How he could still love her after everything she'd put him through, Auraelia would never understand. But it was also something she would never take for granted again. "I love you, too."

Daemon's lips pressed against hers, soft yet demanding as his hands twisted in the strands of hair at the base of her skull. When he broke away, his words were barely a whisper against her lips. "Marry me."

Daemon

It wasn't a question or a demand.

It was more of a plea.

Nothing in this world would have made him happier at that moment than to hear her say *yes*, but instead, she pulled back, confusion swirling in her slate-gray eyes as they flicked between his own.

"What?"

"Marry me, Auraelia."

A small laugh slipped from her lips, but there was a light in her eyes that would rival the sun on the brightest day. "How much did you have to drink tonight?"

"Enough to give me the courage to beg you to be my wife, but not so much that I don't mean every word that I'm saying. Marry me, my star. Please."

"Daemon—" she chided gently, her thumb idly running across his cheek. "There is a war coming. It's right outside our doors, and you're asking me to *marry you*?"

"Yes, I am. Nothing would make me happier in this world than to have you by my side. To know that nothing, not even death, could tear us apart. Please," he rested his forehead against hers. "Say you'll be mine."

Auraelia released a breath and leaned into him. "My love, I have always been yours. From the moment we met, you have had a hold on me. But—"

"But what, Auraelia?" he asked, pulling away once more as a heavy stone settled in his stomach.

"But now is not the time. If we make it through this war—"

"When," he amended, and the smile she gave him had his heart skittering in his chest.

"Ask me *when* we make it to the other side of this. When the fate of our people isn't hanging in the balance. Ask me when nothing else is on my mind but you."

Daemon gave a slight shake of his head, then briefly pressed his lips to hers. "It's not the answer I was hoping for, but it is the one I will accept...*for now*."

"Thank you." She smiled as her lips met his, and when she pulled away, she said, "Come on, we should get back."

"If you insist," he groaned as she climbed off his lap and stood, reaching out her hand to help him up as well.

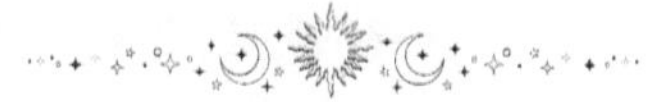

They hadn't been gone more than an hour by the time they returned to the castle, and it seemed as if no one had noticed their absence at all. Though the crowd had thinned some, people were still milling about in groups, and a few remaining couples were wrapped in each other as they swayed to the music.

The ale had run out fairly early in the festivities, so as the night pressed on, it had become more of a gathering of friends instead of the party usually held in the grand room.

As they walked through the doors, Piper ran up to them, her face flushed with a broad smile across her lips. "Well?" she asked as she clasped Auraelia's hands.

Daemon snickered as Auraelia's wide eyes swung in his direction.

"He didn't tell me anything, I saw it, but the vision faded before I could see your answer."

"Piper," Auraelia admonished playfully. "When there is something to tell, you will be the first to know."

"You said *no*?!"

"No, it was more of an 'ask me when the world isn't ending'," Daemon supplied, smirking at the glare the two best friends shared. It turned into a full-fledged, amused smile when Piper softly screeched Auraelia's name.

"*Piper*, stop," Auraelia said with a laugh as she dragged her friend toward the tables of food, casting a smile over her shoulder at him before giving her her full attention.

Daemon watched from a distance as their conversation grew more animated. But the lightness that had filled him from his time at the lake with Auraelia died away as Lord Harland crossed the room to where the women stood. When he extended his hand toward Auraelia, Daemon's jaw clenched with painful tightness, and he was sure his teeth would crack under the pressure. But when she took Lord Harland's hand, her entire body stiff as he led her out to the dance floor, Daemon's shadows revolted against the stranglehold he had on them.

How she managed to allow that man to touch her was beyond him, but he knew there was nothing he could do but watch.

Chapter Thirty-Four

Auraelia

"I can't believe you didn't tell him yes," Piper muttered for what seemed like the fiftieth time since they'd walked away from Daemon before popping a piece of cheese in her mouth.

Auraelia was about to explain *again* how it wasn't the right time, but her words were cut short as the hairs on the back of her neck stood on end, her pulse fluttering in time with the pounding of her heart as her magic seemed to wake, stirring uneasily in her veins. She didn't understand the feelings coursing through her body. The night had been amazing; her mind was calm for the first time in what felt like forever, and she was with her people. With the people who loved and supported her. There was no reason for her magic to be on high alert...for the *anger* she felt filling her body.

Scanning the room, her gaze fell on Daemon—on the tight set of his shoulders, the hard line of his jaw, and the way he continuously clenched and unclenched his fists at his side. It was then that she realized it was *his anger* she was feeling, though she didn't know why. He had been perfectly at ease only moments before. She tried following his gaze, but Piper's sharp inhale pulled her attention—her eyes widening as she took in the look on her friend's face. The color had drained from Piper's skin, her lips set in a tight, thin line, eyes focused just over Auraelia's shoulder.

What the hell is going on?

"Your Majesty."

The hoarse, grating tone of Lord Harland's voice sent chills down her spine, and she had to tighten the hold on her magic. Slowly, she turned to face the man who was determined to see her fall.

With a sickly sweet smile on her face, she asked, "Lord Harland. How may I be of service?"

"Would you honor me with a dance?"

The audacity of his question rendered her speechless for a moment before she remembered the role she had to play. Of the mask she had to continue wearing for a little while longer. "Of course."

Lord Harland gave her a slight bow and extended his hand. Burning rage slammed into her chest as she slipped her hand into his, and she had to take a deep breath to quell the feeling. Daemon's anger was a fiery inferno in her chest, his anxiety a tight ball in her stomach that twisted and twined with her own.

Breathe.

In.

Out.

It's only a dance.

She repeated the words on a loop in her mind, steadying her breathing as she allowed him to lead her to the dance floor. Everything about it felt wrong. The pressure of his hand on her back. Of her hand in his. The longer she was in his presence, an inky feeling of dread coated every fiber of her being.

They'd made one pass around the floor before Lord Harland spoke, his words sending chills down her spine. "You're not planning on running from your problems, are you?"

"Excuse me?" She made to pull away, but his hold on her hardened, pulling her closer as he continued to lead her through the steps.

"You disappeared tonight. With *him*."

"Where I do or do not go, and with whom, is no concern of yours."

"Of course, Your Majesty. I'm just making sure you're not abandoning your people. I'm sure you're concerned about what is to come."

The nonchalant way he accused her of abandoning her people, of betraying her role—her kingdom—had her magic simmering just below the surface. "Lord Harland, you seem to have forgotten yourself."

"Your Majesty?" His brows were drawn together, but a spark in his eyes betrayed the confusion he seemed determined to convey.

His feigned innocence did nothing but stoke her anger, and she decided right then and there that enough was enough. She was tired of pretending. Tired of letting him think that he was somehow getting away with all of the atrocities he was committing against the realm and her crown. Like sand running through her fingers, she let her mask slip away to reveal her burning hatred for the man before her.

"It is not *I* who is abandoning our people. It is not *I* who is betraying the kingdom." His eyes grew wide, a flush coloring his cheeks as a muscle ticked in his jaw. "Is it, Lord Harland?"

"Aurae—"

"It's *Your Majesty.*" Auraelia loosened the hold on her magic. Let heat radiate from her palm as she tightly clenched her fingers around his hand. "I may be young, Harland. But I am far from stupid, and you aren't as clever as you think you are." Her tone was cold as ice, and a malicious smile spread across her face as he groaned in pain. "I know everything that you've done. Everything that you've *tried* to do. Did you think that *your Queen* wouldn't find out?"

A faint white glow emanated from between their palms, the air around them shifting as her power rolled off her. Lord Harland's knees began to buckle, and Auraelia tsked her displeasure, holding him up as she led *him* in the dance.

"I think—" he groaned as pain began to contort his features, "you've proven your point, *Your Majesty*."

"I don't think that I have. You see, *Lord Harland*, I could end your miserable life right here and now, and no one would bat an eye. I wouldn't lose a wink of sleep. Instead," faint tendrils of lightning began to coil around their clasped hands, and he hissed through his teeth, "I think I'll let you slink away like the coward you are. But don't be fooled, Harland. *If* my cousin doesn't kill you, and *if* you somehow manage to survive this war, I will end you. You will not see another day." Auraelia brought them to a halt as the music ended, canting her head to the side. "Do we understand each other?"

Lord Harland tried to pull his hand away and step back, but Auraelia held firm, watching as his eyes widened, nostrils flaring as he blew out a short breath. "Perfectly," he hissed through clenched teeth.

Pasting an unsuspecting smile on her face, Auraelia released his hand. "Good. Now, I suggest you take the grace I've given you and leave before I change my mind."

The ground rumbled beneath his feet, causing him to stagger back a step before regaining his balance and bending at the waist into a low bow. "Your Majesty."

Auraelia closed her eyes and released a shuddered breath when he was no longer in the ballroom.

"Keeping your enemies close, I see." Caius' silky tone wrapped around her, and she whipped around to see him standing no more than an arm's length away.

"What are you doing here?" she whispered angrily.

"Dance with me." Caius extended his hand and raised a brow as Auraelia turned to search the crowd for Daemon. Worry crept in when she didn't find him, and she returned her gaze to Caius. "Don't worry, Your Majesty. He's just making sure that the rat left your home. One dance, that's all. I'll be gone before your precious prince returns."

Caius slowly tilted his head to the side, the movement feline—like a cat tracking its prey before it pounced. "Well?" he asked, wiggling his fingers as a singular brow arched expectantly.

Auraelia took a deep breath, then blew it out as she shook her head in disbelief and slipped her hand into his. As he bowed, he pressed a kiss to the emerald ring on her hand, then pulled her into his hold as the musicians began the next tune.

"What are you doing here, Caius?" Auraelia asked, not willing to let the silence linger when there were questions she needed answered.

"Were you *trying* to enrage her?"

His question caught her off guard, his tone a mix of wonder and anger, and it took a moment for her to process his words before she could respond. "I assume you're talking about Kyra?"

The sardonic look on his face shouldn't have brought a smile to her lips, and maybe it was partially due to the events that had just transpired with Lord Harland, but she couldn't help it when her lips tilted upward.

"You're *smiling*? You just knowingly, *purposefully*, pissed off the woman determined to obliterate you from this realm, and you're *smiling*?" Disbelief filled every word, and the shocked look on his face sent her into a fit of laughter.

"I'm sorry, Caius. Truly, I am. Tonight has been...I don't even have a word for it, honestly. As for pissing off Davina," Auraelia sobered slightly, huffing out a breath through her nose, "I couldn't care less. She brought this on herself, as did Kyra."

A slow, easy smile began to spread across his face, and it made her stomach turn. "You have a darkness to you, Auraelia. One I didn't see coming and one your cousin certainly didn't anticipate." She narrowed her eyes as she tongued a canine. "It's a compliment, I assure you."

"Are you here for a reason, Caius? Or just here to size up my cousin's opponent?"

An amused chuckle rumbled in his throat, and he nodded slightly. "Davina will strike tomorrow before the sun sets. Be ready, Your Majesty. I fully expect you to be the one who walks away from this."

"Purely for your own sake," she scoffed.

Her comment seemed to sober him for a moment, his brow pinching slightly before he smoothed his features back into the mask he donned at every encounter—amusement and indifference jumbled together to create the perfect façade.

"For the sake of all of Ixora, Auraelia. Not just my own." As the song came to an end, Caius bent her backward, dipping her low and bringing his face a breath away from her own. "Until tomorrow, my Queen."

When he straightened her once more, he bowed quickly and backed away, but not before winking at someone behind her and disappearing into the crowd.

"What the fuck did he want?" Daemon asked as he wrapped a possessive arm around her waist.

"He was telling me when Davina was planning to attack."

"And?"

She turned in his arm and wrapped hers around his neck. "Tomorrow, before sundown. I think she's going to try and channel what's left of the new moon."

"Which means she probably doesn't think she can defeat you without it."

Auraelia cast a look over her shoulder, searching the crowd for any sign of Garnet's emissary before turning back toward Daemon. "What that means is that my time to take her down was just lessened significantly. If she channels the moon—"

Daemon pulled her closer. "She won't have the opportunity to, my star. Not if we are together. We will do this *together*."

Though anxiety churned in her belly, a soft smile pulled at Auraelia's lips as she slowly slid her hands down his chest to encircle his waist. "Together."

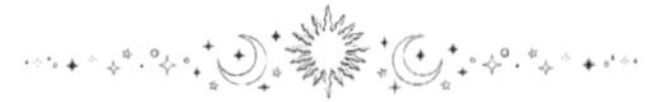

Without the moon, there was little to no way to determine how late the night had gotten. By the time Daemon and Auraelia retired to her suite, her body was exhausted, but her thoughts wouldn't slow down. Events from the evening turned over in her mind in an endless rotation. From Daemon returning to her and asking her to be his wife to the confrontation with Lord Harland and the information Caius supplied.

Auraelia collapsed face down onto her bed and groaned.

"What can I do for you, my star? What do you need?" Daemon asked as he crawled onto the bed beside her and rubbed her shoulders.

Rolling onto her back, Auraelia reached up and ran her fingers across his jaw, relishing in the soft, yet scratchy, feeling of his beard against her skin. Tonight was possibly their last night together. Potentially, the last night, she would see his face, see the love that shone in his eyes. She took a moment to let herself soak in the moment, memorizing each and every inch of his face so that it was emblazoned on her mind, from the bright gold centers of his eyes and the mossy swirls that surrounded them to his plump bottom lip that her thumb was sliding across.

Daemon pressed a kiss to the pad of her thumb, and her chest ached with how much she loved him. How much time she'd wasted trying to push him away when she could have—*should have*—just been with him.

Her throat tightened as tears pricked at the back of her eyes. "You, Daemon. I just need you."

"Auraelia, you're exhausted. You need slee—"

"What I *need* is you. We don't know what tomorrow will bring, and if," Daemon opened his mouth to protest, but she covered it with her palm, and his shoulders sagged with resignation. It was the reality of what they were to face, and though he seemed reluctant to let his mind go in that direction, it was firmly planted in her own. "*If* something happens to us, I want to know that I spent my last night completely consumed by you. *Loved* by you. Sleep can wait. Right now, I need all of you."

"Auraelia." Her name was a plea on his lips, matching the worry in his gaze.

"*Please*, my love."

He loosed a heavy sigh, his eyes raking over every inch of her body before coming back to her face. Heat simmered in his gaze as it latched onto hers, the burning embers of love and lust colliding as his tell-tale smirk graced his lips. "I do love it when you beg."

Daemon's lips were hard and demanding as they came down against her own, his hands sliding along her curves until he reached her hips. Auraelia arched into his touch as his fingers skimmed the top of her waistband, dipping in slightly as he reached the ties at the center. Searing kisses marked her skin as he slowly trailed them along her jawline, down the column of her neck, all while his fingers made quick work of the thin leather strips that held her pants together.

Anticipation clawed at her insides, a pulse settling between her thighs as she waited anxiously for his hand to slip beneath the leather. But as his mouth continued its downward descent, his hands moved upward. His fingers drifted in featherlight caresses along her torso, tracing each and every lace of her corset before reaching the ties that held it together. A low whine rumbled in her throat as he slowly pulled the strings to untie the knot at the top of her breasts before meticulously unlacing each segment down to her navel.

"*Daemon.*" His name was a plea that quickly turned into a moan as his mouth latched onto her nipple through her tunic, his tongue rolling around the sensitive bud before pulling on it with his teeth.

"*Fuck,*" she groaned, her hands flying to his head. Fingers tangled in his hair as he worked each breast in equal measure.

His hands were bruising as he gripped her hips, grinding her against the leg he'd pressed between her thighs, guiding her movements in long, languid rolls, giving her enough friction to drive her to the edge but not nearly enough to send her careening over.

"Daemon, please," she begged as he slowly kissed his way back up her body.

"Not a chance, my star. If this is my last night with you, I'm going to take my time. I'm going to worship every inch of your body. Have you in as many ways as you or I can think of." Each promise was punctuated with a pop of a button on his vest until they were all undone, and he'd tossed the garment to the floor. "I'm going to make you come so many times that you won't think you can anymore—" he pulled his tunic over his head and added it to the slowly growing pile of garments on the floor, "and then you'll give me another one."

Daemon climbed off the bed, and Auraelia watched with rapt attention as his hands slid to the clasp on his trousers...then stopped. The look in his eyes was intense—want mixing with that predatory gaze that lit her body on fire—as he hooked his thumbs into his waistband and stared down at her.

"What do you want, Auraelia? Use your words, or I will put that mouth of yours to better use." A sly smirk lifted one corner of his mouth.

A challenge.

One he knew she would rise to but also struggled with.

She was in control of most things in her life, and letting go—giving Daemon the reins in the bedroom—had always been a comfort she clung to.

"Come on, *Princess.*"

Auraelia pursed her lips at his blatant use of her former title, her eyes raking down his body before meeting his gaze once more.

Challenge accepted.

Pushing up onto her elbows, she said, "Strip."

One word—one command—was all it took for Daemon's magic to seep from his pores, glittering darkness brushing against her as it slid along the mattress.

He kicked off one boot, then the other, his pants following quickly after, then raised a questioning brow.

Auraelia lazily ran her eyes along each line of ink across his chest, then down his chiseled frame to his cock, which stood at full attention with a bead of precum glistening on its tip. When her gaze reached his face once more, she curled a finger in his direction and lifted a booted foot. "Now me."

His smirk firmly in place, Daemon made quick work of her boots, pants, and finally, her tunic. When he leaned forward to kiss her, Auraelia placed a hand on his shoulder and tsked, gently pushing him down. "On your knees, *Prince.* Kneel before your Queen."

Daemon's smirk morphed into a rakish smile as he dropped to his knees. "I would gladly live on my knees at your feet if that's where you want me, *Your Majesty.*"

Before she could even form a response, his face was buried between her thighs. His tongue ran long strokes along her slit before he sucked her clit into his mouth, flicking it with the tip of his tongue.

"*Fuck,*" she mewled, her back arching as her fingers found his hair once more.

Daemon's grip on her thighs was bruising as he pushed one of her legs wider, then lifted the other to drape over his shoulder.

"Fuck, you taste good," he moaned against her, slipping two fingers into her slick entrance and curling them forward to work the spot he knew would send her spiraling. He pumped them in and out a few times before removing them and bringing his hand to her mouth. "Taste yourself, Princess."

Without hesitating, Auraelia wrapped her lips around his digits, sucking them into her mouth and licking them clean. She'd tasted herself on his lips before, but this was different. It was somehow more erotic to suck her arousal from his hand while he devoured her.

Pulling his fingers from her mouth with a *pop*, he thrust them back inside her, working her walls once more as he punished her clit with his mouth.

Heat bloomed low in her belly, her muscles growing taught, breath quickening as her orgasm built.

"Come for me, my star," he growled, dragging his tongue up her center once before returning to assault that sensitive bundle of nerves. Shadows swirled around her. Strands pinching and tugging on her nipples while bands massaged her breasts and wrapped around her throat. The sensation was overwhelming, her senses going into overdrive as she dove headfirst into bliss. Her climax ripped through her so suddenly that her breath caught in her throat, her back arching off the bed as her fist tightened in Daemon's hair.

Instead of slowing his ministrations as she rode the waves of ecstasy, Daemon rose from his knees and flipped her onto her stomach. "We're not done yet, my love. Time to give me another one." Then he slid into her in one swift thrust.

The sensation of him filling her so completely while her walls were still fluttering from her orgasm sent her reeling, stars filling her vision as he worked her back toward the edge.

Daemon slid a hand down her spine, gripping her shoulder as he slammed into her from behind. His other snaked around her hip, slipping between her thighs as he worked her clit in furious circles.

"Oh–oh, God–dess. Dae–Daemon." Her words were stunted with each thrust, his hips driving into her at a punishing pace. "Too–too much."

"Be a good girl, and give me another one, Auraelia."

Black specks swam in her vision, limbs tingling as she dug her fists into the sheets. Her body trembled, her magic raging to be released as the sensations built and her orgasm began to crest. "I–I'm going to come."

"Fuck," he growled as his thrusts became more demanding. "That's right. Come for me, Princess."

The walls of her pussy began to flutter as Daemon slammed into her again. When he pinched her clit, her climax erupted in streaks of lightning that struck walls and ricocheted off the mirror of her vanity, shattering the reflective glass and sending it cascading to the floor.

"Shit," he cursed, wrapping them in a cocoon of shadows as he drove into her again and found his release.

Breathing heavy, skin slick with sweat, they collapsed together onto the bed. Silence reigned for a moment before Auraelia burst into a fit of laughter.

"What's so funny?" Daemon chuckled as he swiped wet strands of hair from her brow. His question made her laugh harder, and a tiny snort accompanied each inhale, causing him to join in.

"I missed that sound," he mused when they'd finally calmed.

"My laugh?" she asked, rolling onto her side and propping her head on a fist as she traced the lines of his tattoos with a finger.

"No, my star. Your *snort*. It's fucking adorable."

"You're joking," she deadpanned, casting him a sidelong glance.

"Not in the slightest." Pulling her leg over his hip, he idly ran his fingertips along her skin. "It happens when you're truly happy, so it's a sound I cherish."

Auraelia's eyes softened as she met his gaze. "I love you."

"I love you, too." He pulled her down, his lips meeting hers in a soft, languid kiss, before pulling away. "Now, shower or bath?" Auraelia raised a questioning brow, and he chuckled. "I'm not finished worshiping you yet, my Queen."

Chapter Thirty-Five

Daemon

The sun barely peeked over the horizon when something pulled Daemon from his sleep. An inky feeling settled in his stomach, roiling and turning over as worry ebbed and flowed for reasons he didn't quite understand. He'd fallen into a dreamless sleep with Auraelia tucked against his chest, her hair tickling his nose with each inhale. It had been the most at peace he'd felt in a while, yet when he reached out of her, her spot was empty. Cold, as if she hadn't been there for some time.

Sitting up, he rubbed the sleep from his eyes and waited for them to adjust to the room's dim light. He was just about to call out for her when he spotted her curled up in one of the armchairs—a blanket wrapped around her shoulders as she stared out the frosty panes of her window. She looked at peace, her features relaxed as she rested her chin on her knees, the early morning glow shimmering through the glass and kissing her cheeks.

"Is everything alright, my star?" he asked hesitantly, not wanting to startle her.

She hummed in response, her gaze never shifting from the window.

"Auraelia, my love. Come back to bed. You need your rest."

"I woke up about an hour ago, and I just...I couldn't go back to sleep." She shrugged, turning to rest her chin on her shoulder as she gave him a small smile.

Despite the uptilt of her lips, he could see the toll everything was taking on her. Stress rolled off of her and crashed into him like waves upon the sand, and the stardust that usually sparkled in her eyes had dimmed.

Pushing up from the bed, Daemon quickly pulled on his trousers and crossed the room. Her smile broadened slightly when he kneeled in front of her, and she scooted to the edge of the chair, wrapping her arms and legs around him and cocooning them in the warmth of her blanket before bringing her lips to his.

"Can I get you anything?" he asked as he tucked a piece of hair behind her ear.

"I'm okay."

"My star, I could see your thoughts churning from across the room. Talk to me."

Blowing out a heavy breath, Auraelia pulled her gaze from his and returned to look out the window. "Something doesn't...*feel* right. I don't know how to explain it." She shook her head, sinking back into the chair as her gaze fell to her lap.

Daemon wrapped her hands in one of his and used the other to urge her gaze back to his face. "You can't plan for everything. It's not possible. We've done the best we can with the information that we've been given."

"I know," she expelled a shuddered breath, the sound a tight grip around his heart. "But it's like we're missing something. We've been so focused on what Davina is doing that it just seems like I've forgotten something."

Daemon watched as she spiraled back into herself, the rapid turning of wheels in her mind evident in the way her eyes flicked back and forth, like she was trying to solve a puzzle only she could see. Never in his life had he wished for his mother's abilities over his own. But the ability to be inside her head, to *know* what kept her from sleep the one night that she needed it the most, would have been more helpful than his shadows on his best day.

Unwrapping her legs from his torso, Daemon stood and scooped her out of the chair, taking her place and setting her on his lap. "If you're awake, my star, then so am I. And maybe we can figure this out together."

Auraelia settled into him, resting her head on his shoulder as they both stared out the window and watched the sun paint the sky in a wash of lavender and pink. And for a moment—one brief moment—everything felt like it would turn out the way he wanted it to. That they would get the ending that Astraea and Killian never got the chance to have. That they would make it through this war together. But that dream ended with the sound of a door ricocheting off a wall and Piper screeching their names as she barreled into Auraelia's sitting room.

"D! Come on man, get up!" Aiden bellowed, evidently close on Piper's heels.

Auraelia jumped from his lap, the blanket falling to the floor as she sprinted to grab her robe from the edge of the bed. Her eyes were wide when she whirled around and met his. Worry and panic swirled in her storm-colored irises, her breath coming in short, shallow pants as her anxiety took root.

Not now. It's too soon.

Not bothering with walking, Daemon pulled on his shadows until he was standing in front of her, wrapping her in his embrace until she could take a full breath. "Breathe, my star. We don't even know why they're here."

"It sure as hell isn't a good reason," she mumbled into his chest.

"D!"

"Rae!"

Piper and Aiden called out in unison. He could hear the urgency in their tone, but he wasn't willing to let Auraelia go. Not until he was sure she was breathing steadily, and he was sure she would be able to handle whatever problem lay beyond that door.

"Rae, I don't care if he's balls deep, I *will* come in there! I will scar myself for life if I have to!" Piper yelled from right on the other side of the door, her tone an octave higher than usual.

"Fuck off, give us a second. *Goddess,*" Daemon hollered before taking a deep breath to calm the irritation that had begun to swirl in his chest. "Are you ready?" he whispered, tilting Auraelia's face up to his.

The panic had ebbed, but worry was still present in her gaze when she laced her fingers with his and nodded.

"Okay." He gave her a small smile, then pressed a kiss to her brow before guiding her to the door. When he pushed it open, Piper and Aiden were pacing the floor.

"What the fuck is going on?" he growled.

"It's your Dad," Aiden began.

"Pearl is on the move, Daemon. You need to go," Piper finished, sympathy filling her gaze as it flicked between him and her best friend.

"What did you see, Piper?" The strength had come back to Auraelia's voice, her spine ramrod straight as she honed in on her friend.

There's my girl. One corner of Daemon's lips lifted as he looked down at her. Despite her fear of what the day would bring, he knew she wouldn't let it hold her back. Wouldn't let it overwhelm her. He knew she was strong, but seeing her step into her strength when she looked like she would break just moments ago was a sight that would never cease to awe and impress him.

"I can show you." Piper's gaze shifted from Auraelia to him.

"Me?" he questioned, his eyes wide as they met the clairvoyant's all-seeing gaze.

"I mean...I can show Auraelia, but it would be faster and more beneficial to just show you directly." Urgency bled into every word, but there was also hesitancy there. Like she wasn't sure about this idea either. When he didn't respond, she rolled her eyes and closed the distance between them, holding out her hand for his. "Just breathe, okay? It's the fastest way."

Before he could even respond, Piper seized his hand, and it immediately felt like he was being held underwater. Like he was drowning, his lungs constricting in his chest from the onslaught of Piper's power running through his system. Auraelia's voice filtered into his mind, urging him to breathe, and he had to force his lungs to draw in air.

White swirls of fog spilled across his vision for a moment before it cleared away to show the bloodbath that was to befall his father's troops. The Court of Pearl had moved sooner than they'd anticipated, catching the Court of Opal and his father's soldiers unaware, ending the lives of so many good men and women. Though as quickly as that vision had appeared, it was replaced with another. One where he was on the field, fighting alongside his people with victory within their grasp as Pearl's forces fell and retreated around them. The differences between the two were drastic.

One led to catastrophic losses, the other—possible victory.

As the fog began to roll across his vision once more, Piper removed her hand, and he had to blink a few times for his vision to clear.

"Why were there two?" he demanded.

"Because you haven't decided." Her voice was low but sure as if she'd seen his question coming—and when he thought about it, she probably had. After taking a deep breath, she continued. "The future... it's not set in stone. It's constantly changing. But one thing is certain; if you do not go to their aid, they *will* fall."

"Daemon," Auraelia breathed, her gaze shooting to his, panic once again swimming in her eyes.

"Can you two give us a moment?" he asked, not bothering to look Piper and Aiden's way. When the door was closed behind them, Daemon tried to speak, but Auraelia cut him off.

"You have to go."

"Auraelia—"

"No, Daemon. This isn't a discussion that we should be having. It's *your father*! Your people! What about them? What about Yvaine? Sariah? You can't leave them to do this alone."

Daemon gently cradled her face in his hands, pleading with her to see reason even when he knew she was right. "Please, don't do this. We're supposed to do this together. We have to bring her down *together*."

"Daemon, my love. I don't want you to go, but you *have* to. They need you."

"*You* need me." Anguish filled every word, his heart cleaving in two at the path that Dalia was forcing them to walk.

Tears welled in her eyes, turning them a bright shade of aquamarine that made her look so much like Astraea at that moment that Daemon's breath caught in his throat.

"They need you more." Her lip trembled as she held his gaze, her voice wavering as she spoke. "I–I couldn't live with myself if something happened to your family. Neither could you."

"I can't live if something happens to *you*. *You* are my life, Auraelia."

"And you are mine. So don't you dare do something heroic and get yourself killed. Do you hear me?" Her words came out around a sob, tears flowing freely down her cheeks.

Daemon crushed his lips to hers, pulling her against his body as her hands wrapped around his neck, holding him just as tightly. It wasn't meant to be a goodbye kiss, but everything about it felt like it was. His heart and magic raged against the decision he had to make.

Leave the one person who meant the entire world to him and help his people...or stay and live with the consequences of that choice. Either way, there was a chance he would lose.

Auraelia broke their kiss, her breathing as heavy as his own as they pressed their foreheads together. "Promise you will come back to me."

"I will always come back to you, my star. Always."

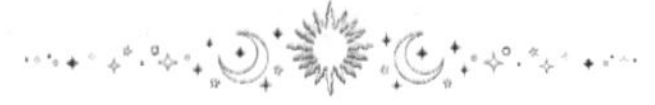

It had taken him longer than he'd hoped to shadow-walk from Lyndaria to the border between the Court of Opal and the Court of Pearl, but as he stood in the center of the battlefield, the scene that was sprawled out around him momentarily froze him to the spot.

Opal's warriors were easy to spot among the fray, their flowing white garb masking the armor and weapons hidden beneath. Magnolia flowers were emblazoned in gold across the chests of Pearl's soldiers, and a sea of silver and blue marked the men who fought under his father's banner.

Agonized screams pierced the air, mixing with a chorus of battle cries as droves of people clashed together in a cacophony of clanging metal.

Formations had long been forgotten as soldiers fanned out around him, meeting enemies from all directions. Bodies of members from each of the courts littered the ground, reducing the once grassy plain to nothing but crimson-soaked mud.

During his meeting with Lady Aesira, they'd decided to set up camp beyond the tree line that bordered her court, but with the chaos surrounding him, there was no time for a briefing. No time to get the lay of the land or the battle plans that had been established.

He'd barely had time to get his bearings, to *breathe*, before a soldier from Pearl charged him from his right.

Daemon's body moved on instinct, his shadows spilling out of him into a solidified mass to block the man's blow as he drew the swords sheathed across his back. Letting the wall drop between them, he blocked the next blow with one blade while parrying with the other. He met each strike from his opponent with a maneuver of his own until his sword met flesh just below the man's breastplate, slicing clean across his abdomen.

The soldier staggered, his sword falling to the ground as he tried to hold his stomach together and sank to his knees. Daemon sneered as he stared down at him, disgust churning in his stomach as he met the man's gaze and plunged his sword clean through the magnolia on his thin armor. He was the first in what would undoubtedly be a long line of enemies that met their end by his hand.

Rolling his shoulders, Daemon turned his head, his eyes locking on another opponent. The sound of metal scraping against metal sent chills down his spine as he removed his sword, spinning it once over his hand and letting a smirk tilt one corner of his lips.

And so it begins.

One by one, Daemon met his enemies, and one by one, they all fell to either his magic or his blade. A warrior's calm washed over him, numbing him to the chaos as more and more people succumbed to the perils of war. He ignored the blood and mud that now caked his clothes. He lost count of how many soldiers he'd slain. He tried not to remember their faces or their garbled final words as the Goddess Keres came for their souls.

Though he'd lost sight of them as the battle raged on, he held onto the glimpses of Yvaine and Sariah fighting side by side and the wisps of his father's magic that mirrored his own. Of the way Lady Aesira and her warriors moved languidly through the throng of soldiers, leaving bodies in their wake.

As Daemon drove his sword into yet another soldier, a deep, guttural scream cut through the tumult, and the world seemed to slow around him.

He knew that voice.

Linked it to the bellowing laugh that used to fill his home. To the stories that were told and the teachings that had been shared throughout his childhood.

Daemon quickly pulled his blade from the man's neck—thick, hot blood spraying his face and coating his hands. But by the time he turned around, he was too late.

"*Father!*" Daemon's scream mixed with those around him.

He watched his father fall to his knees as Lord Kaemon of the Court of Pearl pushed his sword further into his father's chest until it protruded from his spine.

Shock rooted him to the spot, but everything around him seemed to be moving in a blur as if time couldn't decide whether to speed up or slow. Blood rushed through his ears, blocking out the sounds around him, and his thoughts spiraled through every conversation and argument he'd had with his father.

As Lord Kaemon pulled his sword from King Evander's chest, every thought racing through Daemon's mind ceased and was replaced by a deep-seated rage that burned away every fiber of calm he'd been trying to cling to.

His breathing came in harsh inhales and ragged exhales. His nostrils flared as he watched his father's blood drip from the end of the sword.

Drip.

Pure, blinding hatred twisted in his stomach.

Drip.

His shadows responded in kind, turning to frigid darkness in his veins and spilling out of him in waves as he made his way across the blood-soaked battlefield.

Drip.

"*Kaemon!*" he shouted, his voice rising over the noise and echoing across the field.

Lord Kaemon slowly turned his way, a sinister smile painted across his face as his head canted slightly.

Fucking bastard.

Shadows swirled around him, creating a wall of impenetrable night, while tendrils slithered at his feet, striking out at anyone who tried to get in his way. Nothing—and no one—was going to keep him from ending Lord Kaemon's life.

Kaemon's smile broadened as he got closer, and he called out, "Your shadows won't help you here, boy."

Daemon's steps faltered for a moment as his father's teachings about other courts and their leaders sprung to mind.

Lord Kaemon is a siphon, son. No magic can touch him. He simply absorbs it and can turn it against the original wielder. And whatever you do, do not let him touch you with a bare hand. He can draw the very power that runs through your veins and, if he chooses to, drain you of it entirely. No one is safe with a siphon, not even in the shadows.

"Scared, *Prince*? Or should I say, *Your Majesty*?" Kaemon called out, his brows rising as his gaze ran over Daemon from top to toe—as if he was assessing if he was worth his time.

Your Majesty. That phrase slammed into him harder than any blow. In one fell swoop, Daemon's world had been turned upside down in more ways than one. He'd lost his father and gained a kingdom in the same breath.

Tonguing a canine, Daemon pushed that thought aside, and shadow walked the rest of the way to Kaemon, making sure to leave enough distance between them before spooling his magic so far into his veins that it was barely a glimmer.

"I don't need my shadows to end your treasonous life, Kaemon." Daemon took a step closer, his grip on his swords tightening. "As a matter of fact, feeling your blood spray across my face before you drown in it sounds like a much better option."

Daemon struck as Kaemon's eyes widened with surprise, swinging one blade to slice across the Lord's body and following it up with a diagonal, downward strike. Kaemon staggered back a step to avoid the first, then blocked the second, the sound of metal crashing together reverberating through the open field.

They moved together in a deadly dance of blades.

Each strike was met with a countermove. Each step was accentuated by the sound of mud squelching beneath their feet.

Despite his heart pounding in his veins, Daemon kept his breathing steady, his eyes constantly tracking the subtle movements Lord Kaemon would make so that he was ready for a counterattack. This duel wasn't easy—not that he'd expected it to be after Kaemon had taken down the very man who'd put a blade in his hand when he was five. But as it dragged on, the mixture of sweat and blood that coated Daemon's palms made it harder for him to grip his hilts.

Lord Kaemon knocked the sword from Daemon's left hand with one heavy blow and lunged forward. Spinning to the side to escape the full force of the blow, he groaned as the edge sliced through his shoulder, sending rivulets of blood to spill down his arm. White dots flecked his vision as the wound throbbed in time to the beat of his heart. It wasn't deep, but it was severe enough that it would need to be mended.

"Call on your shadows, boy. Seems you can't beat me without them." Kaemon chuckled darkly.

Gritting his teeth through the pain, Daemon gripped the hilt of his remaining sword with both hands and met Kaemon's gaze head-on. "Over my dead body, will you get your hands on my shadows."

"That can be arranged." The cocky smirk on Kaemon's face made Daemon's blood boil.

Taking a deep breath, he calmed his mind and focused.

His breathing slowed, and it was as if time followed suit.

Swinging his blade overhead, Daemon turned his body to the left before switching directions. The maneuver forced Kaemon to defend his left side, leaving his right open for the taking.

As if the Goddess Rhayne herself was guiding his movements, Daemon's blade came down against Kaemon's side, cutting through the leather straps that held his armor in place and slicing through his skin and muscle until the edge sank into his ribs. When he pulled it free, Lord Kaemon cried out in agony, driving his sword into the mud as he crumpled to the ground.

Knocking him to his back, Daemon rested the point of his blade in the center of Lord Kaemon's throat.

"You rose against the rightful queen of this realm. Murdered a king and threatened the next." With each word, Daemon slowly pushed his sword through skin and sinew. Watching as Kaemon's eyes widened, his body shuttering as death slowly claimed him. When he began to choke on his own blood, the crimson liquid spilling out of the corners of his mouth, Daemon squatted down next to him, twisting the blade as he hissed, "May the Goddess Keres have no mercy upon your soul."

As Daemon watched the light fade from Lord Kaemon's eyes, a piercing scream shattered the air, bringing him to his feet. But it was his sister's agonized wail that had his head whipping in the direction of the sound. Hair the color of flames caught his eye, and a crimson stain steadily growing at her side.

Fuck, Sariah.

Before he could bring his shadows to the surface, Yvaine was there, her dagger sliding free from the sheath in the armor on her arm and into her hand. Her strike was quick, slicing through the soldier's neck before she ripped it to the side, relieving the man of his head.

As his sister stooped to support Sariah, Daemon felt a magic other than his own stir in his veins—liquid and warm and rising like the tide.

His whole body went taut, his shadows swirling as the hair on his arms stood on end, and an alluring melody drifted across the field.

An eerie silence settled in the air as every soldier from the Court of Pearl froze. Locked in the clutches of a siren, their weapons fell to the ground, a glazed look falling across their features as his allies dispatched them one by one.

He'd seen Yvaine use her power—*felt it* more than he would have ever liked to—but this siren's song was an entirely different magnitude than he'd ever witnessed.

This was the reason few knew of her abilities.

Daemon smiled as the ones on the outskirts of her range began to flee back toward the border of their court. They wouldn't get far, but he'd at least give them a head start.

Pulling his sword from Lord Kaemon's neck, Daemon sheathed the blade then took a few steps to retrieve the weapon he'd had knocked from his hand. But as he reached for it, a pain so cold it burned bloomed in his chest, radiating out through his limbs and causing his knees to buckle. Daemon's vision darkened, his breath coming in shallow pants, and he attempted to breathe around the unexplained agony.

Nothing about it made sense.

Yvaine had subdued nearly an entire army with her magic, giving them the upper hand. The only injury he'd sustained was a minor one at best, and it had already clotted. There was no reason for him to be in this much...

As the pain subsided, clarity took its place.

Auraelia.

"*Your Majesty!*" Panic-laced words and the sound of an arrow sinking to flesh penetrated what was left of the agony-induced haze around his mind. "Goddess damn it, boy. Get your ass up," Lady Aesira growled in his ear as she hoisted him upright.

"Auraelia," he groaned as he rubbed at the still lingering ache in his chest and met the hardened gaze of a warrior.

"What about Auraelia?" she demanded through clenched teeth, her eyes scanning their surroundings before coming back to drill into his.

"Something's wrong. I've never felt—" Daemon rubbed at his sternum. "I've never felt her from this far away, but it's the only thing that makes sense."

"Goddess help me," she muttered as she hastily stooped to pick up his blade and thrust it into his hand. "You feel her pain because you are fated. Because you have both *accepted* that bond. Knowingly or not, it doesn't matter. But I swear to the Goddess, if she dies, you will be next."

Sheathing his blade down his back, he yelled his sister's name, hoping by some miracle she could hear him. When she turned, he could only imagine what was written across his face as her eyes widened, and she screamed, *"Go!"*

Diving into his well of power, Daemon summoned as much as he could and let it carry him back to Lyndaria.

The sun had barely begun to kiss the horizon when his feet touched the ground, its tangerine glow bouncing off the soldier's armor and lighting up the battlefield like it had been set ablaze.

If he'd thought that the battle he'd just left was a bloodbath, what Auraelia was fighting was a massacre. Bodies were strewn all across the open field, blood soaking into the ground as screams of agony echoed throughout the air.

"D!" He heard Aiden shout.

Whipping his head toward the sound, he hollered, "Where is Auraelia?! You're supposed to be with her!"

Aiden sprinted to his side, his breathing heavy as he swiped blood from his brow, smearing it across his face. "I don't know. Garnet came out of nowhere, and Xander said he had her, so I just—"

"Fuck." Daemon cursed under his breath as he scoured the field, looking for any sign of Auraelia amongst the throng of people. When he found her, his lungs ceased to function.

"No," he breathed on an exhale, his eyes wide as his worst nightmare came to fruition. "*Auraeliaaaa!*" he screamed, his voice somehow carrying over the chaos as he began sprinting toward her.

Her knees buckled, and everything around him went dark.

Chapter Thirty-Six

Auraelia

After Daemon left...

The sun was hardly above the horizon—the war just beginning—and it already felt like she'd lost.

Daemon was gone.

The warmth of his kiss still lingered on her lips, his shadows nothing but wisps in the air where he had been standing mere moments ago. The sound of the door creaking open echoed through the silence that had settled in her sitting area.

"Rae?" Piper hedged, her face the only thing visible through the crack in the door.

"You can come in, Piper. I'm fine."

"Rae—" she breathed, remorse filling her eyes as she leaned against the door until the latch clicked into place.

"Really, I'm fine."

"You're allowed to *feel*, Auraelia."

Auraelia whirled on her friend, her face taut where the streams of tears had dried on her skin. "*Enough*, Piper. I know you mean well, but I can't allow myself to dwell on the things...that *hurt* right now. Too much is at stake. And if I let—" She blew out a ragged exhale, her gaze shifting toward the ceiling in an attempt to quell the tears that were beginning to fill her eyes once more. "If I let myself *really* feel it. Really take in the way my heart is cleaved in two...I won't be the one who walks away today."

Piper crossed the room and grasped Auraelia's hands, strength and determination shining in her hardened, hazel gaze. "Auraelia Rose," she admonished, her grip tightening slightly, "I *know you*. Better than anyone else. That pain you feel, that heartache? It won't break you. If anything, it will fuel you. Let it feed the rage that I know burns inside. Let it build and fester until the only outcome you can see is the one where you walk away from this battle. Davina is fighting for herself. You, my dear sweet friend, my *Queen,* are fighting for so much more. And that alone gives you the upper hand."

"How?" she asked meekly, her throat constricting as she tried to stifle the sob working its way free.

"Because you would gladly give your life for the people you love, Auraelia. You choose to stand between her revenge and the people of your kingdom and this realm. You are *choosing* them over yourself. You will walk away from this, Fate be damned."

"I don't think Goddess Dalia would appreciate that sentiment," she said with a choked laugh.

Piper's brows winged upward, sass bleeding into every word as she countered, "If Dalia sides with that *bitch*, she's not a goddess I want on my side anyway."

With a light laugh, Auraelia pulled her friend into a tight embrace. "I love you."

"Love you, too, Rae."

As Auraelia breathed deeply for what seemed like the first time that morning, a floral scent wrapped around her senses. *Is that...honeysuckle?* In all of the time she'd known Piper, she'd always opted for something soft and refreshing, like eucalyptus and mint. But this was different.

Auraelia pulled back slightly, her head quirking to the side. "Did you get a new perfume or soap bar?"

"Oh..." a flush began to creep into Piper's cheeks, her gaze suddenly anywhere but on Auraelia's face. "Um...it was a...gift."

A brow winged up, a slight smirk playing at Auraelia's lips as she anxiously waited for her friend to elaborate. When she didn't, Auraelia pushed her shoulder gently. "A gift from *who*?"

"Xander," she said his name like a whispered prayer, her shoulders rising toward her ears, nose scrunching like she was anticipating a bad reaction to the news.

Instead, Auraelia squealed—bouncing up and down as she clasped Piper's hands tightly. "Oh my goddess! Are you two..." She left the question open-ended, hoping her friend would fill in the blanks and confirm what she'd assumed for a while now.

"We're not...*officially together*. But there have been...steps...in that direction."

"Oh, Piper." Auraelia pulled her back into her arms as a lone tear trailed down her cheek.

That singular drop of water held more emotions than it should have. She was beyond happy for her brother and best friend. Ecstatic that they'd finally decided it was worth the chance. But as time ticked by, drawing dusk closer and closer with every movement of the hands on the clock, a weight settled in her chest.

How long would they all have? And what would their endings be?

Taking a ragged breath, Auraelia quickly swiped the treasonous tear away and released her friend. "Would you help me get ready today?"

"It would be my honor."

The ride across Lyndaria was nearly silent as Auraelia and her party rode toward Emerald's campsite, the only sound coming from their horses' hooves as they galloped across the hardened ground. As they approached, she saw Ser Aeron and Captain Soren standing just beyond the last line of tents, each dropping to a knee with heads bowed. They came to a stop, and Auraelia dismounted Jasira.

"Commander General Koa. Captain Soren. You may rise." Auraelia ran her hand along Jasira's nose, then handed the reins to the waiting stable hand. As the horses were led away, she asked, "Do you have a report?"

"We do. If you'd follow me this way, Your Majesty."

Captain Soren led them through the rows of tents erected along the edge of the Amber Woods. They were far enough away from where Ser Aeron and the Captain assumed Garnet would attack but close enough that when soldiers inevitably needed care, they would be able to get there quickly. As they made it through the last line of temporary makeshift homes, Auraelia's steps faltered.

Standing toward the outskirts of the others was a larger version of the deep green canvas tents that belonged to her soldiers, only this one had a golden crown embroidered on the flaps.

"Why is it so *big*?" Piper whispered from behind her.

"I don't think I've ever heard a woman complain about something being *big*," Aiden mumbled under his breath, which earned a stifled chuckle from Xander that he attempted to cover with a cough.

"Why are you even here? Shouldn't you be with Daemon?" Piper riposted, her brows pinched so closely together that they'd merged into one as she glared at Aiden.

There was a cocky smirk on his face, and when he opened his mouth to respond—clearly intending to enter into a verbal jousting contest with Piper—Auraelia spoke for him.

"He's here because I need him to be. Just as I need you and Xander. Now," she cut a sharp look around the group, "Can we please be adults? Aiden, keep your comments to yourself unless they are actually useful. Piper? For the love of every Goddess in Arcelia. Let. It. *Go.*" The end of her statement was said through clenched teeth, her eyes flicking toward Xander, hoping her friend would catch the hint.

The sound of a throat clearing had them all looking over to where Ser Aeron and Captain Soren stood a few feet away. The Captain—goddess bless him—was looking away and acting like he hadn't heard the entire exchange between their group.

On the other hand, Ser Aeron shook his head in disbelief and blew out an exasperated breath before saying, "Shall we, Your Majesty? There's much to discuss before the sun sets."

Auraelia gave him a terse smile and made hasty steps to catch up to her Commander General. As they drew closer, she asked, "Why *is it* so much larger than the others? Surely I don't need more than they do."

"Your tent also acts as the war tent. It's where all of your leaders meet before battle to figure out the best strategies and alternate options. They're in there now, waiting for you."

Auraelia took in a deep breath, her anxiety ramping up as she tried to wrap her head around everything.

Never in her life did she ever think that her path would lead here. That she would be stepping into a tent full of her army's squadron leaders and captains. She'd planned for a quiet life on the throne. For ruling in a time of peace and prosperity.

But fate had been cruel and dealt her an unbalanced hand.

Time slowed as she stepped through the tent flaps. Watching as each member of her advisory team bent a knee and bowed their heads, their right arm braced across their chests. Her magic swirled in her veins, heat blooming at her fingertips as she looked over every single person in that tent. These people were willing to die for their kingdom. For *her*. The thought had her stomach clenching.

Closing her eyes, she sent a quick prayer to the Goddesses of Arcelia.

My Goddess Rhayne, please help and guide me through this war if you can hear me. Steady my people's blades and help their arrows fly true. Goddess Inara, Protector of Warriors, please guide my soldiers through this, and should they fall, bring them home to Arcelia to sit at your table.

Stealing her spine, Auraelia let out a steady breath. "You may rise."

As each member of her team rose, she crossed the space to the large table set up in its center. Maps were spread across the surface, weighed down by daggers, swords, and books. Tiny figurines dotted their surfaces, and she scoured over each and every one. It was all guesswork. They had no clue what Davina's numbers were, but with the magnitude of her power, Auraelia wasn't sure if her cousin needed numbers.

Sinking down into her chair, Auraelia blew out a short breath as she steepled her fingers in front of her face and met Ser Aeron's gaze. "Commander General Koa. Report."

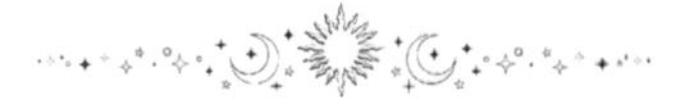

They'd discussed every possible battle plan they could devise over the last two hours. But as conflicting opinions rose, so did tempers. Yelling ensued, and cups were knocked over by overzealous hand motions. Accusations were thrown in every direction—including hers.

Her head was pounding, stars dancing in her vision as the pressure in her skull increased.

These were grown men, and they were acting like children.

When she'd had enough, she glanced toward Aiden and gave him a slight nod. Within seconds, the tension in the air ebbed, and she breathed a sigh of relief.

"Gentlemen, I thank you for all of your advice and counsel. I believe we've come to the best solutions possible with the information we have. I know some—if not most—of you don't think I am ready for this. And I can't truthfully say that I am. You have all trained for moments like this for the majority of your lives while I lived protected behind castle walls. But let me be clear. I have trained just as hard as any of you. I have honed my combat skills under Commander General Koa's instruction. I have fought off and killed assassins who have tried to take my life. I've nurtured my powers and will stand *beside* you on that field today. Not tucked away behind stone walls or cowering in this tent. I am as much a soldier of this court as you are. And if Davina wants my crown, she will have to pry it from my dead hands."

A chorus of cheers echoed through the space, and she breathed a sigh of relief as she met each of their impressed smiles. And though her stomach was in knots, she meant every word.

The only way Davina would get her crown was if she failed.

And failure was *not* an option.

After a quick recap on what plans needed to be set into motion, the council bowed and left to relay the messages to their troops, leaving Auraelia alone with her travel party and Ser Aeron.

"You did well, Auraelia. Your mother would be proud," Ser Aeron said, pride beaming in his eyes.

"I meant every word."

"We know, which is why you make a great Queen. Above life and limb, you put your people first. You already had their loyalty, but today, you gained their respect."

"Do *you* think I'm ready, Ser Aeron?"

A small smile played on his lips as he rounded the table to sit in the empty chair next to her. He engulfed her hands in his, his tone taking on a more serious note as he said, "No one is ready for what war brings, Auraelia. Not even me. It's brutal. It's exhausting. And you will lose more than just people when you step out onto that field. But if you hold on to who you are, you will win this. Just remember, you are allowed to bend, but never the knee. And under no circumstances are you allowed to *break*. Do you hear me? You are a strong, capable woman. And I am *honored* to fight by your side."

"Your sister told me something similar not too long ago," she said with a light chuckle.

"She's a smart woman. Who do you think I got it from?" he replied, the smile returning to his face.

"Thank you. For—" She shook her head, her chest tightening as she held the gaze of the man who had done so much for her throughout her life. Who continued to do so. "For *everything*."

"With my honor and my life, my Queen." With a slight bow of his head, Ser Aeron stood and placed a kiss on Auraelia's brow before excusing himself from the tent. As soon as the flaps fluttered closed behind him, they were pulled aside once more as Master Demir walked through.

"Your Majesty," he said before dropping into the same bow she'd been receiving since she arrived at camp.

"Master Demir, please rise. What can I do for you?"

A smile stretched across his tanned face. "I believe it is I who can do something for you. Here." As he gestured behind him, his son—Atticus—stepped through the opening with a long box in his hand. "It's your sword, Your Majesty. She's finished. As are the other weapons you asked for, though I'm not sure how you'll carry all of them," he said with a chuckle.

"The daggers aren't for me; they're for Lady Piper. She has an affinity for small sharp objects."

"It's true," Piper said with a shrug as she pranced across the space excitedly to take the smaller box from Master Demir. "Thank you, sir."

With a word of thanks, Auraelia took the box from the boy and brought it to the table, gasping as she opened the lid. Inside, nestled on a bed of green velvet so dark it could have been mistaken for black, was the most beautiful piece of craftsmanship she'd ever seen.

As she ran her fingers along the emerald inlay of the blade, her magic sparked in her veins, trailing out of the tips of her hands and setting the stone aglow. The swirls where the blade met the hilt were more defined than the last time she'd seen them, twisting and twining into little vines that translated all the way up the hilt.

"It's stunning," she breathed as she lifted it from the box, testing the weight and balance. "You are an artist, Master Demir. Thank you."

"It was my honor, Your Majesty. May these weapons serve you both well." He bowed his head, untied a sheath around his torso, and handed it to Auraelia. "A woman with a sword is an asset. A woman with *two is* deadly. May the Goddess Rhayne guide you to victory, my Queen."

Master Demir bowed at the waist, but as he turned to leave, Piper called out, "What about a woman with daggers?"

"She is both," he said, throwing Piper a wink over his shoulder before exiting the tent.

Standing outside her tent, Auraelia shielded her brow from the midday sun as she watched Piper walk out into the open field and kneel down in the grass—her head bowed as she slid her fingers across the blades.

"What's she doing?" Xander asked as he leaned on the support post beside his sister.

"I think she's trying to see if she can pull a vision. See if she can ascertain the outcome before it starts and give us an edge."

"Do you think it will work?"

Auraelia shrugged, her gaze still focused yards away on her friend. "I don't know. I hope so, but she's still trying to understand her triggers." Blowing out a heavy sigh, she turned toward her brother and asked, "Has there been any word from the Court of Opal?"

Pity filled Xander's eyes as he looked her way, and that was all she needed.

When she turned back toward the field, Xander wrapped his arm around her shoulders. "Come on, you need to eat."

Nodding, she let him lead her back into the tent where a plate of roast, carrots, and bread sat steaming on the tabletop. "Have the men eaten? Have *you*?" she asked when she noticed only one place setting.

"Yes, and yes. Aiden and I wandered about to meet some of the men and ate when they did. We're fine, Rae. *Eat*, please."

As if on cue, her stomach rumbled, and she gave her brother a sheepish smile before digging into her plate.

She was nearly halfway done when all hell broke loose outside. "What the hell is going on?"

Xander's hands flew to his waist, checking to ensure his blades were where they were supposed to be, while Auraelia scrambled across the room to grab her own.

The tent flaps were thrown wide as Piper—red-faced with panic shining in her eyes—came barreling in. "Garnet—" she panted, taking in a ragged breath, "Garnet has breached the edge of the mountains. They're *here*, Rae. I—I don't know how I missed it."

Auraelia's eyes widened, time seeming to freeze around her as Piper's words sank into her stomach. It was too soon. Too early in the day. Unless...

Fucking, Caius.

Snatching her blade from the sideboard, she slid it into the sheath down her back before grabbing the other from where it was still nestled in its case. Her magic surged to the surface like a tidal wave as rage filled her veins, determination settling in her bones.

"Rae," Xander's tone was curt, jarring her out of her thoughts.

When she met her friend's gaze, the color in her skin bled away, and she quickly crossed the room to frame her face with her hands. "Piper, stay here and collect yourself. I need you focused out there." When she nodded, Auraelia rested her brow on Piper's and whispered, "You do not break. You survive this, do you hear me? No matter what happens to me, you *live*."

Piper jerked her head away, her eyes narrowing as anger swirled in their depths. "Rae—"

"I mean it, Piper. Live. For both of us, if that's what Dalia has deemed."

A lone, angry tear slipped down Piper's face as she let out a resigned breath and nodded.

Placing a kiss on her friend's cheek, Auraelia turned toward her brother, eyes hard as she met his gaze. "One minute, Xander. I need you out of this tent in one minute."

She knew that there would never be enough time for them to say whatever they needed to say to each other. Goddess, she wished she could give them more. But the time for long, sorrowful goodbyes was gone. The war was here, and as she stepped into the sunshine that was a blaring contrast to what the day held, she let the hardened mask of a queen hellbent on avenging her people slip into place.

Chapter Thirty-Seven

Auraelia

The early arrival of Garnet's army had thrown hers into disorganized chaos. Men were filing out of tents, throwing on armor as quickly as they could before strapping on their weapons. Squadron leaders she recognized from earlier in the day and some she didn't, hollered commands to wrangle people into formation. Archers lined the edge of their camp, firing waves of arrows across the field in an attempt to stave off the impending ambush.

Time.

They needed more time.

Turning toward the field, Auraelia dove into her well of power, wrapping a mental fist around the gold and gray threads that connected her to the storm that raged inside her. Dark clouds rolled across the sky, blotting out the sun as thunder boomed above them. Closing her eyes, Auraelia took a deep breath, letting the power grow until it threatened to burst from her skin. When she opened them, she let it all go. Agonized screams pierced the air as lightning streams rained across the field, setting the grass ablaze across the line of Garnet soldiers and striking down those unlucky enough to be in the path.

As a chorus of cheers rang out around their camp, she expelled a relief-filled breath. She hadn't wanted to use her magic—had wanted to let it build until she met Davina on the battlefield—but it would be worth it if it gave them the time they needed.

Her hand fell to the hilt of the sword strapped at her side, but a familiar voice called her name as she took a step toward where her men were filing into formation.

"Auraelia!" Ser Aeron called out again, his voice carrying over the camp, pulling her attention over her shoulder. She could feel the pounding of his horse's hooves as he rode toward her with Jasira in tow, a canvas bag slung across her saddle. Dismounting before his horse had come to a complete stop, he demanded, "Where the hell do you think you're going dressed like that?"

Pulling the bag from Jasira's saddle, he dropped it at her feet, knelt, and began tugging at the drawstrings.

"You're completely exposed." Ser Aeron paused his ministrations and looked up from where he'd crouched next to the bag. "I know you want to be out there. To stand with your people. But you wouldn't last more than five minutes out there without this, power or not."

Auraelia watched as he began pulling out pieces of armor and glanced down at herself to the cotton and leather that covered her frame, internally wincing at the sheer stupidity of what she had intended to do. No trained warrior would walk out into the middle of a battle without armor.

"Where's your brother?" Ser Aeron demanded as he pulled the last of the segments from the canvas bag and began strapping the greaves to her shins.

"He's in the tent with Piper."

"Xander!" he yelled, thrusting the bracers for her forearms into her hands as he stood. "Put these on. Make sure that they're tight, but don't restrict movement."

Within seconds, her brother was barreling through the tent flaps toward them. His armor was already fastened into place, and his brows furrowed in fierce determination. But a red rim was around his eyes from unshed tears, and the sight gutted her. She hated that this was what their lives had come to. That fate had brought them into this battle, forcing them to deliver goodbyes that may never lead to another hello.

Her heart ached in her chest, and when she turned her gaze away from Xander, she met the hard stare of her Commander General—strength and rage burning in the crystalized amber of his eyes.

While she donned the hardened metal of her soldiers, he was dressed in the traditional garb of the Court of Opal's warriors, only instead of the ethereal white they were known for, his was dyed the rich green of her court. Seeing him in the colors of Emerald instead of his natural-born court had Auraelia standing a little taller, her head lifting a fraction higher. This was the most revered warrior in all of Ixora, and he'd chosen to represent *her court* on the battlefield.

As if he knew the thoughts swirling in her head, Ser Aeron's eyes glowed with mirth as a cocky smirk lifted the corner of his mouth, and he sank to a knee with his head bowed. "With my honor and my life, Your Majesty. I will see you on the battlefield, and may we meet again."

"May the Goddesses of Arcelia guide and protect you, Ser Aeron."

As he rose, he clasped arms with Xander and gave him a slight bow of his head. "My Prince. Help her into the rest of her armor. I need to get to the front lines before Garnet's troops figure out a way through your sister's line of fire. Can you do that?"

Xander gave him a curt nod, straightening his spine as he turned toward Auraelia. The commander mounted his horse and rode away.

A tense silence settled between them as he stooped to grab her breastplate from where it rested on the ground. Persisted as he meticulously ran the leather through the buckles at her side, pulling them taut until there was barely a sliver of space between the front and back plates.

His lips were set in a tight line as he worked to protect every inch of her person. Every breath he took was ragged like it was taking everything he had not to run back into the tent and hold Piper in his arms. And if anyone understood what that felt like, it was her. They'd lost so much already, but through time, they'd gained more in return. And because of that, they had all the more to lose. She knew that her battle with Davina would be the hardest to win. Didn't know what the outcome would be. But she knew that Xander and Piper deserved more than their world had given them. And though she couldn't guarantee them the time they deserved, she could at least give them a chance.

As Xander rested the final pauldron on her shoulder, Auraelia released a sorrowful sigh and broke the heavy silence. "Protect Piper."

His gaze shot to hers, his eyes wide before narrowing in confusion. "Auraelia—"

"I mean it, Xander. Stay with her. Shield *her*. She needs you more than I do."

"I can't just leave you, Rae. You know I can't," he spat back angrily.

She firmly wrapped her hand around his wrist when he pulled the last strap taut. "You can, and you will. You both need to survive this. If there is one last thing you ever do for me, make it this. Protect my friend. Love her the way only you can, and see her through to the other side of this war. *Please.*"

His head shook from side to side, his lips pinched together as he blew out an aggravated breath through his nose. "Don't ask this of me, Rae."

"I shouldn't have to. I know what she is to you. What you are to *her*. Protect that at all costs. I didn't when I should have. Don't make the same mistakes I did. Hold tight with both hands and *fight* for what you share. If I don't make it through this—"

"Auraelia—"

"No, Xander, listen to me. If I don't make it through this, you're going to need each other. Davina won't stop at just me, so take Piper and run. *Be* together. Live the life you both crave and deserve away from all of the court politics. Have tiny raven-haired babies with our family's eyes. But for the love of every Goddess, just *live.* Promise me, Xander."

His eyes lingered on hers, resentment swirling in their depths as silence settled between them. With a resigned sigh, he asked, "You're not even going to give me a choice in this?"

"I'm telling you to *choose* her, Xander, not as your Queen, but as your sister. *Choose. Her.*"

Auraelia released her hold as Xander let out a disgruntled huff, his tongue running across his teeth behind his lips. "Your ultimatums really suck, you know that?"

"You can thank me for them later when we make it through this. Now come on, the end of the world awaits."

As Auraelia's blade sliced across the throat of yet another soldier in crimson armor, the world seemed to spin around her in a blur. Time moved differently in the heat of battle. Each second felt like hours, each hour a month that seemed to bleed into a year. She had no idea how long they'd been fighting back Davina's army, but as the hours ticked by, there was still no sign of her or Caius.

Auraelia grunted as she spun to meet another blade with her own, the crash reverberating down into her hand, threatening the hold she kept on her hilt. No amount of training could have prepared her for the exhaustion creeping in with each swipe of her sword. It didn't matter how many times she told herself that lives would be lost; being the one to take their futures from them for no other reason than they were on the wrong side of history would forever be a heavy weight on her soul.

She didn't want *this*.

Didn't want to be the villain in anyone's story. But that's precisely what she'd become as another unknown name was added to the death toll. She knew she couldn't continue to dwell on the hand fate had dealt her. All she could do was walk the path and pray she came out with a winning hand.

So, with a ragged breath, Auraelia let herself go numb.

Let her mind filter out the faces and screams of those around her, and let her instincts guide her. Pulling her dagger from the sheath on her thigh, she let her magic channel into the emerald blade as she launched it into the neck of an enemy who had the advantage over one of her men. When it landed true, she sprinted toward the fallen soldier, thwarting advances with each step she took until her blade was in her hand once more.

She continued to meet each opponent blow for blow, her magic and training guiding her through the movements. Sweat plastered strands of her hair to her face and soaked through her layers. Blood coated the onyx and gold plates of her armor and mud caked her boots. But as she pulled her blade free from another nameless face's abdomen, the hair on the back of her neck stood on end, and a sickly sweet laugh silenced the tumult of battle that had been there mere moments before.

"Hello, *cousin.*"

Auraelia's grip tightened on her hilt as she turned to meet the face of the person who'd brought all of this bloodshed to her front door. Who perpetrated grief and loss throughout the realm.

"I do hope you've saved some of your strength for me. I want to end you when you're at your best."

The sight of Davina's sinister smile had her magic surging in her veins; sparks of lightning ignited at the tips of her fingers as the wind stirred the air around them.

"I see you're still letting others fight your battles for you, *cousin*," Auraelia spat as her gaze raked over Davina. She was all black except for the crimson breastplate and cape fluttering in the delicate wind that drifted over the field.

Davina scoffed as her blood-red lips pulled up into a sneer. "I'm not here for them. I'm here for *you.*"

Auraelia's magic responded before she'd even had time to think, her lightning searing through her veins at the onslaught of Davina's magic that was determined to take root. The battle around them faded into nothing as Auraelia focused on the enemy before her.

Davina's assault on her system pulled her concentration into defensive strategies, channeling her strength into fighting off the ice that threatened to crystallize in her blood. She'd trained for years, but not even Ser Aeron could prepare her to fight something she couldn't *see.*

She couldn't defeat her if all of her magic was going to stave off Davina's attacks.

She needed to attack hard and fast.

What she needed was a distraction.

Grabbing hold of the rich brown thread that connected her to the earth, Auraelia pulled on the ground beneath Davina's feet in an attempt to knock her off balance. It worked, but only enough to give her mere seconds to strike. Throwing out a bolt of lightning, her heart sank as it only grazed her cousin's shoulder.

Davina's assault stopped as she brought her hand to where blood had begun to trickle down from the wound and let out a guttural scream. When her crazed gaze met Auraelia's, she hissed through clenched teeth, "Big mistake, little cousin."

Frigid magic assaulted Auraelia's system harder and faster than her own could respond; her lightning fizzled out as it came close to the icy bands that constricted her veins and wrapped around her heart. Every breath felt like she was sucking daggers into her lungs. Every movement sent streams of ice so cold it burned down her limbs. Blinding agony shot through her, causing her muscles to lock.

Auraelia cried out as she clung to her threads, begging them to aid her against the onslaught. But as Davina's stranglehold over her body tightened, her magic began to slip through her fingers. The fragments of her magic dimmed, growing limp like a wilted flower on a vine. And the more she fought, the harder Davina hit her.

Summoning the strength she had left, Auraelia threw everything she had into one more strike. But it failed, her lightning sputtering as it left her hand and dying completely before it reached Davina.

Lies.

It was all lies.

Davina hadn't wanted her at her best. She'd wanted her at her weakest. She hid behind people who had no stake in this war until she found out Auraelia was worn down. And she'd gotten her wish.

She was exhausted; her magic spent.

And she'd failed.

Failed her family and her people.

Daemon. The thought of him and the future she'd looked forward to exploring with him had her heart stalled in her chest for an entirely different reason.

She could feel the life draining from her body, her heart slowing to stagnant beats. Blood began to trickle out of her nose, the taste of copper filling her mouth as her knees threatened to give out. If this is what the Goddess Dalia had in store for her, then she had no choice but to accept her fate.

Davina's laugh echoed across the field, its shrill tone stabbing into her skull as she staggered to stay on her feet.

"Auraelia!"

She could have sworn she heard Daemon screaming her name, but through the pain-addled fog, it didn't make sense. He was in Opal. There was no way he could be there.

Auraelia tried to shake the cloud of agony from her mind, but it was like trying to uproot a mountain. She heard her name again, closer this time, but her knees buckled, and she sank into the muck as the world around her went black.

Daemon

War was a brutal part of life. There would always be the ones who died and the ones who lived to tell the story. But as Daemon watched Auraelia fall to her knees, every shred of humanity he had left crumbled with her.

"*No*!" he screamed, his voice cracking from the strain. He could feel her fading. Could feel her heart slowing as if it were his own, the thread tethering them together weakening with each draw of breath into his lungs. "*Auraelia!*"

Daemon spooled down to a depth of his magic he'd never explored, letting his power unfurl around him and fill him with a darkness he'd never known. Shadows spilled out around him, shrouding the ground in a heavy blanket of rolling black mist as snake-like tendrils dove into the mouths of their enemies, suffocating their screams as their lives became forfeit.

Drawing his sword, he began to cut his way across the field. It didn't matter if the wounds left by his blade were what leeched the light from soldiers' eyes; his shadows had become a living, breathing entity. They shaped into creatures that would haunt even grown men's nightmares before extinguishing the souls that dared get in his way.

Taking advantage of Davina's focus on Auraelia, Daemon slipped between the shadows until he was in front of her, and his hand was wrapped around her throat.

"Let. Her. Go." he bit out through gritted teeth, his hold tightening around the slender column of her neck. Davina's smile was malicious as she met his gaze, but her assault on Auraelia never ceased; her power was a palpable force surrounding the woman he loved.

"Hello, Prince Daemon. Or is it *King* now? I'm so glad you could join us." He didn't even have time to blink before ice crystalized in his veins. "I must admit, I was a little disappointed to learn that you left your precious *star.* Goddess knows it's going to be *so much* more satisfying to let you watch her wither away in front of your eyes."

Davina pried his hand from her throat and shoved her own into his chest, sending him staggering back to where Auraelia had fallen. Daemon groaned as a burning cold surrounded his heart, causing him to double over just to stay on his feet.

Only together can you do what needs to be done. Narissa's words filtered through his mind as he glanced down at his fallen star. There was blood caked on her armor, and her hair was matted to her face, but she was still so beautiful. It looked like she was just sleeping, but the dimming glow of the bond that connected them told another story. With every slow beat of her heart, each ragged breath she drew into her lungs had her fading further and further away from him.

Open your eyes, Auraelia. Fight this. He mentally pleaded as he took in the soft lines of her face.

"Kneel."

Davina's command had him dragging his gaze from the woman he loved to the one he despised.

With gritted teeth, Daemon forced his body to straighten. "There is only one woman I will ever get on my knees for, and it will never be you."

"I said *kneel*!" Davina shouted, her power wrapping around him in a way he hadn't experienced.

Instead of ice, it felt like his blood was boiling. His heart thundered in his chest. Every breath was suffocating as blood filled his mouth and spilled from his nose. Daemon crumpled, his knees sinking into the mud next to Auraelia as he continued to choke on the very thing meant to keep him alive.

Davina stalked toward him, bending until her face was mere inches from his own. "Last chance, little King. Bow to me, and you can rule by my side. Refuse, and you will die. Either way, you will be on your knees before me."

"Go to hell." Daemon spat, spraying blood over Davina's face.

She sucked on a canine as she straightened, her head tilting to the side before a feline smile stretched across her face. "Have it your way, then."

Being drowned by one of Narissa's creatures would have been preferable to the agony that was being inflicted on every inch of his body. Davina's magic ravaged his system, snuffing out any glimmer of shadows in his veins.

It was like she was playing with him, prolonging his torment as she alternated between the two extremes of her power. One moment, it felt like icicles stabbing his brain while frost bloomed around his heart. In the next, blood would be pouring from his mouth and nose.

Daemon bent over, his fingers digging into the mud as he gritted his teeth through the onslaught. Fighting through the pain, he slid his hand over to Auraelia and curled his fingers around hers.

Auraelia, please, my star. Your people need you. I *need you.*

He wasn't sure if he imagined it, but as stars danced around his vision, he could have sworn he felt the tether tighten.

Chapter Thirty-Eight

Auraelia

Auraelia.

A voice as calm as a summer breeze cut through the darkness surrounding her, replacing it with the warmth of light.

Auraelia, my sweet child, open your eyes.

Hesitantly, she let her eyes flutter open. All the pain she'd felt moments ago was gone, and a soft, buttery glow illuminated the world around her. Gone were the screams of the wounded and the smell of wet earth. In their place were the sound of crashing waterfalls in the distance and the sweet scent of honey. And in front of her was a woman bathed in an ethereal glow, her features masked in the shadows the light cast. She was dressed in simple armor with overflowing silver robes and a sword strapped to her hip, her chestnut brown ringlets falling over her shoulder as she softly tilted her head to the side, a gentle smile painted across her lips.

"Where am I?" Auraelia asked as she met the woman's soft brown eyes.

"You're in the world between worlds, my child."

"The world between—what does that mean? Who are you?"

The woman chuckled and knelt in front of her. Auraelia couldn't help the gasp that escaped as her features became clearer and recognition dawned. The depictions of her goddess were nothing compared to being in her presence. She radiated love and light, but a sharpness to her eyes spoke to why she was also the goddess of war.

"Ah," Rhayne smiled, her head bobbing slightly, "I see you know me now. Hello, Auraelia. And in answer to your other question, your soul is attempting to enter Arcelia."

Panic flooded her veins as she scurried to her feet, her words coming out around a choked sob. "I—I failed. My p—*people*."

"Shhh, be calm now. You have not failed." Rhayne clasped Auraelia's hands in her own, pulling her up as she pushed to her feet. "It is not yet your time. You still have much left to accomplish in your life cycle. So much love left to give and receive."

"But Davina."

"Is but an obstacle you must overcome and one you cannot do on your own. You are a powerful soul, Auraelia. But even those with power need help."

"I—I don't understand."

"Don't you?"

"Even with an army behind me, I couldn't defeat her. How—"

"It's not an army you need, Auraelia. What you need is the other half of your soul. You need to trust in the bond you have with Daemon. After all, light cannot exist without the dark."

"But he's in Opal helping his father."

Rhayne slowly shook her head, a small smile lifting the corner of her lips. "What was once true no longer remains so. Close your eyes and *feel* for him, Auraelia. You felt him as soon as he stepped foot back in Lyndaria. Though you believed you imagined it, you knew he was there even through your pain."

Auraelia's brows furrowed, but she did as she was asked. Closing her eyes, she breathed deeply. The thread between them was there, but just barely. And as she followed the path that pulled her toward him, excruciating pain crippled her, sending her to her knees as she cried out.

"He's...he's–" She couldn't even form the words, her heart shattering in her chest as she felt the pain he was enduring.

Warmth washed over her once more as Rhayne helped her back to her feet. "Go back to him, Auraelia. Reach deep within yourself. Demolish the lock you've kept on the well of power within you, and let it fill every fiber of your being. *Lean* on Daemon. Let him fill the spaces where your power cannot reach. Only together can you accomplish what needs to be done."

Auraelia held the goddess' gaze, and when she nodded encouragingly, closed her eyes once more, took a steadying breath, and let the darkness envelop her senses. She could feel the tether to Daemon strengthening. Could feel his warmth even in the between.

"Trust in yourself and in your bond, Auraelia."

Rhayne pressed a kiss to her brow, and it felt as if she was falling, her soul cascading through time itself until it landed back into her pain-riddled body. She had no idea how long she'd been unconscious, but as her soul settled, the effect of Davina's magic began to melt away. She could feel her power growing, the once dimming embers fanning to life as she took her first full breath.

"Have you had enough, little king?" Davina's snide tone pierced through the remaining fog clouding her mind, filling her with white-hot rage.

Curling her hands into fists, Auraelia opened her eyes. Everything around her was blanketed in white light as her power surged within her. Her lightning wrapped around her limbs as a storm formed overhead, and the wind whipped around them.

"Auraelia?" Daemon choked out as she tightened her hand around his, pulling him to his feet as she stood.

"What? This isn't—it isn't possible."

Auraelia's magic glowed around her like the light of Arcelia, twisting together in intricate ribbons to form a shield around herself and Daemon. She dove further into her power, smashing through the bottom and into a seemingly endless pit of energy. Gradually, she could feel Daemon's shadows sinking into her skin. Could feel his strength returning as Davina's magic faded from his system, his power growing alongside her own.

"You wanted me at my best, cousin, did you not? Be careful what you wish for."

With one final plunge into her power, Auraelia erupted.

Her magic streamed from her in a controlled burst while Daemon slammed a wall of shadows into Davina, knocking her off her feet and wrapping her in a cocoon of endless night. Inch by inch, Auraelia's magic wrapped around Davina's limbs, branding her skin as it burned through her garments.

Auraelia pulled on her earthbound thread of magic with a strained groan, causing the ground to rumble beneath their feet. When roots shot from the earth, she twisted them until they were wrapped around her cousin, holding her in place.

Davina's screams pierced the air as she flailed against the onslaught, the sound of her bones cracking beneath the tightening binds echoing in Auraelia's ears.

But she didn't care.

She'd lost too much at Davina's hand. She'd warned her not to step foot in her court. Had warned her to leave her people be and had hoped that Kyra would have been enough of a message.

But she'd been wrong.

Auraelia could feel the magnitude of Daemon's power as her magic glided along his own, delving into her cousin's mouth and nose to cut her screams into silent gasps for air.

But as time raged on, and the more magic Auraelia threw at her cousin, the closer her burnout became. She could feel it looming just below the surface. Her threads were burning too brightly, and she knew she was diving too fast. Her limbs shook from the quantity of power she was expelling, her vision growing hazy as she continued to spiral toward the bottom of her well. But she couldn't stop. She knew that it had to end.

Auraelia tightened her grip on Daemon's hand, tears forming in her eyes as she turned toward him. She'd never tire of looking at him. At the strong lines of his face and the way, his eyes shone like twin suns on a summer day when he let his magic go. Of the way his eyes crinkled at the corners when he laughed or the smirk that drove her crazy. He was the love of her life, and that life was slowly coming to an unfortunate close.

But if this was her end, she wanted him to be the last sight she took with her to Arcelia.

Tears were streaming down her face when Daemon looked her way, but she gave him a watery smile and whispered, "I love you."

Panic shone in his gaze, his mouth parting around her name as she turned her face toward the sky and closed her eyes. Inhaling deeply, she let herself sink into the final depths of her power. Streaks of lightning streamed down from the sky, illuminating the battlefield in a golden glow as they crashed into Auraelia. Sinking into her skin until she was nothing but the power within her veins. Then, with a vengeful cry, she let every last drop of her magic go, channeling it into a ball of blinding white light as it hurled toward Davina.

As the glow of her assault faded, Auraelia swayed on her feet, the roots binding her cousin fell away as her body stilled.

"Auraelia?" Daemon questioned, wrapping his arm around her waist as his magic slowly pulled away from Davina and spooled back into himself.

Panic laced his tone when she didn't answer as he repeated her name.

Warmth washed over her, blanketing her body in a heavy shroud.

It's over.

Her vision darkened, and her limbs grew heavier with each passing second.

My people are safe.

She could feel her lungs struggling to draw in air as her heart began to slow.

"*Auraelia*!"

She wanted to stay. She wanted to see Daemon again, but his scream was the last thing she heard as she let herself drift into nothingness.

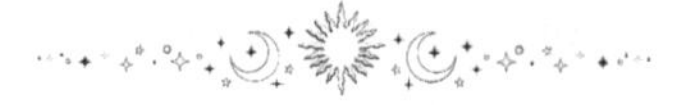

Daemon

Daemon screamed her name as she collapsed in his arms, sinking to the ground as he held her to him. Blood was trickling out of her nose and ears, her breath coming in slow, ragged pulls as she lay limply in his lap.

"No, no, no. This can't be happening," he demanded, stroking the hair away from her face. "Auraelia, *please*. Open your eyes."

His shadows stroked against the power that still glimmered beneath the surface of her skin, coaxing it to rise, to respond. To do *something* to let him know she was still there. Tears landed on her cheeks as he pleaded with her to stay. To come back to him. But the time between the beats of her heart lengthened with each fall of her chest.

Then there was nothing.

The color of her skin began to fade as her heart slowed.

"No!" he screamed, shaking her roughly before pulling her tightly against him. "We were supposed to have more time. We...we haven't had enough time." Sobs wracked his chest as he held her to him. "Please, my star. Don't leave me."

"Daemon!"

He heard someone scream his name, but he didn't care. Nothing mattered anymore, not if she wasn't there to share it with.

"Daemon! Look out!" He recognized the voice then, the shrill tone of Piper's scream piercing through the shattering of his heart.

His magic responded of its own accord, wrapping around him in a protective shield just in time to deflect a knife thrown at him. The whistle of a blade sailed past him, the telltale sound of it landing in its intended target, pulling his gaze from Auraelia.

Anger surged in his chest as he watched Davina's charred hands claw at the wound in her throat. There was only one way she would have managed to survive the onslaught of power he and Auraelia had funneled into her body. She'd taken the one thing that meant more to him than anything in this realm. And somehow, through her blood bond with Caius, she had managed to survive.

Daemon watched in disbelief as Davina pulled the dagger from her neck, blood pouring from the wound as she held his gaze and took aim. But before she could throw it, another dagger flew past his head and landed directly next to where the first had been.

As Davina's body crumpled to the ground, the elation he thought he'd feel was absent. Instead, he felt hollow. It was over, but the cost had been too high. He'd lost too much.

Anguish and rage began to fill the hole that his heart had left, a sob wracking his chest as he silently pleaded with every goddess in Arcelia to give Auraelia back to him.

He was nothing without her.

Wanted nothing if he didn't have her by his side.

Tilting his face toward the sky, Daemon let out a guttural scream and unleashed the power that coursed through his veins. Waves of shadow washed across the field, barreling into any enemy that remained and leaving nothing but the husks of who they once were in their wake.

He didn't want to live without her.

He couldn't—*wouldn't*—live without her.

Be still, my son. Remember that without darkness, there is no light. The velvety voice of his goddess slid into his mind; her words were followed by another he did not recognize. *She has not left you, young king. Just as your shadows need the light, she needs darkness to shine.*

"Daemon?" Piper's voice was watery, her steps hesitant as she cautiously closed the distance between them. "Daem—" His name was cut in half by a gasp, her steps faltering as her eyes undoubtedly landed on the lifeless body in his lap. "Oh my, goddess. Is that? *Nononono.*"

Piper's sobs drowned in the background as he let himself sink further into his magic.

"This was not how our story was supposed to end," he whispered through a sob, stroking his fingers along her cheek. "We were supposed to have what they couldn't. We were supposed to *live.*"

Daemon began unstrapping the blood-streaked armor from her body and tossed it to the side with a heavy clang. Her tunic was singed from where her lightning had wrapped around her limbs, and dirt was mixed with the sweat and blood on her face, but other than that, she was perfect. His arms shook as he pulled her further into his lap, cradling her against his chest as ribbons of shadows wrapped around them.

"Daemon," Piper choked out. "What—what are you doing?"

Resting his brow on hers, he whispered, "I love you, Auraelia. I have loved you from the very first time I saw you across that stupid ballroom. And I will love you until the stars fall from the sky. But I will not live without you."

As he pressed his lips to hers, Daemon released the final hold he'd kept on his power. Let it flow out of him and into Auraelia until the world around him disappeared in a veil of stars and shadows.

Chapter Thirty-Nine

Piper

Piper's tears had long since dried in the week since the battle that had taken so many. But the arguments of what had transpired on the field that day had only grown.

Accusations had been hurled at Xander, questioning why he'd abandoned his sister when they thought she needed him most. Doubts over Ser Aeron's healing abilities had been shared in hushed tones and shouted in crowded rooms.

It didn't matter.

None of it mattered.

No one could have changed the outcome.

No thread could have been pulled to make it end another way.

She'd tried. Goddess, how she'd tried to see another ending for her friend. But only the Goddess Dalia knew how their story would end when all was said and done. All she could do was hold on to the hope that light would shine through the heavy gray clouds that shrouded the realm—clouds that seemed to grow darker with each passing day.

Piper adjusted her position in the armchair next to the bed. Hugging her legs to her chest, she rested her cheek on her knees as she watched the swirls of shadows dance around Auraelia and Daemon.

Pinpricks of light glimmered in the inky black depths of Daemon's shadows, reminding her of how the stars drifted across the sky as the night wore on.

"Any change?" Xander asked as he draped a blanket around her shoulders. She hadn't heard him enter. No vision came to show her the decisions he'd made. But then again, she hadn't had a vision since she saw Auraelia's body lying limp in Daemon's arms, her skin streaked in crimson.

"None," she said with a sigh. "They've been like this for a week now with no change. We don't even know if either of them are alive, Xan. I can't find their threads. I can't even reach them to *try*. And believe me, I've tried, but Daemon's fucking shadows block everything." She angrily threw a hand out toward the bed, scowling into the star-flecked darkness that cloaked her friends.

"Hey," Xander cooed, dropping to his knees before her. "You can't take this on, Piper. You can't control other people's choices."

"But I should be able to control my own magic!" Piper buried her head in her hands as tears began to fall. What was the point of being clairvoyant if the threads didn't give her the answers she needed to save the people she loved? Auraelia was her chosen sister, the one constant in her life she could always count on. She was a piece of her soul, and that piece was gone. At least, that's what it felt like. Watching Auraelia day in and day out with no change—no chance to even see if a soul was left in the body lying swathed in shadows—had stolen a piece of her she didn't think she would ever get back.

"My visions are gone, Xander. My power abandoned me when I needed it most. And I—" A sob caught in her throat, halting the words that had been swirling in her mind over the last week.

She'd failed to protect her queen, and it seemed her magic was failing her in response.

"Piper—"

"You should have saved *her*, not me," she croaked out in a whisper.

She felt Xander's body shudder, but as he released a heavy sigh, his finger found her chin, and he lifted her gaze to his. "No, Piper. I was right where I was meant to be."

"You were where *she told you* to be."

Xander's hand dropped as he inhaled deeply through his nose and pushed to his feet. "I was where I wanted to be, Piper. You can choose to believe that, or you can blame me for something you know neither of us could change. Either way, I was, and still am, right where I want to be."

Xander pressed a kiss to her brow, and her heart sank as she watched him walk away.

She knew that if she could talk to Auraelia, she would call her an idiot. She would tell her that it wasn't his fault, and deep in her heart, she knew that to be true. But she'd already lost one of the most important people in her life. If she let Xander in, how long would it be until she lost him, too?

Another week came and went, and still, there was no change.

Piper was pretty certain she'd become affixed to the chair by this point. Meals were brought to her by either Xander or Liza, and they stayed until she'd finished the plate. Then, they would gather her dishes and leave quietly. But she never missed the sorrow in their eyes as they looked back at the bed. Never missed the tears that brimmed when there was no news of improvement. And with each passing day, the hope she'd held onto faded, and resentment took its place.

Why did I survive?

Who am I to the realm?

I have no power to protect our people, have nothing to offer...

"Piper?" A hesitant voice called out, breaking her out of her spiraling thoughts. When she turned toward the door, piercing green eyes met hers. "May I come in?"

When she nodded, Daemon's sister pushed the door wider and stepped into the space.

A week after the war ended—when there still hadn't been a change with Auraelia and Dameon—Xander sent word to the Court of Opal and the Sapphire Isles to let them know what had happened. But it wasn't until Yvaine showed up a few days ago that they learned of King Evander's death and that Daemon was now King of the Sapphire Isles.

"Would you like to sit?" Piper asked quietly, gesturing to the chair beside her.

Yvaine swallowed audibly, nodding as she slowly sank down into the cushion with a grieved sigh. Her eyes were rimmed in red, the kohl she usually wore smudged beneath, and the fact that she didn't bother hiding her tears brought Piper a small amount of comfort. She was so tired of pretending to be strong when all she wanted to do was crawl into a hole and whither away.

They'd been sitting in silence for a while, both staring blankly at the shroud of shadows cloaking their loved ones, when Yvaine spoke. Her voice was a hushed whisper, but there was no mistaking the relief that flooded each word. "He's still alive."

"How can you be so sure? Nothing has changed."

A small smile tugged on the corner of Yvaine's lips as water began to line her eyes. "A week or so before the war started, I made Daemon bind a promise that he wouldn't keep me from fighting for our people. I'm not sure how much you know about them, but when you bind a promise, the participants exchange a kernel of magic. And I can still feel his. It's weak but growing stronger the longer I sit here. And I can feel mine pulling toward me."

"I wish I had that. I don't know—" Piper choked on a sob as she stared through the shadows at her friend's still body. "I don't know what fate has befallen Auraelia. And I can't see—"

"Piper," Yvaine reached across the small space between them and grasped her hand, squeezing tightly. "My brother would not be growing stronger if Auraelia had been welcomed home by the goddesses. Nothing, and I mean *nothing*, would hold him here if she was no longer present." She squeezed Piper's hand once more, then pushed to her feet. "Have faith, little raven. They will come back to us when they are ready."

Little Raven? *Raven's are birds associated with death.*

Yvaine gave a small chuckle. "I can see the wheels in your mind turning in your eyes. It was a compliment, I assure you. A raven is also the bird of prophecy, Piper."

"But my sight—"

"Will return when you're ready for it to. You don't trust *yourself*, let alone your visions, right now. Believe in yourself, and they will come back."

Piper watched her walk away, her words resonating with something in her soul and fanning the dying embers of hope. But as Yvaine pulled the door open, Piper called her name, waiting until she turned to say, "Thank you."

"We all need a little light right now. I'm glad that I could give that to you."

Yvaine smiled and then slipped through the door, leaving her alone once more.

Though their conversation was short, it lifted some of the weight off Piper's heart, and she felt as if she could finally breathe more easily.

A little while later, Liza brought her dinner, and it was the first time her face wasn't pinched with worry as she watched her eat. Not long after, her eyes became heavy, and sleep slowly claimed her consciousness. But as her eyes drifted closed, she could have sworn she saw a tiny streak of lightning mingle within the shadows.

Chapter Forty

Auraelia

7 days since the war ended...

Everything was heavy.

Her eyes.

Her limbs.

Her heart.

But it was over, and Daemon was safe. He'd survived the war...even if she hadn't.

Auraelia inhaled deeply, but instead of the easy breaths she'd had when she met the Goddess Rhayne outside the gates of Arcelia, pain cinched in her chest and radiated out into every fiber of her being.

It didn't make sense.

She should have been bathing in the ethereal glow of the Goddess Realm. She should have been dining at Inara's table with the rest of the fallen warriors of history or walking the endless gardens with her mother.

Instead, cool darkness shadowed her sight and cloaked her senses.

With each pained breath she took, the world slowly came into focus, sounds and smells tickling something in the recesses of her memory.

Auraelia urged her body to move, to do anything, but it didn't obey.

Tired.

She was still...so...tired.

14 days since the war ended...

Voices bounced around the room, filling her ears with a cacophony of sounds that pounded around in her skull like the dull edge of a knife. But there was one that soothed the jagged edges.

One that her soul seemed to recognize, though she couldn't place the who or why.

Auraelia tried again to move, but her mind and body still wouldn't connect.

Slowly, she drifted back into the abyss that she'd become so accustomed to.

Let it wash over her in cold waves and drag her under.

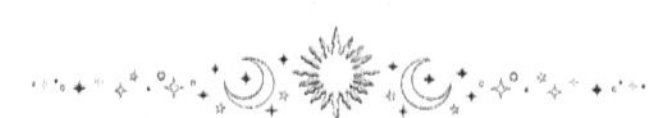

18 days since the war ended...

A steady voice lured her out of the darkness that had enveloped her so completely. It was like listening to her favorite melody—calm and sweet, with all of the notes in the right places, washing over her like a gentle wave.

Something about it felt special, like watching the sun sink below the horizon or seeing a star streak across the sky. She basked in the warmth that voice brought to her heart, letting it sink into her soul and course through her veins.

A delicate touch ran across her cheek, and it was as if the veil had been lifted from her eyes, and everything came rushing back.

Heat flooded her system, like holding her hand close enough to a fire to feel its warmth but not so close that it burned. Tingles pricked her fingertips, and the pain that accompanied her breaths dulled to a manageable ache.

Though the voice was muffled, it floated through her mind, reminding her of crystal-clear waters beneath star-flecked skies, calming the storm that had begun to rage inside her.

"Auraelia, open your eyes for me. I can feel you there; just...open your eyes."

The gentle caress on her cheek continued as each word landed heavily in her heart. She could feel the tears welling behind her eyes, her chest tightening as she finally realized why that voice settled the noise around her. It was the one she never thought she'd hear again. And yet there he was...just as he always had been.

It took more effort than she'd hoped, but after a few tries, she was able to peel her eyes open. Bright, spring-green irises met hers, and she watched as tears began to stream down his cheeks.

Every movement exerted more energy than she had, but she managed to lift her hand to cradle his cheek. When he leaned into it, she felt like she couldn't breathe. It shouldn't have been possible. She'd given every drop of power she had to take out Davina. Had felt her body fade and welcome the darkness as it consumed her. She'd made peace with her fate...and yet...

"Daemon," she breathed through a choked sob.

"Hello, my star."

His lips met hers with an urgency she couldn't answer fast enough. She wasn't sure how or why, but it seemed Fate had given them another chance, and it was one she wasn't going to take for granted. When they parted, Daemon rested his brow on hers, and she breathed him in. His signature scent of sandalwood and salty ocean air was present even among the acrid smell of a battle long since past.

"Daemon."

"Yes, my star?" he asked, pulling back just enough to look into her eyes.

"Marry me. I don't care what it means for our reigns; I just know I don't want to live without you. I don't want to waste—"

Daemon's lips descended upon hers, cutting off her words and every train of thought in the process. When he pulled away, his telltale smirk graced his lips, and her heart leaped in her chest.

"I thought you told me to ask you?"

"Is that a no, then?" she asked, her eyes narrowing as his smirk grew.

"Auraelia, you are the love of my life. Fate might have linked us, but I would have chosen you in this life and every life thereafter. You are the reason my heart beats and for the air in my lungs. I am yours. Wholly and completely."

"So, it's a *yes*, then?"

His laugh boomed through the room, his brow falling to rest upon hers once more. "It's a yes, my star. In every way possible. And I can't wait to see what our forever has in store."

Daemon's hands cradled her face as tears streamed from her eyes, a series of gasps filtering into the room as his lips met hers.

"Auraelia?" Piper's shock was palpable and penetrated every syllable of her name. A collection of "Oh my goddess" and "Thank the heavens" swarmed the space as more and more people filled the quiet of her room.

She felt Daemon chuckle against her lips and couldn't help but smile in return.

"I guess the secret's out."

Daemon pushed into a sitting position and gently pulled her with him. Everything ached, but as his shadows drifted into nothing around them, she welcomed the firm embrace of her friend.

"I thought you died," Piper sobbed into her neck, her hold tightening painfully.

"So did I." Auraelia returned the embrace, tears streaming down her face in rivulets that soaked into the fabric of Piper's dress.

"Rae?" Xander's voice was low—tentative—like he wasn't sure what he was seeing was real.

Peeking over her friend's shoulder, she met his gaze, and as soon as their eyes locked, tears soaked his cheeks, and a watery smile pulled on the corners of his lips.

Auraelia maintained her hold on Piper as she reached out her hand toward her brother, smiling and mouthing, "Thank you."

He inclined his head slightly, but sorrow filled his gaze as his eyes flicked to her friend before they returned to her own. Squeezing her hand gently, he said, "I'll come see you later,"

Nodding, she returned the gesture, then dropped his hand. But as he began to walk away, she called out his name, waiting until he turned to say, "I love you."

"I love you, too. I'll send for Ser Aeron and some food, okay?"

His smile didn't reach his eyes, and as he turned for the door, a million questions filtered into her mind over what could have happened between her brother and her friend. But before she could voice them, Piper pulled away, her eyes bloodshot as she wiped the tears from her cheeks.

"I'll clear everyone out so you two can clean up. You've been lying there for over two weeks, and no offense, Rae? But you smell. Bad. Like, really bad. You both do." Piper scrunched her nose as she backed away, and a laugh tumbled from both of their lips.

"Thank you, Piper."

"I didn't do anything," she said with a shrug.

"You stayed."

"You...you knew? You knew I was here?"

Auraelia shook her head. "Not exactly, but I know you."

Tears renewed in Piper's eyes, and she hastily wiped them away as she ushered people from the room.

"Hey Rae?" she called out before she stepped through the opening. When Auraelia hummed in response, she said, "Thanks."

"For what?" she asked, confusion drawing her brows together.

"For staying."

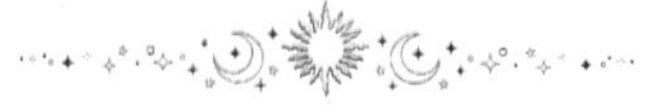

The sun shone brightly, warmth soaking into Auraelia's skin as she meandered through her mother's garden. It was the first day in weeks that she had a moment to breathe.

After a few days of—forced—recovery, Auraelia had thrown herself into the rehabilitation of her kingdom. She'd visited the families of the fallen and held a reception for the ones who'd made it home.

She cleared any misconceptions regarding Ser Aeron and her brother and breathed a sigh of relief when she'd been informed of Lord Harland's demise. Though he'd deserved the end he'd received, after so much death, Auraelia wasn't sure if she would have been able to follow through with her threat if he'd somehow survived.

Breathing in the fresh air, she turned her face toward the sky and embraced the feeling of her magic flowing through her veins. After she'd awoken, she'd barely felt a glimmer of the power she'd held on the battlefield and feared it had been lost. But after a few days, the threads mended, and her magic trickled back into her body like a steady stream.

Warmth blossomed in her chest as her magic flowed languidly through her body, and she smiled. It wasn't long before Daemon's fingers twined with hers, and he pulled her hand to his mouth.

"I've missed you," she said as she turned to meet his gaze. "How's your mother? And Yvaine? Did you discuss the regency?"

"Mother is as well as can be expected. She's been keeping herself busy planning the coronation and her trip here. Yvaine," he let out a heavy sigh, "Let's just say she's not so sure about being Regent. Not that I can really blame her. "

Auraelia nodded and began pulling Daemon along the path with her. "Do you need to go back?"

"No, the coronation and regency ceremony won't take place until after the wedding. Speaking of which." He pulled her to a stop and clasped both of her hands in his. "I think it's high time we made this official."

"It wasn't already?" she asked, quirking a brow.

A laugh rumbled in his chest as he shook his head and slowly dropped to a knee. "Auraelia Rose Morwen. My Queen, my soul, love of my life. I have used the stars to guide me through every journey in my existence, but I never thought that they would bring me to you. You have given me light when all I knew was a world of shadows. I loved you before I really understood what love was, and I will love you until my dying breath."

Auraelia's hands shook as he reached into his vest pocket and pulled out a ring, tears filling his eyes as they met hers once more.

"Marry me, my star. Live this life with me."

As the last word fell from his lips, Auraelia launched herself at him, her lips claiming his in desperation.

His chuckle vibrated against her chest as he pulled away, his hand finding her cheek and wiping away the tears that had slipped from her eyes. "Still waiting on your answer, Princess."

"Yes, Daemon. A thousand times, yes." Time stilled around them as he slipped the silver band onto her hand, the newly blackened tips of his fingers sliding along her own emerald green.

Auraelia ran her fingers along his jaw, then cupped his cheek in her palm, relishing the way he always leaned into her touch. "I love you."

"Even if the stars fall from Arcelia, Auraelia. I am yours."

As they returned to the castle, Auraelia idly ran her fingers along the tops of her mother's bushes. She was so lost in her bliss that she didn't notice when a singular bud appeared and began to bloom.

Epilogue

Daemon

4 months later...

Daemon stood at the foot of the altar, wringing his hands together as he paced in a small line. He'd been awaiting this day for what seemed like a lifetime, his soul restless as he waited for the sun to kiss the horizon.

"Breathe, D," Aiden whispered as he made his way back to his starting point.

Nodding his head, Daemon ceased his pacing and took in the scene around him.

The sanctuary of the Goddess Rhayne looked beautiful. Its towering columns were wrapped in intricately woven vines with sprigs of lavender and delicate white flowers twined within. Ivory candles flickered in tall glass vases that were nestled into rich green foliage that lined the aisle's edge, and white petals were scattered down its length.

It was beautiful, but it all faded into the background as the musicians began to play.

An excited energy ignited the air as people began to stand from their seats, and he had to take a large breath to steady his anxious heart.

One by one, members of Emerald's court, led by Priestess Riona, made their way down the aisle. But the world around him ceased to exist the moment Auraelia stepped into view.

She was absolutely breathtaking.

And as if her presence had demanded it, the sun dipped into the horizon. Its peachy glow washed over the space and illuminated her in an ethereal light, making her look like the shining star he'd always known she was.

A gentle breeze blew through the sanctuary as she took her first step toward him; a cascade of wisteria blossoms fell from the air just like the last time they'd been there together. The memory of the fire in her eyes, as they met his during her coronation, brought a smile to his lips. It broadened as those same eyes locked onto his from the opposite side of the aisle, love and adoration burning brightly in their stormy depths.

Time seemed to slow to a crawl as she made her way down the aisle, but tears welled in his eyes when she was finally before him as he took in every detail.

"My star, you look—" he whispered, his words falling short and evading his mind as his eyes roved down her frame. There wasn't a single word that could accurately describe what he wanted to say, each one seeming less consequential than the last.

Her hair was pulled back in intricate twists with strings of pearls woven within them to pay homage to his court, leaving her face exposed save for a few delicately curled strands. The silvery-blue fabric hugged her torso and cascaded down from her shoulders and waist to pool at her feet, every inch bedecked in intricately beaded stars and constellations.

She had become a living embodiment of the night sky.

The light within the darkness.

The light in *his* darkness.

Words still failed him as he took her hand, nestling it into the crook of his arm as he guided her up the steps to where Priestess Riona waited.

"We're gathered here today, in front of witnesses, loved ones, and the Goddess of Love herself, to celebrate the bond blessed upon this couple..."

The opening words of the ceremony faded into the background as he let himself get lost in Auraelia's eyes.

He still couldn't believe that they'd made it. After everything that the world had thrown at them and all of the obstacles they had to overcome within their own hearts, they'd actually made it.

"King Daemon, if you would, please."

His eyes widened as the priestess' voice cut through his thoughts, and Auraelia let out a small chuckle as she extended her left hand. Anticipation filled his chest as her palm met his. It grew as the priestess draped the long piece of rope from his own ship over their clasped hands and began to loop it into and over itself.

"Your Majesty, would you like to go first?" Priestess Riona asked, a small smile tugging on her lips as she turned toward Auraelia.

With a slight bob of her head and a slow exhale, she turned her eyes back to his, tears lining their rims.

"Daemon Alexander, love of my life and soul of my soul. I thought that I knew what love was before I met you. I thought I knew how I wanted my life to unfold. But I knew I had been wrong from the moment our eyes met.

"You swept into my life, turning it upside down in all of the best ways. You've shown me time and time again what it's like to be loved. To be wanted and needed. You've lent me your strength when I needed it most and stood by my side when I was determined to stand alone. You've been there for me in whatever capacity I allowed, regardless of the hurt I know I caused you."

A sob wracked her chest, and Daemon tightened his fingers around her hand as tears began to flow down her cheeks.

"You are my heart, and I will spend the rest of my life showing you how much you mean to me. I vow to stand by your side and weather the storm of life with you. To be the light in your darkness and the shoulder to share your burdens. To love you wholly and unconditionally in this life and every life thereafter. Forever, and always, I am eternally yours."

Daemon could feel the tears rolling down his face as she finished. He always thought that marriage would be a burden inflicted upon him by his obligations to his kingdom. But as he watched Auraelia slide the twisted silver and onyx band onto his finger, nothing had ever felt more perfect.

More *right*.

His heart skipped when she lightly brushed the tattoo he'd gotten the night before that sat just below his first knuckle, her eyes wide as they met his.

It wasn't much, just a simple sprig of lavender that wrapped around his finger. But its meaning was so much more. He'd been wrapped around her finger since they met, and now he'd carry her with him, always.

Her smile was watery, but as the priestess turned expectantly toward him, he cleared his throat and began.

"Auraelia Rose, my love and my life. I have seen thousands of stars in this realm, but none could ever compare to the bright light you've brought into my world. You've been ingrained into every fiber of my being from the moment you walked into my life. I've been enraptured with the fire in your eyes, your heart's softness, and your mind's stubbornness. You are strong and determined, and I am the luckiest man in all of Ixora to have the privilege of calling you mine. I never knew I could love someone as wholly as I do you."

Auraelia's hand trembled in his, her breaths coming in small hiccups as she tried to breathe through her tears.

With his free hand, he ran his thumb along her cheek. "Fate may have laid this path before us, but we *chose* this. We chose to fight through the trials this world put in our way. And I will continue to choose you in every aspect of our lives, from this one to the next. You own my heart, Auraelia. My soul and magic call to you and yours and are yours to do with as you please. My beautiful star, I am *yours* and yours alone. Forever, and always."

As he finished, he slid her ring—a silver twin to his own—onto her finger until it nestled against the other. Running his finger across the bands, he watched as the last fragments of sunlight glittered in the oval, brilliant-blue sapphire in its center and burned within the emerald shards flanking either side.

A hush fell over the gathered crowd as Riona said, "If you would both, please place your free hands over the top of the knot and repeat after me."

As his hand met Auraelia's, he could feel her magic flutter to life, grazing along his own as she let it seep out around her. A shield of air bloomed around the space, thunder booming overhead as the rain began to fall over their joined hands, and they said their vows in unison.

When they finished, he raised a questioning brow.

"A wet knot is harder to untie," she whispered with a shrug, a sly smile pulling on the corners of her lips.

In a hushed tone, the priestess said, "Your Majesties, if you would now, please remove your hands from the top and grab the ends of the rope." Their eyes never strayed from each other as they did as she asked. "Now, slowly pull the ends as you slide your other hands out from the center."

As the knot between them began to tighten, Daemon's shadows wrapped around the rope in his hand, and Auraelia's lightning followed suit, weaving together until their magic formed a knot of its own.

Auraelia's eyes flicked to the cord between them, a broad smile spreading across her lips.

"May what was joined here today never be undone, and may the Goddesses of Arcelia bless you with love and light for all of your days," Priestess Riona said loudly to everyone gathered.

Applause echoed through the sanctuary as the priestess addressed him in a tone low enough for only their ears. "King Daemon?" Reluctantly, he pulled his gaze from the love beaming in Auraelia's eyes and turned toward the priestess. "Would you like to kiss your wife?"

Wife.

Auraelia is my wife.

His heart soared as he turned back to the love of his life, tears brimming in her eyes as they flicked from his down to his mouth. Daemon closed the distance between them, wrapped his arm around her waist, and pulled her to him. "I love you, Auraelia."

Her hand cradled his cheek as he lowered his mouth toward hers. "I love you, too. Now, kiss me."

The cheers and applause disappeared as his lips met hers. The world faded away until they were the only ones who existed.

Do you want more Auraelia and Daemon, or want to see what happens *after* the wedding?

Scan the QR code for the link.

Acknowledgements

Oh, lord. Where do I start?

To my READERS, thank you so much for coming along on this journey with me. Thank you for taking a chance on a newbie author and for falling in love with my story and characters, then coming back for more. I hope that I did Daemon and Auraelia's story justice, and that you fell in love with them a little more by the end. By reading their story, you helped breathe life into their characters, and I will forever be grateful for the time you gave to them and to me.

To my ARC team, thank you so much for everything! For the ones who came back and the ones who found me later on and couldn't wait to finish Daemon and Auraelia's story. Thank you for taking the time out of your lives to read my story and give it love. I hope you loved it, and I hope that you know you are so, SO, appreciated.

To my BETA crew, you ladies were amazing and I couldn't have made it to the finish line without you. Your insight into the story and its characters brought a new perspective that made my story better, and for that, I will always be thankful.

To my ALPHA and favorite trash panda, DELYNDA. Thank you for always pushing me to be better. For giving me insights that made the story better. For pushing me to finish, and being there when I thought I couldn't get through it. Thank you making time for my crazy rants about time lines and "what if's" and for your excitement over the seeds you found throughout the story. We've both come such a long way in our writing journeys and I can't wait to see where we go next. I love you! I appreciate you! And I am so thankful for you.

SYDNE, this book would not be what it is without you. Thank you for talking out timelines and plot holes with me. For being just as excited about Daemon and Auraeia's story as I was, and for pushing me toward the finish line. Our late night chats and endless gif conversations will forever be a highlight of my life and favorite part of our friendship. I am so grateful that your ARC brought us together, and that we've been able to help each other through subsequent books—even if you make me give you "narrow chicken eyes" on the regular. I love you and appreciate you so much.

To my G.R.I.T.S. girls. The ones who are every piece of Piper and are an intricate part of who I am as a person. Kirsten, Christine, and Alexis, I would not be where I am today without you wonderful women. Each of you are the Piper to my Auraelia, and I will never be able to thank you enough. Thank you for listening to me ramble about this book and the struggles that came with writing it. But most of all, thank you for being there for me every step of the way, regardless of time or distance. I love you ladies.

MOM, where would I be without you? I don't even know where to start. You're my hero and inspiration. You're constantly showing me that I can do anything that I put my mind to, and that it doesn't matter how late you start, just as long as you start. Thank you for being one of the biggest hype people for my books, for recommending it to anyone you think will read it, and for being excited to see what I write next. Your support means more than you know, and I am so grateful that you're in my corner. I love you.

MAKENZIE and LORELAI. My two beautiful girls. Thank you for being patient while mommy followed her long time dream. You won't know it, but you two are all throughout this book. In name, in sass, and stubborn attitudes. It's because of you that I finally had the courage to pursue this dream, and I hope that I will make you proud...just never read it. I don't think I'd survive that. I love you both more than anything, and remember that you can do anything that you set your mind to.

KEGAN. Love of my life and piece of my soul. I would not, COULD not, have done this without you. Thank you for your unwavering support in everything that I do, and for making sure that I follow every dream and crazy idea that I have. Thank you for letting me fangirl at you over my own characters. For letting me become a hermit when I needed to work out chapters or edit my manuscript. Thank you for hyping up my book to guys who would probably never read it, but you have somehow convinced them that they need to. Thank you for letting me read you chapters completely out of context, and for nodding along like you knew exactly what I was talking about.

Thank you for bringing me chocolate croissants and coffee.

Thank you for everything. I love you so very much.

To my editor, SAMANTHA. Thank you for taming the chaos that was my manuscript. I have never had so much fun editing than I did while going through your notes and reading your texts. I am so happy that I found you, and can't wait to work with you again. In Sam We Trust.

To my amazing character artist, STEFANY (@suusliks on Instagram), thank you for being so patient with me while we worked through bringing my characters to life. Thank you for your amazing attention to detail. I can't wait to work with you again.

To the amazing ALEX (@avoccatt_art on Instagram), thank you for bringing my scenes to life. I love them all so much, and I love working with you.

To my amazing cover artist, BIANCA with Moonpress Designs. Thank you for making this cover as beautiful as the first, I can't wait to see them together on my shelves.

About the author

As a lover of life and art, Jessica is constantly looking for the beauty in the world around her.

She's married to a United States Navy Sailor and together, they have two beautiful daughters and a dog. With their military life, they move often, but currently call Washington State home.

When she's not reading or writing, you can find her crafting in one way or another. Whether it's painting, sewing, messing with clay, or working on things for her small shop (Girlie Flamingo Design), she's always got the creative juices flowing.

She's always been an avid reader, using the written word to escape to lands of mythical creatures and happily ever afters. The beach and the bookstore are her happy places, tattoos are her therapy, and though she loves coffee, she could live off of Dr. Pepper. As a Louisiana native, she's a lover of spice...both in food and in her books.

For more information about the author and the books she writes, make sure you follow her on social media.

www.ingramcontent.com/pod-product-compliance
Lightning Source LLC
Chambersburg PA
CBHW030603310726
48979CB00003B/548

* 9 7 9 8 9 8 8 4 1 4 2 5 4 *